11/16/13

Lisa!

Merry Christmas to you -
and proud papa to be!
Congrats to you.

I so hope you
enjoy this story

Biggest cheer and
keep that Dad
of yours healthy

Much Love,
Dan

TAKTSANG

TAKTSANG

DENNIS SNYDER

iUniverse LLC
Bloomington

TAKTSANG

This is a work of fiction. All of the characters, names, incidents, organizations, and dialogue in this novel are either the products of the author's imagination or are used fictitiously.

iUniverse books may be ordered through booksellers or by contacting:

iUniverse LLC
1663 Liberty Drive
Bloomington, IN 47403
www.iuniverse.com
1-800-Authors (1-800-288-4677)

ISBN: 978-1-4917-0151-5 (sc)
ISBN: 978-1-4917-0153-9 (hc)
ISBN: 978-1-4917-0152-2 (ebk)

Library of Congress Control Number: 2013914317

Printed in the United States of America

iUniverse rev. date: 09/23/2013

For Rob
For Karen

The life so short, the craft so long to learn.

—Hippocrates

CHAPTER 1

Paro, Bhutan
Many years in the future

Whether it is fact or fable I may never know, local lore tells of a granite-lined tunnel lying directly beneath my feet.

"The passage begins here, at Ta Dzong," the old sage is telling me, "and ends far below, along the riverbank."

The elderly man standing next to me, whom I met not two minutes ago, uses his wooden cane to point at a circular watchtower perched high on a hill overlooking the Paro River.

"Four hundred years ago, my ancestors constructed Ta Dzong," the man says as he points a crooked finger at my chest, his spirally beard waving in the early-morning breeze. "This watchtower was a surveillance post used to spot any who endeavored to invade Bhutan from the north. Tibetan raiders and savages from other neighboring kingdoms . . . on many occasions, such marauders assailed upon our land."

My newfound friend, clearly reveling in his audience of one, then turns his attention to the imposing white monolith that sits along the near bank of the Paro River.

"That is Rinpung Dzong," the sage says to me, his eyes wide with life. "Rinpung Dzong means 'fortress on a heap of jewels.' It was built by a learned theologian in the seventeenth century, in order to stand guard along the great river you see before us. For countless generations, this garrison was the most formidable outpost in all the Himalayas.

"The walls of Rinpung Dzong," my teacher continues, his steel-gray eyes panning the length of the river, "are impenetrable." My historian friend then used his cane to point back and forth between the two fortifications.

"The underground chamber originates at Ta Dzong, and from there it proceeds deep under the surface, ending far below at Rinpung Dzong." He pulls in closer, our eyes now locked. "Militiamen and weapons, along with water and grain, could move unhindered through this underground cavern. This channel served our land for many centuries, helping our fighters thwart the invader time and time again.

"Without exception, our enemies returned to their homeland telling a tale of defeat. My forefathers," the wise man says slowly, his soft voice receding, "made this land invincible.

"Utterly invincible," the man repeats, his words trailing away as he drifts off in another direction.

Considering the fact that Bhutan has yet to be subjugated by any foe over the course of the past thousand years, I am hardly in any position to question history as chronicled by the victor.

Unknown and unknowable were the words an early traveler once used to describe Bhutan. In fact, Bhutan was for centuries so isolated from the rest of the world that cartographers did not even have a name for it. Ancient Sanskrit referred to the barbarian fringes of Tibet as *Bhotanta*, known also as *Bhu-uttan* or *highland*. Medieval Tibetan scribes told of lush, fertile valleys far to the south, alluding to the Land of Hidden Treasures and the Southern Valley of Medicinal Herbs. The Bhutanese themselves call their country Drul Yul, or Land of the Thunder Dragon. Although the exact origin of this name remains obscure, legend tells of a deafening roar—believed to be the voice of a mighty dragon—that was heard during the twelfth-century consecration of a sacred monastery.

Although this country's sublime isolation has in recent times seen an influx of Western influence—and the beginnings of a constitutional democracy—Bhutan's culture has remained untarnished and its people fiercely self-reliant. Unlike Tibet, its large neighbor to the north, Bhutan has never been conquered. Unlike India, its even larger neighbor to the south, Bhutan has never been colonized. Unlike the former Himalayan kingdoms of Ladakh and Sikkim, Bhutan has never been swallowed up and parceled into oblivion by the will and force of the ravenous giants that surround it. Bhutan remains an insular, independent, majestic realm that sits on top of the world.

Over the past three months, the Land of the Thunder Dragon has shown me a world that I never would have believed existed. Unless the updraft from a distant valley carried the call of herders or the song of schoolchildren, my guide, Lhendrup, and I hiked for days without any evidence that others inhabited the same planet as us. About a week into our trek, we walked through a high mountain plain that looked to be on fire with the bloom of rare orchids and *primulas*. Several days later, we traversed a narrow pass that was lined with blue poppy, an almost transparent, purple-tinged flower that was for centuries thought to exist only in legend. Farther north, sapphire-blue archways of ice could be seen spanning the glaciers that blanketed massive Himalayan peaks.

Every day, at dawn and again at dusk, we would hear the cry of eagles echoing through the valleys.

During the second week of our trek, Lhendrup spotted a monastery that was perched high on a hill along the eastern horizon. This building, along with the group of crimson-robed monks that dwelled within, was the first sign of civilization anywhere along our path through the distant northern reaches of Bhutan. A few days later, we saw clusters of small dwellings dotting the steep canyon walls, each home adorned with hand-painted Tantric symbols and brilliant floral patterns. The children we encountered along the way, clad in a rainbow of *kiras* and *ghos*, were innocence in motion. They would run to greet us whenever we approached a village or township, the beauty of their chant and vibrancy of their laughter still resonant in my mind.

The silence of my days here—a silence broken at times by the song of a prayer wheel whirling in the crystalline waters of a mountain stream—has no doubt left the deepest imprint of all. Like my lasting image of a snow leopard vanishing into the night, I will carry the quiet of this land with me for the rest of my days.

I have waited all my life to trek through this land, and I in every way owe my life to a small group of people who walked along these same paths many years ago. My wife and grown children insist that in coming to Bhutan, I was embarking on a pilgrimage. And perhaps they're right, given my long obsession with the sequence of events that took place here when I was just a child, a very sick child, in a small town back in the United States. It was then that a young Bhutanese girl helped four American visitors—a surgeon, a neurotic scientist, a med school dropout, and a billionaire business mogul—search for a friend who had traveled to Bhutan for reasons that at the time no one understood.

And what they found in Bhutan would change the course of their lives almost as much as it changed the course of mine.

The reason for my coming to Bhutan goes beyond my lifelong desire to experience the splendor of this unbroken land. I have pieced together much of the lives of the four Americans who came to Bhutan all those years ago, as well as the events surrounding the last days in the life of the friend they came here to find. But despite innumerable inquiries to every Bhutanese government agency I could find, I have yet to discover a single authenticated fact as to the fate of the Bhutanese girl who guided that particular group of American travelers. The only response I have ever received is a letter that arrived at my doorstep just over a year ago.

Mr. Jackson Duran
14 North Pamet Road
Truro, MA 02666
USA

Greetings Mr. Duran:

As we have yet to meet each other's acquaintance, allow me to introduce myself.

My name is Yoeden Penjor, and I reside near the town of Paro in my native country of Bhutan.

Kuzuzangpo-la.

The purpose of my correspondence is to extend an invitation for you to attend our National Museum's centennial celebration in September of next year. This momentous occasion shall include a variety of native artisans, archery competition, a number of dance ensembles, and musicians from all parts of Bhutan. Perhaps most of all, honored guests such as yourself will be able to spend time viewing the extensive historical collections housed inside our museum. Within these galleries, the history of our land comes to life.

I would like to mention as well that it has come to the attention of the museum's curator that you have been making inquiries concerning a group of travelers who visited our country many years ago. Our curator has intimate knowledge of these individuals, and as well events that occurred during their stay in Bhutan. Hence, do not be at all taken aback by this invitation, as our curator would be most honored to meet you and have the pleasure of your company at next year's grand festival.

As the centennial festivities begin in the early afternoon on September 21 of next year, our curator would be delighted to meet you in person, if you can avail yourself, at ten o'clock that same morning. The most convenient place for us to meet would be at the eastern entrance of the Paro Dzong bridge, which is quite near to the site of our celebration. I have enclosed all my contact information, a map of the immediate area, and some related material which I trust will be of aid as you prepare for your journey.

In closing, I extend to you my wishes for a safe voyage.

Tashi delek,

Yoeden Penjor
Associate Curator
National Museum of Bhutan
Paro, Bhutan

Although I cannot tell you anything about the person who wrote me this letter, I can tell you that the stamps on the envelope I am holding probably merit all the gushing accolades the collecting community bestows upon them. They are exquisite, each one a work of art. The first one shows a panoply of orchids in full bloom along the edge of a sun-drenched meadow. The second is a rendering of a *takin*, an ungainly, bizarre-looking ungulate that is steeped in Bhutan's religion and mythology. The last is a drawing of a champion archer, in full competitive regalia, superimposed over the five rings of the Olympic Games.

When I first read this letter, I really did not know what to make of it. Truth be told, I still don't. Like I said, I have sent numerous e-mails and letters to the Tourism Council of Bhutan, Bhutan's Department of Foreign Affairs, and assorted other federal and local agencies. But I never sent any solicitation or letter of inquiry to Bhutan's National Museum. Why on earth would I? I wasn't looking for historical facts about the country, nor was I asking about any upcoming nationwide celebrations. I was only trying to find any information I could about the

Bhutanese girl who served as a guide for the American visitors all those years ago.

But in my search I have found someone, more specifically Bhutan's National Museum curator, who claims to have personal knowledge of the American visitors and the events that occurred during their time here. Or maybe that "someone" found me. Perhaps a staff member at the Tourism Council or Foreign Affairs Department passed around one of my e-mails or letters, and somewhere along the way it was read by one of the museum officers. But whoever Yoeden Penjor is, he, or she—Bhutanese names are largely blind to gender—wrote to extend me an invitation to a festival that begins later today at the National Museum here in Paro. Bhutan's National Museum is housed in Ta Dzong, the circular watchtower that is, as I learned just minutes ago, steeped in this country's history.

So in a couple of hours, I am supposed to meet Yoeden Penjor, along with the National Museum's curator, at the entrance to the Paro River footbridge. It is then and there that I hope to find out what happened to someone to whom I, along with countless others, am so indebted. Yoeden and the museum's curator are my only link, my only possible connection, to the events that followed one of the most calamitous days in Bhutan's history. Besides the letter I was sent, and confirming some details of our upcoming meeting in subsequent back-and-forth e-mails, I know nothing about either Yoeden or the museum's head curator. What I do know is that my walk through this timeless land, in every way, began so many years ago. It began the day I was hoisted onto my father's shoulders and brought back home, leaving behind the last of what seemed an endless succession of strange and frightening places. It began the day my youngest sister looked at me without a bewildered stare. It began when I saw the fear at last fade from my mother's eyes.

It began all those many years ago when an extraordinary group of people, none of whom I ever knew, walked through the Land of the Thunder Dragon.

CHAPTER 2

Boston
July 1992

Ivar was looking for any excuse not to go.

It wasn't that he didn't like Doyle's Cafe. What was there not to like about a pub that stocked thirty-odd taps of ice-cold draughts and served wood-fired, brick-oven pizza that one of Ivar's coworkers, a native of Sicily, called "the best this side of the pond." And Ivar enjoyed the company of the neighborhood regulars and twenty-somethings that frequented Doyle's even more than he liked the pizza and beer. A Friday night with his coworkers at Doyle's Cafe was always a hit.

But this Friday night's program had a twist.

Tonight, Ivar and his friends had to stop at a hospital, a *children's* hospital, before they went out for an evening of "pitchers and pizza pie."

"Half an hour tops, Ivar," one of the graduate students said, tugging Ivar's collar lightly. "We're just stopping by long enough to give little Kyle a little squeeze, and then we're outta there."

Little Kyle was the seven-year-old son of the research professor who codirected the immunology lab where Ivar and several other students worked during their summer break. Kyle was an inpatient on the hematology/oncology ward at Boston Children's Hospital, having been admitted a day earlier due to complications from a blood disorder known as thalassemia.

"It's no big deal, man," said another student, this one soon to be starting her fourth year of medical school. "Thalassemia is a benign disease . . . it's a defect in the oxygen-carrying capacity

8

of the red blood cells. I was on a clinical rotation at Children's Hospital last year, and I got to know a couple of the charge nurses who work on the hem/onc floor, and one of them is doing the three-to-eleven shift tonight. I called him about an hour ago, and he said Kyle was being transfused a unit or two of blood and that he would be ready for discharge over the weekend. The charge nurse also said it'd be okay if we stopped by to say hello and good-bye to the little fella. It's just a social call, Ivar . . . not to mention a chance for all of us to score some brown-nosing points by visiting the boss's son."

Ivar was on a full four-year scholarship to the Massachusetts Institute of Technology, and as part of the scholarship program, he was required to work in a health science–related field during his college summer months. Given this requirement, Ivar's academic counselor presented him with three choices: work at the morgue, work on a chinchilla farm, or work at any one of several Boston-based immunology laboratories. Although Ivar had no real interest in the workings of the human immune system, he decided that making busy as a gopher in a research lab was a whole lot more appealing than the graveyard shift at the morgue or chasing around a horde of feral beasts eight hours a day. Besides, Ivar loved science. He was double majoring in physics and music at MIT, and by working in the immunology lab, he would have the chance to learn about a branch of scientific study that he knew next to nothing about.

"We'll be in and out of there in a flash," the med student said as she twirled her long blonde braid in front of Ivar's eyes. "Besides, that ward at Children's Hospital is always hopping busy, and the nursing staff won't want us standing around and getting in their way."

Ivar and his coworkers were seated on a small patch of green grass that fronted one of the Boston University administration buildings, half a block from the immunology lab where they all worked. It was just past five in the afternoon, and the air was still and sticky. Looking up into the sky, Ivar caught sight of a red-tailed hawk emerging from the nest the bird had built on top of a pile of rusted-out wrought-iron beams that lined the rooftop of a nearby abandoned building. This particular building, which had for years housed Boston City Hospital's tuberculosis patients, was slated for demolition later in the year.

"Will you ever find another home?" Ivar said in a low voice as he watched the hawk circle above, the bird landing a minute later on a nearby treetop. "That's the female," he said, pointing up at the hawk. "She's always bigger than the male red-tailed. Her wingspan can reach better than four feet."

One of Ivar's friends made a show of looking at his watch as he loudly cleared his throat. Another began to tap on Ivar's shoulder as she sang the tune "Hot Child in the City."

Feeling the weight of multiple pairs of eyes bearing down on him, Ivar knew it was too late for lame excuses. Even if his evasions weren't evasions at all—as in the stack of quantum physics papers he needed to review for his undergraduate thesis at MIT—Ivar knew that he didn't stand a chance of escaping the trip to the hospital. And mentioning the Dostoevsky novel he wanted to finish, or the Aeschylus tragedy he planned on cracking open, would make him look like an even bigger killjoy.

"We're seated at Doyle's by six," Ivar said as he slowly rose to his feet. "Any later and every slice of the roasted garlic and double cheese is mine."

Although Kyle had a blood transfusion running through an intravenous line that had been placed in his arm, the bright-eyed, freckle-faced redhead had no trouble showing off the multicolored Lego bridge that he had built along the foot of his bed.

"I'm taking this home!" the child announced to Ivar and his friends. "Today . . . today!"

"Maybe not today," the charge nurse said, a stocky middle-aged man who was trying his best not to look harried. "And try not to shake your arm around too much, buddy." The nurse wrapped more tape around the arm board that protected the IV tubing. "You can show all your friends how you put the

Legos together, but you have to be careful not to move your arm too much."

While all of Ivar's friends played games with Kyle, Ivar stood just inside the doorway and tried to look as inconspicuous as possible for a man who stood just over six and a half feet tall. Ivar shuffled his feet uneasily, pressing his back against the doorjamb as he tried to ignore the children ambling in and out of the adjoining rooms, eyeing him.

Ivar looked up at the wall clock mounted above the nurses' station: 5:41.

It wasn't the hospital ward that was making Ivar so uncomfortable, but rather the children on the ward. In the presence of a child, no matter what his or her age, Ivar was self-conscious of his appearance—his towering height, painfully thin build, deep-set eyes, and knotty brow ridge. His eyeglasses, which seemed to take up half his face, appeared askew no matter how he adjusted them. His arms were spindly and exceptionally long, which made it look like he was moving in slow motion whenever he reached for something.

As with his physical characteristics, Ivar's years of social isolation were not a matter of choice. Ivar was born in a town along the southwestern coast of Norway, and he was an only child. Having lost both of his parents by the age of six, Ivar spent most of his childhood homeschooled by an uncle who was a retired teacher and had never married. And a respiratory infection Ivar contracted as a small child had damaged the intrinsic muscles of his heart, which precluded any participation in team athletics with other children. So Ivar's first classmates, or for that matter his first mates of any sort, were the other students he met at MIT's freshman orientation.

Whenever he was around children, Ivar was a stranger in a very strange land.

"They'll be a bunch of long faces up here tonight, I can promise you that," Ivar overheard the charge nurse say to the students who were sitting on Kyle's bed. "On Fridays we always have a musical troupe or juggler or nursery rhyme fabler to entertain the kids for an hour or so. Man, it does wonders for these children. But the duet that was slated for tonight no-showed. Supposedly one of them has bronchitis, and any jester who's coughing his head off is no kind of company for children being treated for cancer."

Ivar again looked up at the clock: 5:48.

"Any of you part-time as a comedian before you went science geek?" the charge nurse asked, looking at Ivar's friends one at a time.

5:49.

"Hell-oh," said the tiny voice from just outside Kyle's doorway.

Ivar startled, looking down at the bald child who was staring up at him.

"Are you the singer?" asked a second child, this one even smaller than the first. The child's entire head was wrapped in a large bandage, with a curled up intravenous catheter secured to the outer layer of the bandage wrapping.

Ivar's back went straight.

"Big man!" the bald child said, giggling as he pointed up at Ivar.

Ivar looked into Kyle's room, hoping one of his friends would move toward the door and take up conversation with two children who were now seated at his feet. But with balloons now flying from one side of Kyle's bed to the other, no one took any notice. With Kyle jumping around on his bed, the Lego bridge's two towers began to sway back and forth as if caught up in a typhoon.

"Which one of you geniuses stopped by the 7–11 to buy balloons?" Ivar muttered under his breath as he looked at his friends, a deep frown across his face.

"He's the circus man," the child with the head bandage said to an older child who was walking down the hall, this one wheeling an intravenous pole that was lined top to bottom with Muppet stickers.

"Hi," the child with the Muppet-decorated IV pole said as he looked up at Ivar, a bright smile across his face. "Do you know Jerry the juggler? He was here last week."

Ivar again looked imploringly toward his coworkers, but still no one noticed him or the gallery of children that was beginning to assemble at the doorway. Kyle was now standing on his bed, chasing after the balloons in every direction. The prized suspension bridge had turned ninety degrees, sinking slowly between the end of the mattress and the foot of the bed.

Ivar noticed the door to a treatment room across the hall swing open, and he saw one of the nurses walk out cradling a small child in her arms. The child, who looked no more than three years old, had a large bandage covering her torso. The girl let out a soft whimper as the nurse who was carrying her kissed the crown of her head. A waft of putrid air emanated from the treatment room, and before the door to the room slammed shut, Ivar saw one of the nursing aides dispose of a bandage that was saturated with a greenish-brown fluid.

Ivar closed his eyes and winced.

"Can you play with us?" the bald child asked, gripping Ivar's pant leg with both hands.

"Jerry did card tricks too," said the child wheeling the IV pole. "He made the king and queen disappear. One of them was hiding under the piano."

"I . . . I . . . I don't know any card tricks," Ivar stammered. "Jerry does all those kinds of things. He does that . . . that and the juggling. All the juggling."

"It was right here," the older child said as he bolted into the nearby game room, his IV pole rattling behind him. "Right under here!"

Looking for any reason to get away, Ivar walked down the hallway a few steps and peered into the game room, tilting his head toward the child who was now pointing under the fallboard of a standup piano that was tucked in a far corner of the room.

"I found the king," the boy said proudly. "The diamond king. He was hiiiidiiiing."

A Knabe. The piano was a Knabe. Ivar hadn't noticed it when they passed by the room earlier, probably because at the time the room was unlit due to the cancellation of the comedy show. But the child with the IV pole had flicked on the overhead light so he could show Ivar where he had found the hidden playing card.

Ivar walked into the game room toward the piano, with the two smaller children following close behind.

"Where did you find the card?" Ivar asked the older boy as he gazed at the piano, his voice more confident.

"I told you," the child said impatiently as he pointed to the middle of the piano's fallboard, his finger directed at the faded inscription that read Wm. Knabe & Co. Baltimore.

"The king was hiding right here!" the boy repeated.

The upright Knabe was nearly identical to the piano Ivar had when he was a young boy. Ivar had learned to play at a very early age, practicing day and night on an heirloom from his mother's side of the family. And although his mother had died before Ivar's first birthday, Ivar told anyone who asked that it was his mother who had taught him how to play the piano. This was in every sense true, because as a young child Ivar would watch reel after grainy reel of his mother, an accomplished musician from a family of accomplished musicians, performing at various concert halls in and around their hometown along the southern coast of Norway. Ivar would sit for hours and play and play, his mind filled with running images of his mother's hands melding into the keyboard. After the death of his father, Ivar played even more, his new home with his uncle resonating with the sounds of Chopin and Liszt as Ivar played in memory of both his parents. At the age of fourteen, Ivar played before audiences in Oslo and Vienna. At fifteen, he won the grand prize at a competition in Strasbourg, and the following year, he played before a capacity audience at Juilliard in New York.

And now, Ivar was going to play before an audience of children who were far too young to be so terribly sick. As he sat down on the piano stool, a five-year-old Nigerian girl sat down next to him. The girl smiled up at Ivar, and after an uneasy moment passed, a broad grin crept across Ivar's face as he looked down into the child's eyes. The child's skin looked like dark velvet, with her smile seeming to light up every corner of the room.

Ivar opened whatever music book was in front of him and began to play, and with that, every child within earshot walked, crawled, limped, or wheeled their way into the game room. Within minutes, there were children on all sides of Ivar as he ad-libbed pieces from Haydn and Bach in between the scores on the music sheets he was flipping through. A teenager from Bulgaria, who was being treated for a malignant brain tumor, sat down on the piano stool next to the Nigerian girl. Another teenager, an Israeli girl on chemotherapy for a tumor of the lymphatic system, leaned against the piano and began to sing as Ivar played "Baby Beluga." Several small children, each in the embrace of their mother or father, bounced to the melody that filled the air. Ivar's friends, some with a dumbfounded look on their face, wandered into the game room and joined in the singing. Kyle walked in holding the arm of the child with the large head bandage in one hand and a collection of balloon strings in the other.

The Nigerian girl, sitting to Ivar's right, stood up on the piano stool and rested her chin on Ivar's shoulder. It was then that Ivar saw the large, irregular swelling that extended down the length of the girl's neck on one side. Ivar then looked at the other children who surrounded him, their eyes hollow and their bodies so frail. Some had undergone surgery, and many were being treated with radiation and chemotherapy. One of the children, a boy with sunken eyes whose complexion was as white as a cloud, placed another sheet of music in front of Ivar.

"My favorite," the child said, slapping his hand against the music sheet.

"Mine too," Ivar said as he placed the small boy on his lap, his long arms again stretching out across the piano keys.

Scouring through the many remnants of Ivar's past—the interviews he gave, the magazine articles written about his research, the half a dozen or so TV documentaries, and at least one less-than-exhaustive biography—I can say with every certainty that there was not a single reference to this chance encounter on a children's hospital ward as being the defining, seminal moment in Ivar's life. I can say with just as much certainty that Ivar's life thereafter became consumed with questions that he would spend every waking hour of his remaining years trying to answer.

Why are some children afflicted with such horrible diseases?

How many of these children will survive their disease, and what's more, how many will survive the treatments that their disease necessitates?

Why, with all the reported advances in surgery, do some tumors remain out of reach?

Why, after surgery and chemotherapy and radiation therapy, do cancers recur?

Ivar swayed from side to side, the child on his lap and the children on each side of the piano stool swaying with him.

If any cell in the human body can transform itself into a potential killer, why can't one's immune system fight off such a process? Isn't that the task of the cells and tissues that make up the human immune structure—to destroy internal substances that produce cancer just as they destroy external invaders that produce infection? Is there not a means of allying the body's own internal defenses in order to reverse such a deadly process?

You make me happy when skies are gray.
   You'll never know . . .
   The Nigerian girl's mother rocked her daughter back and forth as Ivar played on, her faced etched in fear.
   . . . how much I love you.
   Her eyes were desperate and searching
   Please don't take my sunshine away.

CHAPTER 3

Boston
Present day

"I thought Harvard owns this property," Martin said, a gnarl in his voice.

"Harvard leases this property," Ivar said calmly as he adjusted the power setting on his headlight. "I haven't the first idea who owns this building, or for that matter any of the other properties around here. None of my concern, I'm happy to say."

"Well, you'd think the world's richest private institution might have negotiated for a better emergency lighting system than the one you've got," Martin said as he searched for the flashlight application on his cell phone. "It's as dark as a cave in here. How do you expect all the staff you've got scurrying around to get any work done in this place?"

"This place" was the Institute for Pediatric Oncologic Research, also known as IPOR. IPOR was the brainchild of Dr. Ivar Nielsen, who after graduating valedictorian from MIT received combined medical and doctorate degrees from Harvard. IPOR's singular goal was the development of innovations in cancer therapy whereby disease eradication was achieved by the mobilization of a patient's innate immune defenses, as opposed to treating cancer with conventional treatment, such as surgery, radiation therapy, and chemotherapy. Through grants from the National Institutes of Health and the Howard Hughes Medical Institute, Ivar's research had produced hundreds of peer review papers and manuscripts. Ivar's staff consisted of cell biologists, immunologists, geneticists, and biochemists from all over the world, and the IPOR graduate medical program was considered preeminent in the realm of health care research.

IPOR occupies thirty thousand square feet of space on the top floor of the Center for Life Science, located on Blackfan Circle in the epicenter of Boston's medical research community. The Life Science Center is an ultramodern facility with an all-glass curtain wall façade, and the geometry of the building is such that the structure's footprint increases as it rises some three hundred feet above street level. The center is an award-winning, all-green biotech property that has intimate academic connections with every medical center in greater Boston.

What the center didn't have, at 8:15 on a weeknight in early April, was electricity.

"Late winter storm," Ivar said to Martin. "Not the first you've lived through, and it certainly won't be the last. The buildings all around us, the ones with sick people under their roofs, they get full power. This facility stays as green as possible, with just enough juice from our generator to support basic operations. No exceptions. Would you like a headlight? It's loaded with fresh batteries."

"Green wastes my time, which wastes my money. And no thank you on the headlight," Martin huffed as he inspected the sleeves of his Savile Row suit with his flashlight, brushing away a few tiny pieces of lint. "And in case you've been too preoccupied with work to consult your calendar, it is no longer winter."

Ivar and Martin were seated in a small conference room near the entrance to Ivar's laboratory, with Ivar's headlight shining on the pages of data that one of the graduate students had printed out prior to the power outage.

"You could have located your business empire farther south, away from all this arctic air and blowing snow," Ivar said without looking up. "Like Florida or one of the other Gulf states."

"Hurricanes," Martin said, brushing off both shoulders of his jacket.

"How about Texas, inland somewhere?" Ivar asked as he checked and circled various data points on the printout.

"Tornadoes," Martin returned. "And I don't like rednecks."

"Then how about foreign soil, like the Far East?" Ivar asked.

"Typhoons."

"Chile?"

"Earthquakes."

"Panama?"

"Corrupt government."

"Peru?"

"Earthquakes *and* corrupt government."

"What's a blackout in a science center matter to you anyway?" Ivar asked, erasing one of his notations. "I'm the one who works here. You just stop by when you need respite from all those corporate types that you're overpaying. And don't all your facilities have space-age generators to power every light, buzzer, bell, and whistle, no matter what form of natural disaster strikes?"

"You're damn right they do," Martin said as he brushed his hand down both pant legs. "And take note, every last one of you penny-pinching Harvard trustees."

Martin Norris Phyte was forty-three years old and a former classmate of Ivar's at MIT. During his college years, Martin had cut a pretty sharp look, with a mop of curly blond hair, two boyish dimples, and a svelte, solid athletic build. In his younger days, Martin was quick with a smile and even quicker when it came to delivering lines that the people around him wanted to hear. But the good life and all of its trappings, along with a rapidly receding hairline, had taken their toll on Martin. He was every bit of sixty pounds overweight, and any last trace of his once flowing, sandy-blond locks had long ago been claimed by gravity. And Martin's countenance now seemed to alternate between an icy scowl and various degrees of a doubtful stare. His success was undeniable—on a steep upward slope ever since he and two fellow sophomore classmates developed a network whereby custom-made dental implants could be produced and shipped in less than half the time of other supply companies. From that humble start, Martin had built a prosthetics distribution conglomerate that did business in over seventy countries, with headquarters in Seattle, Toronto, and Boston. CEO and sole corporate proprietor Martin Phyte collected antique cars, wore only the finest tailor-made London suits, and flew regularly between Europe and the lower forty-eight on one of his three private jets. Martin had an ex-model, ex-resident physician trophy wife and two young children, and in addition to his gargantuan estate fifteen miles west of downtown Boston, he owned multiple luxury vacation homes. But besides Ivar, very few people, if any, counted Martin as their friend. And that included the two college classmates who had long ago been cut loose from any association with what was now an international business juggernaut.

"Never been there, the Orkney Islands," Martin said, referring to Ivar's upcoming trip to Scotland. "The birding along the coastal cliffs . . . puffins, razorbills, the great skua. Incredible sights and rich breeding grounds, or so I've been told."

Ivar flicked off his headlight and looked in Martin's direction, sensing a hint of jealousy, or perhaps hurt, in his friend's voice.

"Wish I could tell you that the invites were mine to hand out," Ivar said. "It's an extended side trip, organized by the Cancer Research Department in Edinburgh. Just a small group of science eggheads out in the wild before we all give a series of lectures at the medical school. I'm just a tagalong."

"Oh of course, I know I know," Martin said quickly, holding up both hands. "I'm on the road quite a bit over the next few weeks anyway. But send a photo or two along the way, if you think of it."

Ivar and Martin shared exactly one avocation, and that was bird watching. The two first met as college freshmen when they attended an ornithology seminar, and ever since then, they had spent several weekends a year photographing avian life in New England and along the mid Atlantic. Whenever Ivar and Martin were together, any topic of conversation besides "all things birding" was allotted only minimal air time. Ivar had been invited to give several lectures at the College of Medicine in Edinburgh, and the upcoming bird-watching trip in the Orkney Islands, prior to his scheduled talks, was going to be Ivar's first extended vacation in many years.

Ivar stood up from the conference table and placed a hand firmly against his hip as he straightened his back. Although there was enough light in the room for Martin to notice a brief grimace appear across Ivar's face, he acted as if he hadn't noticed.

"But don't think for a second I forgot about you," Ivar said with a slow nod of his head. "I brought you a copy of a guidebook to the birds of Scotland, along with a couple of other manuals that might come in handy one day soon. Thumb through the books and choose any spot you fancy, and maybe sometime later this year, you and I can take a few days and let our eyes wander in a new part of the sky. Maybe Alaska. Or Mexico."

"Melting glaciers. And drug cartels," Martin said, smiling in appreciation.

"Take a copy of each. They're on my desk," Ivar said as he pointed in the direction of his office. "I'll meet you down the hall."

The periphery of Ivar's research facility was made up of rows of small cubicles, each cubicle assigned to either a full-time staff scientist or one of the graduate students. The center of the laboratory consisted of a common work area known by all as "the quad." The quad was a large rectangular space equipped with light microscopes, incubators, autoclaves, electron microscopes, and state-of-the-art imaging devices, with row after row of tiny glass pipettes racked along each of the black granite countertops.

Although he had made untold millions selling high-end medical prosthetics, Martin had very little use for the actual nuts and bolts of advanced scientific study. Accordingly, whenever Martin visited Ivar, he made every effort to steer clear of the quad. So instead of cutting through the center of the laboratory, Martin followed the succession of cubicles along the margins of the facility until he located Ivar's office.

The only difference between Ivar's office and any of the other cubicles was the collection of bird photographs that lined every available square inch of wall space. Martin did a 360-degree turn with his cell phone flashlight, recognizing many of the photos he and Ivar had taken in the White Mountains, along Lake Champlain, and in Acadia National Park.

Martin opened his alligator-skin briefcase and threw in one copy of each of the bird-watching manuals that he found on top of Ivar's desk. While inspecting one of the book covers, Martin accidentally dropped a couple of the texts into an open desk drawer. Without using his flashlight, Martin pulled the books back out of the drawer and tossed them into his briefcase.

Martin found Ivar and one of the graduate students working between two large consoles in the center of the quad. One of the consoles housed an electron microscope, and the other an X-ray crystallography unit. An electron microscope is used to illuminate the ultrastructure of cellular matter by passing an energy source through a series of condensers housed within a large vertical tube. The electron beam produced within the tube allows magnification of biological material by up to ten million times, with the images produced projected onto a computer screen above the console. The X-ray crystallography machine is an approximately one-meter-square box, with large glass windows on three sides and a solid metal casing on the other three sides. An X-ray beam produced within the crystallography unit is used to determine the three-dimensional structure of the genetic material inside a given piece of organic matter.

Martin, while keeping a healthy distance between himself and the center of the quad, watched as a series of images appeared on the console screen above one of the workstations.

"All of this lines up with the data points that you printed out earlier?" Ivar asked the student.

"To the letter," the student responded. "Every code point is incorporated."

Ivar took a blank notecard out of his pocket and wrote out a vertical list of small symbols, shining his headlight along the edge of the card as he made each notation. He eyed the symbols carefully, looked at the various data points on the spreadsheet, and then made a couple more marks along the margins of the card.

"Fine work," Ivar said to the student as he again scanned through the slides. "Have any of the mice been inoculated with this viral prep?"

"Not as of yet," the student said. "I need to review the inoculation protocol for this phase with Myles. I'm meeting with him first thing tomorrow."

Myles Carnot, who had for years spent an average of sixteen hours a day in the lab, was Ivar's director of operations. Ivar had insisted that Myles head home early due to the increasingly treacherous road conditions.

"It took a lot of work to pull all this together, to make this come to life," Ivar said, squeezing the grad student's arm and again congratulating her. "Besides Martin and myself, I think you're the last one here, so please, hit the road. Walking distance, yes?"

"A block and a half," the student said. "I'll send up a prayer that we get full power back by morning. Myles and compromised capacity . . . bad combination."

Ivar grinned.

"Did you say that thing was alive?" Martin asked in a loud voice as he looked at the screen mounted above the electron microscope. The image showed a disc-like structure with spokes projecting from the margins of the disc.

"That's a virus," Ivar said. "One of the viruses that causes the common cold, in fact. When I said 'come to life,' it was just a manner of speech."

"Manner of speech or whatever, when I look at that thing, I see a wild bug on the loose," Martin said, still standing on the periphery of the quad.

"That 'thing' is the end product of everything we do here," Ivar said as he powered down both consoles, "and there's nothing here that can jump onto your skin, if that's what you're worried about. Now I could really use your help with something, so let's go to my office, far away from these creatures you fear."

As Ivar stood, Martin again noticed Ivar applying pressure to his right hip.

"No argument from me," Martin said as he disappeared down the hall, his cell phone app lighting the way.

"I need a big favor," Ivar said once he and Martin were seated across from each other in Ivar's cubicle. "Silas Anthony is arriving next week, and I won't be here to greet him. If you're around, I was wondering if you could meet him when he arrives at the airport."

"That shouldn't be a problem," Martin said, opening his hands and then folding them again. "But if you don't mind me asking, who's Silas Anthony?"

"He's the head of research at the Edinburgh Cancer Center, and I invited him to give a grand rounds lecture at Children's Hospital," Ivar said. "He's the one who's organizing the lecture series in Scotland, and I've been trying for years to get him over here as a visiting professor. This seemed like the perfect opportunity . . . reciprocating for my visiting his research center and medical school. Oddly enough, I've known Silas ever since I was a child, but regrettably we've barely had the chance to see each other over the past twenty years or so."

Martin's eyes narrowed.

"'Silas Anthony' doesn't sound like a Norwegian name to me," Martin said. "Or for that matter, I'll bet there aren't many Scots surnamed Anthony, either."

"You're right on both counts," Ivar said. "It's neither. Dr. Anthony is from the Midwest, an hour or so outside of Chicago. When he was in college back in the early sixties, Silas did a year's study in Glasgow, and while there, he fell for a local girl, and they married a couple of years later. Silas has had a remarkable career, and his work has made quite an impact over there. He's built a powerhouse department, and he's constantly on the go, giving presentations and lectures all over the place."

"As are you," Martin said with a nod of his head. "If the demands on his time are anything like the demands on yours, I can see why the two of you have had trouble catching up with each other. Still, in all these years, he's never once made it to Boston?"

"As you just said, so little time," Ivar said, shrugging his shoulders. "It's just that simple. We see each other at conferences and symposiums but never for very long."

"How did Silas ever get to know your family?" Martin asked.

"He's a pianist," Ivar said in a soft voice. "He met my mother and father just after they were married, at a concert in Oslo. After that, Silas and his wife would get together with my parents before performances, and at other times for dinners and such. They stayed in touch . . . for years."

Martin nodded his head slowly, saying nothing.

"I'm visiting Sloan-Kettering in New York next week, and there's no way I can maneuver an early departure," Ivar said. "I didn't think Silas would arrive here until later in the week, but in fact he's flying in on Tuesday night. If you could meet him at Logan Airport, it would be a great help to me. I want to make a strong first impression, and there's no one better at that than you. I spoke with Joel Morgan earlier today, and he would be glad to join you. Joel would be there as a representative of the Harvard medical community, which would look very official and all of that."

Dr. Joel Morgan, one of the city's most respected physicians and for years one of Ivar's closest friends, was the chief of trauma surgery at Massachusetts General Hospital. Through Ivar, Martin had gotten to know Joel socially, having spoken to him a number of times at charity benefit dinners.

"Say no more," Martin said, putting up a hand. "Give me the details, and I shall accord the royal treatment. Joel and I will roll out the reddest of carpets."

"Thank you," Ivar said emphatically. "After I finish at Sloan-Kettering, I'm taking the late train out of Penn Station, but I won't get back to Boston until after midnight. I'll meet Silas at his hotel first thing the next morning."

Martin sat back and looked intently at Ivar, now knowing why Ivar had asked him to stop by the laboratory despite local news outlets warning of "a blinding late-season Nor'easter." Even through the dim light, Martin could see the concern written across his friend's face.

"You and Silas . . . the two of you working on something, maybe collaborating on a project together?" Martin asked.

"Not really, no," Ivar said. "Not officially, anyway."

"Officially?" Martin asked, raising his eyebrows.

Ivar sat motionless for a long moment, seemingly lost in thought.

"Those pictures you saw down the hall, the photomicrographs above the consoles," Ivar said eventually, pointing in the direction of the center quad, "that's the latest in the line of virus particles we've programmed to kill cancer cells, which is the essence, the sum total, of our work here. We're trying to find a way to treat cancer in children without the limitations and side effects of conventional therapy. We've got years of data and miles of documentation, but the process lacks . . . lacks an accelerant."

"An accelerant?" Martin asked, a sharp inflection in his voice. "What exactly is an accelerant?"

"A trigger. An induction agent," Ivar said. "A spark to initiate the cancer treatment pathway we've been building all these years."

"And you think Silas might know of a way to 'accelerate' all this?" Martin asked skeptically.

"Silas is an authority on the use of chemotherapy to induce cancer regression," Ivar said as he held up a medical journal that was sitting on top of a pile of papers stacked on his desk. "His latest article was published just last month. Even though standard chemotherapy is a step that we've made every effort to bypass, Silas is a great resource on this subject, and he has a wealth of experience. He's a fresh mind, and a brilliant one at that."

Martin shook his head. "Look, Ivar, I don't understand one speck of the work you do here. You show me this or that picture, and even though I may smile and nod, I am in fact lost and clueless. And if you want to know the truth, I get scared shitless whenever I try to wrap my head around the concept of ratcheting up some bug to fight cancer in children. And now," Martin continued, spreading out his arms, "now you tell me that you're asking for help from a man who is a world authority on a topic that runs completely counter to everything you've dedicated your life to."

"They're particles," Ivar said.

"Who? What? What's a particle?" Martin asked, bewildered.

"The viruses. They're particles," Ivar said, grinning slightly. "They're not alive."

"Okay, fine, whatever," Martin said impatiently. "But let me tell you, you've got me thoroughly befuddled. Take no offense here . . . Silas being a lifelong friend, fellow professional, and all that. But you've outlined the perfect reason *not* to invite the man here, as introducing concepts from his field of expertise would be tantamount to you marching backward. I have no doubt that Silas is a renowned researcher and accomplished academician. That said, he's never even been here to see all the work *you* have been doing. It seems to me that he should be the one taking notes, coming away with a better understanding of your world and all you've accomplished."

Ivar said nothing.

"Far be it from me to step into a rarefied world such as yours," Martin went on, "but I simply don't see what you can garner from Silas's world that would in any way enhance yours."

"Silas has traveled more than any scientist I have ever known," Ivar said as he shined a light into his desk drawer, locking the drawer and then pocketing the key. "He's been around people who think on a different plane . . . diverse cultures with a vast array of clinical acumen.

"Our research here," Ivar hesitated for a moment, adjusting his glasses with both hands, "all the research we do here is out of the mainstream, Martin. Unconventional in every way. I've got the best staff you could ever ask for, a really sharp group of graduate students, and plenty of encouraging results to parade in front of our peers. But the larger picture gives me worry. In a very real sense, we are hemmed in, bridled by the same theories and the same line of thinking every time we initiate a new research pathway. The prime mover of IPOR is the belief that the natural power from within a child's bloodstream can be harnessed to cure serious diseases, such as cancer. And everyone here believes that. I believe that. But maybe there's a natural substance from *without* that can jump-start the body's inborn capacity to fight disease . . . some element or compound that isn't a by-product of medical study in a laboratory. Silas has a grasp on the way medicine is practiced in many parts of the world, and it would be enlightening to hear about his experiences, many of which I'm sure are out of the realm of mainstream medicine. I just want to get his thoughts on a few things . . . run an idea or two past him.

"Unofficially, mind you," Ivar added.

Martin stood up and looked down the length of Ivar's facility. The Life Science Center was the tallest building for many blocks in every direction, and as the cubicle and workstation barriers in the lab were no more than five feet high, Martin had an unobstructed panoramic view of Boston. It was still snowing, and the city was largely dark. Except for the nearby hospitals, there was only a scattering of lights in the surrounding neighborhoods.

Martin turned back toward Ivar and shined his cell phone light onto the collection of data charts and photomicrographs that Ivar was packing into his satchel.

"This is all a world that's alien to me," Martin said as he picked up his briefcase. "Much obliged for the bird books. I've got them right here in my case. The next batch of books is on me, and so is the ride home. My driver's got the Hummer out front, ready and waiting. The dusting on the streets is no match for our ride."

"Ever the showman," Ivar said under his breath.

Ivar stood up from his desk, put on his jacket, and threw his satchel over his shoulder. He seemed to favor one side slightly as he stepped out of his office and into the hallway.

Martin eyed Ivar warily.

"You hurt yourself?" Martin asked hesitantly. "Slip on the ice or something?"

"No, I'm fine," Ivar said. "Just a muscle pull."

"Mmmm . . . I know that one," Martin said after clearing his throat. "Well, it's a good thing the Harvard overlords sprung for an elevator with backup power. I'd hate to see you take on twenty flights of stairs with a pulled muscle. Besides, you need to stay in shape for our trip to Mexico."

"Not worried about those drug kingpins?" Ivar asked.

"I'll book us on the Yucatan," Martin said with a quick raise of his eyebrows. "Safe as can be. And the birding . . . simply spectacular."

"By the way, that notecard you had earlier, the one you were writing on while talking to that grad student of yours," Martin said, pointing to the pocket where Ivar had previously placed the notecard. "Can't you just enter all that data into the computer? It would save you a step or two. Why write things down first when you've got a terminal and keyboard at every station? What's the point in using pen and paper first?"

Ivar extended one hand, making a rapid flickering motion with his fingers as if playing the piano.

"Music," Ivar said in a soft voice, moving his hand from side to side. "From mind, to hand, then back to the mind."

"If it was that important, I would think you'd want to enter it all into your databank right away," Martin said, straightening the collar of his jacket.

"Who said it was important?" Ivar asked, now moving his fingers up and down with a slow, deliberate motion. "I didn't say it was important. I said it was like music . . . from mind, to hand, and back to your mind."

Martin grunted.

29

Ivar locked the door to his laboratory, activated the alarm system, and headed toward the elevator with Martin.

"Sure you're okay?" Martin asked again, pointing his briefcase at Ivar's hip as he spoke.

"I'm fine," Ivar said as he pressed the elevator button. "I'm just fine."

CHAPTER 4

Boston
One week later

The Duesenberg J rolled away from Terminal E without making a sound.

Dr. Silas Anthony was seated in the back of Martin's antique limousine with both Martin and Dr. Joel Morgan. Dr. Anthony, after apologizing to his companions for his late arrival from London Heathrow, began to relate the details of his last visit to Boston some twenty years earlier. The occasion was Ivar's MIT graduation ceremony, and Silas recounted how Ivar, as class valedictorian, delivered a segment from Chopin's Piano Concerto no. 1 as his valedictory address. The twelve-minute performance was met with a standing ovation, and after the graduation ceremony concluded, Ivar was surrounded by members of the press corp. One writer described Ivar's execution of Chopin's Piano Concerto no. 1 as "flawless and masterful." Another columnist said it was "a moment of pure elegance." Another pressman wondered if Ivar's slow amble to and from the piano stool was a sign of just how cocky Ivar was, or was he just so nervous that he was trying not to collapse onto the stage floor. What none of the writers knew, or for that matter very few of the audience members knew, was that Ivar's glacially slow gait was due to the cardiomyopathy he had acquired as a result of a childhood respiratory infection.

When Silas found Ivar in the crowd after the conclusion of the graduation ceremony, Ivar was being interviewed by a reporter from the *London Times*. The *Times* reporter asked Ivar how he could have taken such a huge risk, as any miscue or falter at the keyboard could have been disastrous. The reporter pointed out that unlike oration, where the speaker could simply laugh aside a blunder or if need be pause for a moment and compose himself, one could so easily run aground when playing a musical masterpiece before a hushed audience.

Ivar told the *Times* reporter that thoughts of "running aground" had never entered his mind. Whenever he played before a crowd, Ivar thought of his mother and her many recordings that he listened to during his childhood, and how he imagined that it was his mother's hands moving along the keys. Just like he did every time he performed, Ivar played Chopin's Piano Concerto no. 1 in memory of his mother, whom he never knew, and his father, who died at sea when Ivar was six years old.

"By any measure, a truly magnificent performance," Silas Anthony said as he fumbled through his breast pocket, a scattering of papers falling around him. "The window glass rattled from the ovation Ivar received. Without uttering a syllable, Ivar made the rest of the ceremony appear positively turbid. The gathering was spellbound.

"I saved the *London Times* article," Dr. Anthony said as he carefully unfolded a tattered, yellowing newspaper clipping and handed it to Martin. "If I am not mistaken, Mr. Phyte, Ivar was one of your classmates."

Martin, who was seated alone in the rear-facing seat of the limousine, tried to keep a serious look on his face as he looked over the *Times* article.

"I'd like to tell you I have fond memories of that day, but I'm not sure I have any memories of it at all," Martin said as he handed the news article to Dr. Morgan, who was seated next to Silas. "You probably recall the events of that day far better than I do. Some friends and I had been celebrating for every bit of forty-eight hours prior to Ivar delivering his masterpiece. But I'll spare you both the particulars of that fete. And it's Martin. Please, just Martin."

"Of course," Dr. Anthony said, nodding his head. "And please, call me Silas."

Dr. Morgan skimmed through the news clipping, admiring the accompanying photograph that showed a tall, gangly young man seated behind a jet-black Steinway piano. The man in the picture was wearing his MIT graduation gown and mortar board.

"I ran into Ivar the other day, and he happened to mention that you are an accomplished pianist yourself," Martin said, trying to keep his tone casual. "While you're here visiting in Boston, maybe Joel and I will get the chance to hear both you and Ivar play. You know, dueling pianos."

Silas immediately put up both his hands. "I am nowhere in sight of Ivar's craft," he said, looking at Martin and shaking his head. "And I regret to say that both work and travel have pulled me away from my music. I suspect the same is true for Ivar, who is even as we speak traveling back from a series of lectures he was giving in New York. It has been so many years since I have seen Ivar. You mentioned that you saw him recently. How is he doing?"

"Oh fine, fine," Martin said straightaway. "Never better."

The speed of Martin's response to Silas's question did not escape Joel's notice.

"How was your flight?" Joel asked, changing the subject.

"Besides the long delay leaving Heathrow, circling Boston harbor several times, and the high adventure of locating my 'misplaced' luggage, not a glitch," Dr. Anthony said.

"Emerging from the terminal five hours late without a stitch of your belongings," Dr. Morgan said, grinning through his thick, graying beard. "Locally, this is known as 'the Logan welcome.'"

Dr. Anthony shook his head and grimaced as he looked at Martin. "Again, my every apology for being so tardy," he said. "Your forbearance here is more than I can ever repay."

Martin put up his hand and tilted his head slightly. He spoke not a word.

"Any flight is a success when takeoffs and landings total an even number," Dr. Morgan said. "Besides, at 2:00 a.m., you get to bypass the bumper-to-bumper festival that you would otherwise run into between the airport and the city's downtown."

Silas placed both of his palms on the thick leather upholstery, pressing down slowly. Peering out of the side window, Silas saw the car's red luster glow in the light of the Sumner Tunnel.

"The stealth of a cheetah," Silas said as the Duesenberg rolled through the night. "Luxury on this scale would make anyone's airport misadventures quickly fade from memory. This automobile, I have never . . ." His words trailed off.

"It's a 1936 J model, if I am not mistaken," Joel said as he eyed Martin. "Custom-made in the middle of the Great Depression for the family of a tobacco heiress. Only five or six of this model anywhere in the world, and the others I'm told are in museums somewhere. I have also heard rumor of a teal-green 1929 stashed away in a garage nearby."

Martin offered Joel a nonchalant shrug of his shoulders.

"Ivar says there'll be a capacity crowd when you lecture at Children's Hospital this Friday," Joel said, looking at Silas. "I'll be there for sure. And if you're inclined to give us a sneak preview, I promise, our lips shall remained sealed."

Although Martin didn't show it, his interest had piqued.

"There will be no earthshaking revelations, that much I can assure you," Silas said, removing his fedora. "Just our latest research on a line of synthetic agents used to treat tumors in children. Nothing revolutionary, mind you, but I'll present some yet-to-be-published data that will certainly be new to those gathered. Hopefully, I'll enlighten those present on some promising steps forward."

Martin couldn't imagine why Ivar wanted this man here. Why spend so much effort and energy inviting Silas to Boston? Was it just repayment for Silas's inviting Ivar to Scotland? Was it family loyalty? And why now?

The Boston night was windless and its streets nearly empty. Dr. Anthony strained to see the top of the Hancock tower as the limousine moved along Saint James Avenue.

"My day-to-day business is light years removed from the vagaries of medical research," Martin said. "But being a businessman and fretting about the bottom line day and night, I'd have to imagine that there's an enormous expense involved in such innovative endeavors . . . developing agents in a laboratory to fight cancer in children. It would probably take millions just to get a project off the ground."

"It's an endless battle," Silas said, drawing in a deep breath and letting it out slowly. "Fewer and fewer grant dollars chasing bigger and more costly investigatory studies. Ivar, no doubt, feels the same strain."

"Oh, I would imagine so," Martin said, trying to keep his tone positive. "But speaking as a layman here, I just have to wonder about . . . about alternatives."

Joel shot Martin a confused look but said nothing.

"Alternatives?" Silas asked, his brow furrowed.

"I'm speaking as an outsider, of course," Martin said, looking intently at Silas, "but aren't the severe side effects of man-made cancer-fighting drugs common knowledge? In your many years of experience, have alternate means of treatment shown any promise? Perhaps a modality not produced in either a laboratory or a medical center?"

"You mean natural means of cancer therapy?" Silas asked. "As in agents that are not man-made?"

"Again, I know nothing," Martin said, baiting Silas. "I'm just a nonscientist greenhorn."

"Such examples are legion," Silas said, brimming with enthusiasm. "Folklore told of a flowering plant in Madagascar that was used to treat all kinds of ailments, and in the 1950s, this same flower was discovered to inhibit cancer cell division. The two drugs extracted from this plant have been used to treat tumors ever since. Many standard agents are produced by bacteria, and one particularly potent agent is produced from a naturally occurring metal. An entire class of cancer-fighting drugs comes from the bark of a conifer tree in the Pacific Northwest, and another group of agents is derived from a fruit-bearing tree found right here in New England. Many such products have been discovered by accident, including the use of asparagine, a naturally occurring amino acid, in the treatment of certain blood cell cancers.

"Although these examples I just gave may be nature's own products, they're anything but a free ride," Silas continued, looking at Martin with a dour expression on his face. "Every one of these agents has a downside, and in some cases, the toxicity involved can be considerable."

"So there's no way to circumvent potentially deadly side effects?" Martin asked, an edge to his voice. "Whether produced by Mother Nature or in a laboratory somewhere, remedies to treat tumors are going to beat the patient to a pulp? This is predestined, correct?"

Silas let a long moment pass before he spoke.

"Not entirely," Silas said, looking squarely at Martin.

Martin remained impassive, still trying to size up a man he knew almost nothing about.

"So-called 'modern' therapeutic agents," Silas continued, "or more specifically, the standard medications that are used to treat cancer, have only been around for two or three generations. That at most. But our world has an abundance of lesser-known and certainly less scientifically established cancer-fighting substances, many of which have been in use for centuries. I have seen the results with my own eyes . . . remedies discovered in the Amazon rainforest or found in the jungles of Central America, used to shrink cancers of the skin and digestive tract. There's considerable evidence that herbal mixtures from Asia, in particular those found in western China, can be used to treat tumors of the lung and stomach. Ancient cultures from the horn of Africa, Northern India, and the Malaysian peninsula, they have used tree leaves, roots, flowers, bark, and various herbs to treat a host of cancers. Not unlike many of the discoveries in the so-called Western world, the effectiveness of many of these substances was found out by pure happenstance. Although no one knows for certain, most of these agents probably work by cutting off the blood supply to the cancer cells. And many," Silas paused to consider both of his companions, "*many* of the remedies I have mentioned are largely free of toxic side effects."

"All this would seem to beg the question," Joel said, slowly raising an index finger, "where does this leave the patients we treat here? The examples you have given and some of the results you yourself have witnessed, it's all anecdotal, right?"

"Quite," Silas said, peering at Joel over his reading glasses. "But this is only the beginning."

Joel and Martin looked at each other, and without saying anything they looked at Silas.

"Marine invertebrates, sea life along the ocean floor, terrestrial microorganisms and plants found only along high mountain plains . . . over 120 cancer-killing agents have been extracted from these sources alone," Silas went on, spreading out his arms and turning up the palms of both hands as he spoke. "And additional discoveries are being made all the while. What's more, biologists believe that less than 15 percent of the species thought to exist on earth have even been identified and catalogued. *Only 15 percent.* The possibilities in the world we inhabit are boundless."

Martin's Duesenberg moved west along Commonwealth Avenue, past the row of granite statues that memorialized more than two hundred years of Boston's history. Kenmore Square was still and silent, the bounding pulse and echoes of revelry from Fenway Park having faded away hours earlier.

"Why can't this body of knowledge be fused with the medical system we have here?" Martin asked, giving Silas a slanted look. "All you've seen, and no doubt what other medical professionals have experienced, is this not evidence enough?"

"Evidence, yes," Silas said as his fedora fell to the floor. "But proof, no. And that is what *our* system demands—proof. There are only two choices: scientific proof and ultimate acceptance, or disproof and abandonment. And I wouldn't know where to begin when it comes to discussing the hurdles involved in 'proving' something to my medical peers. Traditional therapy utilized by various cultures around the world . . . there is no means of measuring the outcomes of such treatments scientifically. I'd be run out of town if I introduced a mode of therapy that had no scientific backing. I'd also be stripped of every research dollar I was ever granted. And the more recent discoveries of marine life, microorganisms, and rare plants that produce anticancer agents, there are huge problems when it comes to extracting these resources. Only a small number of these substances have been adequately studied because the quantities of each are so limited."

Silas rolled down his window, letting in a rush of the cool night air.

"And then there's the many threats to our fragile environment," Silas said, still staring out the window. "Deforestation, fragmentation of habitat, overpopulation, carbon products soiling our oceans. God only knows how many sources of natural pharmaceuticals have already been destroyed."

"Silas, this is where you've got to enlighten me a bit," Joel said, shaking his head. "I've known Ivar all these years, and yet I've never had the courage to sit down with him and delve into the mechanics of how his work advances the care of children with such terrible disease. As you might imagine, Ivar and I exist in worlds that could not possibly be further apart. All I see are dudes who get shot or stabbed or grenaded by some other dude while walking their crippled aunty to a gospel sing-along. Ivar certainly understands what I do: Joe takes a .38 to the belly, I operate on Joe, Joe leaves the hospital, and I await Joe's return. And believe me, Joe will return. For whatever reason, people just tend to aim their weapons at the poor man, despite the fact that Joe spends every minute of every day minding his own business. Ivar, on the other hand, he has committed all these years to research, yet I really don't have a clear understanding of what his work entails. To the best of my knowledge, limited as it is, Ivar's work is centered on a concept not unlike what you've been discussing, that being the search for cancer therapy that's in every way robust while at the same time far less toxic. But ask me to explain to a fifth-grader what exactly Ivar does with his days and nights? I am shrouded in fog, truth be told."

"Left here, Barnes," Martin said to his chauffeur, the limousine turning sharply onto Lansdowne Street.

"I have been waiting to hear all this myself, and Professor," Martin looking at Dr. Anthony as he punched numbers into his cell phone, "need an appropriate classroom."

For Martin, everything was happening right on cue. Was this guy worth his salt like Ivar said he was, or was he just a chest-beating wind bag? Did Ivar invite Silas here out of politeness, or could Silas contribute something substantive to his research?

"It's me," Martin said to whoever was on the other end of the line. "We'll be coming through in about twenty seconds."

The Duesenberg turned right and disappeared into the bowels of an enormous, unlit brick building.

"Joel, where are we?" Silas whispered in the dim light as Martin continued to give instructions over his cell phone. "There's no one else in sight."

"Martin's got more showman in him than PT Barnum ever dreamed of having," Joel said, laughing. "We're underneath Fenway Park, where the Red Sox play. Ever been to a baseball game, Silas?"

Dr. Anthony took out his pocket watch.

"It is 2:40 a.m. Your team plays at this time of night?"

"No, no," Joel said. "The game ended hours ago. We beat Toronto in eleven innings. Access to these premises in the middle of the night is granted only by permission of the owner."

"Who's the owner?" Silas asked, squinting over his glasses.

"I am," Martin answered as he clicked off his phone.

39

Chapter 5

"He's a part owner," Joel said with a smirk, Martin ignoring the remark as Joel made himself comfortable in a seat on top of Fenway's Green Monster wall. "That said, the World Series trophy from a couple of years ago must look pretty tidy on the top of your desk, Martin. No doubt your corporate office has erected a small altar to house that memento."

"Right next to the one from '04," Martin said with an ear-to-ear grin.

"Ah. The place is looking more like the Vatican all the while," Joel said.

Dr. Anthony stood at the edge of the Green Monster wall, taking in the expanse of the ballpark from thirty-seven feet above the field. The diamond was illuminated by a single bank of tower lights from above center field. The ball field was groomed to perfection.

"Professor Anthony, your class is assembled," Martin said as Silas turned back around. "There are another 37,398 vacant seats," Martin gestured with his arms outstretched, "but we can't blame the others for leaving before you deliver your lecture. We are, after all, a little late getting started."

"Their loss," Joel added.

"Lights, please," Martin shouted, his voice resonating across the ballpark.

Three light towers along the opposite side of the stadium immediately sprang to life.

In over thirty years of lecturing, Professor Silas Anthony figured he had stood in every auditorium and on every podium in every corner of the globe.

Perhaps not.

Perhaps not at all.

"The essence of Dr. Ivar Nielsen's work is a field of study known as cancer virotherapy," Dr. Anthony said, clearing his throat as he began. "Joel, I suspect you are being modest about your knowledge of this topic, and, Mr. Phyte, no doubt you've seen this phrase in any number of news releases concerning Ivar's research."

Martin stared at Silas for a long moment. The professor was poised and his voice confident, not appearing at all intimidated by his surroundings.

"It's Martin," Martin said. "Just Martin."

"Yes, yes of course, Martin," Dr. Anthony said. "Now, cancer virotherapy involves the genetic alteration of a common, relatively harmless viral particle. Such alteration, which is in fact the engineering of the virus particle's genetic sequence, allows the virus to target and kill diseased cells without doing harm to healthy cells. The virus most commonly used is called an adenovirus, and as you may know, the adenovirus is the virus responsible for many cases of the common cold. In an elderly or otherwise debilitated individual, this virus can lead to bigger problems than just nasal congestion and fever, but well more than 99.9 percent of the time, a given patient will recover fully.

"Enter the bad guy," Dr. Anthony said as he began pacing from side to side as was his habit, "or more specifically, the cancer cell. Cancer cells, no matter where in the body they originate, have a series of protein markers on their surface. The first step in virotherapy is to alter the outer covering of the adenovirus particle so it can link up with the proteins that coat the outer layer of the cancer cells. Once this linkage is complete, the virus can enter the cancer cell and do what viruses do best."

"Which is?" Martin asked.

"Make a mess," Dr. Morgan interjected.

"Exactly," Dr. Anthony said. "Once inside the cancer cell, the virus's natural ability to overwhelm the host cell can proceed unhindered. This is step number two in the virotherapy sequence: cancer cell invasion and cancer cell destruction."

"I take it there is an act three," Martin said. "This virus of yours is kicking ass so far."

"Language, please," Dr. Morgan said, turning toward Martin and feigning a look of shock. "Need I remind you of classroom decorum?"

Martin shot Dr. Morgan a glance as he scratched the back of his bald head with his middle finger.

"Professor, please continue," Dr. Morgan said.

"Yes, act three, as you call it," Dr. Anthony said, his pace quickening as he elaborated further. "Now consider for a moment, what makes a person ill when one is infected with a cold virus? It is not the effect of a single virus on a single cell, but the effect of millions of viruses on millions of cells. Viruses replicate, and generally they replicate very rapidly. So now the genetically engineered cancer-killing virus, having entered the cancer cell, begins to replicate. It replicates by the thousands, and eventually by many millions. The virus is then released into the bloodstream, entering countless other cancer cells and destroying them."

"And only cancer cells, I take it," Dr. Morgan asked.

"You are correct, Dr. Morgan," Dr. Anthony said, pointing his index finger skyward. "As the surface markers on the virus are coded to dock with cancer cells and cancer cells alone, normal healthy cells that make up normal healthy organs escape unscathed.

"And there is yet another powerful weapon afoot here," Dr. Anthony continued. "The adenovirus particles are also coded with genes for enzymes that transform harmless chemicals in the hijacked cancer cells into chemotherapeutic agents. These chemical agents then go on to annihilate other cancer cells. This is step number four in the process: chemotherapy being produced *by* the body, as opposed to being introduced *into* the body."

"Like a neutron bomb," Martin said. "It kills the enemy but spares all else."

"That is the concept," Dr. Anthony said, nodding at Martin.

"Like I made clear from the start, all this is far removed from my field of expertise and practice," Dr. Morgan said. "But even I can tell you that it's not all quite that easy. I can see it all on a blackboard, but there's got to be a lot of permutations and details in each of these steps you've outlined, Silas. So many details, so many devils?"

"Countless," Dr. Anthony said, his shadow blanketing the entire section of Green Monster seats. "To start with, the virus particle has to be altered to allow precise linkage with the cancer cell. And there are thousands of surface markers that facilitate such a bonding. And the virus, once it has entered the cancer cell, is programmed to kill the enemy cell, right?"

Martin and Joel both nodded in agreement.

"Indeed it is. But not too rapidly, as the virus needs adequate time to replicate and produce copies of itself. Destroy the invaded cell too quickly and there will be no copies released into the bloodstream.

"From there," Silas continued, "the process only gets more confounding. You have to find the engineered adenovirus strain that replicates most efficiently in a milieu of cancer cells. And the coding for the viral proteins that allow for production of chemotherapy agents within the cancer cell itself . . . God only knows how many sequence variations there are for that process."

The drone from a small fleet of Zambonis could be heard along Lansdowne Street, far below the top of the Green Monster wall. The Fenway clock read 3:07 as the professor took a seat next to his two students.

"What are the chances," Martin asked, shifting in his seat, "what are the chances that Ivar will ever figure all this out? Or for that matter, what are the chances that *anyone* will ever figure all this out?"

"I cannot begin to venture a guess," Dr. Anthony said, shaking his head slowly. "Innovation on this scale faces a host of obstacles. It is a labor of many years, if not a lifetime. If not . . ."

"If not more than a lifetime?" Martin asked.

"If not more than a lifetime," Silas said in a low voice.

"Now you know why I chose to take care of projectile and impalement mishaps," Joel said. "Rather cookbook compared to this virotherapy business. I have neither the disposition nor the patience for such trailblazing pursuits. Mind-boggling, all of it."

"Where exactly does Ivar work?" Silas asked.

As if rehearsed, Martin and Joel pointed in unison to the upper floor of a building several blocks away, south of the ballpark.

Dr. Anthony craned his neck forward.

"The place way over there, with the lights on?" he asked.

"The lights are always on over there," Joel said, "and in more ways than one."

Although only forty-two years old, Ivar had already authored, coauthored, and/or edited a shelf of acclaimed medical texts. This was in addition to the hundreds of scientific journal articles that he and the rest of the IPOR staff had published. Ivar was also the youngest Harvard faculty member, in any medical school department, ever to be appointed a full professor.

Dr. Anthony was still squinting into the distance.

"Ah yes," Silas said, nodding his head slowly. "I am familiar with some of the research organizations that I believe are located in that neighborhood. Some are housed in the same facility as Ivar, if I am not mistaken. Many are quite highly regarded in the medical research community."

"They certainly regard themselves pretty highly," Joel said with a sharp inflection. "And if you listen carefully, you might be able to hear the drums beating even at this hour."

"I'd give Dr. Morgan some room here if I were you, Silas," Martin said as he moved a couple of seats away from Joel. "Wait till you see the foam that erupts out of the center of this sermon."

"If you ask me, Ivar is surrounded by a tribe of phonies over there, awash in a gravy train of grant money that 90-plus percent of the time could be put to far better use," Joel continued. "They spend their days basking in the bliss of endless cerebration and their nights telling the rest of us how impressed they are with themselves. What was it my old mentor used to say? 'Oh so many rivalries and their attendant egos, held forever captive within the confines of three city blocks.' If you ask me, they deserve the pomposity of each other's company. Ivar is cut from a different cloth entirely. He's in a different league, head and shoulders above the rest."

Dr. Anthony put on his fedora, stood up, and buttoned his tweed jacket.

"And to think he was once an orphan in a Scandinavian fishing village," he said, his voice resonating with pride. "If only others from his homeland could see him now."

"Better yet, why don't you see him now?" Joel said. "He's closer than you think."

"Now?" Silas asked, his eyes wide. "Arrive at Ivar's door step in the middle of the night? I have waited this long to see him, I can certainly wait another few hours. Please, I'll go to my hotel and spare him the intrusion."

As Silas was speaking, a metal door at the base of the Green Monster wall swung open, and Martin's Duesenberg rolled onto left field. A moment later, Barnes stepped out of the driver's side and opened the back door of the limousine.

"When it's you knocking, Silas, it's never an intrusion," Ivar said as he emerged from the back of the car. "No matter what the hour of day, or night."

Silas looked down onto the ball field in total disbelief. He then turned back toward Martin and Joel, who were grinning.

"One of your students had his cell phone on speaker mode," Ivar said, looking up at Silas. "I only caught bits and pieces, but from what I heard, you can deliver my own lectures better than I can."

Silas again turned toward Martin and Joel. Martin was dangling his cell phone between two fingers.

"Ivar's late train and your delayed flight," Martin said, cocking his head sharply as he looked at Silas. "Perfect timing."

"Now don't let me interrupt," Ivar said, holding up both hands as he called up to Silas. "But remember, Professor, now you've got three students instead of just two, and as you can see we're somewhat spread out. I'm afraid you'll have to speak up a bit more."

"And what could I possibly teach you?" Silas said to Ivar, a hint of emotion in his voice. "I am on the wrong side of the podium."

"Nonsense," Ivar said, shaking his head. "I was jotting down notes the entire time you were speaking, hoping to hear your thoughts on how to give this research of mine a running start."

Silas considered this for a moment and stared into the darkness of the grandstand before turning back toward Ivar and responding.

"A running start?" Silas asked, leaning over the railing as he called down to Ivar.

"I need your insight on how to . . . incite," Ivar said, stepping forward into the glow of one of the light towers.

"An accelerant," Martin said under his breath, glancing at Silas. "God only knows what that is and where he plans on finding it, but that's what the man is after, Professor."

"It looks to me like the two of you have a lot to discuss," Joel said as he stood up, "and shouting up and down the wall to each other is going to wear you both out. So let's all pile back into Martin's Duesy and head over to the South Street Diner for some vittles. The spread they put out will make Silas forget all about the rubber chicken they served him halfway over the Atlantic, which was probably better than the stale Pringles Amtrak sold Ivar on the way out of New York."

"Of course, if you'd like to bypass those irritating stoplights between here and the diner," Martin said, turning on the laser pointer that he had just pulled out of his pocket, "there are other means of transport at your disposal."

Silas followed the path of Martin's penlight beam across the length of the ball field. A moment later, a searing red glare outlined the black chrome rotor blades of the Agusta Grand helicopter berthed on the far side of the ballpark.

Silas looked at Martin and then at Joel.

"You can't possibly be serious," Silas said, his mouth agape.

"No, no," Joel said as he put his arm around Silas's shoulder. "We've had enough dramatics for one night. No doubt you're sick of air travel, so we'll stay right here on terra firma. Besides, if the Defense Department sees Martin's whirly bird going vertical, they'll probably ask him to give it back."

"We'll meet you down below, Barnes," Martin said, calling down to his chauffeur. "You know the way to South Street. That's our next stop."

Minutes later, the Duesenberg emerged from under Fenway Park and onto the quiet of the streets.

"Gentlemen," Silas began, looking at Joel and then at Martin, "might I ask how long our conversation this evening was on speaker phone?"

"Oh, only after Joel and I were seated above the outfield," Martin said, sounding somewhat apologetic. "We only allowed Ivar in while you were delivering your lecture, Professor. And you can blame it all on me—my idea from the start."

"Like I said, I only heard scattered parts," Ivar said, squeezing Silas's forearm. "I told Joel and Martin that you wouldn't mind if I listened in, and I *was* the only one listening in. So if anyone's at fault in this little caper, it's me."

"Fault?" Silas asked, letting out a laugh. "There is hardly any fault to be distributed here. But, Ivar, when you appeared out of nowhere onto Martin's ball field, I nearly fell over."

"I was feeling left out, you know," Ivar said, looking at Joel and Martin, and then looking at Silas. "I didn't want to miss any pearls of wisdom, so I eavesdropped my way over here after Barnes picked me up at the train station. But there was one part of your talk I just couldn't make out, Silas; the reception was particularly scratchy. I thought I heard something about this or that taking a lifetime to achieve? Could you repeat that one time for me?"

Silas looked baffled, but only for a moment.

"Ah, now I recall," Silas said, springing back to life. "Your research . . . years of study and toil, but it will all come to fruition well within our lifetime."

"Mmmm, I see," Ivar said, pressing his fist firmly against his hip as he sat back. "There's an optimist in the crowd."

Silas rolled down his window and looked back at the stadium, watching the rows of field lights flicker off one by one.

"Well within our lifetime," Silas repeated, nodding as the last of the light towers went dark.

Chapter 6

Boston
Four days later

Ivar had wanted to show Silas around Boston for years, and with Silas's lectures at Children's Hospital successfully completed the previous morning, he thought this would be the perfect day for a city tour. Silas and Ivar started out at the New England Aquarium, getting in line early and taking their time along the walkway that spirals around the giant ocean tank, viewing the sharks, stingrays, eels, sea turtles, and other marine life through the many windows cut into the sides of the barrel-shaped enclosure. Their next stop was in the North End for espresso and cannolis at Caffe Vittoria, and from there Ivar showed Silas the city's waterfront before taking him on a walk through the long corridors of Faneuil Hall Marketplace.

Ivar's favorite Saturday-morning ritual was a visit to Haymarket Square, an open-air fruit and vegetable market that dates back to the 1830s. The Haymarket is open every Friday and Saturday during daylight hours, with over a hundred vendors setting up shop at the end of Hanover Street, one block north of Faneuil Hall. Whenever he visited the Haymarket, Ivar would fill two large canvas shopping bags with fresh fruit and then bring the loaded bags to the lunch room for his laboratory staff to share.

Having arrived at the Haymarket during the midmorning rush, Ivar and Silas were trying to squeeze their way through the throng of shoppers shuffling in both directions along Hanover Street.

"Compared to this," Ivar said to Silas, pulling a plum out of the bag of fruit he had just purchased from one of the street merchants, "biting into produce from a supermarket is like sinking your teeth into a tennis ball. And I'm packing at least one of everything for your flight home tomorrow. When you clear customs in London, everything will have disappeared. Trust me."

"Thanks, pal," the merchant said as he handed Ivar two dollars in change, pointing at Ivar with his other hand as if he were holding a pistol. The man had on a fluorescent-green floppy hat and a pair of wraparound sunglasses, with a weighty gold necklace dangling in an out of his half-buttoned shirt.

"Don't forget me next week, friend," the man said, tucking his index finger under his belt as if holstering the pistol. "We got the best in the house. For you, only the best."

Ivar gave the man a wink.

Silas and Ivar walked through the center of the market and eventually stopped in front of two large vending carts that were parked back to back against the curb. One of the carts had several large vats filled with cod and snapper, along with slabs of tuna steak and swordfish. The other cart had row after row of fresh vegetables—beets, turnips, leeks, yucca, scallions, plantain, avocados, potatoes, and yams. As the vendors and the money they were handling moved freely between the two kiosks, there was little doubt that this was a family-run operation, just like many of the most successful Haymarket businesses.

"I'm looking for a spark, Silas," Ivar said, his tone matter of fact as he looked over the racks of vegetables. "A provocateur."

"Here?" Silas asked, pointing his finger back and forth between the two carts in a dramatic fashion.

Silas knew what Ivar was talking about, and Ivar knew that he knew.

Ivar offered Silas a crooked grin.

"See that table of green leaves over there?" Ivar said, pointing to a vending cart at the end of the street that was loaded down with garden herbs. "You never know . . ."

Silas let out a laugh.

"Tell me what you know, tell me what you surmise, or tell," Ivar hesitated as an elderly woman, bent at the waist, wheeled her hand cart past him, "or just guess. What I'm after, or more to the point what I'm lacking, is an inciting agent. I'm looking for something that can charge the virotherapy pathway. I've been rolling the ball uphill for a long time, Silas. What I need is momentum in the other direction."

"I take it you wanted to get out of the shop to talk about this?" Silas asked, looking wide-eyed at the people who ambled past, some weighed down with bundles of produce. "Best to save talk like this for ballparks and street markets, I guess."

"Yesterday was the day for pure science," Ivar said, referring to the lectures Silas had delivered the day before. "Today is for para-science."

"Whatever that is," Silas said, moving aside as two small children chased by. "As for your accelerant, your provocateur, one place you might look, in case it's not obvious, is the Amazon rainforest."

"A place you've visited, if I'm not mistaken," Ivar asked.

"Recently, in fact," Silas said, tilting his head and nodding. "Don't ask me what I was looking for. I really wasn't looking for anything. I was touring, for whatever reason, in a part of Brazil that's minimally accessible. I went there with a couple of Brazilian doctors after visiting one of the medical centers in Sao Paulo, and seeing the practice of medicine in the middle of a jungle, in a place so secluded . . . just fascinating. I had for years heard talk of the graviola tree, which grows in this distant part of Brazil, as a plant from which acetogenins can be extracted."

Acetogenins are naturally occurring carbon-based complexes that are closely related to compounds from which several commonly used antibiotic and antifungal agents are produced. Another pharmaceutical, which is used to reduce blood levels of cholesterol, is derived from the same family of compounds.

"The acetogenins found within the graviola leaf may—I repeat *may*—inhibit cancer cell growth," Silas continued, "but after visiting this region, I came away far from convinced, and I'm not sure I'd recommend using this line of agents in any cancer-treatment protocol. You can purchase this product here in the United States, but I can't attest to the purity of the product you'd be buying. Getting your hands on bona fide, native-grown graviola leaf, in quantities needed for study and research, is in my estimation close to impossible. The locals in that part of South America remain quite suspicious of anyone taking native products out of their rainforest."

"Canta-*loop*, canta-*loop*, two for three dollar!" a frizzy-haired child began screaming, his arms flailing. "Your canta-*loop* here, give three take two."

"A minute ago, you said the rainforest held promise," Ivar said with his face in a frown, "and now you're telling me the locals chased you away empty-handed. Is the Brazilian Amazon a part of the world that's worth investigating?"

"Oh, I believe it is," Silas said, getting his words out in between the street cries advertising cantaloupe. "The sheer scale of the rainforest makes it promising, but that's also what makes it so intimidating, as in five and a half million square kilometers intimidating, with who knows how many species that may be of utility in medicine."

"Canta-*loop*!"

Ivar motioned for Silas to follow him across the street, finding a somewhat quieter place below a barely legible ad painted on the side of a building at the corner of Hanover and Marshall Streets. Silas looked up at the sign, making out the words *Bostonian Cigars 10 cents* written vertically along the building's edge.

"I wanted to ask you about a species of invertebrate that I read something about a while back," Ivar said, looking over a stack of grapefruit on a nearby cart. "I only breezed through the article, and I'm afraid I don't recall much in the way of specifics. This invertebrate . . . the name begins with a *B*, I think."

"A bryozoan species?" Silas asked.

"That's it," Ivar said, speaking to Silas but pointing at the grapefruit. "I'll take four of those, please," Ivar said to the vendor.

"Bryozoans are tiny aquatic organisms," Silas said, "but it is actually a bacteria found within the bryozoan's tentacle that may have activity against cancer cells. There is some evidence that an enzyme produced by this bacteria may be useful in treating pancreatic and lung tumors, but in my estimation, there's a lot of distance to cover before any of this can be proven. I'd stick to plant life, Ivar. There's more promise on the ground, I believe."

"Thank you," Ivar said to the vendor, placing the grapefruit in his shopping bag.

"Well, that's good to hear," Ivar said, now looking at Silas. "Staying with plant life, that is."

"Glad you agree," Silas said, looking at Ivar over his glasses.

"Yes," Ivar said, pointing up the street. "Because I've called in my very favorite botanist, just to lend us a hand."

When Silas turned to look up Hanover Street, he saw a tall girl making her way through the crowd, her face covered by the dark shield of a motorcycle helmet. The girl was dressed in black leather from head to toe, and as she drew near, she pulled off the riding helmet and shook loose her long locks of coppery hair. The girl immediately embraced Ivar, and she then turned toward Silas.

"Silas, I'd like you to meet Andie McKillnaugh," Ivar said, squeezing Andie's shoulder. "Andie and her Harley caught the early ferry out of Nantucket, just to meet you. I just couldn't imagine you visiting Boston and not meeting Andie, and vice versa."

"Dr. Anthony, it is an honor to meet you," Andie said, extending her hand. "Ivar has told me so much about you. I know I'm a few days late, but welcome to Boston."

"The pleasure is all mine," Silas said, shaking Andie's hand and placing his other hand on Andie's forearm. "Ivar said he had a surprise for me when we were at the market, and indeed he did. So good of you to come all the way here to join us."

Andrea Lynn McKillnaugh had spent her college summers working for Ivar as a microbiology technician, and once she entered Tufts Medical School, she continued to work in the lab two nights a week and at least one weekend every month. Through the years, Ivar had become Andie's mentor and confidant, and to Ivar, Andie was in every sense the little sister he never had. Andie told Ivar everything—every design, every dream, every delight, every hurt. At lunchtime, the two of them would sit in Evans Way Park and play chess, weaving plots for spy novels around those who wandered through the park or frequented the neighboring street corners:

The falafel sheik, I know his face . . . he's an Uzbeki spy, I'm sure of it.

The snow cones sold by the dwarf Rastafarian are laced with surveillance chips.

How can the utility van driver afford a diamond pinkie ring and a $200 hairdo?

The spumoni man was the most suspicious character of all, his zoned-out Timothy Leary façade fooling absolutely no one.

It all seemed so great, and it all seemed so perfect until one frozen January afternoon when something went terribly wrong. That was the day Andie received an urgent call from a nearby hospital's emergency room, and a minute later, Andie was seen doing a full sprint out the door of Ivar's laboratory, racing down Brookline Avenue and never returning. And as far as anybody knew, that was the end of everything—Andie's research, Andie's medical education, Andie's fiancé, and by all accounts, Andie's ebullient smile. Everyone at the lab knew that Ivar had stayed in touch with Andie, but they also knew that Ivar would never divulge any of the details as to what happened on the day that Andie's world came undone.

"No waiting! Step up to the plate!" the rotund vendor bellowed, the rolls of his midsection draped between the lower fold of his shirt and his sagging waistline. "C'mon, we've got eggplant, apricots ten for a dollar, c'mon. Beautiful green grapes, a dollar a bag."

"Excuse me," Andie said to Silas and Ivar, walking across the street and handing the merchant a dollar for a bag of apricots.

"Thank you, m'lady," the salesman said, snapping his index finger against the bill of his visor.

"Beautiful green grapes before they're gone, a dollar a bag, c'mon!"

"Ivar mentioned that you are a botanist," Silas said once Andie had returned. "Considering our line of conversation so far, your arrival is most timely."

"I majored in botany in college, but I won't have much to offer beyond that," Andie said, stuffing the apricots into her satchel. "I do keep a garden, or at least try to."

"Have you heard of the peony?" Silas asked. "You may even have one or two in your garden as we speak."

"I don't, but I ought to," Andie said, peeling off her leather riding jacket. "A big flowering plant, light-colored petals, very fragrant. Originally from Asia, I think."

"You think correctly," Silas said, looking at Ivar and then back at Andie. "And if I might I ask, have you ever heard of PHY906?"

"You've got me there," Andie said, grinning and shaking her head.

Silas then looked at Ivar, searching for an answer to the same question.

"You've got to be kidding," Ivar said, arching one eyebrow. "The single plant in my office is barely surviving, which might give you some clue as to my knowledge of plant life."

"I'll keep it brief, I promise," Silas said, "as PHY906 is a most abrasive name for a substance derived from such a bountiful flower."

A large dolly cart holding a stack of plastic bins rumbled past, ice spilling off from every side. Two men from a nearby kiosk heaved the bins onto their empty table, with a line of waiting customers moving in around them.

"Fresh shucked clams! No wait!" one of the vendors shouted, a cigarillo bobbing between his upper and lower lip. "Oysters, you gotta wait! Clams no wait! They're all a dollar. We got fresh shucked . . ." The vendor looked into another bin that his partner had just sent crashing down onto their cart. "Shrimp! Now we got shrimp, no wait either," the man said through a gap-toothed smile, rocking his head back. "Shrimp and clams, you got no wait, oysters, you gotta wait. All a dollar."

"As Andie pointed out," Silas continued, stepping against the curb as the empty shellfish cart rolled past, "the peony is a flowering plant native to Asia. There is a four-herb combination extracted from this flower that goes by the name PHY906. There are at least sixty active chemicals within this herbal mixture, and there is some evidence that PHY906 is effective against stomach and intestinal cancers. This should really not be a surprise, as medicinal use of the peony flower in China dates back to antiquity. Then of course . . ."

"Comin' through, buddy," another man said as he pushed his loaded cart toward the shellfish vendor, missing Silas's feet by inches.

Silas took out a handkerchief and wiped his forehead.

"Let's find a seat over there," Ivar said to Silas, pointing to the open door of the Bell in Hand Tavern. "We'll take a break and save your toes from getting sheared off."

"Now we got oysters! There's no wait neither!" the vendor called out, waving his shucking knife at the bin that had just landed on his cart. "Shrimp, clams, and now oysters, they're all fresh, and they're all a dollar."

The Bell in Hand Tavern, the self-proclaimed oldest alehouse in America, takes up most of the tiny triangle of space between Hanover Street, Union Street, and Marshall Street. Ivar found a table near a large open window, and although it was only eleven in the morning, he ordered three Harp drafts and offered Silas a toast, thanking him for his visit and wishing him a safe trip home. When the waitress came by, Ivar ordered two more Harps, one for himself and one for Silas. Andie had a long drive ahead, so she ordered a club soda.

"So let's put the peony aside for a moment," Ivar said, looking at Silas after taking another sip from his beer. "I want to ask you about alkaloids. They have a long history when it comes to medicinal uses; that much I know. What I don't know is which one, or ones, might hold promise as our provocative agent."

Alkaloids are a diverse group of naturally occurring nitrogen-based compounds produced by a large variety of plants, animals, bacteria, and fungi. Alkaloids are found worldwide, with over ten thousand chemically distinct compounds identified.

"A long history indeed," Silas said, swirling his pint glass. "Four thousand years' worth, perhaps longer. Ancient writings from Mesopotamia record their medicinal virtues, and ever since then, alkaloids have been used by many cultures as anesthetics, stimulants, antibiotics, and painkillers. They have been used as well in the treatment of heart ailments."

"And to treat cancer?" Andie asked.

"Breast, ovarian, tumors of the head and neck," Silas said, finishing his beer, "and highly potent, as they halt the replication of cancer cells. And highly toxic."

"Does that include the *Lobelia* plant that can be used in cancer therapy?" Ivar asked, handing the waitress his empty glass. "What I'm asking is, are the alkaloids extracted from the *Lobelia* plant in any way toxic?"

"I really have no idea," Silas said. "I'm not sure anyone does. There are probably four hundred species of *Lobelia* worldwide, but as far as I know, only one has shown any evidence of having anticancer properties. The *Lobelia* species you're referring to is found in a dot of a place somewhere off in the Himalayas and nowhere else. Finding it would be enormously difficult, if not impossible. But the utility of alkaloids in cancer therapy is undeniable, and so much remains unknown. There's no telling what potential is still out there."

While Silas was speaking, Ivar pulled two notecards from his shirt pocket and began writing out a line of small symbols on the margins of one of the cards.

"Playing the piano once again, Professor?" Andie asked, smiling at Ivar.

Without looking at Andie, Ivar stretched out his other arm and tapped his fingers lightly against the side of the table.

"Ivar, I must ask," Silas said, edging across the table slightly. "Where are you heading with all this? The graviola tree, the bryozoan, the peony, *Lobelia,* and the alkaloid compounds . . . where do they fit in? Do you really believe any of these can lend a spark to ignite your research pathway? None of these substances have even been studied for use in children. Can anything we've talked about extend the life of a child with cancer for even a day?"

"They don't have to extend anything," Ivar said as he wrote notes on the second card. "They only have to accelerate."

Once they left the Bell in Hand, Andie, Ivar, and Silas mixed in with an even thicker crowd of patrons along Hanover Street. Andie found a nearby kiosk that was overflowing with homegrown garden herbs, the minty scent of basil filling the surrounding air as if the vending cart was parked on a lawn of fresh-cut grass. Andie bought three small bags of tarragon and three bags of sage, handing one of each to Silas and Ivar.

"Just hide these deep in your luggage," Andie said to Silas. "If customs finds them, something tells me they'll believe you when you confess the contents."

"Much appreciated, Andie," Silas said. "And that goes double for my wife, who is the chef in our home. She's a wonderful cook."

"Oh look, mangos," Andie said, eying the stacks of fruit on the cart immediately across the street.

"How 'bout these mangos, they're $1.50, three for $4. Right he-ay. Yes, darlin'," the vendor said to Andie, running a hand through his slicked back, gray hair. "What'll it be?"

"Two mangos, ripe," Andie said, handing the man some cash.

"Comin' up . . . Hey, you—yeah, you—no picking!" the vendor said sharply, making a motion as if he might slap the hand of a customer who was reaching across his cart. "Unless you want my job, I pick. You point, I pick. You can go home and pick anything you want, but not here. Here, I pick." Focusing his attention back on Andie, he said, "Thanks muchly, miss," offering her a wide toothy grin.

"Walk me to my ride?" Andie said to Ivar and Silas, pointing up Hanover Street. "Got lucky. Found a spot at the corner."

Once they reached Andie's motorcycle, Andie shook Silas's hand and embraced him. "A safe trip home, Dr. Anthony, and keep an eye on my best pal while he's over in Scotland with you," Andie said, nodding toward Ivar.

"I'm afraid he'll be on his own for a good while," Silas said, handing Andie one of his business cards. "Ivar's got quite an excursion planned, scouting about for rare birds on several of our islands. But once in Edinburgh, I hope to show our man half as good a time as he showed me here."

When Andie turned to Ivar, she noticed him pressing his thumb into the top of one eye socket. Ivar blinked several times, rubbed his eye, and put his glasses back on.

"Mornings and Harp, maybe they don't mix," Andie said, a sad smile across her face. "I'm going to miss you, you know. Please send an e-mail here and there . . . whenever."

After hugging Andie for every bit of a full minute, Ivar pulled away and looked at her.

"I'll miss you too, but you already know that," Ivar said, again rubbing his eye. "I'll send along some shots of the terns along the shore."

Andie sat down on her bike, put on her helmet, and started the engine.

"And before you leave town, please get your eyes checked," Andie said, flipping up her helmet shield and regarding Ivar with a worried look. "You look really tired, you know. And maybe you need a new eyeglass prescription. You don't want to miss any of those shorebirds out there in the Orkneys."

Andie flipped her shield down and sped off, waving good-bye to Silas and Ivar.

Andie headed toward the expressway onramp, but she stopped short when she noticed something pressing down on top of her head from inside her helmet. When Andie pulled over and took the helmet off, she found one of the notecards that Ivar had been writing on tucked inside. Andie unfolded the card and read the words:

The ragged men in ragged clothes
the sliver thorn of bloody rose,
lie crushed and broken
on the virgin snow.

Andie placed the notecard in the pocket of her riding jacket and put her helmet back on. When she looked in her rearview mirror, Andie saw Ivar standing on the corner of Hanover Street, looking in her direction, and holding a laser light in his hand. Andie then saw four bright bursts of light reflect twice in succession.

short-short-long-short
short-short-long-short

Andie squeezed the tears back into her eyes and gunned the engine, her Harley racing through the tunnel that led away from the city.

Chapter 7

Boston
Five weeks later

Dr. Myles Carnot, Ivar's chief of operations at IPOR, had not taken his eyes off the computer screens in front of him since he arrived at his office four and a half hours earlier. Myles was sitting at his desk, entering data from one series of research trials and setting up the starting points for the next phase of study. In between entries, Myles sent out a stream of e-mail responses to other staff members, each note a one-to-two-syllable reply, such as "yes," "no," "wrong," "forget," "Cme," "now," "rightnow," "redo," "never!" "today," "noway," or "toolate," to mention just a few. Myles had been Ivar's partner in cancer research for over fifteen years, and despite his petulance and not infrequent angular remarks, the rest of the laboratory staff respected his tireless work ethic and his capacity as an on-site troubleshooter. If Ivar's primary task was to innovate and formulate, Myles's primary task was to serve as superintendent of minutiae and lord of every particular through each research stage. Myles had spent the previous evening reviewing a series of protein markers with one of the lab's virologists, Dr. Luc dul Tran, who was supposed to meet Myles the next day at 8:00 a.m. sharp. It was now 8:35, and there was no sign of Dr. Tran.

"Tran. Tran. Where in bloody hell . . ." Myles yelped, sticking his head above one of the cubicle barriers. "Tran!"

Dr. Stacey Ravelle, the lead geneticist on Ivar's team, was down the hall with a group of medical students. Having been witness to Myles's tirades more times than she could count, Stacey acted as if she heard nothing.

Myles spotted Stacey and raced toward her.

"Stacey, Tran has performed another vanishing act," Myles blurted, his mop of red hair pointing in every direction. "There's a three-hour window here, and I'm doing wind sprints in quicksand without those phase-six surface markers Tran has supposedly been slaving over for the past week. These are the markers that are going to be inserted into the genetic code of that latest viral strain we've prepared."

Myles looked away from Stacey, considered the gathering of startled faces standing directly behind her.

"Who are these people?" Myles asked with his own patented brand of impatience.

"These *people*," Stacey said, "are known as medical students. You know, the ones who actually pay for the privilege of being here. Third Thursday of the month, as always, the first-year students spend the day with us. Ladies and gentlemen, allow me to introduce our operations director, Dr. Myles Carnot."

A collection of uneasy smiles greeted Dr. Carnot.

"Of course, of course, good morning," Myles said as he ran a palm across his brow. "I see you've all met Dr. Ravelle, and *eventually* we'll all have the pleasure of Dr. Tran's company. Today, as no doubt you know, we have a lot of ground to cover . . . some basic genetics, and more importantly how it relates to microbiology and our cancer research. We may be limited when it comes to time, but you are never limited when it comes to asking questions. So along the way, ask whatever whenever, and by the end of the day, you'll have some appreciation—" Myles stopped abruptly when he spotted Dr. Luc dul Tran.

"Excuse me," Myles said as he moved away from Stacey and the medical students and walked full stride toward Dr. Tran, who had entered the lab through a fire exit along the far wall.

"Tran, shit, we're at a crucial hour here. You know I need those markers, and yet you pull another David Copperfield on me. What's the skinny?"

Although she was standing at least a hundred feet away, Stacey exchanged glances with Dr. Tran as they both watched Myles navigate his way through yet another "crisis." In Myles's estimation, every hour was crucial and every experiment dire, with the gray cells below his shock of red hair forever stuck in the "on" position.

"Two lef, Myle. On-ly two. Then, we have full see-quence," Dr. Tran said in his thick Vietnamese accent.

"Tran, listen," Myles said, a trace of a twitch beginning to develop above the corner of his left eye. "*This* sequence is the starting gate for phase six; you know that every damn bit as well as I do. All the other gene transfers are just sitting there—waiting . . . *waiting* . . . waiting to be inserted into the genetic sequence of the newest strain of virus we've prepared."

Myles was whispering now, stooping down low in dramatic fashion and looking up imploringly at Dr. Tran.

"Tran, I truly mean it. Come through for me on this, and the world is yours. I promise you, it is. Go ahead and ask, and anything you want, it's yours. If there's some delay, I understand. But I just need to know when—*when* will you have those surface markers ready? Before the noon whistle? Before dark? Before the Fourth of July fireworks?"

Myles whispered yet lower, "When?"

"Two hour, no more. Two," Dr. Tran said.

With that assurance, Myles began rifling through the drift of data that one of the graduate students had just handed him.

Dr. Tran had not moved an inch.

"What?" Myles asked, his face twisted.

Dr. Tran shuffling his feet uneasily.

"I-var, post-cod?" Dr. Tran asked, worry punctuating his few words.

Myles closed his eyes and drew in a deep breath. "No, Tran, no such communiqué. No calls, no texts, no e-mails, no wires. No smoke signals, semaphore flags, or Morse code either. And no postcards. The man is wandering somewhere in the Scottish Highlands, looking for all kinds of rare birds and with any luck at all enjoying the first vacation he's ever treated himself to. Now you will be the first to know if a flock-of-feathers postcard lands at our door, or for that matter if I see a photo of Miss Scotland or the Loch Ness Monster or a bunch of merry chaps in plaid skirts running about. Meanwhile, I would be eternally grateful if you unloaded a pound or two of lead and FedEx me a nice, shiny postcard of that line of surface markers you've been promising."

"Ki my ass, Myle," Dr. Tran said as he did an immediate about-face, leaving Myles to wade through the sheaf of data he was holding.

"Just get me the fucking numbers, will ya?" Myles mumbled to himself, with no one else around to shout at. "And the med students are here today," Myles said as he looked down the hallway, his words chasing after Dr. Tran. "Teach them something while you're perfecting your work, just like you always do. Preferably in English, if it's not asking too much"

Myles did a rapid-fire scan through the pages of trial data he was holding.

Trajan 17	9% cytoreduction
Pertinax 8	11% cytoreduction
Macrinus 1	15% cytoreduction
Otho 2	Aborted
Decius 11	14% cytoreduction
Severus 18b/c	22% cytoreduction
Galerius 4	No measurable change
Julian 7	19% cytoreduction
Julian 22	27% cytoreduction
Macrinus 6	Aborted
Quintillus 29a	12% cytoreduction
Magnus 10	In study
Lucius 5	In study
Otho 5/6	20% cytoreduction
Valens 1	30% cytoreduction

"Who handed me this?" Myles asked, with no one in sight. "You can come out from under the rock," Myles said, a bit louder. "This is what I'm after. This is what *we* are after. Hello? We've got progress here, folks. Will someone please raise a hand?"

At the other end of the lab, Stacey was giving the medical students an overview of the IPOR facility.

"The facility you are standing in exists to pursue a singular objective," Stacey began, tuning out Myles's voice from down the hall, "that objective being: how do you annihilate cancer in a child without sapping the life out of its young victim? The core of our work here is cancer virology, also known as virotherapy. The ultimate goal of virotherapy is to re-format a common virus particle and use it to kill *all* cancer cells and thereby obviate the need for more traditional therapy."

The genetic code in *homo sapiens* contains at least forty to fifty thousand genes housed on the complement of twenty-three chromosomes we inherit from each of our parents. This is the blueprint that largely determines an individual's physical substance, growth, and development. Each gene is made up of the complex chemical deoxyribonucleic acid, or DNA. DNA controls all the processes that take place inside our bodies and does so by producing proteins that carry out a given gene's instructions.

"Cancer," Stacey said, emphasizing the word, "begins when a damaged gene leads to the production of abnormal proteins. In children, some of the most vicious of all cancers are soft tissue malignancies of the head, throat, ear, eye, and neck. These tumors originate in between the deep layers of the skin and the bony skeleton, or more specifically in muscles, joints, blood vessels, and fat. The most common of these cancerous growths is known as a rhabdomyosarcoma, or malignancy of muscle cells.

"Rhabdomyosarcoma generally occurs between the ages of four and fifteen," Stacey continued, "invading the vital structures of the face, ear, and neck. If left unchecked, the tumor will eventually erode the adjacent bony skeleton and then spread to distant sites via the lymphatic system. Conventional therapy for this cancer is as aggressive as it is debilitating, consisting of a combination of surgery, radiation therapy, and intravenous chemotherapy. Even at the most-advanced medical centers, including the one next door, the five-year cure rate for some of these children is 50 percent at best.

"Rhabdomyosarcoma is a killer of children and teenagers," Stacey said, the point hitting home as some of the students shifted uneasily, "and curing this disease by means of virotherapy is the IPOR's ultimate goal. If a malignancy such as this can be cured by virotherapy, then this same technology can be applied to other pediatric cancers."

Stacey was in the middle of fielding a question when Myles appeared out of nowhere. Myles was carrying a stack of microscope slides in one hand and what appeared to be an expense report in the other, with a cluster of phone messages stuffed into his shirt pocket. Stacey also noticed that Myles had rows of phone numbers scribbled onto the back of both of his hands.

In an age when nearly everyone relied on two or more electronic devices at all times, each capable of holding millions of data bits, Myles still wrote down the phone numbers he needed, often on the back of both hands.

"This way," Myles said, arcing his arm in a wide swoop, directing the group of students to the center quad of the lab.

Myles gave one of the medical students a hard look, reading the student's name straight off the ID badge that was clipped to his jacket.

"Doctor, as of today, has any cancer in the human body been cured with virotherapy?" Myles asked. "And in case it is not obvious, you have two choices in answering my question: one of those choices is yes, and the other is no."

The student knew that no matter how long he thought about the question he was just asked, the answer he gave would be wrong. "No," the student answered firmly.

Myles was staring up at a ceiling fan that was making a low grating sound as it slowly spun around.

"Ever hear of Thompson's Law?" Myles asked the student, still looking up at the fan.

"No, I haven't," the student answered.

"Anyone?" Myles scanned the eyes of the other students.

Silence.

"Dr. Milford Thompson was the dean of my school, and he went to his grave bull-headed certain that if you asked a med student any question with a fifty-fifty chance of getting it right, there was a 90 percent chance he or she would get it wrong. So the old crow is still wearing that shit-eating grin of his," Myles said.

"The answer is in fact a resounding yes," Myles continued. "Better than a hundred years ago, a young woman with cervical cancer was attacked by a dog that was believed to be rabid, and immediately after this injury, the woman was treated with an attenuated rabies virus. Within a month or so, the woman's cervical cancer had disappeared. And this occurrence is not unique. In the 1950s, a group of cancer patients who underwent a series of vaccinations subsequently showed signs of tumor regression. Twenty years after that, there was a report of a lymphoma patient showing significant improvement after he contracted the measles."

Myles then walked over to a five-foot black cylinder that was housed on a gun-metal console.

"This, as you all recognize, is a transmission electron microscope. Trade this in and each one of you can expunge that unsightly blot of red ink you've all been accumulating at your local savings and loan. Consider," Myles said, placing a slide on the microscope stage.

The micrograph that appeared on the console screen looked like a cobblestoned flying saucer, with hundreds of jagged spikes projecting from its surface.

"Doctor," Myles said, his eyes taking aim at another student, "what have we here?"

"A virus," the student answered as she looked over at a classmate for encouragement. "Some sort of virus."

"You see," Myles said as he adjusted the magnification, "avoid those pesky fifty-fifty questions, and we begin to make progress.

"This is an adenovirus," Myles said. "The last time either you or your great-aunt Bessy had a sniffle, this was the likely culprit. The projections that you see extending from the body of the virus are proteinaceous fibers, also known as pins. Our first goal is to engineer the adenovirus such that the proteinaceous pins recognize the unique markers along the outer layer of the rhabdomyosarcoma cell. Once the virus has docked with the malignant cell, viral DNA is injected inside the cancer cell, and the virus begins to replicate. DNA strands injected into tumor cells allow viral replication that is a thousand times greater than replication within normal cells.

"This is where the Everly Brothers step in," Myles said as he removed the microscope slide. "And Buddy Holly, Jefferson Airplane, the Doors, Donovan, Yes, U2, the Clash, Zager and Evans, the King, and yes, even Janis herself," Myles added.

"Zager and who?" one of students whispered to no one in particular.

"Zager and Evans," Myles answered. "'In the Year 2525.' You've got to show some respect for the one-hit wonders.

"Unfortunately," Myles continued, "you will not have the opportunity to meet Dr. Ivar Nielsen today. This, as no doubt you are aware, is his facility, his research, and his brainchild. The aforementioned instances of a virus effectively treating cancer are anecdotal, and at the time of their discovery, this entire process was very poorly understood. Cancer virology, as a science, is still in its infancy. Dr. Nielsen pioneered the technology that allows the conjugation of the engineered virus with certain cancer cells, and the trials going on around you will delineate which genetic alterations within the virus allow the most efficacious bonding between the virus and the cancer cells.

"Dr. Nielsen assigns each combination of viral surface proteins, or pins, the name of a celebrated rock band or hall-of-fame legend. This keeps the rest of us totally blinded as to the machinations that altered the virus's genetic makeup."

Another member of the laboratory staff, a Colombian graduate student with jet-black hair that trailed down to her waist, handed Myles a message. Myles stuffed the message into the bundle of notes that was already jammed into his shirt pocket. Myles then handed the grad student the expense report he was holding, which detailed all purchases from the local supply company that stocked Ivar's laboratory.

"So now that our cancer cell is hijacked," Myles said as he used his thumb to jam the last message deeper into his pocket, "the real work begins."

Myles motioned everyone to a workstation lined with state-of-the-art Zeiss microscopes. Each of the microscopes had a large viewing screen mounted overhead.

"I am not even going to ask you what that is," Myles said as a micrograph appeared on each of the overhead screens.

The photograph showed parallel arrangements of striated structures, each highlighted in a light purple stain.

"This you will recognize as normal muscle tissue," Myles said. "You know, the stuff that atrophies during your four years of med school. Now, compare this to exhibit 2."

A new micrograph appeared on each of the screens.

"Doctor, your thoughts on this image," Myles asked as he peered at another one of the students. This student in particular could relate to Dr. Carnot's observation about muscle mass wasting away as the years of academic pursuit marched along, as he had at least ten years and six extra inches of waistline on most of his classmates, with Jolt and Red Bull fueling every extra pound.

"This is not normal tissue," the student said.

While a couple of the other students snickered, Myles gave the small gathering a stern look.

"And why is this not normal?" Myles asked.

"I see muscle fibers, but they're very irregular," the student said in response. "The fibers are arranged in irregular ribbons and dark, haphazard clumps."

The whirl of a centrifuge from an adjoining workstation became louder as the student spoke. Myles powered down the centrifuge and considered his audience.

"One and all, take note," Myles said. "'Not normal,' to quote the doctor. *This*," Myles pointed to the screens above, each showing the identical image of diseased muscle tissue, "is *not* normal. This is a rhabdomyosarcoma, or cancer of the muscle cells. And it is a killer.

"The second part of our research determines which variation of the adenovirus will allow maximal virus replication prior to cancer cell death," Myles explained. "You can't kill the cell too quickly, but you can't let the engineered virus linger too long either. The internal chemistry of the virus has to be engineered so as to maximize replication and thereby propagate the cancer-fighting virus. Once again, there are multitudes of variations in the genetic code that have to be studied and trialed.

"Any takers as to how we designate these variations?" Myles asked. "And keep in mind that the last person who suggested the use of letters from the Greek alphabet is now lathering mustard onto hot pretzels about fifty yards from here.

"Here's a hint," Myles continued. "That dude you saw under the electron microscope, his name is *Jaws*."

"Do you have one called *Shaft*," someone asked after a brief silence.

"He's in the mix somewhere," Myles said, grinning slightly. "The rest you can probably guess: *Casablanca, Shane, Godfather, MASH, Scrooged, Marty, Dracula, Godzilla, Kane* . . . each is given a name from the silver screen. And as with the first phase of this research, every member of the staff is blinded, having no knowledge whatsoever of the genetic code. Dr. Nielsen gives each genetic variation an alias, and our research team runs each trial free of any bias."

Myles ushered everyone into a conference room where a bank of printers along the far wall clattered continuously, sending streams of data onto the floor. Framed photographs of birds from all over the world covered every parcel of wall space.

"A Merlin," one of the students said as she entered the room.

Myles spun around and looked at the student, his face contorted.

"A what?" he asked.

The student pointed to a photo of a powerful-looking bird with a blue-gray crown and a white-tipped tail.

"That's a Merlin. It's a type of falcon. And the dark brown bird with the long wings and forked tail, in the next frame, that looks like some type of storm petrel."

"Mind if I ask how you're progressing in Gross Anatomy?" Myles said, sending the student a harsh look. "Perish the thought that the dead guy you're cutting up might in any way interrupt the regularly scheduled nature walks. It sounds to me like you and Dr. Nielsen have a lot in common, stomping about with your heads pointed skyward. And if you don't mind me asking also, what is the status of your pretzel-vending license application?"

"It's under review," the student shot back, busting up the room.

"So if I may now move on from today's ornithology lesson," Myles said as he motioned everyone to sit down, "and onto the next major part of cancer virotherapy."

The students sat down at another workstation that had individual computer screens for everyone.

"So now that the engineered adenovirus is replicating within the cancer cell," Myles continued, "we alter the virus gene program such that it will produce chemotherapeutic agents within the cancer cell itself. Once perfected, chemotherapy will be produced endogenously within the patient, obviating the need for intravenous medications. Dr. Ravelle has worked with Dr. Nielsen for better than ten years on this aspect of our research, and she will now introduce you to . . ."

"Rome," Stacey said as she stood. "Or to be more precise, Roman emperors. If you scroll through the images on your screen, you will see the extent to which tumor bulk is reduced in groups of mice treated with the modified virus. What we measure is cytoreduction, or the overall regression of tumor load. This segment of our research determines which chemotherapeutic agent is produced and in what quantity. Each sequence of genetic alteration is designated by the name of a Roman ruler. And just like Roman emperors, there are a bunch of them, and they are all unpredictable."

"And unknown," Myles said as he checked the number that flashed across his pager screen. "Unknown to us, anyway. Just like the viral surface pins and replication codes, the genetic combinations that allow for the production of endogenous chemotherapy are known only to Dr. Nielsen. So, with that introduction, anyone care to guess how many permutations there are if you combine the different facets of virotherapy research?"

"A few hundred thousand?" answered one of the students.

"Try a few hundred million," Myles said. "And as to when any of this leads to clinical trials in cancer patients," Myles clicked off his pager as it flashed again, "I'll have to refer you directly to Dr. Nielsen. Once he returns, that is. Excuse me."

Myles gathered up a roll of data that was spitting out of one of the printers and hustled out of the conference room. One of the lab staffers met Myles in the hallway, handing him another message.

"My pager was having a seizure in there," Myles said as he opened the message. "Any idea who . . . wait, it's the same number as the one on my pager," he said, looking at the lab assistant. "It's Silas Anthony."

"I just hung up the phone with him," the staffer said. "He needs to speak with you right away, Myles. That's all he said."

"I'll call him from my office. And meanwhile, for everyone's sake and sanity, do everything you possibly can to find the elusive Dr. Tran for me."

Myles found his cell phone under a pile of journal articles and punched in Silas's number via speed dial. Silas picked up on the first ring.

"Myles, thank God I found you," Silas said.

"I'm either here or asleep at home, Silas. What's on your mind?"

"Has Ivar called in, contacted you at all?" Silas asked, his voice urgent.

Myles shot to his feet. "What are you talking about? I haven't heard from Ivar in weeks. Last I knew, he was off in the middle of that group of islands in the northlands or wherever, birding. Then he was meeting up with you—today or tomorrow, right? What time is it over there anyway?"

"It is just after three in the afternoon, and yes, Ivar was supposed to be here today," Silas said. "Ivar handed me his itinerary a few weeks ago when I was in Boston visiting. After his bird-watching trip on the islands, Ivar was due to arrive on today's early-morning flight to Edinburgh. That was where I was going to meet up with him. When I arrived at the Edinburgh airport this morning and there was no sign of Ivar, I reasoned he would likely be on the next flight. But something just didn't feel right about the whole thing . . . you know better than anyone how exact Ivar is with everything. So I checked with the agent at the British Airways desk at the airport. When I asked about Ivar's arrival, the young woman gave me a wary eye, wondering why I needed information about the flight route of a person who was not related to me. Security is tight, she emphasized, as well it should be. But after I explained to her who I was and showed my identification along with the copy of Ivar's itinerary that I had in my hand, the agent was quite helpful and went out of her way to assist. She searched through their records and could not find Ivar booked on *any* of their flights today, tomorrow, or later in the week."

"Silas, slow down for just a minute, please," Myles said as he paced the length of his small office. "Ivar probably made a side trip to here or there. He's been gone for nearly a month, you know. And how about other airlines, a different airport, or the train? Ivar may have missed his flight, hopped a ride, and is on his way now. Or maybe he booked himself on a different airline without telling anyone. I'm sure there's a—"

"Ivar's not here!" Silas interrupted. "After my conversation with the British Air representative, I was totally at a loss, so I contacted the local agency that puts together most of the side trips and excursions. They work with all the carriers and hotel chains. Myles, there is no record of Ivar arriving in Scotland at all, anywhere, in the last five weeks. I was so concerned at that point that I contacted an old classmate who has been with the Office of Immigration in Glasgow for years. He confirmed all I had been told by the various agents: a Dr. Ivar Nielsen has not made entry into Scotland *at any time* this year. In the midst of all this, I repeatedly tried Ivar's home and cellular numbers back in the States, with both reciting the same message about him being away until such and such date. And no e-mails either. Nothing.

"Myles, what's going on?" Silas asked after an uneasy silence had passed.

Myles stood stock-still, staring down to the street below. A driving rain began to pellet his window, with the only person visible along the avenue below being a young man who was pushing a vending cart through the back entrance of an adjoining building. Despite looking down from the top floor of the Life Science Center, Myles was able to make out the bright red lettering painted on top of the cart: *Hot Pretzels $1.75.*

"I have no idea," Myles said.

CHAPTER 8

The Ocean Street dock slowly disappeared as Myles stared back from the ship's stern.

Myles was able to catch the next day's 6:30 a.m. launch out of Hyannis, and in a little over an hour, his ferry would moor at Straight Wharf on Nantucket Island. Myles couldn't stand boat rides, and he particularly despised this one, having suffered through New England's fierce springtime swells on far too many occasions. The churning seawaters between Hyannis and Nantucket were merciless at this time of year, and Myles knew there would be no escaping the twenty-six miles of heaving hell that lay ahead. He had tried to book a commuter flight out of Boston, but as Nantucket's airport had been fogged in for a couple of hours, all the flights had been put on hold, so air travel was not an option. If he wanted to get to the island, he had no choice other than the morning ferry and the relentless slam of waves across the ship's hull. Myles figured he might arrive at Straight Wharf a little greener in the jowls and lighter at the waist, but at least he'd get there.

God, did he hate boat rides.

In the eighteen hours that had passed since his conversation with Silas, Myles had yet to find any trace of an answer to the two questions he had been asking himself: why didn't Ivar go to Scotland, and if he wasn't in Scotland, then where was he? Myles had spent the previous afternoon and evening with staff members at the lab, recounting to each what little information he had and asking if any of them had any insight into Ivar's possible whereabouts. After staring into one set of bewildered eyes after another, Myles searched through Ivar's office, finding nothing more than piles of glass slides, mounds of data, a microscope, and a bunch of bird pictures. Ivar's PC housed years of research files, but beyond that, nothing. Myles then met with officers from the Boston Police Department and the Massachusetts State Police, reciting the same monotonous answers to the same predictable questions.

No, Dr. Nielsen didn't gamble.

No, Dr. Nielsen didn't buy, use, or sell illicit drugs.

No, no known "street debts."

No known enemies.

No jilted lovers either.

No family. "*We* are his family."

No messages, calls, texts, or e-mails.

After a formal missing person's report had been filed, Myles had a middle-of-the-night meeting with a representative from KMS Investigations, a private firm he hired on the spot to look into Ivar's disappearance.

Along with the building's superintendent, the city police had done a cursory inspection of Ivar's Beacon Hill apartment. Beyond the piles of mail strewn all over the floor, nothing out of the ordinary was reported. There was no sign of life, and blessedly no sign of foul play. As no crime was known to have occurred, a more thorough scouring of the premises was not allowed by Massachusetts law.

As Myles saw it, his only immediate hope for answers resided at 87 Hulbert Avenue on Nantucket. Myles did not even bother to try to find a phone number and call ahead. As far as he knew, Andie neither answered nor returned any calls unless the calls were from Ivar, and Myles had no reason to believe that he would be an exception. Myles found Andie's forwarding residence on the previous year's tax record, and as he wandered down Hulbert Avenue toward the listed address, he was not expecting much in the way of a warm welcome.

Andie's townhouse was perched on the top level of a rambling late-eighteenth-century whaler's home, and to Myles, the place looked nearly identical to the New Bedford homestead he had toured while in high school. Myles remembered how he and his classmates were shown every square inch of that sprawling New Bedford home by the resident caretaker, Mr. Sedgwick. Although Myles thought Sedgwick looked like a drunken vagrant, he had to admit that the man taught him a lot about life at sea while they toured that old New Bedford estate. Mr. Sedgwick, dressed in a convincing whaler's outfit, referred to homes like the one Andie lived in as "seadogs." Myles had never quite figured out where that name came from, until now. And now, with the entire frame of Andie's home trembling from the force of a breaking wave, Myles figured old Sedgwick knew what he was talking about.

Myles banged on Andie's screen door several times, but his efforts fell silent against the roaring surf. Seeing no sign of Andie inside, Myles climbed up an outer stairway, holding the rail with both hands as he stepped along the narrow catwalk that wrapped around the uppermost floor of the mansion. He emerged onto a deck that was alive with color and scent of hyacinths and trumpet daffodils. Andie turned as if on cue, not seeming the least bit startled as she considered her uninvited guest with amusement.

With the endless sea at her back, Andie's long auburn hair seemed to ignite as the morning's rays fired around her. Despite the chilly air, Andie was wearing shorts and sandals, with a blue-and-white checkerboard flannel shirt tied in front above her waist. She was as stunning as Myles had remembered, forever the girl who had just strolled out of every man's dream.

"Myles and Myles and Myles," Andie said slowly as she refilled her watering can. "Myles to go before I sleep. Son of a bitch."

Andie did a slow pirouette as she watered the daffodils dangling in the planters suspended from one of the eaves. The image was enough to rattle even someone as single-minded as Myles.

"So you chose our fair island as venue for your once-a-decade mental health day," Andie said without turning around. "We're honored. Or maybe our famed haberdashery row brings you here. You do look every bit the man seeking a major fashion overhaul. Henri, our renowned coiffeur, perhaps? He opens today at ten, and, God knows, he has been waiting for you."

Andie walked toward the less-than-statuesque Dr. Carnot. Myles was now looking straight into a pair of emerald-green eyes that could, in the words of one love-struck colleague, stop a four o'clock train.

"Just one question, Myles," Andie said softly, now standing inches from her visitor's face. "Why exactly are you standing on my porch?"

Andie then walked over to a corner of the roof deck and watered the flowers that draped over the wooden railing, a stiff onshore breeze arcing some of the droplets in Myles's direction.

"Have you heard anything from Ivar, Andie?" Myles asked. "Anything at all? He's supposed to be in Scotland, but he isn't there, and he isn't here, and all I've got around me is an audience of scared faces and shaking heads."

"Wait, wait, stop," Andie said, setting down her watering can. "Ivar is on vacation, Myles. *Vacation*. I know this is a foreign concept to you, but some people actually get away from work every now and then. And Ivar was way, *way* overdue. I'm sure he took a couple of extra days birding in the wilderness, because once he gets to Edinburg, he won't have a moment to himself. He's the guest of honor over there, and they'll keep him busy day and night. He's in Scotland, Myles. On vacation."

"No, he isn't," Myles said loudly, trying to outdo a sudden gust of wind. "Silas Anthony was expecting him in Edinburgh, but he never showed. He hasn't heard a thing from Ivar, and UK Immigration says Ivar never entered the country. Silas called yesterday, and since then, your former Boston workplace has been a nuthouse. I'm trying to figure out what's going on, and so is the Boston Police Department, the state police, and the private investigator I hired. And right now I've got nothing, Andie. Zero. But I do know that there's no way Ivar left town without seeing you, particularly given the fact that this is the first time he has ever been out of Boston for more than three days in a row. He must have said something, some inkling as to where he was headed or what was on his mind. Something, Andie."

For a long moment, neither of them spoke.

"'The ragged men in ragged clothes, the silver thorn of bloody rose, lie crushed and broken, on the virgin snow,'" Andie said faintly.

"What?" Myles asked as he moved closer. "What was that?"

"I saw Ivar a couple of days before he left," Andie said as she slowly shook her head. "I met Ivar at the Haymarket, and he introduced me to Silas Anthony. The three of us just wandered around for a couple of hours, showing off some of the city's color to Dr. Anthony. I was so happy for Ivar, finally getting some rest, some downtime. For all he told me, it was the long bird-watching trip and then back to business in Edinburgh."

Andie walked over to the deck railing, staring down at the shoreline below.

"Just like every other time we were together, Ivar left me with a quote or phrase of some sort," Andie said, her eyes fixed on the rolling waves as they broke onto the sand. "A mantra, I always called it. He left me a note jammed inside of my motorcycle helmet. Ivar had scribbled down lyrics from a song by—"

"Andie!" Myles interrupted. "I appreciate the man's existential insights as much as anyone, but right now I need something with a little more substance, ethereal wisdom aside for a moment."

Andie looked out again toward Children's Beach, Myles's voice fading into the distance as the words Ivar left behind echoed in her mind. *Silver thorn of bloody rose, lie crushed and broken . . .*

"Andie, I have to believe that you were the last person to speak with Ivar before he . . . before he whatever," Myles said, trying to ignore the vibration of his cell phone as he continued to carry on about how little he knew. "Is there any chance—wait, sorry, hang on for a second."

Myles looked at the number on his cell phone. "Yeah," he said, straining to hear against the repeated wind blasts, pacing from one corner of the roof deck to the other as his cell reception faded in and out.

A shade of a grin crept across Andie's face as she watched Myles's hair form a red sail that shifted direction with each gust of wind. Andie had no reason to dislike Myles; he had always treated her fairly, and he had never in any way wronged her. Myles was a man who everyone seemed to know yet no one really knew, and as with anyone who remained a stranger to those around him, rumor and suspicion filled the void left by the absence of rapport and intimacy. Andie, like everyone who worked in the lab, had heard all the stories, each one a bit more farfetched than the last:

Myles was enrolled as a freshman in college before he turned fifteen.

He became a father on this eighteenth birthday and was married a month later.

He was divorced by age twenty.

His estranged son, once a stunt double in a James Bond movie and for two and a half years a guest at Riker's Island for cocaine possession, now worked as a ski jumping instructor in Lake Placid, New York.

Myles was once a contestant on *Jeopardy*, but the episode never aired because of the scene he created over the answer to a question about Newton's third law of motion.

"Say what?" Myles screamed to whoever was unfortunate enough to be on the other end of the line. "You've got to be putting me on. We cannot possibly be talking about the same guy."

Myles's face seemed to swell as the conversation went along, with the corner of his left eyelid beginning to quiver as he spoke.

"You are 100 percent sure, no way you have the wrong man? No slipup here? I don't . . . Okay look, I'll have to get back to you in a little while. I'll be in my office by noon and will call you from there."

Myles turned off his phone and looked at Andie. His face was sheet white.

"Ivar flew to Nepal," Myles said. "That was Terrance Hayward from KMS. They tracked down Ivar's visa application, and from there they were able to trace his flight route. When he left here about a month ago, Ivar flew out of JFK to Frankfurt, then to New Delhi, and from there to Kathmandu. That's what they've got so far, and this guy is certain that the man he has traced is Ivar."

"Well, he did get out of town now, didn't he," Andie said, letting out a laugh. "Myles, try taking your fret out of overdrive, if it's not asking too much. Ivar is a grown man, as in a grown *middle-aged* man. So instead of buying a Porsche or getting a tattoo of a pirate across his back, he decided to break away into the great unknown for a while. Maybe he's in love. Or maybe it's just wanderlust. So now you know he's on the other end of the planet. Good for him. Are you really, *truly* worried about him, Myles, or do you want to find Ivar so you can keep him updated on your million flippin' trials? And why did you come all the way out here anyway? You think I knew Ivar flew off to Nepal? And if I did, and he wanted to keep it on the QT, do you think I'd tell you?"

Myles closed his eyes tightly and bit his lower lip.

"Don't minimize this, Andie. I heard all the same lines you did—wanting a break from it all, wanting to take some long walks in the wilderness, find some rare birds. I'm sure he told you all the same things he told me, about taking some time to rest up before wrestling with all the projects that lie ahead. But I'm not about to chalk up this little detour of his to some midlife getaway, replete with bushy sideburns and torn sandals and a loopy earring. And after the phone conversation I just had, I am *particularly* glad that I rode that barf-bucket excuse of a boat out here today," Myles went on, now with a sharp edge to his voice.

"You wouldn't know any reason Ivar would take off to such a desolate place, would you?"

Myles was staring straight at Andie, the muscles along the left side of his face twitching slightly.

"Take a load off," Andie said to Myles, pointing at a chair. "I'll be right back."

Andie walked off her roof deck, through the apartment kitchen, and into her bedroom. She stared out the window toward the ocean, recalling again the note Ivar had left her the last time they were together. She couldn't make any sense of the message he wrote to her, and now he'd gone off to parts unknown. Why? And why now? And she knew Myles was right. Ivar was never impulsive. Everything he did was rational and measured, with forethought and a clear blueprint. Andie's emotions began to race. She needed to slow down and think clearly. She had to relax, and she had to focus. This was neither the time nor the place to meditate, and a simple slow count to ten never much worked for Andie. She rarely drank, but if there was a bottle of Stoli anywhere in the house, she was in the mood to make two or three tumblers of it disappear.

Andie went back into the kitchen and splashed several handfuls of cold water on her face. She poured two glasses of grapefruit juice and walked back out onto the deck, handing one of the glasses to Myles. The pain written across Myles's face was almost palpable.

"Thanks," Myles said as he emptied the glass.

"I don't know any more than you do," Andie said in a soft tone. "Believe me, I don't. And this is out of character for Ivar, I'll give you that. Ivar tells me a lot, Myles. But hey, not everything." Andie set down her glass. "What are you going to do now?"

"Maybe I need to hire the next rickshaw to old Kathmandu," Myles said, letting out a nervous laugh. "I guess I'll start by hopping the 9:30 ferry to Hyannis, drive back home, and meet up with that private investigator I hired."

"Take your foot off the pedal for a minute, will you please?" Andie said. "You just got here. C'mon in, and I'll put on some joe and scare up something to eat. When was the last time you ate anyway?"

Myles shook his head and looked up at Andie. "Thanks anyway, but I can't miss that next ride back off the island. And besides, I don't really have much of an appetite right now. And that mother of a ferry ride—the less in my stomach, the better. By the way, do you have any idea how long it takes to secure a Nepalese visa?"

Andie arched her eyebrows.

"You might want to check with some of your Maoist rebel acquaintances back in South Boston. I'm sure they'll cut you a deal."

Myles stood and looked out across Nantucket Sound. The sky to the north had cleared, and the Great Point Lighthouse was now in full view. A trio of sailboats was rounding the northeast point of the island, one flying a brilliant red-and-blue spinnaker.

"Spectacular view," Myles said, squinting. "By the way, how'd you ever find this place?"

"It's a sublet," Andie said. "They're easy to find on the island in the middle of winter. Spend a January here, and you'll find out why. I stayed busy as a private tutor for some high school kids over the past year or so—math and science, even French for a couple of students. I'm taking a break from tutoring for a while, but I saved enough to keep the place for the foreseeable future."

"Are you going to be able to stay here through the high season?" Myles asked, still looking at the sailboats. "I'd think the primary renter would want back in for the summer."

"I guess the guy who holds the lease on this place fell on hard times, so it sounds like he won't be summering here on the island any longer. And the family that owns the house, I'm told that their level of dysfunction approaches reality-TV range. So for now, this is home."

"You'll be the first to know, Andie, whatever the news is," Myles said as he turned to leave. "That much I can promise you. I'll send you a text message this evening, and if by any chance you learn something in the meantime, you know how to find me."

Myles was halfway down the outside stairway when Andie called down to him.

"That investigator you hired told you Ivar flew to Nepal," Andie said. "That doesn't mean he's still *in* Nepal. So ask that private eye to dig around a little more. And if you go off looking for Ivar, I'm going with you."

Myles hesitated for a moment but did not turn around.

"I thought you said you had no idea where Ivar was," Myles said after a long pause.

"I don't," Andie said, leaning against the railing. "I'm only guessing. But if you and I go flying off somewhere to find him, wherever that somewhere is, the window seat is mine."

Without saying another word, Myles hustled down the stairs and onto Hulbert Avenue, walking as fast as he could toward the ferry moored at Straight Wharf.

Andie was again surrounded by the spring blossoms that covered her roof deck, the floral perfume mingling with the cool Atlantic breeze. Between the soft pads of her thumb and index finger, Andie cradled the tiny necklace ornament that was her most-treasured possession. The bright yellow bee had jet-black wings and wore a giant smile, and in her hand Andie was sure she could feel its heartbeat. The little bee did have a heart, and Andie knew his heart would never stop beating. Andie was sure his heart would buzz forever.

Chapter 9

"You're going to have to start over, old man," Dr. Morgan said as he slumped back in his chair. "The famed square one."

Dr. Joel Morgan let out a big puff of his Cohiba Siglo IV as he talked everything over with Myles at Stanza Dei Sigari in the North End. The ninety-plus year old cigar parlor was Dr. Morgan's favorite after-hours haunt, and Joel seized almost any opportunity to rest his considerable frame in one of Stanza's burgundy leather chairs while savoring a few drags of a fine stogie along with a glass or two of his favorite scotch. Nothing like a hand-wrapped Cuban cigar and eighteen-year-old Cragganmore single malt, neat. As this was a weeknight, the standard Cohiba would fit the bill just fine. Between surgical cases at Massachusetts General Hospital, a few clandestine puffs off a Juan Lopez, medium flavor, soothed out any rough spots. Saint Luis Ray, deep and dark, was for weekends only, and the forty-ring gauge Trinidad was reserved for what Dr. Morgan referred to as "the most hallowed of occasions."

> *Dr. Morgan, your patient, initials JJD, DOB 8.2.90, re: his surgery three days ago. Code for procedure required.*

"My friends in billing," Joel said as he read his text message.

> *Good question. Something tells me there isn't yet a code for being skewered by chain-link fence post,* Dr. Morgan returned.

Code necessary. Applies to length of stay, read the next
message.

*Spleen shish-kebabed and a liter of blood sent
northward into left lung. Let me guess, you want him
discharged,* Joel replied.

Coding essential, Dr. Morgan, said the next message.

So is his chest tube, Dr. Morgan returned.

Reviewer requests above referenced information.

"Reviewer," Joel said with disdain as he looked at his cell
phone screen. "Some prick anointed to an administrative post
who immediately morphs into a turncoat slattern, selling out the
needs of the sick for the 'good' of the institution. Go eat shit,"
Joel said as he turned off his cell phone. "Hey, at least I didn't
text back that last little editorial," he said, looking at Myles and
pulling in a puff from his cigar.

Joel Morgan grew up on the streets of East St. Louis,
and over thirty years had passed since his seasons as an
All-American linebacker at Notre Dame ended with sequential
knee injuries during his senior year. With pro football no longer
an option, Joel had worked as a nightclub bouncer and long-haul
furniture trucker while completing the credits he needed to
enroll at Upstate Medical University in Syracuse. As a career
trauma surgeon at Massachusetts General Hospital, Dr. Morgan
was known as a no-bullshit, apolitical, go-to guy that veteran
staff members relied on when the water they were immersed in
suddenly became very hot and very deep.

"Still winning hearts in the front office?" Myles said,
surmising the nature of Joel's repeated text messages.

"The way I see it," Joel said with a twirl of his cigar, "I'm
the treasure hunter who forages through hundred-year-old

outhouses. I know what I'm after, but I'm constantly reminded of what all I have to dig through to find it."

"'The patients, their families, the students, and the residents. All the rest . . . invisible.' I believe that's a quote with Dr. Morgan's name attached to it," Myles said.

"Nine to five," Joel said, still twirling his smoke.

"More like nine to nine . . . to nine," Myles said, taking a sip of his Corona.

"Says the pot to the kettle," Joel said, setting down his cigar in the heavy granite ashtray that was on the table next to him.

"Look, Myles, here's what you've got: your boss is AWOL. No known crime has been committed, and thankfully there is no evidence of foul play. Now, what do you expect from the Boston cops, or for that matter from the state police? Is Ivar *really* a missing person? From what team KMS told you earlier today, Ivar *was* a missing person. The fact of the matter is that in the eyes of the law and the eyes of the private investigators, he's not even missing anymore. As far as the authorities are concerned, the man's on vacation. And hey, the KMS sleuths, they're done here too. You expect more from them? Think they have a satellite office hidden in some pagoda outside Kathmandu? They live for guys like you. 'Hire us to find . . . well, we found. Now pay us.' The one thing you have going for you is the lack of any press coverage. Sure, the *Globe* or the *Herald* might call and poke around a little bit, but the whole thing lacks any fire or romance. No blood, no corpse, no loot, no real story. So at least for now you don't have to deal with all that sort of media aggravation."

Joel swirled another finger of the Cragganmore, letting the Cuban smoke fill his crystal glass before taking a swig and exhaling toward the vaulted ceiling.

"That's all well and good, Joel, but how exactly does any of what you just said help me?" Myles said, pressing two knuckles against the bridge of his nose. "This disappearing act is totally unlike Ivar, and all without a single message of any sort over the past month. What if he's in some sort of trouble? Or what if he's injured himself? Make no mistake, I need the man here, or at least I need access to him. It's his research, Joel. *His* brain. A lot of what we're working on was frontloaded before Ivar went off to 'Scotland,' but that clock will run out soon enough. I'll put all that aside and go back to what I said a minute ago. For Ivar, this is bizarre behavior, and I am really worried."

"Chief, you're back to where you started, and you're going to have to dig," Joel said. "From what you're telling me, you did a pretty good rummaging through Ivar's office, so as I see it, one way or another, you'll have to get into Ivar's apartment and lay waste to the place—his desk, his library, the circular file, the freezer, the mailbox, the lunch box, the soap box, the litter box, the bread box, the juke box, everything."

"How am I supposed to toss Ivar's apartment, Joel?" Myles asked, shrugging. "The building superintendent barely let Boston's finest look through the place. This super, he is one serious control freak, and from what I saw, he's about as congenial as a hive of killer bees. That guy is never going to let me even get near that front door."

Joel signaled the waiter for another round. An evening with Myles, Joel figured, might require a full tank.

"Relax, my man. Just let me worry about getting us past the welcome mat. Thanks, Sandy," Joel said as another single malt arrived, along with a Corona for Myles. "And I think I can help you secure that Nepalese visa you're going to be needing posthaste. After you called this morning, I tracked down Rob Vesley, an anesthesiologist I work with. Rob knows everyone, including an INS big wig he looked after recently in the intensive care unit. Rob said it's easy money, and he'll get it done for you. Wish I could join you on this little venture. Man, do I ever. But a junket like this will not sit well back at the ranch."

Besides a weekly foray to his favorite cigar bar, Dr. Morgan spent what precious little free time he had with his five teenagers. Busy place, the Morgan household.

"So, you've got Andie McKillnaugh to keep you company while you play Charlie Chan halfway around the world," Joel said, offering Myles a wink as he took another puff from his cigar. "Nice going, kid. Talk about easy on the eyes."

Myles looked down toward the ground and frowned.

"She's Ivar's best friend, and to tell you the truth, I would rather travel alone," Myles said. "I don't know what Andie's deal is. She's not in school anymore, and at the moment she's not even working. What she *is* is mad at the world, for one reason or another."

"You know, I've wondered what all happened," Joel said. "Andie was on rotation through our service at Mass General a while back. An excellent student, one seriously bright kid."

"I don't know anything more than you do," Myles said as he took a long hit of his Corona, "except that she lives alone in a rooftop apartment on Nantucket. She did bring up the possibility that Ivar is no longer in Nepal, as in he flew to Nepal to get to somewhere else. Andie said she was only 'guessing,' but something tells me she has a hunch as to where Ivar might be. *Might* be, I said. She doesn't know, but I think she knows more than either you or I do.

"Joel, there's something else I need to ask you," Myles went on, leaning forward. "It's about Martin. Any chance he knows what's going on? I mean, how well do you know this guy?"

Joel took another drag of his Cohiba and considered the question, flicking an ash away from his beard.

"I was wondering when you were going to get around to that," he said. "Tough topic to avoid, I guess, given the circumstances. You know, I never quite figured that one out, Ivar and Martin. Talk about an unlikely mix, the two of them. The only thing they have in common is a MIT diploma with the same year stamped on it. But I have to give Martin his due; he's a born salesman if there ever was one. That man could sell salt water to a Fijian. The head of the New York Stock Exchange would walk barefoot through hot coals to go public with the company he founded, which goes by the modest name *NPhyte*. Martin supposedly came up with that moniker by taking his mother's first initial and the patriarch's surname, but knowing

Martin, you can rest confident that it's all about him. By the way, his middle name is Norris."

"He comes around the lab, maybe once a week or so," Myles said as he watched a group of yuppies inspect a new selection of cigars in the walk-in humidor. "For reasons that I can't quite put my finger on, the man just makes me feel uneasy. He stays out of the way and all, but Martin, he's one of those people whose very presence is in itself a distraction. I know that he and Ivar would go out for a late dinner or wander through the Museum of Science every now and again, but all I ever heard them talk about was bird watching. And on that topic, it's incessant—who could 'out-bird' the other, whose binoculars had the best focus, who was the better photographer. My God, they're only birds."

Myles looked back at Joel and shook his head. "Ivar befriending a scamp like Martin all these years," he said, "it just never made any sense to me. This company Martin owns, what's that all about anyway?"

"Prosthetics," Joel answered, sending another cloud of smoke upward. "If it ain't real, Martin sells it, as in everything you could ever imagine: eyes, hair, limbs, ears, teeth, not to mention boobs and other inflatables that are implanted where it really counts. He supposedly started it all while he was an undergrad across the river, but I don't know how on earth he ever found the time. From what I hear, Martin spent 24/7 with one hand on a Jack Daniels and the other palm-up on some coed's butt. But you know, when you never go to class, I guess you end up being weighed down by all sorts of free time."

During Martin's college years, the grapevine had it that when it came to passing an exam, Martin liberally employed the ends-always-justifies-the-means philosophy. He was accused of cheating on one occasion, but Martin denied the charge, and as nothing could be proven, the allegation was dismissed.

"I was actually at Martin's house in Dover once," Joel continued. "I drove Ivar over there for a barbecue. Martin and his family had just moved into a house that looked like it should have had a 'let's see if anyone can top this' banner strung around it. Martin and his wife invited half the East Coast over for an open house, and son of a bitch, the scale of this place . . . you could land a 747 in their driveway. Martin's children, they love Ivar, they were all over him. Martin's wife was actually a radiology resident once upon a time. She was a resident, anyway, until Martin met her at a party one night and then two months later handed her a ring with a stone bigger than the lime you just jammed into that beer. She's a piece of work too, let me tell you."

Myles shifted uncomfortably in his seat, edgy as ever.

"I called him," Joel said. "Martin, that is. The last time I saw him was a few weeks back when Silas Anthony was here visiting, but a couple of hours ago, I reached him while he was sitting on the tarmac in Seattle. He was about to fly back this way on one of his Gulfstreams. When I told him about Ivar, he sounded as lost as I did when you called me earlier today. He doesn't get in until after midnight tonight, but he'll call me from Logan once he lands. He's one serious resource, Myles, and he can help. He's as worried as any of us, and I know he'll do anything he can to sort all this out."

Joel polished off the last of his Cragganmore while shearing the near end of another Cohiba.

"Care for one?" Joel asked, offering Myles a cigar.

"No, no, I'm good," Myles said, putting up his hand. "Another time, maybe. Thanks anyway."

"As long as we're sitting here jawing, can I send a little friendly advice your way?" Joel asked.

"Speak," Myles said.

"Go home and get some sleep," Joel said. "You're exhausted, pal, and if you want to know the truth, you look like shit. You live only five minutes from here, and I humbly request that you walk out the door and get horizontal for the next ten or twelve hours. I know you have a meeting with your staff tomorrow morning, and while there, do everything humanly possible to convince the masses that all is going to be okay. That's what you have to do, and carry on with their work is what everyone else there has to do. I'll pick you up at around ten in the morning, and then we'll go over to Ivar's place. Let me worry about what we'll do from there. All you have to do right now is go home and get some rest."

"You're right, I know," Myles said. "Thanks for everything, Joel. And thanks for the suds."

Myles stood to leave, his palm disappearing into Joel's hand as they shook and then bumped shoulders. Myles then looked Joel squarely in the eye. "What do you think has happened?" Myles asked. "Do you think Ivar is dead? Tell me straight here, Joel."

Joel was hit with this while using a nearby candle to light his cigar, thankful that he had a moment or two to consider such a question.

"We have to assume that Ivar is alive, and we also have to assume he knows exactly what he's doing," Joel said. "But let's face it, Myles, I don't know any more than you do. And I think it's safe to say that the only person who does know exactly what's happening is at this moment wandering around somewhere in the Himalayas. We cannot do anything more tonight, so unplug the phone and for once, please, unplug your brain. Sweet dreams, partner."

Dr. Morgan sank back into the deep leather sofa, his speculations having remained unvoiced during his conversation with Myles. Joel kept thinking of the first time he ever met Ivar, all those years ago, when Ivar was a third-year medical student on the surgical rotation where Joel was an attending physician. Joel had worked with hundreds of med students over the course of his career, and the primary goal of nearly every one of them was to impress their superiors with their fund of knowledge and untiring work ethic. But Ivar . . . Ivar was different. He connected with patients. He understood their disease process. He had a grasp on what was going on inside the patients he cared for, with the charge to help heal both implicit and inviolate. Joel had the same sense every time he saw Ivar touch someone who was sick: He got it. Ivar really got it.

And seemingly in an instant, that part of Ivar's life was over. Once his career path turned toward medical research, Ivar no longer had any contact with the sick, or with the injured, or with the dying. And that was what Joel wondered about most of all, Ivar's career in scientific research. Was that Ivar's choice, or had fate chosen it for him? Had this man's massive intellect and physical limitations conspired against him, precluding any real chance at a career that involved clinical work and direct patient care? Ivar's research could one day bring a cure to thousands—or maybe to millions. But when? And worse yet, the crushing possibility of a life's work advancing nothing more than false hope.

Dr. Morgan sat alone with his thoughts, another waft of Cuban smoke arching toward the rafters.

He listened.

He got it.

The bond that eluded so many . . . he *had* it.

CHAPTER 10

"Myles, the last time I was this close to someone, I nearly ended up with a sixth kid," Joel said as he jimmied the lock on the door to Ivar's apartment. "Back up a step or two, will ya? It's been a while, but I'll get it."

Myles could feel pellets of cold sweat roll down his back. When a moth flew past the hallway ceiling light, Myles startled as if he had spotted a spy plane overhead.

"There," Joel said as the door gave way. "I still got a little street hound in me."

Once inside Ivar's flat, Myles found immediate refuge behind the front window curtain, his eyes raking the street below in both directions.

"Need the powder room, Myles, or did you take care of that out in the hallway?" Joel asked.

Looking down from the third-story window, Myles saw Andie, the building superintendent, and two male pedestrians all standing in front of the apartment building. Twenty minutes earlier, Joel and Myles had let Andie out of the car a couple of blocks away from Ivar's apartment, and with little effort, Andie was able to engage the superintendent and the two passersby in a long dialogue about a paper she was writing on the history of Beacon Hill and all its varied architecture. Andie's conversation with the gentlemen had allowed Joel and Myles unhindered entrance into Ivar's apartment building. Joel walked to the front window and looked over Myles's shoulder, peering down onto Chestnut Street and the enraptured audience that stood before Ms. Andie McKillnaugh. Andie was wearing a pair of weathered Calvin Klein jeans and a skin-tight, canary-yellow Bebe long-sleeve top, tossing her long auburn locks from side to side as she carried on about how friendly Bostonians were.

"She's a natural, that one," Joel said with a wry grin. "Those boys wouldn't have noticed a horde of Mongols charging through the front door on horseback. C'mon, kid, let's get a look around."

Ivar's single-level apartment consisted of six rooms, and with floor-to-ceiling shelves in five of the rooms, the dwelling had the look of a library wing in a centuries-old manor home. The rows of books on history, music, geology, cartography, ornithology, philosophy, and classic literature left little doubt in Joel's mind that he had picked the door lock at the right address. Framed family pictures covered much of the wall space that didn't house Ivar's collection of books and manuscripts. In one of the pictures was a tall, fair-skinned woman with a warm, confident smile, her photograph having been taken against the backdrop of ocean waves breaking onto a rugged shoreline.

"Must be Ivar's mother," Joel said, pointing to the woman in the photo. "Exquisite lady.

"And look at this," Joel continued, thumbing through one of the volumes he had just pulled off a nearby shelf. "This is a 140-year-old first edition, and I bet some of these other books are even older. They're classics. And this one is actually written in Greek. I didn't know Ivar could read Greek. And check out these plates and the print quality. Fantastic stuff."

Myles did a rapid tiptoe toward Joel, grabbed the text out of his hands, and immediately re-shelved the book. "What are you doing?" he said in a high-pitched whisper. "We just became felons, and you're acting like this is an antiquarian tour. This was your idea, Joel. Andie didn't like us breaking in here any more than I did, violating a friend's privacy like this. But since there's no other place to look, let's just get on with it. And by the way, what exactly are we looking for, anyway?"

Joel slowly shrugged as he took one step down into Ivar's study, his considerable heft causing a floor board's groan to resonate in every direction.

"We're dead men," Myles said. "We're going to jail!"

"Chill it, will ya?" Joel said as he scanned Ivar's office. "Ivar's my friend too, and that's why we're here, remember? You're worried about him, and quite honestly, so am I. The same goes for Andie and Silas and your staff at the lab. And since you found nothing in Ivar's office, it's either search this apartment or await Ivar's return. And to answer your question, chief, we're looking for something different, all right? A surprise—you know, like a skeleton or something. Now turn over those file cabinets and see what shakes out, and I'll scrounge my way through Ivar's desk."

Myles carefully opened one of the three antique file cabinets that stood behind Ivar's rolltop desk. The papers inside the cabinets were a chronology of genetic studies and peer review journal drafts that dated back to Ivar's undergraduate days. Myles rifled through the files at a manic pace, squinting through the growing cloud of dust that emerged from the top of the oak cabinets. He wiped his brow and eyes as he turned back toward Joel.

"This is the same business I stare at day and night," Myles said, suppressing a cough. "I see this stuff in my sleep. Anything with you?"

Joel's search through the rows of cubby holes on the upper part of the desk produced an assortment of unpaid bills, several old visa applications, and a pile of rumpled airline boarding passes. The visa applications and boarding passes were all for trips to Europe and South America, with no evidence of previous travel to Nepal or any country that bordered Nepal. Joel also found a couple of expired passports along with a stack of scrap papers that had formula equations scribbled in every direction. He was tempted to comment on the craftsmanship it took to build Ivar's antique desk, but he thought it better to keep such observations to himself. Myles, he knew, was all business, teetering ever more on sanity's edge.

"I thought you said Ivar didn't travel all that much," Joel said, the desk chair he was sitting in letting out a squeak whenever Joel swiveled from side to side. "This is quite an archive for a supposed homebody. And take a look at the wallpaper lining this old passport. From the looks of all this, Ivar has visited countries on every continent."

"He has," Myles said, laying waste to another stack of files and journal articles. "But with every trip, it's the same revolving-door routine: travel on day one, lecture on day two, return home on day three. And sit still over there, will you please. The creaking joints in that chair you're in are loud enough to be heard down the block."

"Sure, sure." Joel nodded as he looked through one of the lower desk drawers. "Hey look, there's all kinds of different currency in here. We could exchange all these shekels for green backs and treat ourselves to one feast of a lunch. Is there a federal bank open today?"

Myles squatted down next to Joel, who continued to clear out the contents of the bottom drawer.

"The federal prisons are sure as hell open today," Myles said in a high-pitched squeal. "We gotta get out of here!"

Joel ignored the dread in his accomplice's voice as he fingered through a file stuffed with dozens of lecture invitations Ivar had received through the years. "Everyone wants him," Joel observed.

"Yeah, including me," Myles mumbled as he rolled one of the file drawers shut.

Joel found another stack of letters along with three small books that were bound together.

"Who's Norling?" Joel asked.

"Who?" asked Myles.

"Norling. It's on the return of a bunch of these letters, but I don't see any street address or city listing. These postage stamps, look at them. They're spectacular."

When Joel unwound the string that was wrapped around the three books, a stack of news clippings fell out from between the pages. He put the newspaper articles aside and then read the book titles aloud. "*The Tibetan Art of Healing* by Ian Baker, *Quintessence Tantras of Tibetan Medicine* by Barry Clark, and *Dreams of the Peaceful Dragon*, written by Katie Hickman."

Along with the books and letters, there was a large folder containing a collection of photographs and magazine articles. Joel's eye brightened. "I'd call all this different. Any of this subject matter ring a bell with you?" he asked.

Myles shook his head.

"Me neither," Joel said. "We're outta here, partner. Best not to overstay our welcome. Since getting in here was this easy, we can always come back should circumstances so dictate. Just remember to tuck that fire-engine toupee of yours under a ski hat next time. It nearly gave us away when we slithered through the foyer."

Myles's forehead began to twitch as his eyes bulged outward. "You wouldn't catch me dead in here again," he said, beating a path toward the apartment door.

"Another few minutes in here, and you'd likely be dead of a stroke anyway," Joel muttered to himself as he stuffed the papers, books, and photographs under his jacket.

After closing the door as gently as they could, Myles and Joel hurried down the two flights of stairs that brought them back out onto Chestnut Street. En route, Joel punched in a text message to Andie's cell: *Charlie's. 15 minutes.*

Chapter 11

Charlie's Sandwich Shoppe on Columbus Avenue was a South End landmark, having served chocolate chip griddle cakes and its signature turkey hash to local patrons and visiting celebrities for five generations. Andie had waved down a cab at the bottom of Beacon Hill and hightailed it to Charlie's in less than ten minutes, arriving well before Joel and Myles. When the two cat burglars finally showed up, they found out in a hurry that the coed bimbo act had not left Andie in good humor.

"I just got eye stripped by three guys who haven't gotten laid since bell-bottoms first hit the shelf," Andie said, her jaw tight and her eyes narrow. "Let me hear it. *Please*, tell me you found something in there."

Joel filed the unsmoked half of a Cohiba in his shirt pocket.

"Andie, you were a star over there," Joel said. "Oscar worthy, I'd say. The two of us would still be begging on the stoop if it wasn't for you. And all this cloak-and-dagger business has given me an appetite," he continued as French toast, sausage, pancakes, and bacon sizzled on the griddle less than an arm's length away. "How about a couple of major helpings of that hash and a double order of high-test Tanzanian java to help settle your nerves, Myles."

Myles was seated with his elbows on the counter, the palm of each hand pressed like a vice against his temples. His chest was pounding. Myles asked the waitress for a large iced coffee, and when it arrived, he quaffed it as if he was competing in a chugging contest at a Friday night fraternity party. He then set down the empty glass, and without saying another word, Myles began thumbing through one of the books that he and Joel had lifted from Ivar's apartment.

"Not sure what to make of all this," Joel said to Andie after taking a sip of his coffee, "but it's all news to me, that's for sure. These letters look like they go back quite a few years, and there's a bunch of them."

Andie opened one of the letters and saw the word Norling inscribed at the top of the stationery. The letter was short, and although handwritten, it was quite legible.

> *Nga-to delek, Ivar:*
>
> *My friend, the morning sky here is truly a gift from heaven. As I write to you, I see Mount Jomolhari ahead of me, its peak well above the clouds. The air was perfectly silent earlier, but I now hear herders in the valley as they begin out on their long, weaving trail. A great day awaits.*
>
> *Ivar, my thanks knows no bounds. The medications and supplies you have sent are pure gold. You cannot imagine. Tandin, who is caring for so many people here in the highlands, sends his every thanks.*
>
> *But I do not want you to imagine.*
> *Let your eyes see it all one day soon.*
> *It is a long trek to TN, so I must go now.*
> *A cup of butter tea awaits you.*
>
> > *jema jay—youg,*
> > *Galen*

Andie sifted through the rest of the letters, slowly running her fingertips over the postage stamps affixed to the envelopes. One of the stamps was a painting of a mandala in deep forest green, another the image of a blazing red-orange dragon guarding the entrance to a mountainside cave.

"These letters, it looks like they're all written by the same guy. Someone named Galen. I've never heard of him. Have you?" Andie asked, looking at Myles and then at Joel.

"A stranger to me," Joel said.

Myles shook his head and kept turning through the pages of *The Tibetan Art of Healing*.

"A bunch of these letters are on stationery from someplace called Norling," Andie continued. "Some go back to the early nineties."

"So Norling is a place, not a person?" Joel asked.

"So it would seem," Andie said as she pulled out her iPhone. "I'll check it out."

"So much for my Holmes-and-Watson delusions of grandeur," Joel said as he speared a nearby sausage. "I figured Norling had two legs and took regular nourishment. Wrong again, and you can spare me your comments about me keeping my day job."

"These are all postmarked from Bhutan," Andie said, holding up the stack of letters in one hand. "And if you cross Norling and Bhutan on the Web, you come up with a place called Norling Handicrafts."

"Bhu-what?" Myles asked, his brow furrowed.

"Bhutan. It's a country between India and Tibet," Andie said to Myles, her head slightly cocked and speaking in a tone that a school teacher might use to right a stray student. "But hey, Myles, I know you don't get out much. I'll bet that round-tripper to Nantucket was a real eye-opener. I hate to be the one to break this news to you, but there's a big world due east of here."

Myles frowned and kept on reading, putting away fork loads of homemade hash as he turned the pages. The cook dropped a large stack of griddle cakes onto the counter, sliding the plate in Joel's direction. Dr. Morgan doused the pancakes with maple syrup and then topped it all off with a hefty block of butter.

"Much obliged," Joel said as the cook turned his attention back to the crowded griddle.

"Have at it, kids," Joel said to Myles and Andie, pointing at the plate with his fork. "These don't stand a chance in front of me."

Andie opened another letter, scanning halfway down the first paragraph.

> *Just back from Mongar, and the things we saw, the people we touched. Ivar, every last parcel was used, and on my return there was a fresh stock waiting at Norling. I will deliver everything you sent, personally, to Tandin. He will be overjoyed, as the need is greater than ever. Thug je-chay, my friend.*

Andie then read the closing paragraph from another letter:

> *As you can well imagine, we are all saddened by the passing of Tandin's brother, Denzin. He died a week ago today, and many lamps are burning today in front of this small stupa. I had the honor of this man's friendship during his final years, and in my heart I know we did all possible to help him through his long illness. You were part of this, Ivar, with the donations you sent to aid Denzin and all the more the supplies you sent to assist so many needy children that are under Tandin's care. All these many families, they are terribly grateful. After a day or two here in Bumthang, we will again head toward TN to assist Tandin, and then back to Paro.*
>
> *Time to rest a bit now.*
> *ta do-ran-sha, my brother Ivar*
> *Galen*

"Whoever this Galen guy is," Andie said as she continued to read through the letters, "he keeps referring to someone named Tandin and someplace called TN. Whatever TN is, he's either coming from it or going to it. If I could find the man's full name buried in here somewhere, we could probably track him down pretty easily. He can't be that hard to find."

"Yes, he can," Joel said. "He's dead."

Andie and Myles turned away from their breakfast and reading materials as Joel shared with them a news clipping he had found in one of the file folders. It was an obituary from the *Philadelphia Inquirer*, dated April 9, 2007.

> *Vossner, Galen Lee—66, lifelong resident of Bethlehem and beloved husband of the late Eva M. (Hawthorne). Cherished son of the late James L. Vossner and Margaret S. (Lee). Loving father of Eric L. Vossner and his wife Diane of Salem, WA, and Sharon E. Taluson and her husband Warren of Raleigh, NC. He is also survived by five grandchildren, two brothers, a sister, and many other relatives, friends, and colleagues. Mr. Vossner began working at Bethlehem Steel as a teenager, and in 1965 he volunteered for service in the Vietnam conflict. Mr. Vossner served as a medic during three tours of duty in Vietnam, and upon honorable discharge he founded a mountaineering school and as well a company that specialized in high-altitude travel. Mr. Vossner dedicated over twenty years of his life to the passionate pursuit of providing aid to the people of Tibet, India, and Bhutan, where he volunteered his time helping various charitable organizations. Expressions of sympathy may be made in his memory to the Bhutan Relief—Save the Children.*

"He didn't even live in Philadelphia," Myles observed, looking over Joel's shoulder. "Nice tribute in such a large metro paper. Even a photograph of him in his military uniform."

"This Bethlehem paper gave him a half-page obit," Andie said, pointing to another article in the same folder, this one from the *Bethlehem Post-Gazette.*"

"How do you think Ivar ever connected with this fella?" Joel asked, thumbing through the stack of articles. "I mean, a steelworker, a Vietnam vet, chasing around in the Himalayas and all that. It doesn't—"

"My God, I'm a moron," Andie interrupting with a slap of her palm on the linoleum countertop, the reverberations causing ripples in nearby coffee cups. "That name, Tandin, I've seen it before, a bunch of times. Ivar used to have crates and boxes in his trunk and strewn all over the place in his car. I don't ever recall seeing the address, but I know I saw the name Tandin, as in 'attention: Tandin.' When we went to Doyle's Pub or wherever, Ivar would toss the packages into the backseat. I didn't think much of it at the time because people were sending him stuff all the while, you know, the latest and the greatest to try out in his lab. I figured he was returning the supplies because they were of no real use to him. But I saw that name time and time again. They were donations—*his* donations, not someone else's."

Myles began to shake his head, making a low, grumbling noise, and gripped his hair with clenched fists.

Between Andie's rattling of the breakfast counter and Myles's now escalating theatrics, other customers seated nearby were beginning to take notice. Joel put a thick index finger to his lips and made a slow patting motion in the air with his other hand. Myles made a show of folding his hands in front of him, and after a minute or so, he leaned over in front of Joel and Andie, speaking in a strained whisper.

"We are heading down a blind alley here. In all these years, Ivar has never once mentioned this or that or anything about anyone named Tandin. Same for this Vossner fellow. No disrespect intended. I have no doubt Galen Vossner was a fine humanitarian, and I'm sorry he ended up on the horizontal page. No matter what the circumstances, his death was tragic and untimely. But please, I mean, look at all this," Myles continued as he did a rapid finger flip through the book he was reading, the resultant breeze causing both Andie and Joel to blink and rear back a bit. "Yogins wandering all over the place with herbs and roots, spinning mandalas and meditating their way to human wholeness. Ivar is a scientist—*the* scientist. He will someday bring therapeutic medicine to an entirely new place. You of all people, Joel . . . man alive, you're a surgeon. Take a look here." Myles opened another one of the books to a random page. "I'm still looking for a chapter on snake oil. These Tibetan books aren't about medicine. They're about spells and incantations."

"No, Myles," Joel said in his unmistakable baritone, "they're about healing. All of this, everything you see in front of you, is about healing. It isn't about surgery or cutting or some historic breakthrough in genetic engineering. It's about the sick. It's about healing the sick, Myles. And you better believe that there are plenty of ways to get there, hombre. Plenty."

Joel took another swig of his coffee as he spread an upturned hand across the letters strewn between the pancakes and turkey hash.

"Somewhere along the line, Ivar made a connection with a steelworker who for years helped minister to those in need in a very far-off land," Joel said, slanting in a bit toward Myles. "A *steelworker*, mind you. I read through a bunch of these letters while we were stuck in traffic on the way over here, and I didn't see any reference as to how or where or when Ivar and Galen met. Hell, they may have never met at all. But however they found each other, Ivar saw something in this guy that stirred him. And let me ask you this," Joel continued, picking up one of the letters Andie had been reading, "who do you think this Tandin guy is? Maybe that's the question we should be asking ourselves. We know Galen Vossner reached out to the people of Bhutan, and in reading these letters, it looks like Ivar helped him do it. But if Ivar was going to dedicate himself to charity work, why choose a place so remote? You can hear the élan in Galen's voice in his letters to Ivar. He clearly had a passion for this type of work. But Galen, if I'm reading this right, was a conduit. An intermediary. He connected those in need with much-needed supplies, but the supplies had to make it into the hands of a caregiver. And by all indications, that caregiver was, and maybe still is, Tandin. But why Tandin, and why Bhutan? From what Andie's saying, Ivar has carried on as a champion for this Tandin gent, and the people he cares for, for many years. That said, if Ivar was going to support a third-world clinic, he could have chosen one that was far more accessible. There's something else at play here, and I don't think this is a simple one-way street where Ivar sends whatever is needed time and time again, gaining nothing beyond the satisfaction of helping his fellow man. He could have done that right down the street. Look a little deeper into those books we lifted out of Ivar's apartment, Myles. Ivar had those books for a reason. Tandin . . . I'll bet you the next Charlie's breakfast that he's a native healer, trained in the ways of traditional medicine. It may not have been Galen's intent, but I think he brought together two people of kindred spirit. Ivar and Tandin may be worlds apart in many ways, but they share a bond as caregivers. *Healers.* And if Ivar is up there somewhere in those colossal mountains, he didn't go there just to chase around a flock of condors."

Myles looked away from Joel and Andie, distracted for a moment by a gust of wind that followed a group of roller bladers and a pair of suits through the front door.

"My friends," Myles said, still staring out onto Columbus Avenue, "you have no idea. Nearly twenty years of study, and Ivar is so close—*this* close." Myles squinted at the one millimeter space between his thumb and index finger. "You have no idea," he repeated.

"You're right, we have no idea," Joel said. "But Ivar does, that's for damn certain. How many times have you said it yourself, Myles. Ivar working and thinking in places far beyond those around him. Well, you're right again. Consider for a minute that when it comes to treating the sick, Ivar sees all kinds of things happening beyond the four walls of IPOR. Why did he choose now to go to the other end of the planet? At the moment, I haven't a clue. But I think we'll learn more if we sift through the rest of those letters."

Myles looked back toward Joel, staring him straight in the eye.

"So what now?" he asked. "What exactly am I supposed to do with all you're telling me, hmmmm? Just go back and tell the whole crew that their leader has decided to become a Sherpa doctor, so we'll all have to just forget about the cancer research that we've been working on for half our lives. I *need* him, Joel. All the research designs—they belong to Ivar. All the grant money—it's Ivar's. Oh yes, and the mind behind all this research—that's Ivar's too. So in case you haven't noticed, I am just a little worried that Ivar is ten thousand miles away and totally out of reach. So if you can forbear my asking, just one more time: what am I supposed to do?"

"Nothing," Andie shot back. "He needs some room, Myles. When I last saw Ivar, just before he left, he looked exhausted, as in *really* worn down. He's getting a break for a while, and if he's in Bhutan, which it looks like he is, then he's touring one spectacular part of the world. He's safe over there, if that's what you're worried about. It's a Buddhist kingdom, for crying out loud. Unlike the inhabitants of most everywhere else on the planet, these people are nonviolent pacifists. Myles, I have to believe that Ivar will be back soon. Besides, I thought all the next phase trials were set up before he left. Ivar told me all the designs were in order, and you said as much yesterday when you were at my house. Has something changed? I mean, do you need Ivar here this minute to keep each and every trial on course?"

Myles let out a deep sigh and sat back in his chair, seeming for the first time to be a bit more at ease.

"No, I guess for the moment we're okay," he said. "There's a million or so questions I would like to run past the man, but as far as the phase trials go, for right now, we're good. There's certainly plenty to keep everyone busy. Ivar did go to incredible lengths to have everything set up before he left for . . . for wherever."

While Myles was talking, Andie opened another one of the letters and scanned through the contents. This letter, as with the others she had read, had been written by Galen and made mention of both Tandin and a place called TN. Paper-clipped to the envelope, however, was a series of data tables that were handwritten on thick, off-white paper. All of the tables had been X'd out with a red pen except the last table, which listed seven different entries chronologically:

1Sept'09 MT 4.0—2.5 41days>**LO**
14Nov'09 RR 4.5—2.5 31days>**LO**
09Jan'10 UT 3.5—2.0 32days>**LO**
23Feb'10 KW 5.0—2.0 39days>**LO**
17Aug'10 PY 5.5—3.0 29days>**LO**
03Mar'11 LW 3.0—1.5 42days>**LO**
03Jan'12 GT 5.5—2.5 37days>**LO**

The data tables had no signature, name stamp, or date.

"You see," Joel said to Myles, spreading out his arms, "this isn't a crisis. There's no call for alarm bells. You have to be patient, Myles, and let Ivar walk back. And meanwhile, don't panic those who are looking to you for guidance. Take a few minutes tonight and read through some of these letters, because they speak volumes about a part of Ivar's life that's news to all of us."

"LO," Andie said under her breath. "LO, LO, LO."

"And if you're worried about Silas and the oncology lectures, please put that out of your mind," Joel went on, still looking at Myles. "I'll call Silas this afternoon and square all this with him. Silas is a pro through and through, and no doubt he's very good on his feet. He'll have no problem figuring out something to tell the masses at the meetings and lectures."

"The decreasing numbers, the days," Andie said, her voice still so low that no one could hear her. "Why would someone send this to Ivar, with no explanation or key? And each entry, this boldface **LO.**"

Although Andie had never seen any of it before, the inscription of the letters **LO** at the end of each line had a strange, almost chilling familiarity.

"You just need to worry about the masses at your place of business," Joel continued, putting his hand on Myles's shoulder. "Let whatever's going on up there in the Himalayas be a concern for a later day."

Andie looked at Joel, sensing a jolt of fire along the length of her spine.

"The Himalayas," Andie said as she shot out of her chair. "Holy shit, the Himalayas. Haymarket, Ivar at the Haymarket. A tiny dot somewhere in the middle of that mountain range. LO. *Lobelia.* That's what he's after. *Lobelia.* Ivar's looking for *Lobelia!*"

Joel and Myles looked at each other and then at the same moment looked at Andie.

"Who, or what, is *Lobelia*?" Myles asked over the jangle of his cell phone, a dazed look on face. "And what in God's name has . . . has this *Lobelia* got to do with Ivar or Galen or Tandin or any of this Bhutan stuff?"

Myles clicked on his phone. "Yes, it's me," he said, still staring at Andie. "What?"

"Myles, this is Stacey. I need you here now," Stacey said, her voice loud enough for Andie and Joel to hear.

Myles stood up and swiveled on his heels. "Have you heard from Ivar?" he asked, his eyes darting back and forth between Andie and Joel.

"No, but I need you here now," Stacey said, her voice yet louder.

"Has he—"

"*Right now!*"

Chapter 12

"It's only you and me, Stacey," Myles said as he looked around the IPOR complex, no one else in sight on a Saturday afternoon. "Talk to me."

"I started with Ivar's office," Stacey began, "and I'm here to tell you there was nothing to be found. I know you went through his office two days ago, but I turned it upside down, four hours' worth, late last night. Absolutely zero."

"So then I checked his personal e-mail," Stacey said in a matter-of-fact tone.

"You got into Ivar's e-mail?" Myles asked. "His password and all that, how did you—"

"Easy," Stacey said. "Ivar, for someone so damn smart, he's real predictable. Well, he's usually predictable. Anyway, he keeps all his usernames, passwords, and access codes on a small printout sheet that's rolled up like a cigarette and hidden in the base of that sandpiper carving behind his desk. You know, the sandpiper is one of his favorite avian families. Reminds him of his home, I guess."

"And?" Myles asked.

"Nothing," Stacey said back. "I mean, not a thing. Every message was about this or that theory, experiment, or design. No strange names or bizarre requests or people looking for money. Same old day-to-day stuff, plus the usual ton and a half of junk mail."

Myles began to quietly thump on the floor with his toe, one of his countless nervous habits.

"Keep it rolling," he said.

"Okay, so next I opened Ivar's bank account statements online," Stacey said.

"Ho . . . you got into his bank account?"

"Sure I did. Nothing to it."

"Let me guess, the username and password were *hidden* under the bird."

"Right."

"And?"

"Nothing."

"Rads!" Myles said with his signature high-pitched emphasis.

Somewhere through the years, Stacey's sixth sense had earned her the nickname Rads, her more nostalgic colleagues figuring that this must have started when someone first noticed Stacey's resemblance to the iconic *M.A.S.H.* character, Radar O'Reilly.

"Myles," Stacey enunciated slowly, "how many times have we all heard it: when it comes to research work, if you stray from order, you've strayed for good."

"Apologies," Myles said as he listened to his own words come back to bite him. "I won't interrupt again. Please, go on."

"Then it came to me," Stacey said as she wheeled her desk chair to another workstation, her tiny frame allowing her to move around like a pinball. "His T. Rowe Price account. Ivar spent a lot of time all those years ago opening up that IRA account for everyone, and I know for a fact that Ivar has a personal investment account with that same firm. So I checked that out also."

"Another password under the sandpiper's wings?" Myles asked.

"Got it on the first try," Stacey said.

"I'm waiting," Myles said.

Stacey had a printout of the previous month's statement, tracing through the entries chronologically.

"Six weeks ago, Ivar transferred $58,600 from a series of stock sales to his core cash account. Two days later, he drew a check for that same exact amount. Almost 60K, Myles. That's a lot of money if you ask me. Ivar was clearly planning on being away for quite some time, and he wanted to keep it all very, very quiet. That must be why he withdrew the funds from a personal investment account. I mean, who would ever think to look there?"

"Who besides you," Myles said.

"Whatever. And something else," Stacey said as she lined up several of the statements across her desk. "There's a list of donations, going back quite a few years, to several foundations that benefit really remote mountain communities in places like Nepal, northern India, and—"

"Bhutan," Myles said, finishing the sentence, "which I heard about for the first time about an hour ago."

"Right," Stacey said, a surprised look on her face. "How did you ever hear about—"

"Because it's suddenly the hub of all human activity, or so it would seem," Myles said in a haughty tone as he again interrupted Stacey.

"Well, for whatever reason, Ivar wanted to keep all these donations hush-hush," Stacey said. "He sent money directly out of his personal investment account, so he didn't channel any of the donations through his regular bank account. Same with that big cash withdrawal last month."

Myles pulled up a chair and sat down next to Stacey.

"Rads, on top of everything else, you are one hell of a cyber sleuth. But you and I both know that you're not spilling it all here. There's something else tugging on the line, and I heard it in your voice over the phone. Whatever suspicion or query you have, now is the time for me to hear it."

Stacey looked up at Myles, her large dark eyes betraying the angst that was churning inside her.

"I got here real early this morning, Myles. Before four o'clock. I just couldn't sleep. I had to keep moving with all this. I kept poking around, but when I didn't find anything beyond the T. Rowe Price accounts, I kind of gave up for a while. I still help out coaching the men's and women's gymnastics team down at Brown in Providence, and since there's a meet-and-greet with a new member of the coaching staff this evening, I decided to stay here and catch up on some of my own work.

"When I went to get some pipettes from the supply room," Stacey explained, "I noticed that the biohazard bags were overstuffed with vials and samples. Ben or one of the other techs usually seal up all that material at the end of each day, but then I remembered that the Casella Company hadn't been here in over a week to pick up the bio waste. There was a trucker's strike or some kind of problem, so our bio trash had started to accumulate. Just to get it all out of the way, I grabbed a couple of the red biohazard bags and cleaned the place up a bit. I used two pairs of gloves and all that, believe me."

Stacey shifted uneasily in her seat as she continued.

"When I was bundling up the waste samples, I noticed three vials designated as 111570, with two of the vials having the letters BM after that six-digit number. There was no stamp, no processing date, no locator, nothing else written on the tube, which is really strange. I wanted to find out where the vials came from so I could identify whoever disposed of the samples and remind them of established protocol. So I typed the blood, starting with the usual (AB) and (Rho) system."

One of Stacey's favorite lectures to the first-year medical students was her presentation on human blood cell typing. Stacey would present a series of diagrams that detailed the surface proteins that coat red blood cells in humans. These proteins are also known as antigens, and in addition to the (ABO) and (Rh) antigens, there exists about two dozen other genetically determined blood cell antigen markers, including the MNS(s), Lutheran, Kell, and Lewis designations.

"The bottom line is that the blood in the tubes belongs to someone with a blood type that isn't all that rare, maybe one in seventy or eighty people. So you could never call this result a virtual fingerprint for a given individual. There are plenty of people running around with this lineup of blood antigens."

Stacey's hand quivered as she handed Myles three glass slides.

"Last summer, when we calibrated the new Beckman system, we took a blood sample from everyone here and ran all the samples through," Stacey said. "Well, the system stored every marker from every sample. So about an hour ago, I ran the blood cell antigen combination through the Beckman system, figuring it might give me some clue as to who was being careless with standard labeling procedure.

"The blood smears from the tubes marked 111570BM," Stacey said with a dark look across her face, "they're his. They're Ivar's. The antigen match is perfect. Like I said, the blood antigen lineup isn't particularly rare, so you could never say it's a positive ID for this person or that. But that doesn't really matter. 111570, that's Ivar's birthday: November 15, 1970. And BM means bone marrow, which two of these three samples proved to be. They're aspirates from someone's bone marrow, and the only match that came up on the Beckman system was with Ivar's blood type. When I saw what came up, my heart just about stopped. Myles, why would we have samples of Ivar's bone marrow and blood here?"

Myles sat motionless, staring off into space.

"Worcester," Myles said slowly, shaking his head. "I cannot believe it."

"Worcester?" Stacey asked,. "What on earth does Worcester have to do with any of this?"

"Ivar loves to teach the students and residents out at U Mass Medical Center in Worcester," Myles said, now looking squarely at Stacey. "I drove out there yesterday after I got off the Nantucket ferry, just to ask around and see if anyone could help us out. My day was shot anyway, so I figured I had nothing to lose. I caught up with a few of the fourth-year students, and one of them happened to mention that Ivar had let him draw a bone marrow aspirate from him. I know that might sound a little bonkers to you, but some docs actually let students and interns do procedures on them as part of their training. Not many, but a few do. Stoic Norwegians, you know. They know no pain."

Myles let out a deep sigh.

"For whatever reason, Ivar wanted a sample of his own bone marrow, and he didn't want any of us or even his own doctor to know anything about it," Myles said. "He got a med student to take a bone marrow aspirate, so only Ivar himself would be able to analyze the blood cells within the aspirate. Ivar no doubt figured the original sample would be trashed along with everything else."

"That is a smear of the sample taken from one of the unlabeled vials," Stacey said, pointing to the first of the slides that she had just handed Myles. "I can look at cell markers and blood antigens and chromosome maps all day long, but I have no idea what this and the other slides tell us. That's why I called you, Myles, and I don't mind telling you that this whole deal has got my stomach coiled in knots."

Myles placed the slide on the microscope stage and flicked on the light source, adjusting the eyepiece and swirling the objective to the right power setting. The beam gave life to a sea of bizarre, primitive blood cells.

Myles knew this one in an instant. It required no weighing of evidence. None whatsoever.

"Stacey," Myles said, trying to clear the gravel in his voice, "what are the chances that this sample is from someone . . . someone besides Ivar?"

"Myles, the samples had Ivar's date of birth on them," Stacey said without the slightest hesitation. "And the antigen match parallels his blood type."

Myles blinked slowly, his eyes unable to will away the invader that was staring back at him. Myles flicked off the light and squeezed Stacey's hand, his feigned grin not nearly as convincing as the snow-white blanch that was creeping toward the edges of his flame-red hair.

"Stacey," Myles said, his firm grip warm against the beads of cold sweat that had pooled along the back of Stacey's tiny hand, "this is big trouble."

Chapter 13

"Acute lymphoblastic leukemia," Dr. Arnold Schreiber said, his tone somber. "Not that there's any such thing as a good one, but this character is really ugly. The malignant cell count is essentially immeasurable. The cancer cells are climbing all over each other, pretty much wiping out everything else in sight."

Dr. Schreiber, a former roommate of Joel's in medical school, was the chief of medical oncology at Dana Farber Cancer Institute in Boston. Dr. Schreiber had received an urgent call from Joel and left his weekly tennis match so he could review the bone marrow slides that presumably belonged to Ivar.

"And this tissue sample, you're certain about where it came from?" Dr. Schreiber asked as he looked through the rest of the slides.

Joel nodded. "Like I mentioned over the phone, Arnie, I'm one of two agents on Ivar's health care proxy. And since I need to consult an authority in cancer care, you being that authority, I'll tell you everything I can here. But I've asked everyone else who knows anything about this to keep it all completely confidential. Ivar's privacy has been violated big time, and as you're about to hear, the biggest of the violators is me.

"Ivar's been away for over a month, and for all I knew—or for that matter all anybody knew—he was on furlough in Scotland," Joel continued. "Turns out his sabbatical took a turn five thousand or so miles farther east to join some volunteer organization in the country of Bhutan. This charitable outfit he's apparently working with, Ivar's been donating to them on the sly for years. As you might imagine, this Bhutan business came as quite a jolt to all of us. Earlier today, through a string of unrelated circumstances, we got a pretty good picture as to where Ivar is and what all he's involved with over there. But our collective sigh of relief got sucked out in a hurry when by complete happenstance, one of Ivar's staff stumbled upon the tissue samples you just scrutinized."

"You're telling me that these were found by accident?" Arnie asked, pointing at the slides.

"Let's just call it a rather unlikely trail of discovery," Joel said, putting up a hand. "The bottom line is that Myles and another member of Ivar's research staff now know that their boss, who clearly went to great lengths to keep his private life very private, is really sick. Like you said yourself, this information was found by accident, so there was no meddling or malintent involved. But we, Myles and I, were so worried about Ivar that we broke into his apartment earlier today to see if we could find any hint as to where he might be. What we found was plenty of documentation that Ivar has been very involved in helping a medical clinic in Bhutan, and at this point, we're reasonably sure that's where he is. But all this information has come at the cost of those closest to Ivar, most egregiously yours truly, trashing the man's privacy. You know, it's very possible, I'd say even likely, that Ivar does not *want* to be found."

"When you said 'no meddling or malintent,' Joel, perhaps you should include yourself under that same umbrella," Arnie said after a long pause. "From what you mentioned over the phone, Ivar has otherwise never been away for any length time. Any reasonable person would see your concern as very well founded. As for confidentiality, you've already cautioned Ivar's staff members. Besides that, there's you, Ivar's designated proxy agent, and myself, a consultant. As far as tossing Ivar's apartment goes, whenever you next see Ivar, I suspect he'll understand."

Joel, although far from convinced, nodded just the same.

"In regards to Ivar's symptoms, are you aware of anything significant, like weight loss, fatigue, chest pain?" Arnie asked. "Had Ivar been complaining of headaches or nausea, anything like that?"

Joel shrugged. "A mutual friend had noticed Ivar having hip pain a while back, but that was probably from the bone marrow aspiration. No other symptoms that I know of," he said, "but I'm not around Ivar every day. His team at the lab is with him day and night, and apparently no one there had noticed anything out of the ordinary. But with what you're telling me here," Joel went on as he picked up one of the glass slides, "that sounds nearly impossible. If Ivar is that sick, is it possible that he would have no symptoms whatsoever?"

"Anything is possible, Joel. You know that as well as I do," Arnie said, peering over his wire-rimmed glasses and reading the unease on his friend's face. "The leukemic cells are everywhere on that slide you're holding, and with time, they'll infiltrate multiple internal organs. Tumor cell spread to the brain is a major worry, which is why I asked about whether or not Ivar was experiencing any headaches. But remember, Joel, this disease is called 'acute' for a reason. This entire process may have started only a couple of months ago, or for that matter just a couple of weeks before Ivar himself had any sense that something was wrong. Some people have no symptoms at all, and then a routine blood test ends up shocking their socks off. Believe me, I have been down that road with patients more times than I care to recall. It's devastating. They simply cannot believe it's happening to them."

"I can't believe *this* is happening at all," Joel said as he stood and walked to the other end of Arnie's office. "Best I can figure, Ivar had some inkling that he was sick, had a blood sample drawn, saw the bad news, and then confirmed it by having a med student do a bone marrow aspirate on him under the pretense of teaching him or her how to do the procedure. As you might imagine, Myles and the rest of the staff over there are really shook up. Myles is trying to keep everyone calm, not letting on anything about Ivar's presumed diagnosis. Of all people, Myles is left to still the waters. That ought to be a sight."

"He does go into a frisson often enough," Arnie said, grinning through his perfectly trimmed Van Dyke beard. "Although I don't envy the task he has before him. Not for one minute."

Joel stood in front of Arnie's office window, taking in the street scene eight floors below. Throngs of pedestrians were filing up and down Brookline Avenue on both sides. "Graduation week," Joel said in a low voice. "Happy days. Happy times."

"On the day we graduated, you told me that someday you'd have a kid with an arm like a rifle and a yard full of wolfhounds," Arnie said.

"Yeah. And I ended up with five teenagers who can't throw and a pug who eats my furniture," Joel said as he turned away from the window, rotating an unlit Cohiba between his teeth.

"Don't let a citywide smoking ban stop you," Arnie said. "There's no one up here except you and me, and since that Cubano is contraband to begin with, you might as well fire it up."

Joel flashed a crooked grin and took a seat across from Arnie.

"I appreciate the offer but better pass," Joel said. "With the luck I'm having lately, the whole place is likely to get torched. It can wait for the ride home.

"Arnie, even if we find Ivar, and given what we know so far that is one helluva big if," Joel said after an uncomfortable silence had passed, "can this thing be cured?"

"Is this curable? Yes," Arnie said confidently. "You can beat this form of leukemia with a combination of three or four chemotherapeutic agents, and more often than not a bone marrow transplant. Focused delivery of radiation therapy is a consideration in some patients as well."

Arnie removed his glassed and leaned forward.

"But I have to tell it to you straight, Joel," he said, "we will be swimming against a very big current here. The blast cell count on these bone marrow slides is enormous, which speaks of one fierce malignancy. If it's as aggressive as I think it is, we could discuss any number of investigatory protocols, but there's a considerable increase in toxicity with any such therapy. And let's face it. Ivar is not exactly a robust specimen. The cardiomyopathy he has will complicate anything and everything we do. Just getting him through the pulses of standard chemotherapy will be a challenge. A big challenge."

Joel began tapping his cigar lighter on Arnie's desk.

"And if left untreated?" Joel asked.

"If he hasn't already, Ivar will soon begin to experience abnormal bleeding from the gums, from his nose, and possibly from his stomach or lower GI tract," Arnie said. "And as you know, he's at considerable risk for contracting a major respiratory infection. There is no way his immune system will be able to stave off a bronchitis or pneumonitis. And before long, this tumor will spread, very likely to his brain, as I mentioned. The leukemic cells will essentially destroy the normal blood cells, and with time wipe out everything they latch on to."

"So how long," Joel asked evenly, no longer tapping his lighter.

"Without treatment, a couple of months. Four or five at the outside," Arnie said, affirming what Joel had already suspected.

Arnie placed the microscope slides into the top drawer of his desk.

"I need to know something, Joel," Arnie said, rubbing his eyes. "What's really going on here? You and I both know that Ivar's work is unparalleled—pre-eminent in every way, if you'll pardon the melodrama. Every time you look at him, his sphere is expanding. The innovation you see, not to mention the limitless potential . . . I've never seen anything like it. No one has.

"So with that as a backdrop," Arnie's voice rose an octave, "you are now telling me that the tissue sample you just showed me is Ivar's, and instead of treating his illness, Ivar has decided to trade in over twenty years of peerless science so he can hand out decongestants to a cloister of monks on the top of some mountain that's a million miles from here?"

"I was asking that same thing a couple of hours ago," Joel said without expression. "I'm thinking along the same lines as you, that there's a piece missing here. A big piece. When we went through his apartment earlier, we found a stack of letters indicating that Ivar has been assisting a Bhutanese doctor named

Tandin for years. Ivar's best friend, a former med student named Andrea McKillnaugh, is the one who helped us get into Ivar's apartment this morning. Afterward, we all went out to breakfast, and just before we got the news about Ivar's bone marrow slides, Andrea found something in one of the letters that might explain why Ivar went to Bhutan. Assuming, of course, that's where Ivar is right now.

"Then again," Joel continued, easing in toward Arnie, "maybe he's just handing out decongestants to a cloister of monks."

"So one part comedy to go along with ten parts tragedy," Arnie said, letting out a nervous laugh.

"And sadly, zero part fiction," Joel said as he stood up and pulled a random journal off a nearby bookshelf.

"Arnie, consider this from Ivar's perspective for a moment," Joel said, holding up the journal. "Over twenty years of scientific quest. *Twenty-plus years.* And for what? In all that time, has anyone, any patient, ever been treated or cured from the end results of his research?"

"Not yet, no," Arnie said. "But it's close, Joel. I'm telling you, it's closer and closer all the while."

Joel leaned onto Arnie's desk with both hands. "Closer and closer, Arn. I believe that you believe that—you and an untold number of others in the field," Joel said. "But think of it from where Ivar's standing. I ask you, how many more days does he have left to wait?"

"Plenty," Arnie replied immediately. "If Ivar gets on a chemotherapy and bone marrow transplant protocol, he can beat this."

"Come on, pal, who are we trying to fool here?" Joel said. "Ivar has had compromised cardiac function ever since he acquired that viral infection as a small child. Why a heart transplant was never considered in all the interim years—that's a damn good question, and I haven't the first clue as to an explanation. Maybe Ivar never saw himself as confined or limited by the cardiomyopathy, or maybe it's always been a 'hand that I was dealt' sort of thing. So now I ask you, what are the chances of Ivar getting through several rounds of chemotherapy and returning to full-time research? With his performance status and the side effects of treatment, Ivar will likely never get back on his feet fully, if he survives at all."

"But there's a chance, Joel, and that is more than he's got now," Arnie said. "It's a terminal path without proper treatment. Where he is now, his chances are zero."

"That's where you may be wrong," Joel said.

Arnie narrowed his gaze and gave Joel a long, hard stare. "What the devil are you talking about?" he asked.

"Ivar has a chance," Joel said as he again took a seat across from Arnie, "a chance to get back to where he started. You didn't see him as a med student, Arn. He had a caring touch with patients. All the sick folks that you and I see every day—I think Ivar has truly missed being with them all these years. With his physical limitations, Ivar found a home in medical research, and he's doing wonders there. But all that has changed now. Ivar is running out of tomorrows. He's been supplying a medical clinic in Bhutan for years, and there's some bond, some connection, between Ivar and the practice of medicine over there that goes beyond him sending medical supplies to some remote mountain clinic. I don't know what that link is, but I'm beginning to understand why Ivar might now see his being in Bhutan as an imperative. From his perspective, the time is right now. And after what you've told me here today, Ivar might not be putting much prospect into life after 'right now.'"

Arnie continued to stare at his friend, wearing the look of a man not yet convinced.

"He hasn't examined a patient in years," Arnie said. "So if you don't mind me asking, what exactly do you think he's going to accomplish off in the hinterlands of Asia?"

"Don't sell him short on that count," Joel said as he reached for his jacket. "It turns out that Ivar has been teaching physical diagnosis to the medical students for years, and he also makes rounds at times with the residents and fellows. He's not as distant from clinical medicine as you might think. The question isn't whether or not he *can* take care of sick people. The question is *why* he chose to go to Bhutan to care for sick people."

Arnie turned off his desk lamp and leaned back in his chair.

"You know, your old chums have been trying to get you to take a few days' respite from that cauldron you work in day and night," Arnie said. "Looks to me like Ivar may have succeeded on that count."

"Well, I'm not out of Dodge just yet," Joel said, searching for his car key. "Procuring travel visas to Bhutan can be a bit of a chore, but I'm pretty sure I know someone who can pull it off. Martin Phyte, as in the NPhyte zillionaire Martin Phyte, has more connections than anyone on the planet. He'll get it done, believe me. He was the one who found someone who found someone else who found another someone else who confirmed that an Ivar Nielsen purchased a ticket on Druk Air out of Kathmandu about a month ago. And although said contact could not 'confirm or deny' this man's flight route, Druk Air only flies to one airport."

"An airport in Bhutan?" Arnie asked.

"*The* airport in Bhutan," Joel returned. "So like I said, we have a pretty good idea where Ivar is.

"Can't tell you how much I appreciate all this, Arn," Joel said as the two shook hands and embraced. "You're as clutch as ever."

"For you, no charge," Arnie said. "That said, the next time you haul me away from my tennis game, the first round's on you."

"I'll go you one better," Joel said, pointing a finger at Arnie's chest. "Next time, *every* round will be on me. And that includes covering whatever our favorite Norwegian is drinking."

"One query, along that same line," Arnie said as Joel was opening the door to leave. "How do you plan on finding Ivar, let alone persuading him to come back here with you?"

"You mean, how am I going to find a man who doesn't want to be found and then convince that man to leave a place he doesn't want to leave?"

Dr. Morgan mouthed the words "good question" as the door closed behind him.

Chapter 14

At exactly 9:00 p.m. on Saturday, Martin Phyte called to order a meeting of his entire senior staff, motioning for all to take their seats behind the massive oak conference table. The table itself was supposedly commissioned by a seventeenth-century viscount and crafted by a master Bavarian woodworker, and it had been salvaged from a British estate on one of Martin's many objet d'art reconnaissance trips. The piece was a signature Martin acquisition: over-the-top, garish, and right in everyone's face. No one present had ever quite figured out how Martin had managed to move this monstrosity into the center of his Rowe's Wharf waterfront penthouse. One member of his staff, while downing late-night double martinis with his fellow NPhyte executives, suggested that Martin had hired one of those giant cranes, with the four walls of the apartment and the cathedral ceiling built around the table once it was in place. Another member of Martin's executive team, who on more than one occasion was heard characterizing the table as "the ugliest piece of furniture ever created," thought Martin had it dismantled and then reassembled, piece by piece, on-site. Other members of the senior staff disagreed, saying they could never imagine Martin taking a saw to one of his precious antiquities.

One thing was certain: none of NPhyte's staff ever expressed their opinion of the office suite's décor in the presence of the company's chairman and CEO, Mr. Martin Norris Phyte.

"There it is," Martin said, casually pointing in the direction of an eight-acre parcel of land to the east of Rowe's Wharf. "Pier IV, ladies and gentlemen. And it is as good as ours."

Martin stood at the huge picture window that fronted his palatial waterfront suite, using his fingertip to slowly trace out the row of light posts that outlined the perimeter of Pier IV.

"You see this rectangle?" Martin asked in a smug tone. "You can nail a sign right to this glass. Home Sweet Home."

Pier IV was, in the estimation of NPhyte's one and only shareholder, the most illustrious of all possible locations for a long-sought-after corporate world headquarters. Martin had musings of such a prestigious site since his company's inception, and through a reliable source he had learned that this priceless length of harbor-front real estate would soon be put on the market.

"That's what we are about tonight, comrades," Martin continued. "Before any of us see our front door again, we're going to have every last particular of this deal in dark ink. So the minute the official For Sale sign goes up, we strike.

"Why so quiet over there, Hal?" Martin asked as he looked directly at Harold Halder, NPhyte's chief financial officer. "I'm waiting to hear something really substantial from your corner. We both know you can make this happen, Hal, and you're about to tell me how."

Harold was, by requisite, first deputy on all of Martin's weekend investment rampages. And although Harold could sense plenty of squirming in the seats around him, he remained as untroubled as ever. Harold's golden parachute would spring open in less than a year, and a just-completed Sonoran ranch house on twenty-seven acres of painted desert awaited his arrival. Such thoughts—along with a pack and a half of Camels per day and the tranquilizer he took with every capricious move his boss made—kept him at perfect ease.

"Hal?" Martin asked, his arms crossed over his chest as he leaned in Harold's direction.

"On the way over here, one of the loan officers from JPMorgan Chase returned my call," Harold said calmly. "Before I even got the words out of my mouth, she began grilling me about the eight-figure loan we just took out to develop our facility outside of Toronto. After the initial dust storm passed, I managed to articulate our investment plan of the Pier IV property, and she said she'd run the proposal up the line to their next level of management. But the voice I heard rang of neither optimism nor enthusiasm. 'Already max'd out' was the refrain I kept hearing."

Martin walked over to the sideboard and pulled out a stack of papers from his briefcase. One of the other executives in the room eyeballed the gothic images carved into the sideboard's eight tree-trunk-size legs.

"That's not acceptable," Martin said imperiously. "We've been one of their top clients since their stock was eleven dollars a share. If they don't want our business, that's fine with me. What about Citigroup? They're a hungry bunch of slags when it comes to this sort of transaction."

"Not that hungry," Harold said without hesitation. "They're even bigger hard-asses when you talk about the kind of money it will take to pull off this sort of purchase and development. If you'll recall, Citi was the first bank to show us the door when we looked for backing in Toronto. 'Clearly overextended,' to quote the undersong."

"They're whores, all of them," Martin said, giving his CFO a dismissive wave as he slid a pile of papers down the table. "If those monkeys didn't have venturers like us, they'd spend their careers depositing Social Security checks and foreclosing on overpriced Florida condos that are slowly sinking into some mosquito-infested swamp. Take a long look at these plans. There's a copy for everyone. These were drawn up for a different site a few years back, but the design and dimensions are a perfect fit for the pier property. We've been waiting a long time to break ground on an international corporate home, and we're not about to let a couple of chicken-shit bankers get between us and our collective vision."

Much to his staff's silent distaste, Martin frequently used the word "our" when outlining points of action that he was initiating without ever consulting members of "his" executive team.

"I'm tired of getting slapped around," Martin intoned as the heat in the room began to rise, "by a bunch of piss-ant—"

"Mr. Phyte," the soft voice of Martin's administrative assistant came through his earpiece. "It's the call you said to send through immediately, no matter what. Go ahead, sir."

"Martin, it's Joel. No doubt you're somewhere on the monopoly board, so I'll keep it brief. First off, your contact at that international travel agency came through big time. Ivar did fly from Nepal to Bhutan a little over a month ago, so it's safe to assume that's where he is. Second, when you mentioned to me a while back that it looked like Ivar had a sore hip, well, now I know why. It was the result of a medical procedure, but more on that later. The bottom line is that I think we need to find Ivar, and if we're ever going to do that, you'll need to be all in on this. There's a flight out of JFK to New Delhi early tomorrow morning, so the first thing we'll need is a car or a plane to get us to the city sometime in the next few hours. And on the way to New York, you'll need to pull some strings at the UN, or maybe at the State Department, to secure us all entry visas into Bhutan. That's where Ivar is. Meanwhile, the hospital's emergency travel department will finalize our flight details, and I'll cash in the chits needed to get an escape pass for the next ten days or however long all this takes. So whatever universe you're in the middle of mastering, put it on a shelf, and we'll meet in my office as soon as you can get there."

"I understand," Martin said as he clicked off the phone line and rose from his seat at the head of the table.

"Excuse me, ladies and gentlemen."

Martin Phyte walked from the conference room and out of his rooftop suite, not even breaking stride as he picked up the Gucci travel bag that was parked in the foyer.

Harold Halder poured himself a glass of water from a nearby Baccarat pitcher. Without anyone noticing, Harold slipped a small white pill between his teeth and swallowed.

The rest of NPhyte's abandoned financial team sat dumbfounded around the antique table, the dim lights of the now orphaned Pier IV barely visible over the gloomy waters of Boston Harbor.

CHAPTER 15

Seven miles of cloudless sky separated Joel Morgan's sixty-third-row window seat from the endless expanse of glacial ice below.

Greenland, he figured. A long ways to go.

Having never had much luck sleeping on a plane, Joel spent some time reading through more of the letters that Galen had written to Ivar. In some of the letters, Galen had gone into detail about which medical products were in shortest supply at Tandin's clinic: ace wraps for minor injuries, anti-inflammatory agents, instruments to drain skin and dental abscesses, non-narcotic painkillers, antibiotics for a host of respiratory infections, and nutritional supplements for small children. Galen also referenced Ivar having sent much-needed iodine packs, gauze pads, tape, and medications for nausea and diarrhea.

Several of the letters also made reference to patients with far more serious illnesses, including people who presented to Tandin with what Galen described as "effects from the betel." Betel nut is the seed of the areca palm wrapped in betel leaf and flavored with lime powder or clove. It is a mild stimulant and used much like chewing tobacco, and as with chewing tobacco, it is known to cause cancer of the mouth and throat. Galen, in a number of letters, requested Ivar's assistance in the care of those afflicted by the effects of the betel nut, stating that Tandin was treating these patients with "available remedies" and then sending them on to a hospital in Thimphu, Bhutan's capital city.

Joel again looked out his window, surveying the seemingly boundless white layers of Greenland's snow scape.

"Is that Iceland?" Myles asked, leaning over from the adjoining seat.

"Shit on rye, where'd you come from?" Joel said, bolting up in his seat. "A minute ago, you were buckled and comatose. I mean you were *out*."

"There's *out*," Myles said as he brushed crumbs off his shirt, "then there's *really* out. What you reading?" Myles yawned.

"Oh, just an article or two about Bhutan—trekking, mountaineering, historical tidbits, stuff like that," Joel said, not wanting to raise Myles's ire by mentioning anything more about Tandin's letters to Ivar. Joel knew that such a discussion would only set Myles off on a tirade about how Ivar would never waste time studying the "voodoo and witchery" of traditional medicine. Although it was still a long ways to New Delhi, it was not long enough to break Myles's ironclad agnosticism when it came to medical care delivered anywhere outside the walls of the Western world's ivory towers.

"I take it these articles don't include any particulars about physician volunteers arriving recently?" Myles asked as he picked up one of the magazine articles that was on the floor in front of Joel's seat and rifled through the pages.

"Rather lean when it comes to such specifics," Joel said.

"Well then, let's just get to this place and find him ourselves," Myles said, placing the magazine article into the seat pocket in front of him. "At least we can fly there, wherever exactly 'there' is. Anything but another one of those bastard ferry rides."

"Speak for yourself," Joel said, firing down two more Rolaids and taking a swig of water. "Personally, I'd rather have a paddle in my hand and a bamboo raft under my ass. If the missus and I ever see the promised land of retirement, we're springing for a couple of kayaks and two pairs of the best hiking boots we can find."

"No more adventure spirit inside you than that?" Myles asked. "You can't sink into the leather and smoke cigars every night."

"Yes, I can," Joel said as he took another quick look at Greenland's shoreline. "Besides, there's always my favorite row of

Sicilian bistros in the North End of town. I can stay plenty busy in and around my own backyard. So believe it or not, there's at least one thing my lady and I actually *do* agree on."

Myles looked at Joel with a blank expression.

"Flying," Joel said, flapping shut his window shade, "is for the birds. Although flying sure doesn't seem to bother Andie much. She's been slumbered since they closed the door."

Andie, seated two rows ahead, was sound asleep.

"Even though I'd rather avoid air travel altogether, it really isn't so bad back here in the cheap seats," Joel went on as Myles began to fidget with a plastic fork he found on his seat. "I'll bet you don't get anywhere near this much peace and quiet at work. And by the way, the last time I crossed the pond, I ended up sitting next to Sammy the sumo wrestler and the screaming quintuplets. So it could be a lot worse."

"It could be a lot better," Myles said, straightening up in his seat. "Just ask Martin, who's sitting up there in a different zip code, relishing his roast duck, polenta, and Grand Marnier. I'd expect him to be in full recline any minute now."

"Hey, when you've successfully kiboshed all your competitors, you can travel with your feet up," Joel said. "The demand for prosthetics and implants is colossal, and therein, no doubt, lie colossal profits. And where there's profit, there's Martin. To him, it's all commerce, and believe me when I tell you that the man has never once been freighted with a moment's remorse over his 'no one else shall be left standing' maxim."

"Believe me when I say that I believe you," Myles said with a slow nod. "Bears remarkable similarity to the precept that got him through college, that 'earned' Martin his diploma."

"Hearsay," Joel said, putting up a finger.

"Hearsay, my white French ass," Myles said. "Look, we've both heard it from plenty of reliable sources. Martin a bottom-rung student whose weekends usually began around Tuesday noon. Ask any of his classmates, and they'll all tell you that during his sophomore second term, Martin was circling the drain academically, and I know for a fact that he was flagging his

Developmental Biology course. When the final exam came up, he probably needed a map just to find the classroom. But somehow, miraculously, Martin escaped with a C in Developmental Bio. What couldn't be proven was that Martin, after the fact—after the exam, that is—pinched one of the test booklets out from under the nose of the moderator and returned later that evening to exchange the old answer sheet for the new 'revised' edition. As the story goes, one of the custodians facilitated this little sleight of hand after Martin flashed him a couple of Ben Franklin photos. What *could* be proven was that the lot numbers on the completed exam answer sheets were not consecutive. There was a perfunctory investigation of sorts, and after a brief hullabaloo, Martin was granted the proverbial benefit of the doubt. The official review referenced 'any number of other explanations' in regards to the jumbled answer sheet sequence. Those most familiar with this little escapade thought Martin should have been graded an S for the course instead of a C."

"S?" Joel asked.

"As in Switch," Myles said as he wrapped a blanket around his head. "And don't try and tell me that this is the first time you've ever heard that little term of endearment."

Five minutes later, Myles was once again slumped low in his seat, fast asleep with his body contorted. Joel was always envious of people like Myles, who was now snoring. Joel hadn't seen a wink of airborne sleep in his life. To kill some more time, Joel searched through the overstuffed file of letters and clippings that he and Myles had looted from Ivar's apartment. Jammed in between the yellowing stationery was a news piece about the sudden passing of a local author who had, just weeks prior to his death, gained celebrity for being the playwright of a sell-out West End London drama. Joel stopped when he found a color photograph of the man in a *Boston Magazine* article written about two years earlier.

At the time of his death, Bradford Zachary "Buzz" McKillnaugh was twenty-four years old.

Chapter 16

Fifteen miles due west of Paro, Bhutan

"Judas Priest, did you see that?" Myles shrieked as he reared back from the plane's window. "Those tree branches bloody near scraped the wing tips. I'm not sure I can take much more of this shit."

"And I'm supposed to be the one who's scared of flying," Joel said, gripping the armrests and staring down at the floor. "Indulge me just this one time, Myles, and close your eyes. It'll all be over soon."

"It'll all be over, all right—over in a wink if we clip one of those treetops. Are you kidding me? Joel, look, he's nearing even closer to—"

"I found it," Andie interrupted, leaning over from the seat across the aisle. "I knew this travel guide made some mention of the landing into Paro: *The approach into Paro International Airport, Bhutan's only landing field, can give pause to even the savviest of travelers.*"

"It's giving my heart pause right about now," Myles said, still looking out the window, straining to see as far forward as possible.

"*Powerful wind currents surge continually along the length of Paro Valley,*" Andie went on, "*causing varied degrees of aircraft turbulence. The valley's steepness demands a series of banked turns close against the north and south rims. Given the airstrip's position deep between the valley walls, an unusually sharp angle is required for both approach and takeoff.*"

"Located that *Welcome to Bhutan* guidebook, did you, Andie?" Joel asked without looking up.

"*Five of the seven planes within the Druk Air fleet are British Aerospace 146-100s, a medium-sized jet with four enormous engines mounted on a high wing above the fuselage,*" Andie read from her travel guide. "*Such design facilitates steep, high-altitude approaches.*

"That explains why this plane looks so bizarre, almost like something you'd see in a cartoon," Andie said, closing the book, looking over at Myles and Joel.

"I never saw this thing on any episode of *The Jetsons*, that's for damn certain," Myles said, his face pressed against the window. "Tell me there's a flight control tower out there somewhere. Anywhere."

About half an hour later, the forty-one passengers who had disembarked from New Delhi were standing in the middle of the Paro tarmac. The luggage had already been offloaded, and the plane was now being wheeled away by a small tow truck. No other aircraft was anywhere in sight.

Martin did a slow circle, surveying the surrounding mountainsides.

"In Delhi, I thought I was going to go deaf from all the noise and blind from all the smoke," he said. "And now . . . now, it looks like the time machine has landed."

"Check out that monastery along the river," Andie said as she looked upstream, her hair strewn back in the valley's breeze. "I saw the inner courtyard on our approach. It was packed with children, all wearing long, crimson robes. Students and monks, I'd imagine."

"I must have missed that on the way in," Joel said. "But that was probably about the time I had my eyes shut while praying for our collective lives."

"I don't feel so hot," Myles said in between shallow breaths. "This air might be cleaner than the air in India, but at least in

India there was a lot more of it. How high is this place anyway? I'm starting to see stars up here."

"Not quite 7,500 feet, and you'll get used to it soon enough," Andie said. "Slow, deep breaths, Myles."

Inside the terminal, Martin had a brief meeting with a liaison from the Ministry of Foreign Affairs, a gentleman who introduced himself as a Mr. Dharmo.

"We're in," Martin said, turning back toward Andie and Joel. "Our ride is waiting out front, so let's load up. Where's Myles?"

"I think that's him half-piked along the side of the building, heaving lunch," Joel said. "Mercifully upwind, I might add."

"What a goddamn cruiser," Andie said, shaking her head. "No wonder he never leaves home. I'll go get him. Just give me a minute."

While Martin was speaking with Mr. Dharmo, Andie pulled Joel aside.

"*Lobelia*," Andie said, looking at Joel with fire in her voice. "Ivar is here to find an herbal remedy called *Lobelia*. This is what I started to tell you and Myles about while we were at Charlie's Shoppe. That's what the boldface LO stands for on these tables."

Andie unfolded the paper she was holding and showed it to Joel, pointing to entries listed on the last table:

> 1Sept'09 MT 4.0—2.5 41days>**LO**
> 14Nov'09 RR 4.5—2.5 31days>**LO**
> 09Jan'10 UT 3.5—2.0 32days>**LO**
> 23Feb'10 KW 5.5—2.0 39days>**LO**
> 17Aug'10 PY 5.5—3.0 29days>**LO**
> 03Mar'11 LW 3.0—1.5 42days>**LO**
> 03Jan'12 GT 5.5—2.5 37days>**LO**

"This was attached to the letters that you and Myles lifted out of Ivar's apartment," Andie went on, "and it was written by someone besides Galen Vossner. Galen died two years before any of these entries were recorded. This table seems to indicate regression in the size of . . . of something. And whatever that something is, it was treated with *Lobelia*. When we were wandering through the Haymarket, Ivar was trying to get Dr. Anthony's thoughts on all kinds of natural medicines, and *Lobelia* was the one that seemed to pique Dr. Anthony's interest the most. The problem, as Dr. Anthony saw it, was access to this herb. He said it was only found in 'a dot of a place' in the Himalayas, or something along that line. But Ivar had that problem solved. He knew he could come here and find it himself, if someone of authority thought it held promise. And that someone was Dr. Anthony. Ivar wanted his blessing, I guess, for lack of a better word."

"I take it you haven't said anything more about this to Myles," Joel said, looking at Myles bent over along the side of the building.

"No way," Andie said as she shook her head. "Not a word since we left Charlie's a couple of days ago. That's when Myles was heading out full speed to catch up with Stacey, and it's safe to say he doesn't have use for any of this *Lobelia* discussion. But there isn't a doubt in my mind why Ivar came to Bhutan."

"You'd get further taking up conversation with the Sphinx than you would trying to sway Myles on this topic," Joel said, "so you might just as well keep this between the two of us. He'll blow a gasket if you bring this issue up again, and it won't help us find Ivar any sooner.

"Looks like Myles is back to vertical," Joel said, again looking over Andie's shoulder. "Why don't you lead him back over this way, and we'll catch our ride to the hotel."

Fifteen minutes later, the group arrived at the Hotel Druk's front entrance.

"Anything you need, sir, I would be honored to assist," Mr. Dharmo said, nodding his head slightly as he handed Martin his business card. "At any hour, and please, do not hesitate."

Mr. Dharmo politely declined when Martin tried to discreetly hand him a fold of bills.

"Haven't seen that before," Martin said as the car drove off, Mr. Dharmo waving good-bye.

"I'll bet not," Andie said in a stern voice just loud enough for all to hear. "I guess there are some things in this world that you just *cannot* buy."

"Okay, a suggestion," Joel said quickly. "I know we're all tired as hell, but while we're all still on our feet, let's wander around town a little bit. It's all well and good that we have no set schedule, but a word of caution here. We cannot start banging on doors and interrogating the locals about Ivar. There's liable to be some level of suspicion to begin with, because it's pretty obvious that we aren't sightseeing or mountaineering or rafting or anything like that. If we get too aggressive, folks might even think we're cops or under the auspices of Uncle Sam. Word like that will spread like wildfire in a place like this, so let's keep a low profile and try not to become part of the local rumor mill."

"What's wrong with just being direct with people, Joel?" Myles asked, coughing and clearing his throat. "I mean, what's the harm, being straight with everyone? For all we know, someone right here at the hotel may have seen Ivar in the past day or two, or have knowledge of his whereabouts. Maybe we could start by interviewing the hotel manager. We've come halfway around the world, and you're suggesting that we traipse our way through the center of town like a bunch of tenderfoots? We're here to find Ivar, right? So let's get on with it."

Before Myles had finished speaking, Andie dropped her travel bag and approached him.

"Myles, ease up here, please," Andie said, now standing right in front of Myles. "You can't just waltz in wherever you please and demand information about Ivar. Marching into the hotel manager's office to shake out information will get us nowhere. I mean, what do you plan on saying? 'Excuse me, sir, hate to interrupt, but have you seen a guy who measures in at around six-six, binoculars around neck, big glasses, IQ about 185? He fancies bird watching, and let me tell you, he plays one serious classical piano.' Wherever Ivar is, he's actually *doing* something for the people around him. And what are we doing for them? Ever consider that for a minute? Well, in case you haven't, we're trying to take him *away*, that's what we're trying to do. Once there's a whiff of that in the air, everyone will clam up, and shortly thereafter we will all be taking our seats on that favorite plane ride of yours, only this time headed due west."

"Looks to me like you're getting some of your color back," Joel said as he looked at Myles, trying his best not to laugh. "Look, pal, we just have to notch it back a bit, okay? Remember, we're not in Boston. From what I've read, the Bhutanese do not take kindly to a commandeering approach. Unlike the place we call home, this society treats others in a civil and respectful manner."

"Listen," Martin said, tilting his head and pointing into the air.

"Listen to what?" Myles asked impatiently.

Martin gestured for the others to follow him down a footpath that began along the side of the hotel. The trail weaved through a large grove of weeping willows and emerged along the edge of a cliff, the deep murmur of the Paro River welling up from a hundred meters below. To the north, the Paro flowed down from its source along the slopes of Mount Jomolhari, and from the cliff's edge, the valley itself appeared to fade into the endless expanse of the Himalayas. Wood-framed dwellings and rows of terraced rice paddies punctuated the lush mountainside that bordered the eastern side of the river.

"Listen now," Martin said.

An instant later, the timbre of a pair of cymbals could be heard from a monastery along the far embankment. A minute or so later, a series of three chimes resonated through the air, the first two soft and the last a bit louder.

"The music, it's walking along the water," Andie said, turning her ear toward the river below.

"How'd you ever hear that?" Myles asked, looking at Martin.

Martin's gaze remained fixed on the monastery below.

"I listened," Martin said as another succession of chimes faded into the distance.

"The person we're looking for is named Tshering," Martin went on, without looking up.

"Who's Tshering?" Joel asked after he exchanged a confused look with Andie and Myles.

"While the three of you were summiting back there, I introduced myself to the hotel manager," Martin said. "During the course of our brief conversation, I happened to mention that I was keen on picking up some native artifacts and souvenirs. He was quite accommodating. In fact, he handed me this stack of business cards from local vendors."

Martin pulled out one of the cards and held it up in front of the others.

"The manager of the hotel said he's known the proprietor for over forty years."

K. Tshering Norling Handicrafts
Paro Town Center
Paro, Bhutan

"If we're ever going to find Ivar," Martin said with complete calm, "this might be a good place to start."

ChAPTER 17

"That is poppy jasper," said the soft voice that neared Joel as he sifted through a vase of marble-sized stones. "The red and orange hues are much like the color of the sun just after dawn, and the swirls of black are reminiscent of tempest clouds encroaching from all sides. Each stone is, in nature's own way, a miniature storm."

The young girl standing next to Joel was barely five feet tall, her round face and dark eyes framed by medium-length black hair. The ankle-length garment she was wearing, made of a single rectangular piece of woven fabric, was a traditional Bhutanese dress known as a *kira*. The *kira* the girl had on was vermillion red, with an intricate pattern of deeper red along her tiny waistline. A silver *koma*, forged in the likeness of a dragon, was fastened across the right shoulder of her *kira*. To Joel, the girl's facial skin had the appearance of burnished porcelain, glistening in the afternoon sunlight. And despite the fact that she didn't have violet-colored streaks through her hair or a metal bolt piercing her nose, the girl could have easily passed as one of Joel's tenth-grade daughter's classmates.

Norling Handicrafts was located in the center of Paro town, immediately across the main thoroughfare from the town's largest outdoor market. Like all the surrounding businesses, the Norling shop was housed in a wood-framed building with elaborate hand-carved trim and richly colored patterns of Tantric symbols painted on the exterior walls. The population of Paro town proper was no more than five thousand, but with local vendors and merchants in the street markets supplying every trekker, mountaineer, white-water rafter, and wayfaring merchant, Paro's streets were always bustling. Some café and restaurant owners would boast that their staff could greet customers in over twenty languages, a useful skill when serving travelers from the diverse cultural regions of Nepal, Tibet, and the surrounding Indian states.

"Please, take your time and inspect all the beads and gemstones. Each of the glass containers holds a different jewel," the girl explained. "That is rose quartz in the smaller vase, next to our poppy jasper. Some of the quartz stones have a pinkish-red tint that is so fine the gem is nearly translucent in the sunlight. On the shelf nearest the door, you can find lemon agate, amethyst, many types of jade, river stone, and also tiger eye. All of our jewelry is custom made and handcrafted.

"Lapis is the best known of all our native gems," the girl continued as she picked a cobalt-blue stone out of one of the vases, balancing the gem on the tip of her index finger. "Lapis has been fashioned into artwork and objects of adornment for many centuries."

After plucking a fist full of jade stones off a nearby shelf, Martin stepped forward and offered the young girl his hand.

"Good afternoon," Martin said, dropping one of the beads onto the floor. "My name is Martin Phyte, and allow me to introduce my friends and fellow travelers, Andie, Joel, and Myles. The Hotel Druk manager gave me the card of your shopkeeper, and we could not resist stopping by and seeing what treasures you had in store."

Martin pulled out the business card and handed it to the girl.

"You are looking for the proprietor?" the young girl asked.

"Yes, yes," Martin said quickly. "The hotel manager said your store owner could assist us with all of our needs."

"Your hotel manager is quite correct," the girl said as she handed the card back to Martin.

"*Ngi ming Karmaing.* My name is Karma, and I am the proprietor. *Kuzuzangpo-la*, and welcome to Norling."

The four visitors exchanged brief, awkward glances.

"You will have to pardon us, Karma," Joel said, putting up both hands. "When the manager back at our hotel gave us your name, I assumed—we all assumed, incorrectly—that K. Tshering, the proprietor, was a man. More than likely an older man. Older, well, kind of like me."

Karma offered a warm smile. "There is no cause at all for apologies," she said. "This jewelry shop and the boarding house on the floor above have been in my family for many years. As my father has been in ill health, I became the proprietor a little over two years ago. And in regards to my name, I am in fact named after my great uncle. It surprises some visitors to learn that either a newborn boy or newborn girl can be given the name Karma. This is similar, I believe, to many American names like Frances or Jean or Chris. Or Andie, as I have now learned. So I believe it is I that must ask *your* pardon, as I did not know that Andie could be a girl's name also. It is a very pretty name, and if I might add, most appropriate."

For the first time in three days, ten thousand miles, or for that matter anyone's recent memory, Andrea McKillnaugh actually laughed.

"Thank you, Karma," Andie said, blushing. "That's a sweet thing to say. My given name is Andrea, but as a small child, everyone started calling me Andie. It probably all began . . . with my brother, somewhere along the line."

Karma invited everyone to take a seat, and despite the spare dimensions of the shop, everyone found room to sit at the small table near the window that faced Paro's main thoroughfare. The shop was filled with the subtle fragrance of citrus grass from an incense burner on a shelf in the corner of Karma's shop. Once her guests were seated, Karma began pouring a rich, thick, white liquid into the five bowls that were on the table.

"Karma is in fact a quite common name, which may have created some confusion when you were in conversation back at the hotel. My great uncle and Sanjay, your hotel manager, were classmates many years ago. You see, in Bhutan, we do not carry what you refer to as a family name. Each person you meet has only a first and second name. A proper last name is reserved only for the family of His Majesty the king."

Karma pointed to a framed photograph above the shop's front entrance.

"That is His Majesty, Jigme Khesar Namgyel Wangchuk, the Fifth Dragon King, on the day of his coronation," Karma said. "His likeness is seen above the doorway of every dwelling, business, and temple in Bhutan. Seated to the king's left is His Majesty's father, who ruled our nation for thirty-four years. In every photograph, the king is dressed in yellow vestments, as bright shades of yellow are worn only by royalty in Bhutan. Our country remains the only Buddhist kingdom anywhere in the world. Please, my friends, enjoy some tea."

Karma looked at the expression on the faces of her guests as they each took a careful sip from their bowl.

"Do you find our butter tea to your liking?" Karma asked as she looked at Joel.

"A bit of a gamey concoction," Joel said, wincing and setting down his bowl. "Back where I come from, Karma, this might be referred to as an acquired taste."

"That is a phrase I have heard a number of times before," Karma said. "But in a short time, nearly all find butter tea an essential ingredient of their daily lives. In Bhutan, butter tea is known as *sudja*, and it is a simple brew consisting of tea leaves, yak butter, and salt. Regular ingestion of butter tea helps ensure a long, vigorous life."

"I like it," Myles said, fooling no one as he forced down another swallow. "A little on the salty side, but it's working for me. By the way, do you get many visitors from our part of the world coming through here, sampling your tea?"

Myles, as impatient as ever, was already dropping hints as to why he and the others had come to Bhutan. After Andie gave him a sharp kick to the ankle, Myles, getting the message that this was the wrong tack, let out a brief grunt as he smiled and took another sip of his tea.

"Oh, many visitors, yes. And perhaps your ancestors were from a mountainous land," Karma said as she reached for the kettle at the center of the table and topped off Myles's bowl. "Yak herders throughout Bhutan and Tibet ingest as many as forty servings every day."

"Forty helpings of this, and I'd turn into a yak," Joel said, taking another cautious sip. "I think it's best if I stay in the slow lane."

"Just thirty-nine . . . make that thirty-eight, more to go, Doctor," Andie said as she poured Joel a refill.

"Those are *thangkas*, unique to Bhutan," Karma said, looking over at Myles as he thumbed through some of the paintings that were stacked on a shelf near his seat. "Some are pictures of Buddha, others are paintings of mandalas. All are made here in our shop, and each is unique. My brother is an excellent artist, as is my niece, who is but eleven years old."

"*Kadinchhey-la*, Norbu," Karma said to the cherub-faced youngster who brought out a tray of crisped rice. "You must be very hungry after your long journey. Please, enjoy some rice cakes."

"Is that a kite of some sort?" Andie asked, looking up at a triangular object hanging from the ceiling.

"That is a *dzoe*," Karma said. "To fashion a *dzoe*, one ties two twigs together in the shape of a cross. A rainbow of fine thread is then woven like a spider's web between the four corners. A *dzoe* will capture many evil spirits, trapping them in its tangle and casting them away forever. It shall rid one's home of all forces that would malign those that dwell within."

"I'd spring for a *dzoe*, if I were you," Joel whispered to Martin as he set down his butter tea bowl. "Dangle one of those above your desk, and you'll turn that last annoying competitor of yours into a troll."

Karma pointed out the *kiras, ghos,* and uncut lengths of richly colored fabrics that covered the walls of her shop.

"In Bhutan, we have a tradition of producing some of the finest handmade textiles anywhere in the world," Karma explained. "Most weaves are cotton, but the finest are elaborate patterns of pure silk. As with fine Persian rugs, no two cuts of textiles are identical. And the dyes, they are all natural. Red dyes are resin extracts from an insect, and blue dyes are made from the leaves of an indigo shrub. Shades of yellow, such as those used to weave the royal garments, are derived from turmeric or other vegetable sources.

"But you will have ample time to choose items that you wish to bring back to your families," Karma said. "Please, my friends, you are in need of sleep. The rest of your group, I suspect, are now in a deep slumber at the hotel."

Joel and the others knew that sooner or later, someone somewhere would ask about their "tour group."

"Believe it or not, Karma, we're pretty much on our own," Joel said. "I work with a hospital in Boston, back in the States, and we're trying to develop a humanitarian program in various parts of the world. One of the sites chosen was Bhutan, and we came here to survey local medical practices and available care. I hope we can learn about traditional means of medicine practiced here in your country, and perhaps see if there is any place for Western medicine in the more remote areas of Bhutan. Who knows. Maybe Western medicine is already making a significant impact in the less accessible parts of Bhutan.

"And since we're here in Paro," Joel continued, "we would appreciate any suggestions you have in regards to sightseeing in the immediate area."

"There is much to do here," Karma said with a flash of her perfect smile, a teardrop dimple appearing in the middle of each cheek. "I am close friends with the owner of a small but very experienced travel agency, so perhaps we can arrange a trek to the north of Paro town. We could follow the river northward toward the foothills of Jomolhari, which is a very sacred mountain. Nowhere in the world shall you see such a peak, as it is the home of our creators. Jomolhari has been climbed but twice, and I pray that it is never again trodden upon. Much of Bhutan farther to the north has never been explored or charted, and many peaks in that region of our country have no name and remain untouched by any human. Ganghar Puensum is nearly 7,500 meters in height, and this great peak has yet to be summited. It is far better that Ganghar Puensum has remained unconquered, as many spirits dwell there."

"It might be best if we stay close to town, Karma," Andie said. "There must be plenty to see and do right here, in and around Paro. In fact, just before we landed this morning, I saw a large building along the river that has a central courtyard. It looked like a school or temple, with a crowd of students running around inside."

The building Andie saw from the airport tarmac was Rinchen Dzong, considered by many to be the finest dzong anywhere in Bhutan. Dzongs are the country's great fortresses, and much like castles in Europe, they were built long ago to protect the native people. Rinchen Dzong means "great fortress upon jewels," and its foundation is said to be over one thousand years old. Dzongs are most often built along the banks of a large river, and each has massive, inward-sloping walls that are coated in pure white. Wooden joints secure every segment of the dzong, with neither iron bolts nor metal nails within any part of its structure. It is said that each dzong within Bhutan originated in the mind of a master builder, requiring no written plans or artist's design.

"The building you are speaking of is Rinchen Dzong, and I am sure a tour can be arranged," Karma said. "The monks who reside there will receive us most kindly, I am sure, and with some good fortune, we can watch the archers as they prepare for competition. In our country, archery is known as *datse*, and it is our national sport. A Bhutanese archery field measures three times the length of a standard Olympic range, and from such training ground come the most skilled archers anywhere in the world. Experts in *datse* are so accurate that during practice, teammates flank each side of a target board that is no larger than an average-sized dining table. From this proximate distance, fellow competitors will watch as arrows fired from 140 meters strike a small wooden target.

"We can as well journey to Ta Dzong, our National Museum," Karma continued. "It is high above Rinchen Dzong, on a hilltop overlooking the Paro River. Our history is told through the many ancient *thangkas* and paintings that hang on the museum walls. Although it is but a short walk to Ta Dzong, the pitch is steep, so I will ask that we proceed slowly. You have just arrived, and therefore you must allow adequate time to adjust to the altitude."

Karma poured more butter tea into each of the bowls. She then set down the clay kettle and considered each of her guests.

"Throughout the many centuries," Karma said, now speaking in a low, solemn tone, "our great scribes have written that the life force of Bhutan lies below the ground we tread and that the true treasures of our land are housed within the sacred caves that span beneath us. So as we walk about, consider with every step all that exists below the simple footpaths we travel upon. As you may know, my country goes by a number of names, the most fitting of which is the Land of the Peaceful Dragon. And as do all who dwell here, I wish every visitor peace in their heart and in their mind, both while traveling in Bhutan and in their lives at home."

A brief silence was broken by the sound of Myles quaffing down the rest of his tea. Karma smiled and refilled his bowl yet again.

"My friend, you need not finish," she said. "This bowl is poured for the next time you honor my family with your presence. It awaits the hour of your return, as do I."

"Weren't you the one doing the big heave-ho just after we stepped off the plane?" Andie asked Myles in a low voice as everyone stood up from the small table. "Take it easy on that stuff, will you please. I don't want to watch your retinas pop out while we're wandering through that dzong later this afternoon."

Andie, Joel, Myles, and Martin each thanked Karma as she waved good-bye from the threshold of her shop.

"One detail, if I may mention," Karma said as the group was leaving. "Appropriate footwear will be needed for our walk, and if you are in need of trekking shoes, there are a number of vendors in the marketplace that sell such apparel. And do not hesitate to haggle with the merchant, no matter what you are attempting to purchase."

"That's just the kind of advice we need, Karma," Joel said. "Before we head back to the hotel, we'll stroll through town and shop around until we find boots that are sturdy enough to climb Annapurna."

"I believe it is best to leave Annapurna's summit to the Nepalese Sherpas," Karma said, laughing. "There is no need to spend so much on such a high-end item. Although, if your schedule allows and you desire a more robust trek, we could traverse along an alternate route, perhaps to the Tiger's Nest."

Joel and Andie immediately looked at each other, recalling some of the lines written by Galen Vossner in his letters to Ivar:

> *It is a long trek to TN*
> *. . . we'll again walk toward TN*

"Trek where?" Joel asked, taking a step closer and cocking his head.

"To Taktsang, the Tiger's Nest," Karma said as a sudden blast of wind ripped through the street. "This is a more vigorous walk, and all the more now as a recent flood damaged the only access road. To get there, one must walk every kilometer from Paro town."

"I guess that pretty much wipes out the dzong tour," Myles mumbled, again waving good-bye to Karma.

"Not to mention seeing the exhibits at the museum," Martin added.

"Not to mention getting some sleep," Joel grumbled.

"Well, c'mon," Andie said as she headed across the street toward the outdoor market, her eyes tearing from the biting wind. "Sounds to me like we might need some gear."

Chapter 18

The sound of the monks' hymn broke through the morning air, its low rhythm welling up from the shrouded valley far below. Karma stood at the edge of the Tremo Pass overlook, her eyes following the faint shadows that began to appear in the depths of the vast corridor that reached northward to the Himalayan peaks along Bhutan's border with Tibet. As the day's first light reflected off Jomolhari's sheer white eastern slope, the chanting slowly faded, and the morning was again silent.

It was just after six the next morning, and Joel, who in addition to experiencing insomnia during air travel suffered from jetlag whenever he left the Eastern Time Zone, had accepted Karma's offer to visit Tremo Pass at daybreak. Martin, Andie, and Myles, despite going to bed early the previous evening, were still sound asleep back at the hotel. Tremo Pass, by road just over an hour's drive north of Paro town, offered visitors an unparalleled view of several Himalayan peaks that pierced the northern sky. It was a clear, windless morning, and Dr. Joel Morgan was wide awake.

"And I thought the view from Smuggler's Notch was impressive," Joel said between heaving breaths once he had reached the wooden viewing platform. "Now I can say that I stood on top of the world to watch the sun rise."

"And this Smuggler's, it is a mountain located near your home?" Karma asked.

Joel turned toward Karma, still struggling to draw in a breath. "Smuggler's Notch, I am just now learning, would be best described as a hill," he said as sweat streamed down his brow.

"*That*," Joel said, pointing over his right shoulder, "is a mountain."

"We have the good fortune of a clear daybreak," Karma said. "As you can see, this mountain pass is quite close to Paro town, and I much enjoy bringing visitors here. As the others in your party are still asleep, we can perhaps return once more during your stay, so all can take in this sight. I am mindful that you and your friends dwell near the sea, so I hope this climb was not too arduous."

"I haven't climbed this many steps in the past two years," Joel said, squinting as he looked at the glacial blanket that coated Jomolhari's upper ridge line, a mesh of enormous ice crystals visible against the azure sky.

"And don't give me an easy way out here, Karma," Joel said. "Living at sea level is incidental compared to the eighty extra pounds I have on board, not to mention the barge load of stogies I've inhaled in my lifetime. But I'm scoring this experience as my first go at mountaineering. At least that's my story when I get home," Joel said, again wiping his forehead.

Karma pointed to a spec of snow, farther to the north, that pierced the now cloudless sky.

"That is Gieu Gang, also along our border with Tibet," Karma said. "Gieu Gang is at the end of the Shakyapassang Valley, and it is a giant nearly on the scale of Mount Jomolhari. Seeing this peak is a very rare sight from this pass, and we are most fortunate to be part of an unclouded morning."

"Fortunate does not come near close enough to describe any of this," Joel said, searching for the distant peak through the viewfinder of his camera, zooming in and out and clicking repeatedly. "I don't know why I'm bothering to take pictures, as they won't do this vista an ounce of justice."

Karma stepped off the viewing platform and moved to the edge of the cliff, finding a seat on a granite boulder that straddled the ridge line. The chime of a prayer wheel, powered by water coursing down a nearby mountain brook, could be heard in the distance.

"There are many thousands of prayer wheels throughout our country," Karma said. "Each one is inscribed with a long list of devotions and supplications and kept in perpetual clockwise motion by water, wind, or the human hand."

Karma let a long moment pass, all the while looking in the direction of the chiming prayer wheel.

"You are here to find the man who came to Bhutan to cure many ills, are you not?" Karma said, her tone completely calm. "And I must believe that you, like Dr. Ivar, are also a physician."

Joel's eyes went wide. "Yes, and yes again, I am. How on earth did you know all this?" he asked.

"It was, in my mind, only a question of time," Karma said. "From what I have learned, your friend is a remarkable man, and regrettably, it is most unusual to have such a gifted healer stay with us for very long. With time, it was a certainty that others would have concern and come here in search of him."

"But how did you know it was us . . . our group?" Joel asked, shaking his head slowly.

"There were a number of clues yesterday while you were visiting my shop," Karma said. "The gentleman who first introduced himself, Mr. Martin Phyte, it was quite evident that he is no ordinary traveler. On his wrist he wears a gold bracelet that bears the image of Sitalces, the great Thracian king. The king's crown has within it an ancient emerald, and it is exquisite. This jewelry of Mr. Phyte's, it is authentic. This bracelet is a priceless antiquity, which by providence should be housed in a museum for all to admire. But some antiquities, I know, are in the possession of very wealthy people. Such a person as Mr. Phyte would hardly be in search of the simple items in my shop. If a man of such means was merely a tourist, he would have private attendants about him. But as Mr. Phyte was with you and the others—who were, from all indications, friends of his—I had some suspicion that he was one important man looking for another important man."

"But how . . . how did you know . . ."

"How did I know that you too were a physician?" Karma said as Joel stumbled over his words.

Joel nodded.

"To start, you did mention that you worked at an American hospital," Karma continued. "But also, in my country, as most of a person's body is covered by clothing, one must closely study an individual's face, eyes, and hands in order to learn about those who surround you. From these parts of the body, much can be gathered. And as well, as my craft concerns the design of jewelry, it is easy for me to spot any bodily adornments that a visitor may be wearing. While we were sitting and sharing some butter tea yesterday, I noticed that the skin to the sides of your fingertips show many parallel breaks, indicating frequent abrasive motion with potent cleansers. I also observed the small blemishes and scores on your ring that represent more than just the wear of passing years. Such tarnish comes only from countless washings of the hands, and who else but a doctor washes his or her hands so many times day after day. Seeing this tells me that not only are you a doctor, but you are as well married and that you treasure your family enough to wear your gold band at all times. Excuse my boldness, Dr. Joel, but this is most admirable."

"Twenty-seven years and still happily a pair," Joel said. "So by looking at Martin's wrist and my beat-up wedding band, you came to the conclusion that we were here for reasons other than souvenir shopping," he said as a tiny wisp of ground fog passed between him and Karma.

"There is one more detail to mention," Karma said. "Your companion Myles, while you were visiting yesterday, his every motion seemed pervaded by apprehension. Although our encounter was brief, he struck me as a most reluctant traveler, and so jumpy he nearly rattles. I suspect his mind, much like his hair, often proceeds ungoverned," Karma continued with a slight giggle, "and his unusual curiosity about other travelers who may have paid visit to my shop struck me as peculiar. We do at times have international policing agencies making inquiries about individuals pirating our nation's treasures. In some cases, they are looking for thieves who have pilfered relics that date to the ninth and tenth centuries. For a brief moment, I wondered if your group represented such an agency, but such authorities would never send out an envoy as restive as Myles, who to me showed evidence of being here out of painful necessity. I therefore had suspicion that Myles, like you, Dr. Joel, might be in search of someone very close to him."

"Myles forgot to get in line when they handed out subtlety and style," Joel said. "But his work with Ivar is his life, and he's as loyal as they come."

"Dr. Ivar has devoted friends, and the spirits will help in your quest to find him," Karma said with a warm smile. "Our traditional ways cannot cure all ills, and from what I know, your friend has helped heal many needy people. We need such a person here in my homeland, but I sense that this man may be in greater need elsewhere. And in case you have wondered, I have never met Dr. Ivar myself."

Joel stepped off the viewing platform and walked toward Karma, still keeping a healthy distance between himself and the cliff's edge.

"Karma, this is where I could use your help," Joel said in a somber tone. "Although Ivar has been supplying a medical clinic around here for many years, there's still a lot I don't understand about his reasons for coming to Bhutan. Ivar received many letters from a man named Galen Vossner, who I'm sure you knew when you were a child because his letters to Ivar had your boarding house's insignia on them. From what I gather, Galen delivered medical supplies to a man named Tandin, and Tandin, by my best guess, is a practitioner of traditional medicine here in Bhutan.

"In Galen Vossner's letters to Ivar," Joel continued after again catching his breath, "he repeatedly referenced traveling to a place that I now know to be Taktsang. All I know about Taktsang is that it's a very old and very remote monastery. There's a lot more to the story than that, Karma, including the fact that this place has a lot to do with Ivar being in Bhutan."

Karma again looked out across Tremo Pass, the gorge below now a pulse of verdant green in the brilliant morning light.

"There was a time in our history when our land was ruled by a most vile force," Karma began. "As our sky was sunless and void of the moon's glow, there was no substance to either the day or the night. Evil vapor spilled down from every summit, and the great mountain lands fell under the rule of powerful demons. The gloom was so complete that even our mighty King Sendka became possessed by the most evil of spirits, remaining ill until the arrival of the great Tantric master, Guru Rinpoche.

"Guru Rinpoche was born from a blue lotus on Lake Dhanakosha, far to the west," Karma continued, "and in the eighth century, he subdued all demons while meditating in caves throughout Bhutan and Tibet. With time, he because known as Precious Master, flying on the back of a tigress and ridding our sky of darkness and evil. When the heavens were again clear and sunlight had returned to our land, the tigress took refuge on the edge of a cliff that overlooks Paro Valley. For three months, Guru Rinpoche meditated in the Dubkhang, a sacred cave hidden deep within the mountainside high above Paro River. With all evil spirits extinguished, monasteries could now be erected throughout the mountain kingdoms. The holiest of all shrines, Taktsang, was built above the Dubkhang cave. It is the Tiger's Nest, and a place of singular power, where pilgrims go to seek healing and enlightenment. It is the most sacred of all Buddhist monasteries, and it has no equal anywhere in the world."

Ignoring for a moment his proximity to the canyon's edge, Joel sat down next to Karma and looked her squarely in the eye.

"No more ruse, Karma," Joel said, "and I apologize for that charade in your shop yesterday. We are not here on some medical fact-finding mission. We came here to find Ivar and to try to persuade him to return home with us. Ivar is a renowned leader in the field of medical research, and he is, without question, the most gifted individual I have even known. Andie, Myles, Martin, and I know Ivar better than anyone, yet none of us had any hint as to his affection for your homeland. After reading the letters that Galen sent to Ivar, and with all I have seen since our arrival yesterday, I can now understand why Ivar chose to come here and all the more why he chose to stay. But there's something you need to know, Karma. Ivar is sick. He is very sick. He has a form of blood cancer, and without proper treatment, he will not live long. If Ivar chooses to remain here and forgo any therapy, so be it. That's his choice. But we must find him, because he is our friend and he may need our help. The four of us are, in every sense, Ivar's family."

"If it is assistance you seek, Dr. Joel, you need seek no further," Karma said. "I will arrange to have my sister take over my shop duties, and I can serve as your travel guide. I am quite familiar with the trail that leads to Taktsang, but we will need to procure some extra supplies in Paro town, as the trail to the monastery was flooded recently, and hence we must trek there on foot. It will require two days' travel, and the climb in places is quite steep. And along the way, should I see fatigue across your countenance, I shall simply ask you to imagine that we are traversing the length of Smuggler's Peak. This thought shall remind you of your home and no doubt put you at ease."

For the first time in many days, Joel looked visibly relieved.

"If you can help us find Ivar, Karma . . . if that is in any way possible, we would all be eternally grateful."

"Remember, you are now in the Land of the Peaceful Dragon, Dr. Joel, and it is all possible," Karma said, looking out again toward Mount Jomolhari. "It is all possible."

Signaling that it was time to leave, the driver from the hotel waved Karma and Joel back toward their small van. Minutes later, the three of them began weaving down the lone mountain road that led back toward the Hotel Druk.

"There's something else that I'm curious about, Karma," Joel said as he braced himself for another switchback turn. "Are there any straight roads in this country?"

Karma appeared to be enjoying the ride down the mountain pass, the look on her face reminding Joel of his daughter's expression while descending the Tower of Terror at Disney World.

"If there are," Karma said with a broad smile, "they are most unfamiliar to me."

"I was afraid you'd say that," Joel mumbled.

"One last question," Joel said as the van slowed to navigate another 180-degree turn. "How can you be so sure that we will find Ivar at all?"

"The path to Taktsang is, in many ways, a slow caravan of those who seek healing," Karma said. "Healing of every sort. And you yourself agreed that your friend is an exceptional man, did you not?"

"Yes," Joel said as he clutched the van's tattered upholstery with both hands.

"As of late, I have heard of exceptional things," Karma said softly, wearing a look of perfect calm. "Most exceptional things."

Chapter 19

Tandin Lehto placed both of his hands on the elderly man's neck, pressing firmly enough to gauge the dimensions of the bulbous swelling along the lower border of the man's chin. The patient Tandin was examining appeared gaunt and unsteady, and there was a thin malodorous discharge emanating from the side of his mouth along with a heavy, rubbery coating piled up on his lower lip. Although the man's skin was ashen, his eyelids were violaceous and beefy. The inside of the man's mouth was coated with a substance that looked like black tar, and whatever teeth that remained on the gum line behind his swollen lip were hanging on by a thread.

Tandin measured the size of the growth, jotting down notes to himself on a chart that listed data from dozens of patients. Tandin then opened two glass jars, one containing a small red seed, and another an off-white crystalline powder. Tandin crushed the seed into a bowl of butter tea, added the white powder, and handed the tea bowl to his patient.

"Sir, please," Tandin said to the man, speaking in the native language he and his patient shared. "I will prepare some remedy for you to take with you, with instructions on its use at home."

In an instant, Tandin wrapped some of the red seeds in a small piece of cloth. He handed the seeds to the patient and immediately re-shelved the glass jar that contained the seeds.

"Sir, the other doctor here with me," Tandin said, nodding his head in Ivar's direction, "he has medications that can as well be administered and bring you some relief. This can be done today, right away, should you so desire."

The man shook his head, quietly declining any further assistance.

"Then return in three days' time, please," Tandin said as he helped the man to his feet. "Sooner if need dictates. As your family is waiting for you outside, I shall give them details of the care required at home."

Tandin and the elderly gentleman walked past Ivar and out of the clinic. Ivar, who was seated not five feet away, was examining another patient.

There was no mistaking the shrill sound audible in the lower part of the young man's neck. Through a stethoscope, the flow of blood into the left upper extremity was as loud as a passing freight train, and Ivar could actually feel the turbulent circulation with gentle palpation. Dorje, a local farmer in his early thirties, was brought to the hut by his family after he had repeatedly collapsed while tending his fields of buckwheat and rice. Dorje's children, with unmistakable alarm in their voices, described their father's episodic loss of consciousness and right-sided paralysis. The loss of mentation and one-sided paralysis they had witnessed occurred only when their father was tending his fields. Dorje's symptoms, although striking, were always temporary in nature. In fact, Dorje had no difficulty at all walking for several kilometers in order to see the doctor who lived in the hut high above the valley floor.

Once the history and physical exam had been completed, Ivar needed no sophisticated imaging to establish a diagnosis. Ivar was certain that Dorje had subclavian steal syndrome, a vascular disease caused by an obstruction in the main artery to the upper extremity on one side. When Dorje used his arms vigorously, circulating blood was siphoned off from one of the two main arteries that supply blood to the left side of the brain. This "stolen" volume of circulating blood to the brain was enough to compromise cerebral function and produce symptoms of a stroke, including incapacitating weakness on the right side of the body. Correction of such an obstruction required a team of interventional radiologists and vascular surgeons at a tertiary care center. As this option was an impossibility, Ivar considered a more viable alternative.

"You have, no doubt, worked these same fields since you were a young child," Ivar said to the farmer seated in front of him. "Through your tireless efforts, your family has thrived, and to you they owe everything. Yet there is one need unfulfilled, and that is your children's quest for direction. Their quest for guidance. Their quest for wisdom, the wisdom of their father and the wisdom of the many generation that preceded him."

Ivar placed a hand gently over Dorje's left collarbone, his palm again feeling the coarse thrill of blood pumping through a critically blocked artery.

"Your place, as head of your household, is no longer in the rich fields you have toiled in all these years," Ivar said. "We have now a clear sign, a clear direction. Your children are strong, and by all I can see, most capable. Your labors are now their labors. The day's work is now their work, and as their father is near, they shall not fail."

Dorje's fear and resignation seemed to ease, his face now wearing the look of fatherly pride.

"*Ta do-ran-sha, drog po,*" Ivar said. "I am here to help, should any need arise."

As Dorje and his family shuffled away, a lone figure limped through the burlap barrier that covered the entranceway to the only medical clinic anywhere within a two days' walk. The limping man's face was riddled with beads of icy sweat, and his mouth was as dry as desert sand. He was shaking from head to toe.

Mance was an otherwise healthy herdsman who had begun to experience abdominal pain and vomiting two days prior to his presentation. His gastrointestinal symptoms had progressed to the point that he could no longer hold down water, and by the time Mance arrived at Ivar's doorstep, his flank and back pain were so intense he could barely walk. The man's midback was tender to palpation, and his skin almost hot to the touch.

Mance had wandered away from the other herdsmen in search of help. He was alone, he was frightened, and he was very sick.

Mance was seventeen years old.

Ivar knew immediately that Mance had a bacterial infection of the kidney commonly known as pyelonephritis. Over the past weeks, Ivar had seen several similar cases, and given the fact that dehydration was a key ingredient in the disease's evolution, this was hardly a surprise. A yak herder's endless days of grazing half-ton beasts were followed by nights spent in the arctic cold, with the consumption of large volumes of a local brew known as *chang* being an invariable part of each evening's ritual. And as clean drinking water was at times a luxury, the herdsman's dry kidney was fertile ground for any number of native bacteria.

The progression of Mance's symptoms was classic for pyelonephritis: swift, severe, debilitating, and, if left untreated, potentially fatal.

As with the other herders that Ivar had seen, Mance needed a hospital.

And as with the other herders that Ivar had seen, all Mance had was a thirty-square-meter roughhewn clinic that had "opened" many years earlier when two complete strangers showed up at Tandin Lehto's three-room home. One of the strangers, an eleven-year-old boy and son of a Paro merchant, had fallen out of a tree while playing with friends. The other was a foreigner who had stumbled upon the boy while hiking solo along a nearby stream bed.

The boy's name was Padma Weng, and he left the next day with a homemade cast on his wrist.

The foreigner's name was Galen Vossner, and he in fact never left.

Galen had for years worked as a volunteer medical assistant at a small Nepalese hospital, and after venturing into Bhutan, he created a conduit whereby donated supplies found their way to places as remote as Tandin's improvised clinic. Tandin was a diminutive man with a triangular face, a saddle-shaped nose, and a coarse, irregular facial contour. The skin folds around both of his eyes sagged so much that no one could ever tell if Tandin saw you when you approached him. No one knew how old Tandin was. Whenever he was asked, he ignored the question, and whenever the same question was put to Dru, his wife of over forty years, she seemed to give a different answer. But Tandin's most-telling feature was not his spare stature, rough weathered countenance, or evasiveness when it came to answering personal questions, but rather the speed in which he did everything. His every motion seemed to be in overdrive, as if he had no gear between neutral and fifth. When Tandin prepared mixtures of the various medicinal herbs that were stored in the glass jars shelved along one wall of his clinic, he did so with a rapidity that reminded anyone watching of a movie reel playing in fast forward. Tandin collected roots, flowers, tubers, seeds, leaves, powders, bulbs, and bark strips from all parts of Bhutan and Tibet, concocting one mixture after another that could be either applied or ingested in order to treat any number of ailments and injuries.

All who entered Tandin's home did so under the vigilant gaze of Namthose, the gold king of the north, whose image adorned the moth-eaten *thangka* that hung on the wall opposite the clinic's entrance. Through the years, Tandin's home became a place of *troten*, or healing, where malnourished infants, children with respiratory infections, farmers with tuberculosis, backpackers with amoebic dysentery, travelers with infected insect bites, and mountaineers with altitude sickness were all given aid.

And, from time to time, a place where yak herders with pyelonephritis and impending blood sepsis were patched up and sent on their way.

Ivar placed a large bore intravenous line into Mance's arm, and over the course of ninety minutes, his patient received three liters of fluid and two grams of broad spectrum antibiotic. Within a couple of days, Mance would be back on his feet and in the mountain wilderness with his fellow herdsmen, once again guzzling *chang* under the light of the dragon's moon.

Since his arrival at Tandin's home, Ivar had attempted to make a catalogue of as many of the native medicinal herbs as he possibly could. This proved a daunting task, as there are at least three thousand species of plants used to prepare traditional medicines in Bhutan. To complicate this effort, Tandin's skills in written English were very limited, and although Ivar had become proficient in Dzongkha, Bhutan's spoken language, the faded labels on the glass jars that stored the native herbs were printed in Choekey, which is the written language of Bhutan and unrelated to Dzongkha. Tandin had great appreciation for Ivar's keen interest in the ancient art of herbal medicine, corresponding with him for years on this subject with the help of Galen Vossner, and sending letters directly to Ivar himself after Galen's death. Knowing that Ivar's medical expertise centered on cancer research, Tandin sent Ivar notes of how he treated patients who presented with large, firm swellings that he could only presume to be malignant. Although Tandin encouraged all such patients to seek care at the National Referral Hospital in Thimphu, many patients whose family had lived in the mountain communities for untold generations distrusted the doctors in the large cities and had no desire to leave their home. This left their care in the hands of Tandin, whose resources consisted of the rows of glass jars that lined one wall of his clinic and any supplies that Galen and Ivar could procure for him. Most patients who presented with large facial and neck swellings were inveterate users of the betel nut, and through his many years of practice, Tandin had tried various native herbs to reduce the size of what he believed to be cancerous growths caused by the betel nut.

And as with everyone he treated, Tandin kept detailed records on the progress of all his cancer patients, documenting the extent of tumor progression or tumor regression.

Ivar's interest in medicinal herbs centered around *Lobelia nubigena*, which is a large flowering plant that has dense white leaves and a fleshy, berry-like fruit with tiny seeds. Ivar, through years of study, had read anecdotal evidence suggesting that the powdered extract of the *Lobelia nubigena* seed can impede the growth of, and perhaps even cause the regression of, certain drug-resistant tumors. *Lobelia nubigena* is unique to a tiny region of the Trongsa District in the very center of Bhutan, as the soil, air quality, temperate climate, and relatively low altitude at this specific site are optimal for its growth. Tandin had never traveled to the Trongsa District, as it was at least a full day's trip by road and he preferred not to leave the environs of his clinic. But to Tandin, this was no impediment. Tandin and a small group of native healers had spent a lifetime learning about the medicinal herbs that thrived in any given region of Bhutan, and as with the masters who taught them, they would gather together at least once every month to exchange the various homegrown products that had for centuries been used to treat the people of Bhutan. This was not a business relationship or latest version of some age-old bartering forum. This was a kinship. This was a reciprocity that kept no ledger. This was about seeking ways to heal their own people, and it happened every time these practitioners of the ancient art of medicine gathered together to pray, chant, and meditate.

And they always gathered at Taktsang.

As there were no more patients to be seen, Ivar walked out into the midday sun. The early afternoon had proven the ideal time to spot any number of bird species that roamed the highlands of western Bhutan, and in recent days, Ivar had seen a pair of blue whistling-thrush and a lone Eurasian kestrel diving repeatedly toward the floor of Paro Valley. As Ivar approached the edge of the gorge, a Pallas's fish eagle could be seen against the vertical wall that dropped over one thousand meters from the base of Taktsang. Ivar followed the bird as it arced into a serpentine path along the string of multicolored prayer flags that hung between the roof of the monastery and the small *chorten* on the far eastern edge of the cliff.

Ivar cleared his throat in the dry mountain air, noticing a bit more blood in his handkerchief than had been present the day before. No matter, really. If anything, the internal bleeding seemed almost trivial compared to the searing eye pain that had lasted most of the previous week. The lacerating pulse behind Ivar's right eye had ended as rapidly as it had started, claiming his right-sided vision at the very moment the pain had ceased.

Ivar's world was now flat and two-dimensional. Taktsang itself appeared as an apparition suspended between the mountains and the sky, with a thin film now passing across the prayer flags that fluttered along the roofline of the monastery. The color and motion of the flags faded away briefly but then reappeared a few seconds later.

"Ivar, Ivar," Tandin shouted, his arms flailing as he scurried in Ivar's direction. "Another child, a small girl, please . . . the baby is in distress, and her mother quite in a panic."

Ivar spotted the Pallas's eagle soaring upward from the depth of Paro Gorge. The bird seemed to vanish momentarily but then returned into view along the base of the monastery.

"Ivar!" Tandin insisted.

"*Lho lho, ngay drogpo,*" Ivar said. "Relax, my friend. We will attend to her now."

When Ivar turned around, he knew that the streaks of film cutting across Tandin's face were not caused by layers of moisture from an early-afternoon fog.

"We shall get this child on the mend and return her and her mother to their home as quickly as possible," Ivar said, not pausing to consider how long it might take for the malignant cells to advance into the blood vessels that flowed to his one remaining eye. "Then you and I can enjoy an unhurried walk along the trail together. Perhaps we can hike to Taktsang, and at long last I can tour the monastery with you. We have spoken of this so many times."

"Not possible, not possible," Tandin said, his head whipping from side to side. "The journey to and from Taktsang requires several hours, and the remaining sunlight today is inadequate for such a walk. But soon, Ivar. This I pledge to you."

Tandin knelt down on the grass and pulled a small cloth sack out from one of his pockets. He then produced a large green leaf from a paper wrapping that he had tucked under his belt. With a tapping motion so quick that it appeared to be a muscle spasm, Tandin spread the dark powder that was stored in the pouch onto the surface of the leaf. He folded the leaf three times, shot to his feet, and then handed the leaf to Ivar.

"This shall aid in your care of the young girl." Tandin said, pointing his head sharply in the direction of his clinic. "I am sure you also have medicine that will help the child, but apply this for one hour to the back of her neck. One hour, no more. Dru shall assist you, if need be."

With that, Tandin turned and hurried down the narrow trail that led out from behind his home.

"Then perhaps tomorrow we can trek to Taktsang," Ivar said, his words chasing after Tandin. "Or if not, then maybe the day after."

Tandin stopped, spun around, and looked at Ivar. "Yes then, yes, tomorrow," Tandin said, nodding his head in the direction of Paro Gorge. "I shall join some friends there, and you shall join us tomorrow at Taktsang."

"Excellent. I would be so honored," Ivar said, his visual image of Tandin seeming to wobble as the two spoke. "Honored to be with you and meet others you share knowledge with, and learning more of the remedies you use to treat your patients with growths caused by the betel nut."

"No mixture can eliminate these types of growths," Tandin said, shaking his head vigorously. "At times, a temporary reduction. At times, the progression slowed. Often, some brief respite for those afflicted. But the disease is never arrested. Never vanquished. All succumb."

Ivar nodded, watching the outline of Tandin's body waver from side to side.

"Ivar, please, the girl," Tandin said as he turned back around and rushed down the trail. "I am in search of a small plant, which grows deeper in the forest where there is less wind. I shall be back soon."

As Ivar reentered the clinic, he looked up at Namthose, the great king who now appeared to be smiling down upon the sick young girl seated on her mother's lap in the center of the room. From Tandin's doorway, Ivar glanced back again at Taktsang, the monastery's small wooden dome seeming to dissolve from view as the Pallas's eagle continued to sweep the sky above the Tiger's Nest.

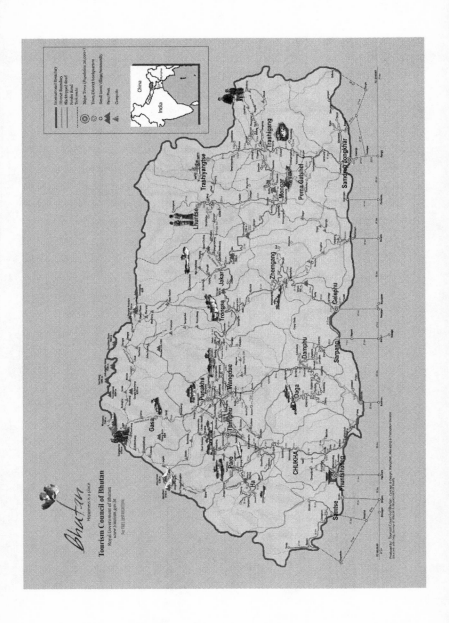

CHAPTER 20

Jhapa, Nepal
Present day

Sandu needed a drink, and he needed one badly. Jhapa was a miserable place even on a decent day, and neither Sandu nor any of the other refugees he lived with had seen a decent day in months. The leeches he could handle, but the snakes, they were a different matter. There were more of them all the while, including the cobra that his wife recently found curled up under their sweat-soaked mattress. As the last jug of *rakshi* had been emptied the previous night, Sandu was hoping that the *ganja* roll he was about to light would provide a couple hours of stuporous relief from the incessant smell of sewage that permeated the air above his tent city. But eventually, after whatever high he had inhaled had worn off, Sandu would have to again face the reality of another sweltering afternoon in the cesspool that the United Nations and Western press referred to as a refugee camp. Camp . . . bullshit this was a camp. This was a prison. In fact, this was worse than a prison. At least prisons were *in* a country—in *some* country. According to everyone's map, Jhapa was in Nepal. But in reality, the squalid Jhapa shantytown that Sandu was forced to call home was in every sense disavowed by both Nepal and India.

Sandu was standing in the middle of a low grove of trees that lined a hill along the camp's northern border. The air was still and dank, rife with a stench that one of Sandu's bunkmates called "downwind latrine." It was not as hot as it had been earlier in the week, but it was still plenty hot. It was just past two in the afternoon, and Sandu was bored out of his mind. Time for light.

"Don't even think of taking a drag of that shit," said a grating voice not ten feet away. "Where the fuck have you been?"

Sandu snapped around and faced Drapche Dorn, the *ganja* roll that fell out of his mouth all but forgotten before it had hit the ground.

"I told you by noon today, pal," Drapche said as he inched closer to the now-trembling Sandu. "Noon. Know what time it is now, numb nuts?"

As with everyone else in camp Jhapa, Sandu knew that Drapche never needed to raise his voice when he was angry. The deep scar that traced downward from Drapche's receding hairline, a scar that penetrated even deeper as it divided his eyelid into two unequal segments, always told the story of Drapche's escalating displeasure. The wound had formed a full thickness cleft into the frontal bone, with the edges of the scar appearing as a bright red arc whenever Drapche was angry.

"Apologies, Drapche," Sandu stuttered. "I was just now on my way to—"

"Save your war stories for someone who gives a shit," Drapche said. "Now tell me something useful for a change, or I'll make chasing snakes out of your bunk look like an afternoon at your favorite whorehouse."

Drapche knew about the cobra in Sandu's tent, but that was no surprise. Drapche knew everything that went on in the camp, no matter what the hour or what the circumstance. If anything was bought, sold, or traded in the camp, Drapche got his cut. If it came into the camp, the top slice was his. If it went out of the camp, it did so only with his blessing and only after he had gouged out his share of whatever profit lay on the table.

"Sapkota, he came through, Drapche," Sandu said, nodding rapidly. "We met late in the night yesterday, and he has done all that you requested. The border guard that Sapkota made contact with, he is a young man whose mother is widowed and whose family is in desperate need of cash. This guard, he was easily swayed, and his cooperation is assured. Four thousand rupees and the trapdoor switchblade you promised. This will get you through the border crossing, there is no question."

The Italian stiletto trapdoor switchblade was one of Drapche's favorite knives, often critiquing it as a light piece with one fine motion. "With this in hand, you'll never forget the look on the face of the man who's facing you," Drapche would occasionally say when trying to sell one of the blades from his collection, adding the words "and neither will he" to help close the deal.

"Some progress, then," Drapche said through a smile of rotting, black, betel-nut-stained teeth. "So if that little tot is stationed at the border every other night, the next thing you're going to tell me is when he'll be there next. And you've got two choices here: tomorrow night or the night after. And do not screw me here, Sandy."

Jhapa was less than four kilometers from Nepal's eastern border with India, and at the request of the Bhutanese monarchy, the Indian government had placed a military patrol along the entire length of the border region. Until "permanent arrangements" could be made, the refugees were to stay where they were, never to return to the land that they had called home for generations. As decreed by the king of Bhutan, Bhutanese citizenship could only be claimed by those able to trace their residency back to at least 1958. In becoming "one land with one people," Bhutan had given birth to the Jhapa refugee camp, which was located well beyond Bhutan's western border. To Bhutan's royal family, this was most fitting, as the vast majority of those expelled were ethnic Nepalis. Enforcement of the king's edict had converted the mustard fields and mango groves of Nepal's southwest corner into living quarters for thousands of outcasts.

"So keep your jaw moving," Drapche said. "Tell me about the rucksack."

"Of course," Sandu said quickly, "it is now ready."

"Good," Drapche said. "As soon as I have it, you'll get enough moonshine to float you and the other urchins in your neighborhood all the way to the Ganges."

"Drapche, I plead with you, reconsider," Sandu said, initiating the discussion that he had been dreading for weeks. "The plan you have, where will it lead? I fear your plot will endanger all who are left behind here in Jhapa. We are all Nepali by ancestry, Drapche. Our blood is that of one people, just as the Bhutanese claim they are of one line. As a brother, I entreat you, spill no more blood on either side."

The novelty of Sandu's bold petition actually amused Drapche.

"Reconsider?" Drapche asked. "And what exactly would you like me to reconsider? What tack would you like to see here, Sand my man? Another march to beg the great king's audience? Surely you recall the last such fiasco, when two hundred of us trudged our way uphill through the mud for three fucking weeks, only to have the most royal one tell us that he was busy that day. And then we all had the fine pleasure of turning tail and walking right back into this hellhole, all us 'undesirables' going back to where we belonged."

"But negotiations are in progress, and this time they are in earnest," Sandu said. "Arum, the United Nations officer, he has traveled from one campsite to the next, telling everyone of his latest petition. But for there to be any dialogue concerning our return to Bhutan, all talk of changing the form of government there must cease. The government of Bhutan has already transitioned to a representative system, so there is hope for us. But all such internal changes must be on their terms, not ours. If either the royal family or the newly elected officials see us as upstarts, we will have no chance at all of returning to Bhutan."

Shortly after the king's "one nation, one people" directive, Drapche led a small group of ethnic Nepalis in a plot to topple the royal family and install a system of self-governance. When reports of this campaign reached Thimphu, the king's position on deportation only hardened. Drapche and his band of insurgents were banished immediately.

"Arum Lasson," Drapche said, pronouncing the name in a slow, mocking tone, "our most esteemed UN representative. Exactly how much hooch did you have to inhale before you started believing a single word that came out of the lying mouth of a limp prick like him? When are you going to wake up and smell the sewage?"

Drapche neared closer and began to slowly wag his index finger in Sandu's face. Sandu saw the stubs of Drapche's other fingers aimed directly between his eyes, wondering if the same weapon that caused the boomerang-shaped forehead gash had also claimed the better part of those three fingers.

"Let me enlighten you on a little historical fact, my *brother*," Drapche began. "My *father* worked his whole life as a farmhand in Dorokha. The flatlands of Dorokha, as no doubt you are aware, see nothing of that cool Himalayan zephyr that the rest of the country enjoys. Unlike the rest of Bhutan, where all the faggot tourists go to convince themselves they're Buddhists, no one wanders off toward Dorokha so they can meditate in lotus position and commune with the cosmos. It's bloody hot in those fields, and my old man worked them from dawn to dusk his entire life. He made a home for us, Sandu. A *home*. Our home. Ours anyway until a pile of horse-shit decrees came down, telling us what to wear, how to speak, and who to marry."

To underscore his point, Drapche, in a single motion, produced an eleven-inch Gurkha knife from its sheath. The blade had a semilunar curve with an elaborate Sanskrit inscription on its thick outer edge, with a razor-sharp surface along the inner arch. Gurkha warriors of northern Nepal had employed these blades for centuries, and through the years, Drapche had found the weapon both persuasive and efficient. The blade was now so close to Sandu's face that he could hear a low whirling sound as Drapche spun the handle between his thumb and the remnant stub of his middle finger. Sandu's eyes followed the faint black streaks of coagulated blood that trailed off from the weapon's inner bow.

"We worked the skin off our hands to feed the Bhutanese," Drapche said, "tilling every inch of those farms and being paid peanuts. We asked for nothing, except for a little regard for our culture, our dress, our heritage. And then the great thunder king sent a bolt straight up our collective asses, taking away land that was—*is*—rightfully ours. Plenty of room for us to work like slaves, but no room for a Hindu who refuses to wear a woolen *gho* in hundred-degree heat. And offering to pay us if we forsake our way of life and marry their wenches. A pathetic ploy to keep us serfs in our proper place and keep all that grain flowing. It was either transfigure yourselves into a bunch of Bhutanese gnomes or be forever excluded."

Drapche rested the blade's bloody edge on the tip of Sandu's nose.

"To keep the ways of our Nepali ancestors," Drapche said, re-sheathing the knife as quickly as he had drawn it. "That is all we ever wanted."

Drapche looked down at the ground for a long moment, as if waiting for a puddle to collect around Sandu's feet.

"Negotiations," Drapche sneered, "are why we are still living here with a couple of billion mosquitoes and the encyclopedia of diseases they carry. The UN-Bhutan circle jerk has brought us nothing but a deeper pool of shit to pitch our tents in."

Drapche spat the remains of a betel nut over Sandu's shoulder, reloading another one in the gap between two of his remaining teeth.

"Now tell me about this weasel who's going to hand me that loaded rucksack," Drapche said. "Tell me when, tell me where, and tell me now."

Sandu had no interest in another Gurkha knife viewing.

"Anytime, Drapche," Sandu answered immediately. "Tonight, if it is your desire. The man who will hand you the rucksack, he worked for many years near Xi'an, along the Longhai railway. He learned much from the Chinese masters while renovations of the rail line were underway."

"Chinamen," Drapche said as he spat out another fragment of betel nut, "they damn love explosions."

Despite the fact that Sandu and Drapche were alone on a hilltop at the northern edge of the refugee camp, Sandu lowered his voice to a whisper.

"Yes, the explosives," Sandu said, "they are prepared. All is packaged safely for transport. But you must pay him in full, Drapche, given the nature of this purchase."

"Loosen up your panties over there," Drapche said as he wiped his mouth on the sleeve of his shirt. "He'll get every dime that he's got coming to him."

Drapche looked over at the far end of the camp, eyeing three trucks that were being inspected at the main entrance gate.

"If I'm not mistaken," he snorted, "one of those loads contains a serious supply of your favorite libation."

"Drapche," Sandu said, ignoring the remark, "I must again mention: once you cross that border, I can no longer be of aid in your passage. It is over three hundred kilometers to your destination, and the terrain . . . you know how difficult the terrain—"

"You're damn fucking right I know the terrain," Drapche interrupted, his tone scornful. "That fool's errand we embarked on all those years ago is the last march to nowhere you'll ever see me on. Just get me across that border, and I'll worry about hitching a ride the rest of the way."

Drapche again placed his crippled hand on the Gurkha knife's bolster, regarding Sandu with the same unblinking stare that he gave everyone he did business with. Sandu could see nothing but the scar that bisected Drapche's left eyelid. The depth of the arcing scar, Sandu noticed, was beginning to brighten.

"Make this happen, Sandy, and that clear brew you crave will be yours by the barrel load. I'll even throw in a few branches of your favorite herb, just to facilitate your journey into eternal chemical bliss."

Drapche's grip on the knife bolster tightened as the arc across his face grew a deeper red.

"But fuck me here, Sandu, and the next draw of hooch you inhale will be through your own pecker. Better yet, I'll save myself the bother and make sure your missus hears tell of that teener you were boinking while she was chasing that cobra out of your bunk."

Sandu felt his face start to burn. Drapche *did* know everything that went on in the camp.

"Here, give this to that loyal little wife of yours," Drapche said as he pulled a jade ring off his belt. "You know, when you're not sloshed or higher than the moon, you're actually a pretty good foot soldier."

Drapche Dorn had, for years, decorated his leather belt with trinkets that he casually referred to as mementoes. Evidence of any business transaction in which a trading partner did not see eye-to-eye with Drapche would, more often than not, end up dangling from one of the irregular rows that circled Drapche's waistline.

"My thanks," Sandu said as he pocketed the ring.

"Just make the next forty-eight hours happen, or that jewel will be back on me with interest," Drapche said.

"Yes, yes," Sandu replied with a curt bow of his head. "Safe travels to you, Drapche."

Hearing this, Drapche reared his head toward the sky and bellowed with laughter.

"Nice try, *brother* Sandy," Drapche said. "My guess is that you'd rather see that knapsack I'll be carrying send my giblets in a million different directions. But I sure do appreciate the heartfelt bon voyage.

"Now go on back to your negotiations," Drapche said as Sandu started to scurry down the hill and into the cloud of mosquitoes that surrounded the camp. "Personally, I never had much use for that sort of thing. I find the maggots in the food they serve more appealing, but don't let me stop you. You just go right on and negotiate with those nice folks from the U-nited Nations."

Drapche stood alone on the hill that overlooked the Jhapa camp, above the sea of scraggly tents that housed his fellow Nepalis. They had all been abandoned by what they once knew as their homeland, left to fight off the swarms of insects that enveloped their camp, all of them slowly rotting amid the morass of human waste.

"Have no fear, Sandu," Drapche shouted as he eyed the road that trailed eastward from the camp.

"When I am done, you won't see a single drop of blood."

Chapter 21

Boston
Present day

In Neville John's dream, he was driving a pink Ferrari in reverse, slamming it repeatedly into the Washington Monument.

"Neville . . . Neville . . . open up," Stacey said in a high-pitched whisper as she continued to bang on Neville's apartment window.

"Tell me you're in there, Nev. It's me, Stacey."

Neville looked up and saw Stacey Ravelle standing on his fire-escape landing, peering through the blinds with her hands cupped around her eyes.

"I didn't have collision coverage for that thing anyway," Neville grumbled to himself as he searched for the switch on his desk lamp.

"Hold, wait," he said as the light flicked on. "I've got to find my glasses."

Stacey slammed her open palm against the window. "Open!"

"Flippin' A, enough already," Neville said, raising the blinds and unlocking the window latch. "Stacey, what ti—"

"It's three fifteen," Stacey said as she vaulted through the window and into Neville's living room, "and to answer the next question you're about to ask, I didn't bother ringing from the front stoop because we both know that there's nothing there to ring. I believe 'that burdensome apparatus' was disengaged some time ago, lest an old flame makes an untimely appearance."

"Yeah, well at least none of them ever climbed six flights on the fire escape just to scare the skin off me," Neville said as he closed and locked the window. "And whatever is going on, you could have texted me or called my cell."

"Like it's actually *on*," Stacey said, clearing her throat loudly. "If I am not mistaken, your cell phone, that 'other annoying contraption,' is powered down at this hour for the same reason you disconnected your doorbell."

"How'd you ever access the escape ladder from the ground level anyway?" Neville asked, staring down at the faint lights that lined the alley behind his apartment building.

Stacey cocked her head and gave Neville a twisted frown.

"Oh yes, I almost forgot," Neville said, putting up both hands, "Spider Woman on speed. A thousand pardons to you, oh lithe one.

"Well, whoever you *didn't* arouse while running gazelle-like up six flights of metal stairs, you probably *did* arouse when you tried to break through my window," Neville went on. "So in all likelihood, we can expect a visit from Boston's finest any minute now. At least they use the door."

"You're probably the only person in this building who isn't in a Jose Cuervo coma right now," Stacey said, not appearing the least bit out of breath. "Excluding of course the gentleman who resides in the pad three levels down. I only caught a quick glance, but I can tell you with all confidence that he did not need me to become *aroused*. Now are you awake? Because I damn well need you to be awake."

"Acrobats leaping through my window at three in the morning have a bad habit of waking me up," Neville said, yawning. "And my guess is that you've been up all night—as in up all night again. Stace, look, I know the last week has been really rough on you, but you have got to get some sleep every now and—"

"Listen to me, Nev," Stacey interrupted, her teeth clenched, "I have to work dusk to dawn just to get anything done over there. I can't accomplish jack shit during the daytime—everyone preoccupied with all things Ivar, which is of course the only topic of conversation. And I can't believe I'm saying this, but I actually miss Myles."

"So to keep me appraised of your latest trials, you hiked all the way over here in the middle of the night, dodging the street sweepers and all the various vendors who make hay in the alley you just walked through."

"I didn't walk," Stacey said, her tone now calm. "I ran. I needed the air. I needed the run."

"Not that I was too worried about you getting jumped," Neville said, his words trailing off as he put on a Dallas Mavericks cap and headed toward the kitchen. "Unless Usain Bolt was in pursuit, I doubt there's anyone out there who could have caught up with you. So now that you're here, make yourself right at home. And say the word if you get chilly; I'll crank on the heat. And since we're having such a nice chat, how about an espresso to really put you into high gear? And hey, if you're in the mood for something with a little more fist to it, I'm all in. Anything liquid goes at this time of day."

While Neville was filling the espresso machine, he heard Stacey mumble something from the other room.

"What was that?" he asked as Stacey again said something faintly. "Stace, I still didn't get that. Something besides espresso?"

"Chinatown . . . Chinatown . . . Chinatown . . ."

"Chinatown?" Neville asked, looking at Stacey from the kitchen. "If you're hungry, you should have said so in the first place. I'm game for a trip to Emperor's Garden or whoever's open down there. On the way, we can talk about whatever it is that's on your mind."

"Sabbath twelve, Clash nine, Chinatown, Valens four, Licinius five," Stacey murmured as she rocked back and forth on her feet.

Neville sat down on the corner of an overstuffed chair and gave Stacey's arm a squeeze.

"Hey, Stace, have a seat, will ya please," Neville said softly. "Espresso and Chinese food can wait. Just tell me what's going on."

"Sabbath twelve, Clash nine, Chinatown, Valens four, Licinius five," Stacey repeated without looking at Neville.

"What?" Neville asked, leaning in. "Rads, now you've got me a little worried here. What in the world is going on?"

Without turning her head, Stacey met Neville's gaze.

"Sabbath twelve, Clash nine, Chinatown, Valens four, Licinius five," she recited once more, her tone still even.

Neville stood and grasped Stacey's other arm, imploring her to sit down and take a deep breath.

"Slow it all down, Stace," he said after a long moment had passed. "Now, how about you enlighten me as to what exactly prompted your breathtaking entrance into my humble home at this early hour."

Stacey went over to Neville's computer and punched in the word Chinatown in large block letters. She gave each of the letters a different color, and then she made the word bounce from side to side off the margins of the computer screen.

"I take it this isn't about the emperor's crab Rangoon or the two-for-one after-midnight special," Neville said as Stacey took a seat on the opposite arm of the overstuffed chair.

"Nev, I need to know something," Stacey began. "That latest line of rhabdo cells, designated five-something-whatever."

"Line 55-T," Neville said, rubbing his eyes.

"That's the one," Stacey said, nodding. "That's the latest isolate of resistant rhabdomyosarcoma cells that you cultured and implanted, right?"

"Right," Neville said.

"And the same tumor cell line was implanted into every one of the mice?" Stacey asked.

"Yes, that's right," Neville said.

Stacey pulled a spreadsheet out of her sweatshirt pocket and unfolded it on the seat of the chair.

"The genetic modifications that alter the virus's capacity to lock onto the cancer cell proteins are given the name of rockers from the sixties, seventies, and eighties," Stacey said as she pointed to the various graphs and tables on the spreadsheet.

"Tran has been at the helm of this research stage since day one, and he can at any time tweak the exact genetic lineup, depending on what alterations maximize viral docking. But even he is blinded to the so-called 'parent sequence,' designated by names like Ringo, Grace, Jimi, B52, Skynyrd, and such the like."

"Whatever happened to the Greek alphabet?" Neville asked.

"You don't want to be the one who's heard asking that question," Stacey said, shaking her head. "There are too few of them, and besides, the music never dies."

"'Make the music,'" Neville said as he looked over one of the tables on the spreadsheet.

"That's 'mark the music,' if I'm not mistaken," Stacey said. "Shakespeare, *The Merchant of Venice*."

"Right, right," Neville said, nodding. "Brit Lit was early a.m. on Tuesdays and Thursdays, and well, you know, those Wednesday night blowouts . . ."

"Maybe I know of them and maybe I don't," Stacey said, pulling out another stack of computer printouts, "but for now we'll both have to shelve such memory-lane particulars. Look at this."

Stacey flipped through several pages of data, pointing out one of the graphs printed on three different pages. "It's the same process with the genetic alterations that control the chemical composition of the cancer-killing oncotoxins that are released inside the rhabdo cell," Stacey continued. "This is my end of the research, and although I can add one molecule or subtract another, I have no idea as to the genetic reordering that's assigned the name of this or that Roman emperor.

"The middle step in all this," Stacey said, unfolding the last spreadsheet, "has proven to be the biggest bear of all. The objective is simple," Stacey went on, Neville squinting as he tried to follow along. "You try to identify the gene sequence that maximizes viral replication within the cancer cell. The challenge is finding the combination of gene insertions and deletions that will allow the virus to adequately replicate *before* it overwhelms and kills the rhabdo cell. This stage of the process has to be damn near perfect, because if it isn't, the new anticancer virus won't have any chance of breaking out into the bloodstream and begin the chain reaction whereby millions of malignant cells are knocked off."

"This is the step where every variation is assigned the name of a movie," Neville said as he flipped his cap around.

"And just like the movies," Stacey said with a sharp nod, "there are far too many of them, and the vast majority are overrated and just plain suck. But some," Stacey said as she rolled the spreadsheets into a baton, pointing to the word Chinatown as it ricocheted across the computer screen, "some turn out to be real gems."

Neville shrugged, looking back and forth between Stacey and his computer screen with a dazed look on his face.

"It's almost as if we live in parallel worlds," Stacey said as she stood up. "You know enough about what I do to sound reasonably intelligent when you make presentations about your work, and the other way around. But, Nev, right now, close enough isn't nearly good enough. I have to ask you again, and you have to be 100 percent on this: are you absolutely certain that the entire group was inoculated with the 55-T resistant rhabdomyosarcoma line?"

"That certain," Neville said without a moment's hesitation.

"And when the inoculation was completed, each of the mice had a full tumor load?" Stacey asked.

"Every one," Neville said. "Every last one has resistant rhabdomyosarcoma."

"Well, they don't anymore," Stacey said, her voice thick with emotion. "Sabbath twelve, Clash nine, *Chinatown*, Valens four, Licinius five. It's gone, Nev. The tumor, the rhabdo. It's gone. Nothing. Zilch. Complete response, every last one. And every last one is living to tell the tale."

"*Do what?*" Neville screeched as he shot to his feet. "That quick . . . not possible, not possible . . . holy . . .

"I guess that's why you're blinded to what I do and Tran to what you do and on and on," Neville said, scrambling for his keys. "That way, when it all comes together, we know it's the real deal. Pay dirt. Untainted, unprejudiced pay dirt. Mother of God, tell me I'm not still crashing that pink Ferrari. Now I know why you said you missed Myles. Man alive, do we ever need him. Un . . . shit, unbelievable. That satellite phone he leased, the number is in the office. I'm sure of it. Isn't it tomorrow over there, or yesterday, or something like that?"

"Believe it or not, it's today in Bhutan," Stacey said calmly. "They're eleven hours ahead of us."

"So it's 2:30 p.m. their time—perfect!" Neville said with one hand on the door. "The satellite phone number is on Myles's desk. My car can't run as fast as you, but we'll take it anyway."

Stacey hadn't moved.

"What?" Neville asked as he took off his cap and scratched his head. "What am I missing here?"

"We've got two problems," Stacey said. "First off, Myles doesn't have the parent sequences."

"Sure he does," Neville said. "Of course he does. Myles has the answer to everything."

"Not to this," Stacey said.

"They're somewhere in his office or on his computer. They've got to be," Neville said.

"They aren't," Stacey said.

Neville took his hand off the door handle and walked toward Stacey, stopping halfway.

"Myles is blinded, just like the rest of us," Stacey said. "That's what makes the whole thing work. Myles can organize, supervise, analyze, and criticize, but above all else, he must remain objective. And for Myles to remain objective, the parent sequences must remain buried. Nev, Myles doesn't have them."

"Then who does?" Neville asked, his tone almost desperate.

"Ivar," Stacey said.

"Then let's get into Ivar's computer," Neville said as he walked back toward the door. "You had no problem doing that a few days ago, right? His e-mails, his bank accounts, all of that business. You've been there already, Stace. Remember?"

Stacey still hadn't moved. "If Ivar keeps a backup copy of the genetic codes on a computer program, no one can find it," Stacey said. "I certainly can't, and trust me, I've tried."

"Backup?" Neville asked. "What do you mean backup?"

"Ivar is constantly tweaking the codes and the sequences," Stacey said evenly, "and he keeps all that in his birding guidebook. That's his workplace, his moving workplace. To Ivar, mapping out the potential genetic algorithms is akin to writing music. It's an energy pathway or whatever . . . from your thoughts to your hand to your paper and then back to your brain. So those codes and sequences are stuffed between the pages of whatever bird book Ivar is using. That's where it's all distilled, Nev—on the scratches of paper he carries with him."

"Okay," Neville said, sinking into a nearby chair, "so that's one problem. Tell me the second one isn't as bad as the first."

"It's not," Stacey said, sitting down next to Neville. "It's more of a caution, to you and me and everyone we work with."

Neville looked at Stacey, motioning for her to continue.

"When I looked at those mice, scampering around without any big tumor lump on their backs, I was as shocked as you were just a minute ago. But we have to remember, Nev, that they're only mice. *Mice.* We still have no idea how well any of this will work when it comes to treating children. We still don't know how far we are from bringing this home."

"I think we better find Myles," Neville said after a long pause.

Stacey nodded slowly.

"I think Myles better find Ivar," she said.

Chapter 22

Bhutan
Present day

The tip of the white-hot, solid-gold applicator touched the skin along the outer surface of Parash's right knee.

Ten seconds later, there was a second application.

Then a third.

Throughout it all, Parash stared directly into the eyes of *Chenmizang*, the Buddha whose image adorned the fraying, two-story-high painting that hung on the opposite side of the monastery's great room.

Parash hadn't flinched.

Karma and Martin were taking a tour of a monastery that was just off the trail that led from Paro town to Taktsang. Karma had suggested that Joel, Andie, Myles, and Martin all take their time along the trail, as the rapid change in elevation would likely make all fatigue quickly. As the afternoon was sunny and pleasant, Andie and Joel decided to take a walk along the river, while Myles meanwhile would continue to search for a signal on his satellite phone. They would all meet up later and set up camp for the night.

"Throughout the ages, the great masters have passed on knowledge of several thousand herbal remedies," Dechen, the monastic leader and native healer, said to Karma and Martin. "Parash's affliction, however, has proven resistant to medicinal therapy," Dechen continued, "and although he is but a boy, Parash suffers greatly from joint inflammation."

Karma and Martin had just watched Dechen administer *gser broc*, or heat acupuncture, to one of his students.

"This," Dechen said as he held up the bullet-shaped applicator, "is a remedy many centuries old. Since initiating *gser broc* some weeks ago, Parash has gained much function, and he now experiences far less pain. *Chenmizang* gives the boy strength, and hence Parash feels neither heat nor any other form of discomfort while the treatment is being administered."

Dechen pointed to the three tattoo marks that formed a perfect equilateral triangle on the skin just to the side of Parash's right kneecap. Parash gave Dechen a slight bow before joining the other monks who were reading in the loft above the monastery's great room.

"That is *Chenmizang*," Karma said to Martin while looking up at the enormous painting that extended from floor to ceiling. "He is lord of all serpents, and one of the Guardians of the Four Directions. *Chenmizang* is the fierce warrior who has the power to subdue any force which may bring us pain or might in any way threaten our well-being."

"Parash," Karma said, now looking at Martin intently, "experienced no pain."

"Herbal remedies and heat acupuncture share a common thread, a common power," Dechen said as he squinted and moved closer to Martin, "and that is that both harness nature's infinite capacity to heal. Plant life, native animals, and minerals of the earth—they are all used in the preparation of therapeutic mixtures. But life is never sacrificed in the formulation of a cure. Either a plant's bark or its leaves may be used, but the plant lives on. A small patch of an animal's skin or hair may be used, but the beast lives on. It is the flow of life, not the taking of one to preserve another.

"And as herbal therapy allies nature's external elements," Dechen continued, "heat acupuncture calls upon the energy meridians housed within us all. When Parash arrived here, he struggled just to walk through the fields, stifling cries of pain while trying to fall asleep at night. And now," Dechen nodded toward Parash, who was now seated with the other monks, "his youth has been restored."

Once Dechen had returned to his students, Karma went on to explain to Martin that the monastery they were visiting, like many throughout Bhutan, had no name. Although the exact date of construction was unknown, Karma was certain that the artwork along the inner walls of the monastery, including the *Chenmizang* painting, dated to the fifteenth century. The structure itself had six-foot-thick walls, and it was built on a granite mound that overlooked a long plateau dotted with small groves of weeping cypress. The building's interior consisted of one large room and an upper loft that served as a communal bunk space. Dechen's eleven students were seated together in a semicircle below a single large window.

Besides Karma's low whisper, the only other sound in the room was the faint clicking of wooden slats being piled onto one another.

"The students are reading sacred religious texts," Karma said as Martin stumbled through the cold, dim room with a dazed look on his face, "and the ancient books you see are unique in many ways. Bhutanese paper is known as *tasho*, and as it is made from ground bamboo pulp, it is very thick and sturdy. *Tasho* will last for over a thousand years, as insects cannot penetrate its fabric."

The eldest of the monks removed the brilliant orange-and-yellow silk cloth that was wrapped around one stack of rectangular cedar wood board. The image of a man dressed in threadbare clothing, who was wearing a mask of Buddha and clutching a beggar's bowl in his right hand, was carved into the grain of the uppermost wooden slat.

"What you see is the image of Shakya Senge," Karma said in a low voice, "the Lion of the Shakya family. This man abandoned all the treasures of his boundless kingdom, forsaking everything, and meditated in a distant mountain cave for many years. His image is etched into many of our sacred texts."

"The calligraphy, the script," Martin stuttered, "is that Sanskrit?"

"The script you see is Choekey, the written language of Bhutan," Karma said. "Choekey dates from the eighth century, and to the outside world, it is known as Classical Tibetan. Through the many centuries, this language has remained unalloyed, and our monks become masters of this script at an early age. Much of the literature throughout the Himalayan kingdoms has been penned in Choekey. Look, please," Karma continued as she pointed at the large window on the opposite side of the room. "In every Bhutanese monastery, you will find a single large window oriented to the east, allowing sunlight in for daytime reading. At night, the monks continue their studies by candlelight. The students seated before you entered monastic school at the age of nine or ten, and as they will become our spiritual leaders, they have many years of learning ahead."

Martin's eyes shifted nervously between Karma and the monks who continued to unwrap the silk covers that sheathed the carved cedar wood containers.

"The books," Martin whispered, "they have no bindings. The wood casings are magnificent, and I would imagine that each is a unique work of art. But to stack every page between them . . . I mean no disrespect, but just reading a single page seems cumbersome."

"As with *tasho* paper, the ink used to inscribe the Choekey characters can last countless generations," Karma said. "It is a formula of yak blood and herbs, and it penetrates the parchment completely. Therein lies the problem, as the ink's rich mixture provides a perfect breeding ground for small insects. By placing each sheet of *tasho* paper between dry cedar, there will be no such contamination and therefore no erosion of the documents. These texts are all original and must remain alive with the wisdom of the lamas who authored them. These volumes contain more than a chronology of our history and our religion. Each book bears the imprint of every eye that ever beheld it, and therefore each one is itself a vital life force. Every page passes on knowledge, and in so doing, every page draws knowledge into its weave. The families of these students are very proud, knowing that their child has been bestowed a rare privilege and that in later years their offspring will be entrusted with a yet-greater charge."

After thanking Dechen for the tour, Karma and Martin exited onto the footbridge that led away from the monastery's only doorway. Martin stopped in the middle of the bridge and pointed out a fortress-like structure that was perched on the edge of a mountainside a couple of kilometers farther to the north.

"I cannot imagine the engineering it took to build that," Martin said. "It's a monolith hanging from the clouds. And there's another similar structure that you can just make out, a bit more to the east. Why are these buildings erected in such precarious places?"

Karma walked Martin to the other side of the footbridge and pointed out another monastery, on an even higher peak, several kilometers to the south.

"The locations of the monasteries you see are not random," Karma said. "In the seventh century, our land was ruled by a mighty king whose name was Songtsen. Songtsen was lord over all the Himalayas, and for many years his power was supreme throughout all the ancient mountain kingdoms. But there arose a day when an evil demoness engulfed every corner of his vast kingdom, and it took all of King Songtsen's will and strength to subdue the ogress by pinning her under the foundations of the many monasteries he constructed. There are over one hundred points of entrapment, and each is marked by the monasteries you see across our landscape. Although the monasteries you see have been rebuilt a number of times throughout the ages, the foundation of each is an original point of the beast's entrapment."

"That might explain why they're all built like military gun towers," Martin said.

"Perhaps," Karma said. "But the monasteries you see before you today were never constructed for armaments and battle. The foundation of each serves to imprison the demoness, and the door of each welcomes all who seek enlightenment."

Martin looked back at the monastery that he and Karma had just visited.

"I suppose every one of these places would carry a foreigner like me back into a world where the clock has stood still since well before the European monarchies colonized the so-called New World," Martin said.

"I believe our mountains have kept Bhutan free from such conquest," Karma said. "Being bestowed such protection has been a most-fortunate blessing."

"Four thousand miles of the deepest blue sea didn't prevent the slow but certain evisceration of any last remnant of native America," Martin said with a distinct edge to his voice. "From all you've shown me, Karma, it took a lot more than ten centuries of luck and a string of mountain peaks to preserve this world."

Karma offered a slight grin as she motioned for Martin to follow her across the bridge.

"Dechen has granted our request," Karma said. "He has given us permission to set up camp on the field below the monastery. As you might suppose, Dechen does not own this land, as he and all in monastic life have disavowed personal property and possess no land themselves. But asking permission was the respectful thing to do, and I passed onto Dechen the appreciation of all our group."

Before leaving Paro town, Karma had hired two Sherpas to assist her group with the cooking and campsite preparations. Karma excused herself while she gave the Sherpas instructions on where to set up the tents and campfire.

"I have a question, Mr. Phyte," Karma said after she returned, she and Martin now standing under the lengthening shadow of the monastery.

"It's Martin, Karma," Martin implored. "Please, just Martin."

Karma nodded. "Then I have a question, Martin," she said.

"I have all the time in the world," Martin said, looking straight up into the sky with his arms outstretched.

Karma let a brief moment pass before she looked up at Martin. "Why are you here?" she asked.

Like an enlisted man caught off guard by an officer on patrol, Martin snapped to attention.

"You certainly know how to enliven a conversation," Martin said. "I take it you've hit the others with this same question."

"There was no need," Karma responded. "The others in your group have a career path that is intimately aligned with the science of life, sickness, and death. And therein, if I am not mistaken, your three companions have a distinct alliance with Dr. Ivar. Dr. Joel had mentioned that you are a businessman, and I have little doubt that in your ventures you have achieved much success. For a man of your stature to take leave of his many responsibilities, even for a brief time . . . this is a remarkable sacrifice. You must have many people under your employment."

"Yes—3,920," Martin said firmly.

"And you must pay each of these individuals on a regular basis, yes?" Karma asked.

"They wouldn't miss it for the world," Martin said with a smirk.

"This is an immense obligation, and one that I cannot begin to fathom," Karma said. "If I may ask, then: Does Dr. Ivar's study aid this large business of yours?"

"No, no, not at all," Martin said, shaking his head. "Ivar spends his days where few, if any, have ever ventured. I spend mine peddling fake body parts. It would be hard to find two spheres further apart."

"Prostheses," Karma said. "This is the proper term?"

Martin nodded.

"Should your business ever expand to this part of the globe," Karma said, "I am afraid my country will not prove to be a particularly robust customer."

Martin grinned. "From what I see, I would have to agree. Not much of a market for artificial parts around here."

"So the reasons for you not coming to Bhutan are apparent to both of us," Karma said. "All that remains, it would seem, is the answer to my original question."

Martin walked over to the footbridge stairs and sat down on the edge of the bottom step.

"Much of my life involves deal making," Martin said. "Probably too much of my life involves deal making. One day I'm crafting a deal, the next I'm negotiating a deal, and the next I'm closing a deal. That's business, Karma. It's one deal followed by another. You can never stand still. If you do, you sink. As it's so often said, the only constant is change.

"Except for Ivar," Martin continued, casting his eyes to one side. "Ivar, to me, is a constant. A rock. A chum. A friend. No deals, no negotiations, no business. He's my friend, Karma, and I just want to find him. I want to find him because I think he's in real trouble, and he may need my help."

Karma smiled slightly, saying nothing.

"Now if *I* may ask," Martin said, meeting Karma's gaze, "just how certain are you of Ivar's whereabouts? You have no firsthand contact, you have no photographs, and you have no verification that he's anywhere along the trail we're following. You must have more than one person telling another person who told another person about someone they know who went off to the most distant place imaginable and came back cured of some lifelong malady."

"Not someone," Karma said, looking at Martin intently, "but some*ones*. Despite the many natural obstacles to travel, our land is small, and word travels fast. Those that dwell high in the mountains do at times come to Paro town, and I have heard some remarkable stories of children and their mothers and fathers being healed at distant medical clinics. And if you will recall, you and your group originally came to my shop because of letters sent by Galen to Dr. Ivar, many of which reference a man named Tandin who cares for people out of his home near Taktsang. It would seem therefore a remarkable coincidence if the sick individuals to whom I refer were treated by someone besides Dr. Ivar, who I very much suspect resides with Tandin. However, as with the many deals your business necessitates, proceeding on this endeavor involves a certain level of faith. As well as an element of chance," Karma added as she became distracted by something about a hundred meters away.

"What?" Martin asked. "What are you looking at?"

"Your friend," Karma said. "It's your friend Myles. He is standing in that clearing over there, and he appears distressed."

"Myles was born distressed," Martin said as he quickly looked back at Karma.

"No," Karma said. "I feel he needs assistance. Whatever is the matter, I think you need to be with him. I will catch up directly behind you. We will have ample opportunity to speak again later. Please."

As Martin approached Myles, he heard a faint noise in the clearing where Myles was standing. A voice perhaps, but it was not Myles who was speaking. It was a woman's voice he heard, and as Martin neared, the staccato pattern of the voice became louder and more familiar.

Martin found Myles leaning against a large cypress tree, seemingly frozen in place. Myles was staring vacantly into the distance.

"*Myles,*" Stacey said, her voice emerging from the satellite phone that was faceup on the ground. "Are you there? Did you get all that? Can you hear me? Myles? . . . Myles?"

CHAPTER 23

"It's just me," Joel said as he stumbled on a rock along the edge of the riverbed. "Hope I didn't startle you."

Andie jumped at the sight of Dr. Morgan, who was standing not ten feet away and carrying two armloads of fishing gear. Joel was wearing an army surplus camouflage vest and a black terrycloth floppy hat.

"Where did you come from?" Andie asked. "And all that equipment, is that an Okuma?"

"Indeed it is," Joel said, snapping together the fishing rod. "It's the real McCoy, and that's a gold star for you. I take it you're a bit of an angler yourself?"

"In the spring, we used to go fishing around Lake Willoughby," Andie said. "You had your choice of all kinds of streams and ponds in that part of Vermont. Once the top layer thawed, the brookies and rainbows were there for the taking. But fishing was the last thing on my mind while I was packing to come here. I can't believe you actually hauled that tackle all the way here from Boston."

"Didn't have to," Joel said, gnawing at an old Cohiba that he had just pulled out of his shirt pocket.

"Is there any country in the world where you *don't* smoke, Dr. Morgan?" Andie asked, grimacing.

"Worry not. I wouldn't dream of polluting this pristine air," Joel said. "Lit or unlit, it still packs a punch."

"Not to mention packing oral cancer," Andie mumbled.

"That does ring a distant bell," Joel said, rummaging through his tackle box in search of a lure. "And if it makes you feel any better, Cuban tobacco products are a not-infrequent topic of lectures delivered in the domestic woodshed."

"I'd feel better if you quit," Andie said. "And so would you, ya know. I can only imagine what the other docs at the hospital—whoa, those lures. They're Bombers! That is some serious outfitting you've got there. Where did you get all that?"

"That gypsy back in Paro," Joel said as he rolled the unlit stogie between his teeth. "Same guy who sold us those five moldy sleeping bags and the three-hundred-pound tent. I went back a bit later and picked up a few other essentials. The guy claims he's from Kathmandu, but I swear he's Hungarian or something like that. 'My friend, every price for you is most special,' and, 'What are your needs, as my stock is now full.' I mean, did that dude look Nepali to you?"

"What exactly is a Nepali field-and-stream supply merchant supposed to look like?" Andie asked, her forehead in a tight knot as she held up a hand to block out the sun.

"He's supposed to look . . . hell, I don't know," Joel said, still fumbling through the collection of lures. "But there's no chance that fella is from these parts. That Cheshire-cat grin and beach-ball belly, complete with the carnival accent, and that poor schlep assisting him, who he had running around all over the place. Davie, I think that was the underling's name. If the boss man told Davie to fetch a housemaid, he'd probably have wheeled out his own mother and haggled over the price.

"But I'll give the man his due," Joel went on as he loaded a lure onto the end of his line. "He had everything a guy or gal would ever need to do a little fishing. So how could I say no? Karma wants us to climb at a slow pace today, given that we're all sea-level dwellers and might all feel the effects of this thin air. So I figured sending out a cast or two would be the perfect way to kill a little time. Besides, I never really get the chance back home anymore, given that my offspring have far too many irons in the fire to go casting for bullhead with dear old dad. And hey, we can surprise everyone with some fresh grub for dinner. If I could land us a few copper mahseers, we'd be in fat city. They're scrumptious, I'm told."

"Told to you, I suppose, by the same two guys who were high-fiving each other the minute you walked out of their shop?" Andie said.

"Something like that," Joel said, nodding. "But when you look down at your plate tonight, it'll either be mahseer or a slab of native yak meat. So what's your choice?"

"Don't make me heave," Andie said, her face twisted. "Say no more and feel free to catch all the fish you can. But if you come up empty, I'll eat tree bark before I try yak steak."

The chime of a prayer wheel, powered by water cascading into the river from an adjoining stream, could be heard along the opposite bank. Andie watched the wheel as it began to spin faster and faster, its chime growing louder with the shifting wind current.

"Hope you don't mind a little company," Joel said, fiddling with one of the lures.

Andie was sitting on a rock along the riverbank, her bare feet immersed in the icy rapids. She looked up at Joel, gave him a faint smile, and shook her head. "No, no. Not at all."

Andie ran her cupped hand along the water's edge, as if trying to catch one of the tiny waves before it broke onto the shore. A moment later, she heard a loud sloshing sound next to her. Andie looked up again at Joel, who had taken off his boots, rolled up his pant legs, and waded into the river.

"Didn't the Bhutanese Walmart have a pair of waders to match that natty vest they sold you?" Andie asked. "They might come in handy if you're going to catch dinner in there. The water's a little chilly, in case you hadn't noticed."

"You have your toes in the same river," Joel said as he cast his line.

"Yeah, and nothing else," Andie said. "You know, you might end up waist-deep before you land anything."

Joel wedged the handle of his fishing rod between two rocks and then grasped Andie's forearm as he sat down next to her.

"Tell me about him, Andie," Joel said. "Buzz, Andie. Tell me about Buzz."

Andie tried to stand and walk away, but Joel firmed his grip.

"Andie," Joel said softly, leaning in, "you can't live with this forever. You wear it, you walk with it, and no doubt you live every minute with it. Don't let this destroy you. You have to let it go, and the time to let it go is now.

"Tell me, Andie," Joel said, easing his grip. "I'm right here."

An uneasy moment passed, Andie slowly shaking her head as she looked out toward the rippling waves.

"We had a family farm in Vermont," Andie said, "where we raised buffalo. It was this postcard-perfect homestead in the center of this bucolic spread of farmland, all kept manicured 24/7/365 by a small army of house staff and stable hands.

"About thirty miles north of our farm in Sheffield," Andie continued, "there's a crossover where all traffic passing into Canada is inspected. And that included all commercial vehicles heading toward Montreal, arguably the western hemisphere's premier party-till-the-next-dawn town. And let me tell you, the end product from a sleepy, family-run buffalo farm can look mighty unfamiliar to a crew of border guards. What they're looking for are hidden weapons and illegal immigrants and such. Refrigerated buffalo meat would routinely get waved through with little fanfare."

Andie scooped up another handful of river water, letting the droplets sift through her fingers.

"My family trafficked cocaine from a Medellin cartel into Canada," Andie said in an even tone. "Or more specifically, my father and his youngest brother, my dear uncle Sean, spent their careers moving that white gold over the border. That was the fuel that fed the burgeoning family farm engine.

"And it gets even better," Andie said in a caustic tone. "For years, no one, and I mean no one, had the first suspicion that any of this was going on. Not the local authorities, not the feds, not the Canadian government, and certainly not the rest of my family. My own mother, Asian history scholar and tenured college professor, was actually naive enough to believe that the E-Class Mercedes and Tiffany chandelier were purchased from the proceeds of the bison steak market. There wasn't enough profit in that business to pay for her yoga instructor.

"My dad and my uncle, they were good," Andie went on. "Very good, apparently. They stowed their precious cargo under the refrigeration coils or compressed it neatly between those tender bison patties. And they wanted to be wealthy without being too greedy. They limited their drug smuggling to three shipments a year, four at the most. That was sufficient enough to perpetuate the consummate homespun family business success story ruse. It was all so clean, so smooth, so professional.

"Enter one James Bryant 'JB' McKillnaugh, my older brother," Andie said with feigned amusement. "My *very* older brother, as in thirteen years older. I was one of those mishaps you hear about from time to time: 'Oops, guess what, honey. It's not the flu or food poisoning from that pasta the Colsons served us last night.'"

"If you were an accident, I've seen worse," Joel said, squeezing Andie's hand.

Andie forced a grin.

"Well, if I was a surprise, the real shock to the system came a few years later when JB became wise to the true source of the family's good fortune. I don't know if he just got suspicious, or if he was dragged into the mine shaft by our father. And I don't know which is worse in a family, blackmail or betrayal. But I do know that after a decade of private school and three years at Princeton, JB dropped out of sight, only to resurface in . . ."

"Colombia," Joel said, finishing the sentence.

Andie nodded.

"Who needs a middle man when you can streamline the whole industry, right?" she asked. "Why settle for a few hundred thousand a year when you can pocket half a million every month. And those clodhoppers up near the border? They don't facilitate. They complicate. So let's move past such hindrances and show Montreal a really good time."

Whatever was tugging on Dr. Morgan's fishing line was long gone by the time he reeled in. Joel waded into deeper water and recast in the direction of the pealing prayer wheel on the opposite side of the river.

"Bet you didn't expect a chronicle like this when you wanted to know about Buzz," Andie said as Joel secured the Okuma handle between the same two rocks.

"Hey, I'm the one who asked," he said.

Andie nodded an acknowledgment. "Buzz was my uncle's only child and my only cousin," Andie said. "We were born three days apart at the same hospital. Buzz and his family lived in a second farm house at the other end of the property. He and I spent every afternoon and every weekend together—horseback riding, swimming, hiking, cross-country skiing. But what we both loved most was writing. I think we were eleven years old when our school enrolled the two of us in a state-wide writing contest. I wrote some sappy futuristic fable but won an honorable mention anyway. But Buzz, he won it all. Gold medal in the Vermont middle-school writing contest. He wrote a story about this miser of a businessman who's moved to generosity after being stuck in an elevator with a crippled young girl. While waiting to be rescued from the broken-down elevator, the little girl reads the man a poem she wrote about how much small gifts mean to those around us. So this businessman proceeds to load his private plane with boxes of chocolate truffles, intending to surprise all of his employees and corporate associates. But his plane crashes in the wilderness of Montana, buried without a trace in several feet of fresh snow. The man's found three weeks later with two broken legs, having survived by drinking water from melted snow and making small fires from what was left of the plane's cockpit. He had water and he had shelter, but he would have starved to death if not for . . ."

"The chocolates," Joel said with a wide grin. "He ate the chocolates."

"Imagine a little kid writing a story like that. He was a beautiful writer. He . . . was beautiful," Andie said, her voice trailing off as she looked up into the sky. "God, the stories Buzz could have told the world if he had lived to see this place."

Andie looked toward Joel, her face and her voice now all emotion.

"I'm working with Ivar one day, and I get this call out of nowhere that Buzz is in the ER with an infection that is 'extremely serious,'" Andie said, gritting her teeth. "When I get to the ER bay, I'm greeted by the sound of a flat-lined monitor and this horrid odor. Buzz's face was as gray as slate, and his tongue looked like a hunk of raw meat that someone had jammed into his mouth.

"A *sore throat*," Andie said. "My cousin had a sore throat. To you or me, that may be no big deal. But Buzz was diagnosed with ulcerative colitis at age seven, and as we both know, the treatment regimen with ulcerative colitis leaves you open to all kinds of respiratory infections. Between his underlying illness and the medications that he was taking, Buzz's immune system wasn't worth a rat's ass. And when things went bad, they went real bad real fast. Buzz's family had him evaluated at one of the downtown Boston hospitals, and he was followed by the same physician for years. But everything changed in this new and ever-efficient era of ours. Buzz was assigned a new doctor, someone who knew nothing about him. It turns out that Buzz did call his new physician's office, and when he finally found a human voice on the other end of the line, he was told that all office slots were 'blocked.' I have to imagine that whoever Buzz had on the line was probably reading straight off their bright, shiny computer screen. 'Your throat hurts? Well, if you really need to be seen, check into our emergency room, have a seat, and read a magazine while you watch the calendar turn. We'll get to you soon enough.'"

Without looking, Andie reached for the jewel on her necklace, cradling the bright yellow bee between two of her fingers. Buzz had given Andie the necklace for Christmas two years earlier.

It would be the last gift Buzz ever gave her.

"The best medical care on the planet, and my cousin choked to death because no one listened," Andie said as she lowered her gaze, fighting back the tears. "And when no one listens, no one looks. All someone in 'the system' had to do was take a minute and consider the possibility that this was a man with an immune system that had no way out of first gear. But Buzz didn't need a system. He needed a doctor.

"He was my heart, my life, my sanity," Andie said, her voice steadier. "We were just kids and knew nothing of this thriving enterprise at the Canadian border. But when JB disappeared, it was madness at home. My father had to confess the whole criminal enterprise to my mother, who became totally unglued. JB ended up getting nailed outside Bogota by the national police, and for what he thought was an exchange for immunity, he spilled his guts about all the goings-on in Vermont's northeast kingdom. But in the end, that wasn't enough to save JB from the Colombian slammer. And believe me when I tell you that I haven't lost a minute's sleep over big brother's fate. By the time the DEA found their way to the family farm, Dad and my uncle had vanished. The whole thing, as you might imagine, was a supreme embarrassment for both the US and Canadian governments. With two of the guilty parties on the lam and a third jailed in South America, there was no one left to arrest. There wasn't a shred of evidence against my mother, who has spent her subsequent years trying to find both solace and answers at the bottom of a bottle. And just so you don't have to ask, I never saw my father again.

"But I had Buzz," Andie said with a sad smile. "I don't know which I hated more . . . my parent's roof-ripping fights or the dead stone silence that followed. But I really didn't care at that point. All I cared about was smiling at me from the other end of the farm. Ironically, because of Buzz's chronic illness, we actually got to live on the farm for a while before the feds seized the property. And amidst all the insanity, every night when I went to bed, I'd see the flashing green light from Buzz's window. Four flashes . . . short, short, long, short, saying Good-night-ANN-dee. That's how he said goodnight to me, every time. And every time, I knew I'd see Buzz the next day.

"When I walked into that trauma room, it was like touring the field of a defeated army," Andie said, covering her eyes with her hands. "You could tell that the staff there had done everything humanly possible, but Buzz was essentially dead before he even got there. So I ask you, how could something like this happen in the middle of Boston? How could a twenty-four-year-old suffocate and die in his apartment stairwell?"

Andie shot to her feet, her eyes meeting Joel's dead on.

"Hurdles, that's what all this is about. Hurdles. Set up enough hurdles, and eventually some of the jumpers stop jumping. I know Buzz called his own shots—not always vigilant, needing frequent reminders. But just to take a minute and listen. Good God, they're supposed to be vigilant. They were supposed to take care of him. How could they let him strangle to death? They should have known. They . . . *I*," Andie covered her eyes once again, "*I* should have known!"

Andie was standing barefoot in the water, her face buried in her hands. Joel approached and put his arms around her, neither of them saying anything for several minutes.

"He'd still be here," Andie eventually said. "He would still be here with me."

"Andie, it's not your fault," Joel said. "You have to let go. You can do so much. Just look around you."

"When I look around, the only person I want to be with is gone. And when I close my eyes," Andie said, "all I see are his eyes, dilated like saucers. It just won't go away."

"I know he's gone, Andie," Joel said. "Seeing someone die so young is far too familiar to me, and trust me when I tell you that familiarity does not lessen the pain. But you're here, Andie. And there are a lot of people calling you."

"Don't," Andie said, shaking her head. "That's a speech I do not need to hear. 'Buzz wouldn't want this' or 'he'd want you to do that.' I was about to become part of an industry that fails those most in need. Contract restrictions and codes and the rest of the endless bullshit. I wonder what the response would have been if that phone call was about some new venture bringing in a pile of fresh patients, as opposed to an already assigned patient who might require urgent care? No thanks, Dr. Morgan. That's not what I signed up for."

Joel held up all five fingers of his right hand and the index finger of his left hand.

"Sixth," he said. "You were ranked sixth in your med school class when you dropped out, Andie. Sixth out of 150 plus students at one of the finest medical schools anywhere. Doesn't that tell you something?"

Andie stood silent.

"I'm not going to preach to you about what Buzz would or would not have wanted you to do," Joel said. "Maybe I would if I had had the good fortune of knowing Buzz, but I was never blessed with that opportunity. And in regards to this 'system' of ours, you are on the mark all the way here. It did fail him. But don't let it lay claim to you, Andie. That would be a loss equally as great.

"I'm asking you to stop and take a long look at the world around you," Joel went on. "Or for that matter, the world right in front of you. Look at all we've seen since arriving here just two days ago. Bhutan isn't considered impoverished by anyone's standards, yet look at the need here. Why do you think Ivar came here? All those years of giving donations and supplies, yet that wasn't even enough. You and I both know that Ivar came here because there's something about Taktsang that he believes will advance the research he's dedicated his life to. But he also came here because they *need* him. And a few weeks ago, when Ivar waved good-bye to you, what did he do?"

Andie shot Joel a surprised look.

"The light," Andie said eventually. "The four flashes of light I saw in the rearview mirror when I was driving away on my bike. Whenever we parted, wherever we were, I'd look back at Ivar, and he'd shine those four beams in my direction. How in the world did you know about that?"

"Silas sent me a letter of thanks a while back, and he happened to mention it, just in passing," Joel said. "He said he had never seen such an exchange between two close friends."

Andie looked down into the river and nodded slightly.

"And why does Ivar do that?" Joel asked. "The light, Andie. Why?"

Andie looked up at Joel, hesitating for a moment.

"To honor Buzz," she said in a soft voice.

"To honor Buzz," Joel said, placing a hand on Andie's shoulder. "To honor him," Joel repeated. "Your pain will ease when you ease the pain of those who need you most. And they do need you, more than you know. Show them all, Andie . . . for the sake of those who've left and for the sake of those left behind."

Andie splashed two handfuls of river water across her face, easing the sting that was circling around both of her eyes. She walked onto the riverbank, dried off her feet, and began lacing on her hiking boots.

"I did have one more question," Joel said as he held up another lure for inspection.

"I hope it's easier than the last one," Andie said with a straight face.

"This plant or herb that Ivar is after, do you really, truly believe that it can—"

"Did you hear that?" Andie asked, jumping to her feet.

"I heard something," Joel said.

Andie and Joel looked up toward the trail that Karma, Martin, and Myles had started to climb a couple of hours earlier.

"It's Martin," Joel said, pointing at a clearing that was a couple of hundred meters away. "He went up to tour that monastery with Karma. If he walked all the way back down here, it's for a pretty damn good reason."

"Tell me they've found him," Andie said as she gathered up her gear and began running to the head of the trail. "Just tell me Ivar's all right."

Joel jammed his gear into the tackle box and cut his fishing line.

"Looks like it's yak meat for dinner," Joel said to himself as he ran off after Andie. "I like mine medium-well."

Chapter 24

"'The immediate reporting of any unforeseen circumstance is the sworn charge of every entrepreneur,'" Joel said, quoting a line from Martin's recent interview in *Investor's Business Daily*. "You weren't bullshitting, were you?" Joel added, looking at Martin. "You sure know how to interrupt a nice afternoon of river casting."

Martin was seated on one of the unrolled sleeping bags, his chest heaving as he searched for air.

"Let me guess," Joel said. "You even skipped your college gym class if it involved anything more vigorous than ping pong."

"Something like that," Martin said between gasps.

"Well, you're buff compared to me," Joel said. "Those damn switchbacks are going to do me in. Up one side and down the other, back and forth, this way then that. And you had to make another round trip on those things, trying to find Andie and me. My hat's off to you, man. I get winded just trying to start my snowblower."

"If we could put the couch-potato diaries on ice for a minute, if you don't mind," Andie said, waving her hand. "It's going to be dark soon, and Myles is out wandering around somewhere. You were the last to see him, Martin. Do you think he's *still* on the phone with Stacey?"

"That's the problem, from what I gather," Martin said, still struggling to catch his breath. "That satellite phone of his keeps losing its signal. When I left to find the two of you, Myles was roaming around helter-skelter, getting bits and pieces from Stacey whenever the connection was strong."

Martin, Andie, and Joel were all seated inside a tent that one of the Sherpas had assembled in a clearing below the monastery that Martin and Karma had visited earlier. A campfire had been lit, and its warmth had started to filter into the tent. Karma and another one of the Sherpas were busy preparing hot *sudja* and dinner for everyone.

"You worked with Ivar for a long time," Joel said, looking at Andie, "and I'm sure you worked with Stacey here and there. Any chance she's overreacting here, jumping the gun on the results she saw in Ivar's lab earlier today?"

Andie began shaking her head before Joel had finished speaking.

"Not in a million years," she said. "If Stacey Ravelle walked in here and told me that the Martians had landed, I'd believe her. She doesn't know how to overreact. That's Myles's wheelhouse, in case you hadn't noticed."

"Andie and Joel, *chhoe gadebe yoe*?" Karma said as she entered the tent. "Hello and how are you? Everyone, please, come out for some hot *sudja*. Butter tea will help lift any traveler who is noticing the effects of our mountain air. Please, the tea is fresh, and you will feel better quickly. And for dinner, we have prepared *ema datse* and *khule*, which are my own special favorites. In your country, you would call this dish green chilies and cheese with buckwheat pancake. Plenty for all, and you must eat heartily, as tomorrow is a long day for us. Pema, one of our Sherpas, is a most excellent cook. But Dr. Joel, Pema tells me he must apologize in advance, as yak meat is available only in the winter months."

"There'll be no mahseer in the pan either," Andie said, looking squarely at Joel. "Next time, I'll choose the lure and cast the line."

"But we do have *chhurpi* to serve with the chilies," Karma said. "You will find its flavor quite unique, as *chhurpi* is the finest yak cheese anywhere. Again, there is plenty for everyone. And once we have finished our dinner, if I may ask your assistance in regards to one of our fellow travelers."

"Anything," Andie said, looking at Karma.

"You may have noticed the large herders' yurt at the far end of the meadow," Karma said. "There are fifteen or twenty in their group, and they know something of us, as we are traversing through land that is very familiar to them. I am told that one of the yak herdsmen, who is on in years, has a painful swelling along the side of his hand. As I mentioned before, there is little medical care anywhere nearby, and the leader of the herdsmen is aware that there are physicians in our group. If we could lend some assistance and complete an exam of the ailing man, and perhaps suggest a means of treatment. They would be most grateful, as would I."

"You should see these creatures," Martin said, his eyes wide. "The yaks, I mean."

"I saw a couple of them heading my way across a narrow footbridge a few hours back," Joel said.

"Then you know what I'm talking about," Martin said. "When I was out chasing after Myles, I accidentally startled a couple of those beasts while climbing up one of the trails. They sound like thunder when they're on the move. Scared the crap out of me. Myles didn't seem to notice, but I sure as hell did. They're monstrous."

"This is excellent grazing pasture," Karma said, "and there is no need to fear. The yak is indeed a very large animal, but they are very gentle creatures. And the herders are never far behind."

"Those nice firm nuggets under your sleeping bag," Joel said, grinning as he looked at Martin. "That's not silver and gold you're bedding with."

Martin shifted uneasily.

"I don't like the sounds of the hand swelling you're describing, Karma," Joel said, "and it's all the more a worry when the hand belongs to a mountain man. Show us the way over there. I don't have much in the way of supplies, but we can get a look and figure it out from there."

"The herders will be camping here for the night," Karma said, "and we can walk over after our dinner. Please, some tea and Pema's chilies first."

Karma turned to leave, but before the torn canvas flap had swung shut, Myles walked through. Myles tossed the satellite phone onto a stack of blankets that were piled up in one corner of the tent.

"Battery just died," Myles said as he sat down, the others exchanging glances at the calmness of his tone.

"You okay?" Joel asked.

Myles shrugged. "I should probably leave the shop more often," Myles said, forcing a smile. "Put a few continents between you and your work, and there's no telling what might happen.

"So here's the skinny," Myles said after he had taken a long pull from his water bottle. "From the very start, Ivar's premise has been simple. You first create your worst enemy, and then you build your best weapon to fight it. The latest tumor cell line is highly resistant, untouchable by conventional therapy. The genetic sequences Ivar constructs are the road maps by which a virus's capacity to kill tumor cells is determined. And everyone, and that includes me, is blinded to the details of those genetic variations. There's no peeking, there's no cheating, and there's no way of knowing the city father's street plan.

"Think of a patient with a potentially deadly recurrence of their cancer," Myles went on, looking directly at Joel. "They've been operated on, irradiated, and filled with chemicals. They then undergo every test known to man, and then they're loaded with more chemicals. And now, you are out of bullets. You know it, they know it, and their family knows it.

"But this is more than just a bullet." Myles leaned in, meeting everyone's gaze. "Granted, what we have at the moment is in a laboratory and not in a human. But there's a door here that leads into a world that is boundless. What we have is . . ."

Myles hesitated, took another swig from his bottle, and then poured the rest of the water over his head.

"What we have is buried somewhere in between the pages of the warbler and sand grouse sections of some bloody avian guidebook!"

"Myles, Myles, there's got to be a backup to the code sequence key somewhere," Joel said emphatically. "I'm about as computer unsavvy as they come, but even I keep duplicates of files a helluva lot less important than the one you're talking about. A log of all this has to be on a program somewhere."

"Yeah, sure, *somewhere*," Myles said, his voice pitched. "But where exactly is somewhere? And while we're on the subject of wild goose chases, we are no closer to finding Ivar than we are to finding Jimmy Hoffa. Everyone back home thinks that locating someone around here is like knocking on the door of a guest at a Club Med resort. They have no idea what a time warp we've stepped into. And let's face it, this expedition into the clouds is based on little more than a hunch.

"If it gets any more bizarre, notify me," Myles said as he reclined against his rucksack, covering both eyes with one hand.

"I am glad everyone is together," Karma said upon re-entering the tent. "And if I may now enjoin you all, I believe it is best if we visit the herders' tent prior to our dinner. I have learned more from these men, more than just their concerns about the man with the injured hand."

"What man with the injured hand?" Myles asked, peering between two fingers.

"Sounds like one of the yak men is working on a cellulitis of the upper extremity," Joel said. "No worries, Karma. Pema has spent the better part of the day cooking up a feast for us. Let's all have some nourishment, and then we'll pay the yurt a visit."

"My friends," Karma said, "there is another man, much younger, that the leader of the group would like you to see. Just a few days ago, this man was very ill, but to the amazement of all, his health has been restored."

"Hear that, Myles," Joel said, wagging a finger. "Local herbs and fifty generations of remedies can probably cure as much as we can back in our venerable institutions."

"The young man they speak of was not mended with herbal remedies," Karma said. "Baldev, the lead herdsman, tells me that this man was revived by a medicine that flowed through a tube that was placed in the man's arm. And although he sought aid at the home of a local healer, this young man was not treated by one of our doctors. He was treated by someone he describes as a foreigner."

Joel, Andie, Myles, and Martin all looked at each other.

"I think it just got more bizarre, Myles," Joel said.

"A very tall foreigner," Karma said.

CHAPTER 25

Baldev introduced Karma and the four visiting Americans to the twenty or so herdsmen who were huddled inside the large yurt.

"Baldev is Hindi for 'supreme in power,'" Karma explained. "He is Indian by birth, and like many nomadic herders, the highlands of India, Tibet, and Bhutan are all equally his home. As the leader of the group, Baldev serves as both spokesman and mediator, but regrettably he converses in a dialect in which I have limited familiarity. This much, however, I can say with certainty: he welcomes you to his home."

Baldev was a squat, thickset man with a black beard that spiraled in every direction. He was garbed from head to toe in heavy animal fur, and when Baldev removed his cap in Andie and Karma's presence, he uncovered a completely bald head with an anvil flat crown. Baldev's shaved scalp and massive beard gave his head a trapezoid configuration, and when Baldev motioned for his guests to sit, Karma, Andie, Martin, Myles, and Joel each nodded their thanks and immediately sat down around the fire that was smoldering in the center of the tent.

"His mother must have been clairvoyant, giving that dude a name that means 'supreme in power,'" Joel whispered to Martin. "Do a search under 'guys you'd never want to mix it up with,' and I guarantee you his mug would pop up."

Although an opening in the yurt's dome allowed an exit flue for the burning campfire, there was still enough smoke inside the tent to partially shroud the men seated along the periphery. When one of the men tried to lure Joel into taking a belt of *rakshi* from a passing wineskin, Andie delivered a sharp elbow to Dr. Morgan's flank as a reminder as to why they were visiting.

Dr. Morgan politely declined.

Through a mix of several languages, Karma was eventually able to introduce her group to Paljor, the herder who had sustained a hand injury. After examining the man, Joel assured Baldev that there was no evidence of a broken bone or evolving infection. In all likelihood, Paljor had a badly sprained wrist that was the result of an acute injury on top of a chronically arthritic joint. Joel carefully wrapped the herder's wrist with a length of animal pelt that to Joel seemed much thinner that the man's leathery, weathered skin.

"Please, my friend, patience," Karma said to Myles, who was clearly growing uneasy. "This is not a temporary shelter we have entered, but a sovereign domicile. You are an honored guest, and hence your visit necessitates a certain level of ceremony. This is the only home, the only existence, these men will ever know. Serving as host to guests who have traveled from such a great distance is an exceptional experience for these herdsmen, and your time here will be the subject of stories told for many years."

"Try and mash yourself a comfortable seat on a nice block of yak turds," Joel said, looking at Myles. "Look at Martin. He's right at home here."

"Son of a bitch," Martin growled as he lifted up his poncho and looked down at the ground where he was seated. "I thought this was just a pile of wet leaves. Son of a . . . I'm in a pile of animal shit here. This sucks, man."

After the *rakshi* had made another round, Baldev motioned for Mance, the youngest of the herders, to stand and tell his story to the assembled crowd.

Mance, although taller than most of his mates, had a wire-thin build. As with the other herders, the scourges of a nomadic existence had plundered Mance's youth, with the wind, sun, and arctic chill having claimed every parcel of exposed skin. Mance's weathered features belied his true age, and if you could peel away the layers of grit, smoke, and sweat, you would probably find a teenage boy no more than sixteen or seventeen years old.

Mance was now on stage, and with Karma translating, he soon had the rapt attention of all present. Some parts of what Mance recounted were likely embellished, and other parts more than likely pure fabrication. But what Dr. Joel Morgan heard was a young man describing the symptoms of rapidly progressing pyelonephritis and impending sepsis. There was no question as to the illness the man had contracted, and there was no question as to how he got better.

Mance had found Ivar, and Ivar had made him well.

With Mance's narrative complete, Andie slipped out of the smoke-filled tent and into the moonless night. It was a stargazer's dream, she thought, with not a hint of light from the Paro Valley below. From the corner of her eye, Andie saw a candle appear in the large window of the monastery that was high above their campsite. A moment later, the candlelight cast a shadow on one of the robed monks as he climbed the inner stairway, the apparition becoming larger and then vanishing suddenly once the man reached the top of the stairs. A few minutes later, Andie watched the same robed man descend the stairs, his shadow at first enormous but then quickly receding to outline the monk's actual body size. Through the dim light, Andie could see that the man was carrying one of the cedar wood boxes that stored the sacred writings of centuries past. When the man again disappeared, a brief flicker of candlelight gave sudden life to the great Buddha whose painted image adorned the far wall of the monastery.

Chapter 26

The truck was the first vehicle Mandar Sarai had ever owned, and it was his most prized earthly possession.

It took every dime of Mandar's savings to purchase the Tata 1613, buying it second hand from a distant relative in Raikot, the Punjabi city that was his father's ancestral home. The cab's pale color was the perfect virgin canvas, and buried somewhere beneath the layers of Mandar's artistry lay the truck's original lusterless orange tone. Within hours of taking possession, Mandar had painted dark, tapered eyebrows above the dull chrome that surrounded the truck's headlights. From there, the rest of the frame became a swirling riot of green, purple, blue, and every imaginable shade of red. Rhinoceros horns were etched across the top of the hood, and peacock feathers were painted along the surface of both front fenders. To assure good fortune and a safe journey, metal talismans dangled from the canary-yellow cowling that hung above the windshield. A dancing fish graced the driver's side door, offering a wink to every passing traveler.

Mandar saved his best work for the side panels of the truck, where he painted an image of the Punjab's five rivers flowing through a verdant pastoral mosaic. Each of the rivers ebbed its way to the tiny village of Sirsa, the home that Mandar had all but forsaken for a life of travel along the worn, perilous roads of northern India.

His truck was his bread, his masterpiece, his partner.

It was his machine.

Mandar knew no life outside of life on the road, having helped his father and older brothers transport freight from northern India to both Nepal and Bhutan ever since he was nine years old. Mandar and his road partner of many years, Ranjeet Vadal, on-loaded their goods in the city of Ludhiana, which was the industrial center of Punjab and the state's largest city. From Ludhiana, they drove east through the states of Haryana, Uttar Pradesh, and Bihar. The crossroads town of Siliguri was their last stop before heading northward onto a sixty-kilometer U-shaped traverse of crumbling switchbacks. A single lane diversion off Road 31 would bring them to Chengmari, a border town along the western edge of Bhutan. Mandar and Ranjeet knew that they had many road miles ahead, and besides the two of them, they had picked up a decrepit hitchhiker who was sound asleep in the back of the cab.

"Outrageous. Scandalous, if you ask me," Ranjeet said, spilling coffee on himself as he carried on once again about the spiraling cost of fuel. "I ask you again, Mandar, when was the last time we refueled in Siliguri, and the price had not increased from the time before? That man is a thief! And our consignors, do they in kind pay us more? The lines are beginning to meet, my friend. This fact is undeniable."

Mandar rolled up his window after throwing out another cigarette butt.

"The man is no thief," Mandar said, puffing the last of the smoke into the cold night air. "He's merely passing along the bad news. But it's trouble for us no matter where the fault lies, I'll give you that. Our only means of countering this trend is to put more road miles beneath us."

"More road miles?" Ranjeet asked, arching his head upward. "How and where? We traverse this pass so often that this beast could probably run the route on its own memory. My family sees a stranger enter the house when I walk through the door during the light of day. I am there just long enough to set an ever-shrinking pile of rupees on our table."

"Needn't tell that tale to me," Mandar said as he lit another *Capstan*, the cigarette he bought wholesale from a friend who hauled tobacco and liquor along the same routes that he and

Ranjeet traveled. "Every time I set foot in my home, I seem to shake hands with yet another mouth to feed, some long lost relative whose only refuge is my kitchen. And who knows how long he or she will stay under my roof? I am back on this trail, rolling with you, before I even learn their name."

"Saudi sheiks with their palaces, each Russian his own private jet," Ranjeet mumbled as he strained to take another sip of coffee between the cavernous ruts that riddled the highway. "Meanwhile, we take it up the ass, purchasing their fuel. I curse them all. And the same goes for that shylock in Siliguri, grinning like a toad each time we refill our tank. Looters, the whole lot!"

To Mandar, Ranjeet Vadal's diatribes were the ultimate in free entertainment. If he wasn't protesting the rising price of gasoline, Ranjeet would surely be blustering on about his latest abdominal malady or the lack of discipline his grandchildren demonstrated at their most recent family gathering. Although Ranjeet was nearly a generation older than Mandar, both men came from a long line of haulers, and the parents and grandparents of both men never squandered an opportunity to recount their many years of sending goods across the border in horse-drawn lorries. Compared to the painful monotony of such lore, Mandar found Ranjeet's incessant carping a welcome diversion.

"You have to admit one thing," Mandar said, changing the subject as his partner continued to grumble. "This computer age of ours has helped us in ways we never could have imagined. The Bhutanese have no internal access to computers, nor the availability of any related electrical supplies. And there is always a demand in Bhutan for our traditional machine tools and fertilizer. Over the past year or so, we have had more and more consignors, which is never bad news for men in our line of work."

Ranjeet growled something toward the bottom of his coffee cup.

"Textiles," Ranjeet exclaimed, having exhausted the topic of rising fuel costs. "Now there is a product line where we can find a two-way street. Once we off-load in Paro, why can we not negotiate the transport of Bhutanese fabrics back to the markets of Ludhiana? We all know the superb quality of Bhutan's textiles, and just think of the demand, particularly in the large cities throughout the western states. Such centers abound with tourists whose pockets brim with currency. With a solid trade arrangement, we will not have to drive back home with an empty truck, tails between our legs. *That* would be true commerce, and to the benefit of all."

"Not so fast, I beg you," Mandar implored. "We have spoken of this many times before. You know as well as I do that Bhutan has very strict regulations on such exporting. But if time allows, we can again make inquiries. Patience and time, my friend. Patience and time."

"Tell that to my grandchildren, the ones' whose hands are out every time they lay eyes on me," Ranjeet said, draining his coffee cup. "Patience is to them a foreign concept. The cost of providing for our families, like the money we pour into this guzzling truck, only escalates by the day. And then there is the cost of the doctor who attends to my digestive needs, selling me those putrid pills to silence this savage belly of mine. He makes the gas man of Siliguri look like a saint of charity."

Mandar slowed to nearly a halt as a loaded semitrailer emerged along the outside of another switchback. The large truck inched past, its driver so close at one point that Mandar could see the ash dangling from the end of the man's cigarette. Once past, the playful melody of the big truck's horn sounded off in appreciation.

Mandar knew that if the night remained clear and the roads stayed uncongested, they'd hit Paro by eight the next morning and be off-loaded by ten or so. Then they would be either on their way back home, or with some luck, they'd have the chance to line up with a local freighter for a shipment farther east to Thimphu.

"You're exhausted, old timer," Ranjeet said with a sideways grin. "Pull over and let a pro navigate these roads."

Mandar put the pack of *Capstans* up to his mouth and drew out another cigarette, lighting it off the one he had just finished.

"Look in that mirror above your head, and I'll show you the old man," Mandar said as he sent a fresh trail of smoke out the window. "I'm just fine in this seat, hours to spare. You can take over after we cross the border.

"Care for one?" Mandar asked as he extended his arm into the cramped space in the back of the cab, offering a *Capstan* to the stranger they had picked up a couple of hours earlier.

"No. Thank you," the precise words emerged from the darkness.

The hitchhiker had been so quiet that Mandar nearly forgot he was even back there.

"Last chance." Ranjeet tapped the gearshift with his index finger. "You young bucks fancy that you can go on forever, and then—smash. Fatigue overtakes you, and we flip over the edge." Ranjeet slapped his knee and roared with laughter.

It did strike Mandar as strange that the man just said 'thank you' in Nepali. When they picked him up, he had spoken briefly in Limbu.

"Wake me once I am slumbered, and you will have aroused a great snake," Ranjeet taunted. "You have been so warned. Speak now, or silence the rest of the night."

Mandar and Ranjeet were always glad to pick up hitchers, and in particular a bedraggled man such as this one, who could barely get himself into the cab.

"Then I shall enter a fine dream," Ranjeet said as he closed his eyes and let out a slow moan. "Fair lasses shall soon be dancing about me."

This man was unusually quiet, which Mandar appreciated. Most stragglers were by nature lonely people, and all too frequently they would carry on and on in conversation, having had no one to talk with in many hours.

"Feel free to negotiate on your own at Chengmari," Ranjeet said through another deep sigh. "My offer just expired."

But something else about this man was peculiar. When they helped him get into the truck, he mentioned that he might try to hop a train into Bangladesh. That train left out of Siliguri, which was the town they had already passed through.

To his right, Mandar heard a faint cracking sound, as if a hollowed-out eggshell had been slowly squeezed to just beyond its breaking point. Looking toward Ranjeet, Mandar saw a fist, its skin cadaveric white, at the base of Ranjeet's neck. A jet of crystal clear fluid pulsed from Ranjeet's left ear.

The truck fishtailed wildly as Mandar stood on the brakes. When the truck had spun to a halt, Mandar was staring straight at the deep crimson scar that bisected Drapche Dorn's eyelid.

"He said the magic word," Drapche said as he unwedged the Gurkha knife, the edges of the blade grinding against the crushed fragments of Ranjeet's skull base. "Chengmari. You're crossing at Chengmari," Drapche repeated, Ranjeet letting out an agonal gasp as his bulging eyes swiveled frantically. "I so appreciate the updated travel log."

Drapche twisted a tuft of Mandar's hair and lifted him out of his seat, wrenching Mandar's neck sideways and piercing the outer layer of skin with the tip of his Gurkha knife.

Ranjeet slumped forward and onto the floor of the cab, a current of spinal fluid streaming slowly from the pith wound in the back of his neck.

"Now that I have your attention," Drapche jeered, "tell me that you can get this thing across that border."

Mandar nodded as he shrieked in agony.

"Nothing to fear," Drapche said, holding the knife at a constant level. "Tell me everything that I need to know, and I'll have no cause to go any deeper.

"The payload," Drapche now gritting the stubs of his teeth and tightening his twist on Mandar's hair. "Electrical parts and all the shit that go with a computer?"

Mandar nodded again.

"How about fertilizer?"

"Only a little," Mandar mouthed slowly, the cab beginning to reek from the smell of excrement.

"Anything else?" Drapche demanded.

With what little mobility he had, Mandar shook his head.

"Nothing?"

Mandar shook his head once more.

Drapche gradually released his grip on Mandar's hair.

"Documents," Drapche said in a mockingly soft tone. "You have documents for all the rot you're dumping off in Bhutan?"

Mandar looked over at the deep pile of papers stuffed into the side pocket of the passenger's side door. As Drapche rifled through the stack of documents, Mandar eyed the stump-like remnants of three fingers on the killer's right hand. Drapche used his other hand to hold the knife blade perfectly steady against Mandar's lower neck.

"And here it is," Drapche said, satisfaction filling his voice. "A full manifest, along with all the required permits. Excellent."

"So it's off to Paro," Drapche said as he pulled the Gurkha blade back slightly, a trickle of blood coursing down Mandar's neck and onto his darkly stained pant leg. "Just the two of us."

Unconsciously, Mandar shot a momentary glance northward along Road 31. The look, however brief, did not escape Drapche's notice.

"What is that glimmer I see?" Drapche hissed. "Is that hope I spot in those eyes? Perhaps a distant set of headlights coming to your aid?"

Mandar let out a piercing squeal as he felt a crushing vice grip on both of his testicles.

"If I may make a suggestion," Drapche said, easing his grip one genital at a time. "Drive. Drive us over that border and into Bhutan, and then you can run your worthless Punjabi ass off anywhere that is not in my direction."

For the first time in several minutes, Mandar actually felt air flow into his lungs.

"Just one question, before our relationship progresses any further," Drapche said as he neared closer to Mandar, the boomerang scar across his forehead flushing a deeper red as he spoke. "If I have all these papers," Drapche said, making a pendulum motion with the crumpled manifest, "why do I need you?"

In one deliberate motion, Drapche turned the Gurkha knife ninety degrees and plunged it into Mandar's neck. The blunt side of the blade compressed the carotid artery, the vessel now torqued against the lower wall of Mandar's throat. Drapche twisted the blade once more, lacerating the artery lengthwise so that its entire blood volume erupted into the lining of Mandar's voice box. Drapche listened to the whirling torrent that flooded into the depths of the man's airway, the terror in his victim's eyes slowly fading as Mandar gurgled to death in his own blood.

Drapche would have no difficulty crossing the border at Chengmari, and from there he would proceed northward to Paro. He had no interest in Bhutan's seat of government, or its king, or its military, or its treasury. Drapche would strike in the midst of the nation's people, impaling the core of their very being.

He would be immortal.

"Perhaps this would be a good time to drop off the fertilizer," Drapche said to himself as he re-sheathed the Gurkha knife. "And that includes the two of you."

Before rolling the two bodies out of what was now his truck, Drapche ripped a gold ring off the hand of one of his victims and a bracelet off the wrist of the other dead man, sliding the two jewels onto the outer edge of his belt and watching them clatter against his other mementos.

Chapter 27

Choeden used both hands to lift the steaming cup of *chiyaa* off the breakfast counter.

He had slept fitfully the night before, jolted awake in the middle of the night by the same thoughts that had tormented his sleep for years:

> *You ran away.*
> *Your family, forsaken.*
> *Disowning your own blood.*
> *What kind of eldest son would abandon . . .*

Choeden's parents had immigrated to Bhutan in the late 1970s, leaving behind the squalor of a Kathmandu shantytown in search of a better life for Choeden and his two younger brothers. Several years after settling in Bhutan, Choeden's father had saved enough money to buy a tiny plot of farmland along the Tarsa River, fifty kilometers southwest of Paro. Having each been born into a family of illiterate street dwellers, Choeden's parents watched their dream come to life as they secured both an education and a promising future for their three children. Choeden and his two siblings grew up in the Bhutanese culture, learning the native language from their schoolteachers and traditional song, dance, and sport from their classmates and friends.

But Choeden and his family were not Bhutanese.

Choeden's family was Nepali, and as such, the king of Bhutan's "one nation, one people" decree all but assured their eventual banishment.

They had no provenance, and therefore they had no rights to their land.

They would soon be exiles, and Choeden could not bear the thought of life as an exile, where he and his brothers would be forced to endure the indignity that their parents had known all those years ago in the gutters of Kathmandu.

So from the moment he slipped away from his family's farm on a howling September night, Choeden began to weave a tale that told of a deceased mother and a drunken, violent father. He managed to pass himself off as a lost soul who had escaped a childhood that was marred by abuse and tragedy, the ruse made all the easier by Choeden's fluency in the Bhutanese language and his familiarity with local customs. Choeden wired on a smile every morning and feigned contentment, working long hours as a hired farmhand for a couple of years before taking on odd jobs in and around Paro. He took part in every holiday celebration, participating enthusiastically in National Day, the December festival that marked the ascension of Bhutan's first king. Choeden's deception was made complete on the day he married a young Bhutanese girl, a union born more out of fear and necessity that one founded on any sense of love and devotion.

You are a fraud.
Your life, a masquerade.
Your mother, your father, your brothers . . . left stranded.

Choeden drank deeply, the *chiyaa* streaming a trail of fire through his chest.

"Narayan."

The word emerged from the darkness that filled the far corner of the cafe, its acquaintance hitting Choeden like a bayonet through his gut.

Choeden dropped his teacup and spun out of his seat, his eyes shooting toward a small booth near the cafe's rear entrance.

"Na-RA-yan." The name pierced the air once again, spoken slowly this time, phonetically, with a deliberate overemphasis on the middle syllable.

Choeden looked over both shoulders as he approached the cafe's back booth, stopping for a moment when one of his footsteps crushed a shard of porcelain from the shattered teacup. Choeden's eyes went wide when he saw a fist thrust up into the air from behind the booth, pellets of ice water trailing down the ghost white hand that held in it a bottle of Black Knight lager.

"Drapche," Choeden said as he straightened, the reverence in his voice unmistakable.

"Drapche Dorn."

"See that place over there?" Drapche asked as he pointed over his shoulder toward the cafe's front window. "Take a good look. It's that second-story watering hole across the square, the one with the flowers hanging out of the window."

Drapche motioned for Choeden to take a seat opposite him.

"It's called the Rendezvous," Drapche said, eyeing Choeden for the first time. "The Rendezvous," Drapche repeated with a sneer, downing the rest of the Black Knight as he arched his head back. "Please, someone tell me I'm in the middle of a bad dream here. Talk about pandering to a bunch of corn-holing tourists. Take yourself another real good look out there. Does that look like fucking Paris to you?"

Drapche snapped his fingers and pointed at the empty beer bottle that he had just set down on the table.

"I'll spring for a refill on your tea if you think you can manage to keep a handle on it," Drapche said with a slow grin. "Or if you'd prefer something with a little more heft to it, order up."

"Tea would be most appreciated," Choeden said, his eyes darting in every direction.

"Found myself one fancy ride over the border," Drapche said after the waiter had set down another beer and a fresh pot of *chiyaa*. "I believe I made it here in record time. And I can tell you this for damn certain, it was one hell of an improvement over the three bloody weeks it took me a few years back, when I trudged eastward with a couple hundred other 'untouchable' types, begging His Majesty's audience."

Drapche kept Choeden's eye as he took a long swig of Black Knight. He didn't even appear to swallow.

"Now just think about that for a minute," Drapche said as he wiped his lower lip with the back of his hand. "Back all those years ago, it took our faithful little band twenty days to cover two hundred puny kilometers. That's all it is, you know. The Jhapa to Bhutan express, a mere two hundred kilometers. Only difference is that this time," Drapche leaned in toward Choeden, "I decided to hitch me a ride."

Choeden used one hand to steady the other as he poured himself some tea.

"Now, let me lighten your load here, mate," Drapche said. "Your ma and pa have not the slightest inkling as to what all you're into here. They don't even know that you and I have been sending smoke signals back and forth all this time. They just wanted me to somehow, someway, get a message to you that they were doing just fine."

Choeden shot bolt upright in his seat.

"Please, Drapche," Choeden pleaded. "I must know. To carry on, I need certainty."

Drapche swirled the last of his beer as he slowly stretched back in his seat. Except for the visible stumps of the three fingers that held the Black Knight bottle, no one who had ever known Drapche Dorn would have recognized the man who had for years been czar of the Jhapa refugee camp. He was clean-shaven and sporting a fresh haircut. He had removed all of his jewelry, and to camouflage his sliced eyelid, he was wearing a pair of thick rimmed sunglasses. The *gho* he had on seemed to fit him perfectly, as if the garment had been tailor-made for him. This in particular was a remarkable coincidence, given the fact that Drapche had torn the robe off the back of a drunk he rolled a few days earlier. This same gentleman was even carrying enough *ngultrums* in his pocket to finance the forest-green skullcap that Drapche was now wearing. Although not particularly fashionable, the hat did serve to cover one bone-deep forehead scar.

Drapche held up his other hand, as if swearing an oath in a court of law. "On the souls of my departed ancestors, you have my word: your family is safe. They dream of the day when their clan is again whole, dwelling once more on the land that is rightfully theirs."

"Thank you, sir," Choeden said, visibly relieved.

Drapche gave Choeden a slight nod as he began to tap on the table, the thick callous at the ends of his three mangled fingers producing a low, thumping vibration that reverberated across the room.

"Narayan," Drapche said, his tone soft as he again leaned in. "Your name is Narayan. Your father and your mother send their affections to Narayan. They don't know anyone named Choeden, and neither do I. And oh yes, your two brothers, including that squashy milksop with the gimp, they know nothing of a man named Choeden. These are, if I am not mistaken, the same two brothers, the same two *younger* brothers, who were left to console their aggrieved mother after their *big* brother vanished into the night."

Choeden hung his head low as Drapche's words gave voice to the shame that had come to consume his life.

> *You fled.*
> *Your crippled, sickly brother left to fend for your*
>   *parents.*
> *The family that gave you everything, deserted in an*
>   *airless cesspool.*
> *Flushed into hell, like so much sewage.*

"Look at me, feather dick," Drapche demanded, cuffing Choeden across the temple. "You are Nepali, you got that. Your family, my family, our people—we brought a much-needed body part to this country. Dragon Land here may have had a heart and may have had a brain, and to give the flag its full due, it may even have had a swinging set of 'nads. But what it did *not* have, Na-RA-yan, was a backbone.

"Our blood worked every acre of this land, and I mean every square meter," Choeden winced as Drapche's words sprayed across his face, "be the land fertile or barren or something in between. Can any of us count the hours we collectively slaved in the fields, the toil of the harvest ours to bear, year in and year out? And what did we ask in return? Was dominion over this nation ever on our minds? Did we ever once seek a voice in the affairs of state? No, Narayan, we sought none of these things. All we ever wanted was some regard for our ways, our culture, our heritage."

Drapche inched his skullcap back to the middle of his forehead, the violaceous edges of the jagged cicatrix seeming to swell as he spoke.

"Ten minutes," Drapche said, his eyes boring into Choeden. "That is all I need. Your one and only task is to make it look like we both belong in there. For you, that's pretty simple, being an adopted son and all. But if anyone should ask, you just say that I'm some long lost uncle in search of redemption or nirvana or whatever comes into your mind at that moment. I'll follow your lead, pasting on a virtuous front, looking more pious with every step. Make a show of meditating with anyone else who's in there, but above all else, stay alert. At some point, I'll duck out of sight, and then you can commence the countdown. Give me those ten minutes, then stand up, give the worshiping world one of your signature bows from the waist, and haul your ass out that door."

Drapche reached down and lifted up his knapsack, placing it carefully on top of the table.

"They raped us," Drapche said as he removed his skullcap, the steady calm of his voice sending a chill along the length of Choeden's spine. "To right such a wrong," Drapche continued, placing the skullcap on top of his rucksack, "is reason enough to live."

Drapche then crouched low in his seat, his chest nearly touching the table as he peered up at Choeden.

"And while we're sitting here debating the assorted rights and wrongs of this world," Drapche said, barely above a whisper, "you might recall a correspondence I sent a while back that referenced a young man by the name of Dreyver. This Dreyver, he's a big guy, impressive sort. The man actually keeps himself looking pretty spiffy, which is nothing short of miraculous in that urinal of a camp they have us all sardined into. But a funny thing about this Dreyver fella. No one, and I mean not a single guy I know, has ever once caught him eyeing any of the half-clad pussy that's always running around seeking shelter in some distant patch of good old Club Jhapa. See Dreyver, well, it turns out, he's a bit of a tike squeezer, prowling about the little boys' guild like a famished wolf circling a pen of spring lambs. The grapevine tells of his penchant for the young, marshmallowy types, you know, the ones with a little extra bulk in their hind quarters. And who knows, maybe those rumors are spot-on— this naughty devil plumping for the little nippers whose defenses are, shall we say, somewhat compromised. So while you're lying all warm and snug with that squinty little tart of yours, young studly Dreyver, he's fixing to saddle up next to—"

The pummel of Choeden's fists on the table was forceful enough to send Drapche's empty Black Knight bottle rolling to the table's edge. Drapche caught the beer bottle in midair.

"We shall compel them to listen!" Choeden said, wiping the tears from his cheek, his eyes wild with anger. "We shall astound them, Drapche Dorn. We shall astound them all!"

"Astound?" Drapche asked, removing his sunglasses and offering his minion a slow wink of his lacerated eyelid. "Oh, you have no idea."

ChApter 28

"I am a weak man," Tandin said to Ivar, his voice breaking as he ambled through the small room that was just beyond the entranceway to Taktsang. "I am the weakest man I have ever known. The footprints of the saints surround us here, and as I follow their path, they can sense my weakness just as surely as I can sense their might."

Tandin and Ivar stood alone in the atrium of the Taktsang Monastery. The room was an austere, windowless space, without any evidence of a mural, *thangka*, or icon on any of its four walls. The only object in the room was a *chorten*, which is a type of obelisk built to memorialize a great religious figure. Each of these monuments consisted of five distinct segments, each segment representing one of the five essential elements: a square base, the earth; the half-sphere dome, water; etchings of the sun and moon, air; the pyramidal-shaped steeple, fire; and the vertical spike at the pinnacle, ether, or the eternal light of Buddha. The *chorten*'s five parts form a stairway-like structure known as the thirteen parasols, which are the thirteen sequential steps, or degrees, that must be ascended to attain enlightenment. These are the steps that liberate and bring freedom from all that is negative: ignorance, malice, hatred, jealousy, and desires of the heart. The *chorten* in the center of the room where Tandin and Ivar were standing housed the ancient relics of Pelkyi Singye, Guru Rinpoche's first disciple.

"Weak," Tandin repeated yet again, with a hint of an echo in the barren space. "My every step through Taktsang reminds me of the long and arduous journey that lies ahead."

The thirteen temples housed within the Taktsang Monastery represent the thirteen parasols of enlightenment, and of these temples the most venerated of all is the Dubkhang. The Dubkhang is the cave where Guru Rinpoche, the Precious Master, subjugated eight evil spirits by meditating for three months. Deep within the Dubkhang cave rest the remnants of many saints, and these relics are Bhutan's greatest treasure. Guru Rinpoche, standing on the back of a tigress in his most terrifying form of Dorje Drolo, guards the cave's entrance.

Whenever Tandin entered Taktsang, he became a different man, with the breakneck pace in which he approached every other facet of his life nowhere to be found. His pensive demeanor and somber words were not otherwise typical of the man, and whenever he approached any of the ancient relics housed within the confines of the monastery, Tandin was visibly moved.

A certificate of official permission was necessary before any non-Bhutanese citizen could be allowed entrance into Taktsang. Any foreigner petitioning for a special permit for entrance had to go through a long and tedious approval process at the government offices in Thimphu. This procedure required time that Ivar didn't have, and all the more a measure of luck that Ivar couldn't count on. And how could Tandin not invite Ivar on his pilgrimage to this sacred monastery? His American friend was further along the path to ultimate liberation than perhaps any Bhutanese citizen he had ever known. And Tandin could not deny what he and his wife, Dru, had witnessed since Ivar had arrived at their home some weeks earlier—the progression of their friend's illness, his faculties failing bit by bit with each passing day. Tandin was not going to make Ivar stand in line for permission to enter Taktsang, where his friend would have to wait for who knows how long while the spools of red tape were being untangled.

Tandin shuffled into the next room, motioning for Ivar to follow.

"That is Guru Rinpoche," Tandin said with a deep reverence in his voice, bowing as he pointed to a statue in the adjoining room. "On the day that this image was consecrated, words from the Precious Master's mouth were heard by all present. To this day, his wisdom reigns supreme in every corner of Bhutan, and throughout all the Himalayas.

"Look also," Tandin directed Ivar to a painting that hung on the wall opposite the doorway. "That is our great teacher and his Eight Different Manifestations. The manifestations detailed in this masterpiece trace Guru Rinpoche's life, beginning with his birth from a blue lotus on Lake Dhanakosha in northern India. As you can see, Guru Rinpoche is wearing elaborate royal vestments, and on his head there is a cap with flames radiating from the cap's brim. The hat is surrounded by bolts of thunder, with a solitary eagle's feather visible above. The master's headdress signifies the union of solar and lunar forces, with thunder from the sky telling of a formidable soaring wind, penetrating like an eagle into the highest realms of reality."

Several elderly men sat in deep meditation around the altar that stood on the far side of the room. Along with statues of two saints, an assortment of lighted butter lamps and a rainbow of silk fabrics covered the top of the altar.

"The altar you see is constructed of cypress," Tandin explained in a low voice. "Cypress wood is sacred in our land, and by heaven's plan a cypress tree which died by natural causes was destined to return to life as a temple altar. A living cypress tree is inviolate, and the felling of a live cypress by the human hand is a grave sin.

"These men you see gathered about the altar, they seek *sarvajna*," Tandin said with a forlorn look in his eyes. "*Sarvajna* is the cognition of the true nature of reality, where any limitation on one's ability to help other living beings is eliminated. It is here where such wisdom can be found, and perhaps one day my sojourn will end at this very place. These pilgrims," Tandin again observed the men seated in the room, "they are closer to *sarvajna* than I. Much closer, this I know. But not as close as you, this I know as well."

On seeing Ivar and Tandin standing at the room's entrance, two of the men who were seated in front of the altar stood up and walked toward the entranceway. The two men greeted Tandin, and when Tandin introduced Ivar to the two men, they all offered one another respectful bows. All four then left the main altar room and gathered in a nearby foyer.

"My friends, Selden and Gopal, they have traveled far," Tandin said, looking at Ivar but nodding in the direction of the two other men. "They are from the Trongsa and Bumthang districts, which are located in the heart of our country. And Ivar," Tandin now looked at Selden and Gopal but cocked his head toward Ivar, "he has journeyed farther than any of us can imagine. During his time here, Ivar has learned much about our medicine, but I in turn have assimilated much knowledge from him. Ivar has aided our people for many years, and perhaps now we can lend aid to those entrusted into his care."

Ivar watched as Tandin, Gopal, and Selden each reached into the large front pocket of their *gho* and produced several small cloth pouches. Each pouch contained a powder, granule, seed, or crystalline material of distinct color and texture. The men examined the contents of each pouch, inspected the attached labels, and without saying a word, they exchanged several of the cloth pouches. Selden and Gopal, again offering Ivar and Tandin a slight bow, then walked back into the altar room.

Tandin, after asking Ivar for a pen, marked a two-letter abbreviation next to the Choekey inscription that was written on each of the pouch labels:

> **GU** for Gudee, a rare plant-based herb that grows only in the Bumthang district.
>
> **TS** for Tseod, which is a root found in the most fertile soils of western Bhutan.
>
> **PI** for Pipling, an herb produced from a fruit that grows only at low altitude.
>
> **TR** for Thro, an herbal extract from a flower found only in central Bhutan.

LO for *Lobelia nubigena*, the rarest of all the herbs, derived from the seeds of a flowering plant that is unique to a very small area of the central Trongsa district.

Tandin handed the five herb pouches to Ivar, drawing in close before he spoke.

"Although it would appear that it was I who brought you here, in truth I believe it was you who brought me here," Tandin said as he clasped Ivar's hand, his eyes glimmering. "I must now join these faithful in meditation, and while I remain here, please, there are two other temples you must visit.

"Follow the stairs and you will approach Tshemo Lhakhang," Tandin said, pointing to a corridor that led away from the monastery's main complex. "This is the first of the two upper temples. From there you can proceed to Taktsang's highest point, which is Zangto Pelri. Zangto Pelri is named in honor of Guru Rinpoche's heavenly abode, and it too is a very holy shrine. There you will also find pilgrims in meditation and prayer. Go at your own pace, and I will rejoin you a bit later."

Tandin then gripped Ivar's sleeve with both hands and whispered into his ear. "But I beg you, Ivar," Tandin said, his forehead tightly knotted, "do not attempt to enter the Dubkhang. The Dubkhang is the cave below where we now stand, and all access is forbidden. Please, make no attempt to proceed."

"You have my solemn promise," Ivar said with a slow nod of his head, leaving Tandin to meditate with the men who were seated around the altar.

A wooden walkway led Ivar past Tshemo Lhakhang and toward Zangto Pelri, the centuries-old temple built on the highest point of the Tiger's Nest cliff. Ivar sat down on the stairs below the temple's entrance, retrieving a pen and crumpled sheet of stationery from the outer pocket of his backpack.

I can hear him, Andie, Ivar wrote.

I saw him yesterday, but I can hear him today. He has a cry that could startle a dead man, his voice running the length of the river in whichever direction the wind chooses. He is, by the way, a male Pallas's eagle, and as I write to you, he's circling somewhere below me. And trust me, there is a lot of somewhere below me.

I remember touring the fjords as a small child, and later when I first visited the States, I stood with my uncle along the north rim of the Grand Canyon. But when I speak of an assault on the senses, today's experience is singular—beyond any in my life, and well beyond what my written words allow.

Ivar reached down and picked up a small white blossom that had fallen off a nearby vine, tossing the flower over the railing and watching as it drifted past the outer edge of the monastery.

If only you could see the flowering vine that is draped along the ledge next to me, Andie. Its blossoms have teardrop petals that feel of pure silk, and the vine's tendrils have found their way into the mountainside's every crag and crevice. One of the flowers just faded out of sight, and once it floats downward for a half mile or so, it will seed the ground somewhere along the banks of the Paro River.

Taktsang has no healing waters rushing through it, and there are no masses of robed followers filing in and out its door. It has no gilding, no frescoes, no marble columns, and no stained glass. It has neither statues of gold within its halls, nor priceless gems lining its interior. Taktsang is elemental, a nucleus of faith born

> *at the confluence of the earth and the sky. The nest of*
> *the flying tiger and the soul of a nation are perched on*
> *a seemingly endless wall of granite, as if thrust out from*
> *the mountains that are the vital substance of this land.*

Even well into the twenty-first century, international mail to and from Bhutan remains notoriously slow. But there was a sense of urgency in Ivar's letter to Andie, given the day's events. And as Ivar had no access to e-mail or a satellite phone, he kept writing.

> *I am staying at a small home near Taktsang, Andie,*
> *and my hosts are two of the most resolute people I*
> *have ever known. Tandin Lehto and his wife, Dru,*
> *have operated a makeshift medical clinic for years,*
> *and their home, a.k.a. their clinic, is located across*
> *the gorge from Taktsang. Although Tandin's training*
> *is in traditional herbal medicine, he welcomes any*
> *assistance I can offer from "our" medical world. But*
> *today, in fact just minutes ago, I had an experience*
> *that until recently seemed unimaginable. Tandin and*
> *several lifelong colleagues of his, all natively trained,*
> *regularly exchange herbal products indigenous to the*
> *region in which they practice medicine. When you,*
> *Silas, and I spent a morning at Haymarket a few*
> *weeks back, I spoke of an extremely rare plant that is*
> *known to arrest the growth of some malignancies or*
> *even induce tumor regression. With Tandin's invaluable*
> *assistance, I was able to obtain the seeds from this*
> *flowering plant, which . . .*

There was a light in the distance.

Ivar saw a flash of light from across the gorge. He was sure of it.

It was not a hallucination, nor was it a deception created by the invasion of malignant cells into his one remaining eye.

There it was again. And again.

Ivar opened his rucksack and spilled the contents onto the creaking floorboards, rummaging for his headlight. As soon as he located the headlight, Ivar felt a sudden congestion deep within his chest.

Ivar coughed violently, covering his mouth with a spare T-shirt, and he picked up the headlight with his other hand.

Once Ivar had cleared his throat, he turned on the headlight and directed it toward the opposite side of the canyon.

Chapter 29

"Dr. Joel, allow me to introduce *eutigel metos hoem*," Karma said as her eyes followed the soft purple striations that radiated from the center of an ice-blue flower that was growing along the edge of the mountain pass.

"This blossom is also known as the blue poppy," Karma said, "and it is the national flower of Bhutan. I last saw one as a small child, while traveling with my family in the far eastern part of our land. We share an uncommon privilege today, Dr. Joel, as sightings such as this are extraordinarily rare. The blue poppy takes several years to fully grow, reaching at times a full meter in height. Once the poppy flowers, it sheds its seeds and dies shortly thereafter. We must stay on the path so as not to trample the freshly seeded ground.

"Farewell, my beauty," Karma said as she stood, blowing a kiss in the direction of the poppy blossom.

"What's going on?" Myles asked, tapping Joel on the shoulder.

"You're looking at a flower of legend," Joel said to Myles while fumbling with his camera. "You've got a better chance of spotting a woolly mammoth than you do of ever seeing another one of these, and I'll thank you not to stampede the seeds that are trying valiantly to propagate the species."

"The thing looks artificial," Myles said, looking over the top of his sunglasses.

"Weren't you a biology major in college?" Joel asked with a grunt as he looked away from the viewfinder.

"Affirmative. What of it?" Myles asked, still inspecting the flower.

"So after spending your university days studying the natural wonders of our planet," Joel said while adjusting his camera lens, "you stand here today, in the midst of nature's glory, and suggest that someone wandered all the way up here just to plop down a plastic flower—their intent, no doubt, being to pull the wool over the eyes of us green city folk."

"I'm telling you, it looks like one of those dust-collecting fakes that Miss Hamville had next to her desk in junior high," Myles said.

"Who? Do what?" Joel asked.

"Miss Hamville, a.k.a. Hamville the anvil," Myles said. "And trust me, if you ever saw the chassis on that old hen, you'd know how she got tagged with that nickname. Shoulders like a nose guard and a beehive coiffure . . . what a battle ax.

"But back to this poppy business and your passing reference to my undergraduate pursuits," Myles continued, looking squarely at Joel. "My mentor in *college* used to toss the flower in question into the same myth bin as the yeti and other such creatures."

"Far from a myth, as you can now appreciate," Karma said to Myles, watching a pair of large, golden-winged butterflies flop lazily between them. "Through the centuries, the blue poppy was believed by much of the world to be founded only in legend. But many years ago, a visitor from Britain, a scientist, trekked the length of our country, studying and photographing the many plants and animals he encountered along the way. His guide was in fact a schoolmate of my great-grandfather. This British scientist, together with his Sherpa guide, proved to all the world that the blue poppy was as real as the mountains that surround it."

"Did they get any shots of the big hairy guy?" Myles asked in a doubtful tone.

"The Bhutanese yeti is known as the *migoi*, and no, there is no such proof of his existence," Karma said. "But unless I am mistaken, such a creature resides somewhere in your American forest, yes?"

"Bigfoot's his name, and he's an invention of the Pacific Northwest's tourism industry," Joel said as he waved a finger in the air. "One charlatan even dressed his Uncle Seth up in a monkey suit and set him loose in the wilderness, producing 'original footage' and proclaiming to all civilization that he had bona fide proof of the nine-foot-tall beast's existence. It's the biggest crock of tripe I've ever heard tell of. The whole thing is a scam that dry shaves pensioners out of a slice of their retirement as they set out Lewis-and-Clark-like, stalking into the wild in search of their elusive prey.

"But the yeti, or should I say, the *migoi*," Joel continued, his tone softer, "that's a different kettle of fish altogether. Look around you, Myles—this vast, unknown world, an endless expanse in every direction, unexplored and uncharted. Snow, ice, and mountains, followed by deeper snow, thicker ice, and higher mountains. Wouldn't surprise me if old *migoi* had his eyes on us right now."

"Who'd ever have thought a major in mythology and a minor in delusional thinking would give you a leg up when it came to filling out your med school application," Myles said.

"As it took many generations to discover the blue poppy, we must remain both vigilant and patient," Karma said as Joel stuck his tongue out at Myles. "Confirming the existence of the *migoi* may necessitate many more years of search through the wilderness of our most northern districts. Then again, it is conceivable that Dr. Joel is correct. Perhaps Bhutan's yeti lies just ahead, awaiting our arrival."

"May be best if I lead the way," Joel said as he moved past Karma and Myles and entered the clearing that marked the trail's end. "I shall be your shield and armor. Bring him on. I'll . . . my God . . . my God," Joel said, his eyes transfixed on the sight before him. He felt as if every molecule of air had been siphoned out of his lungs.

Myles stopped cold in his tracks, his mouth agape.

"As you can see, there is no yeti to be found," Karma said as she and her two guests now stood along the rim of Paro Gorge.

"But I promise you, the life force before you is unlike any other in all the Himalayas.

"My friends, welcome to Taktsang."

Joel had no idea how far of a drop it was to the Paro River below, and he had no intention of looking down and hazarding a guess. All he saw, his only focus, was the cluster of red-and-white buildings that had seemingly grown out of the mile-high black granite wall that lined the opposite side of the canyon. The elaborately carved gold and bronze turrets that canopied each segment of Taktsang were at eye level, and to Joel they seemed close enough to touch. Against the enormity of nature's cathedral, the several hundred meters' distance between Joel and the monastery's spires had appeared to narrow to a mere arm's length.

"How . . . how did they . . . ," Joel whispered, his voice barely audible.

"Build it?" Karma said with a hint of amusement. "As you might imagine, I have been asked this question many times in the past. Within the monastery lie thirteen holy places, signifying the thirteen steps required for one to attain nirvana, or Buddhahood. Taktsang is the melding of many temples, built over the course of several centuries. The highest points of the complex, to the right of the main building, are known as Tshemo Lhakhang and Zangto Pelri. These two shrines are deeply venerated, and they are latched to the lower temples by a small outer walkway. And although the edifice you see was created by the hands of many faithful men, the monastery's sanctum lies beneath, deep within the cliff rocks. The chamber below Taktsang's wooden temples is known as the Dubkhang, and it is the cave where our Precious Master, having flown to this precipice on the back of a great winged tiger, meditated for three months. Throughout all the mountain kingdoms, this is the most sacred of places. The heavens and the earth become one at Taktsang, and it is the polestar of our land."

"But I just cannot imagine, hundreds of years ago, hauling every nail, bolt, and slat up that sheer rock cliff," Joel said, his eyes still wide with amazement. "And with nothing more than their bare hands. It's just not possible."

Karma looked across the gorge, watching the whorl of prayer flags that waved across one of Taktsang's spires.

> *Blue, green, red, yellow, white.*
> *The five elements.*
> *The five wisdoms.*
> *The five directions.*

"It is all possible, Dr. Joel," Karma said as the coils of bright fabric rippled slowly in the shifting mountain breeze. "It is all possible."

Joel found Martin standing in the middle of a separate clearing about a hundred meters away.

"That is one serious set of eyes you're toting," Joel said, pointed to the enormous pair of binoculars that Martin had slung around his neck.

"I've found every avian species you can name with these babies," Martin said, scanning the length of the gorge.

"I wouldn't bet against you finding the space shuttle with those things," Joel said. "And while you're sweeping the mountaintops, feel free to keep an eye out for Scandinavian scientists of above-average height."

"What do you think I've been doing for the last hour and a half?" Martin said without looking away from the eyepiece. "And as of this moment, no such luck. Before we left the yak herders' tent, I slipped big Baldev a few shekels, trying to get a few more specifics as to where that kid Mance was treated for that kidney prob . . . thing . . . infection."

"Pyelonephritis," Joel said.

"Right. Pyelo . . . whatever," Martin said quickly. "The kid found his way to a hut that has served as a sort of makeshift clinic for years. The herders and mountain dwellers know of it, but the place doesn't exactly have a Park Avenue address. It's somewhere off one of the trails that lead . . . there."

Through his binoculars, Martin could see every detail of the hand-carved wooden turrets that topped Taktsang's roofline. "Now I know what an opium dream looks like," Martin said as he followed the jagged shelves of charcoal granite that hovered over the monastery's edifice.

"I could have told you that without the million-dollar eyewear," Joel said as he took a seat on a nearby tree stump. "By the way, where's Andie?"

Without looking away, Martin pointed to a rock ledge that jutted out beyond the canyon rim. Andie was sitting along the edge, sending out repeated pulses from a strobe light that she was holding in her hand.

"Mind if I ask what that's all about?" Martin asked, now thumbing through the copy of Ali's *Field Guide to Birds of the Eastern Himalayas* that he had brought with him. "She's been over there flashing that light for over half an hour."

"Not sure you want the whole history here," Joel said after he drew in a deep breath, "but suffice it to say that Andie and Ivar bid each other adieu by sending a sort of light signal to each other. It's a very personal thing, and it certainly has more pizazz than the traditional distant wave."

"Such a private exchange of affection is all well and good," Martin said, his guidebook in one hand and binoculars in the other, "but I don't know what she thinks she's going to accomplish by . . . oh no, will ya look at this."

"Look at what?" Joel asked, looking between Martin and Andie.

"My kid's homework," Martin said, setting down his binoculars and thumbing through the pages of his guidebook. "My sixth-grader left part of his history lesson in here. He's always rummaging around my office at home, mixing up papers and making a mess. Great. The old lady will somehow make this my fault."

"Hope he doesn't fail history," Joel said, grinning.

"Weird," Martin said, holding up his son's homework lesson, turning it back and forth in his hand and then jamming the sheets of paper back into the guidebook. "I'm looking for a picture of the whistling thrush, and I find this.

"Anyway, back to Andie," Martin went on, again scanning the horizon. "I'm not sure she'll get very far sending beams of light off into the void."

"And what exactly do you have to show for greasing the chief herder's palm and investing in a set of *Star Wars* zoom-oculars?" Joel asked Martin as he stood up. "For all we know, Baldev-the-mighty rehearsed the entire act with that Mance fella, telling us exactly what we wanted to hear. 'Oh yes, yes, the medicine man you seek, he is here. Indeed he is! For a small fee I shall selectively recall the particulars you require to locate him.' The two of them have already invested your graft money in a few leaves of Himalayan hooch and a keg of that hydrogen fuel elixir they were passing around last evening. So let's not knock 'the low-yield Andie approach' just yet. From her vantage point, she can probably see half the planet. A flash beam from the past might be just enough to catch the man's eye. Provided, of course, he's actually here."

"My friends, please," Karma said as she approached, "a photograph before we proceed any further. From this clearing, we have a perfect image of Taktsang in the background. I can set my camera timer and capture a photo of us all against the Paro Gorge, with the monastery visible along the opposite wall."

Karma set her camera on the same tree stump that Joel had just rested on, and after setting the timer, she hurried over to join the others.

"Say seasick," Karma said.

Everyone laughed as the camera flashed.

"Seasick?" Myles asked. "Where did that come from? Right now, we're probably farther from the ocean than any other point on earth."

"You smiled, did you not?" Karma asked.

Myles grinned and nodded.

"Works every time," Karma said.

"So let's see it," Martin said, impatiently.

Karma picked up her camera and retrieved the image. As she was about to show the photo to Martin, something in the right upper corner of the frame caught her attention. Karma zoomed in and out, slowly moving the camera closer to her face.

"Andie," Karma said calmly.

"C'mon, Karma, enough suspense," Martin said, snapping his fingers. "Let me have a look."

"Do we need to take another?" Andie asked as she picked up her knapsack.

"Andie," Karma repeated, "you need to see this."

"You and Andie don't have to try and look good in photographs," Martin said to Karma. "But I do, and I want to frame this one and put it in my corporate office. If I look that bad, we can take a couple more. Trust me, you cannot hurt my feelings."

Karma now stood with the camera only a few inches from her face.

"*Ann-diee*," Karma said again, her deliberate tone catching everyone off guard.

As Karma handed Andie the camera, she pointed to a bright flash of light in the upper corner of the picture, zooming in and out several times.

"That is not the sun's reflection," Karma said. "Nor is it the camera flash."

"It is from Taktsang."

All at once, everyone turned around and looked across Paro Gorge. A moment later, four crisp beams of light—short, short, long, short—appeared beneath a stairway that led to the highest point of the monastery.

Chapter 30

Neither Ivar nor any of his classmates would likely ever forget the day they were first introduced to Dr. William Gitan.

Dr. Gitan, a native of the civil war–torn hinterlands of Guatemala, was the chief of cardiac surgery at one of the Harvard teaching hospitals. As he did at the beginning of every academic year, Dr. Gitan delivered the last in a series of introductory lectures to the first-year medical students. And although he had the body habitus of a pear and stood no more than five foot three, Dr. Gitan had the command of his surroundings comparable to that of an undefeated heavyweight circling an opponent thirty seconds after the opening bell. Dr. Gitan opened his lecture with a film showing a seventy-four-year-old patient undergoing an aortic valve replacement, and then followed with a segment on a teenager receiving a heart transplant. This was all pretty heavy stuff for a bunch of early twenty-somethings who didn't know the difference between a Band-Aid and a bypass, and predictably, all gathered were awed and inspired by the chief surgeon's presentation.

But what Ivar remembered most was Dr. Gitan introducing the first-year class to a precept that was steeped in the wisdom of untold generations of clinicians.

Specifically, Dr. Gitan introduced his students to the principle of *KISS*.

It was as if those deep, penetrating, blue eyes were zeroing in only on Ivar—though he was sure every student felt the same way—as Dr. Gitan's Latin-accented intonation of the words *keep it simple stupid* resonated between the two halves of Ivar's brain.

Keep it simple.

That mantra became imprinted into the deepest recess of Ivar's mind.

Complexity only serves to obscure and deceive, implored the professor.

At every turn, simplicity.

Another volley of lights from the opposite side of the gorge put to rest any last doubt as to what Ivar had seen.

This was no mirage.

Without making a sound, Ivar exited the monastery, leaving behind everything except the letter he had been writing and the headlight he had clutched in his hand. Ivar said nothing to Tandin, who was by nature an alarmist and easily rattled by any unforeseen circumstance. Besides, he would return later and introduce Tandin to his dear friend who had come thousands of miles just to visit Bhutan.

He wouldn't be long.

The access trail to Taktsang winds along the side of Paro Gorge, coursing off in any number of directions along the opposite wall. Ivar passed under the veil of a ribbon-narrow waterfall that was at least three hundred meters in height, the waterfall's spray as welcome as a cold canteen in the desert. Ivar continued to click his headlight on and off, following the blips as they appeared haphazardly along the far rim. The gap between him and Andie was considerable but narrowing all the while.

Ivar didn't know which was more responsible for fueling his effort up the switchback footpath—some subconscious reserve of internal energy, or the sense of guilt he felt for making Andie travel halfway around the world just to chase him down with a penlight.

But a minute later, none of that really mattered.

Ivar stopped in his tracks, spun 360 degrees, and collapsed in a heap. His chest heaved, and a moment later, a torrent of blood fired like a projectile from the base of his left bronchial tube.

Ivar felt no pain, and the pounding in his chest actually seemed to ease.

He was breathing slower now, his breaths shallow and quiet.

It doesn't get much simpler than this.

So much in medicine, Ivar knew, was uncertain—teachings and practice based on little more than the traditions and experiences of the generation that preceded you. In truth, much of what the medical community embraced was nothing short of downright drivel.

But for whatever reason, Ivar never doubted the commonly held belief that in the setting of multiple internal organ failure, one's ability to hear was the most enduring of all the human senses. It was, after all, a well-known fact that hearing was the last sense to be blunted by the induction of general anesthesia.

One could therefore easily conclude that an individual's hearing would be the last of the five senses to fade when the final curtain, at last, began to descend.

And there was an undeniable sense of morbid justice to the whole concept.

Compared to the other senses, the human ear was, beyond any doubt, accorded the narrowest margin for error.

The ear could not squint.

The ear could not stare.

The ear could not luxuriate in the flavor of an exotic spice, or discover a passing scent by pulling in another deep breath of air.

The ear could not take its time and find its way through a darkened room.

One's auditory sense was far less forgiving, forever compelled to perform on a more exacting stage.

There was a sound, and then the sound was gone. And it was gone forever.

The human ear, quite simply, could not cheat.

So perhaps it was true that like the stern of a foundering ship, one's capacity to hear was the last part to vanish beneath the surf, as if by the laws of nature, the human ear had earned the right to savor any last hurrah before waving a final surrender.

And now, the sounds that circled in the air above Ivar were impossibly clear.

The song that flowed from Taktsang's great room was pure poetry, its liquid surrounding Ivar as he lay motionless on the edge of the towering cliff. Ivar could hear the deep timbre of Tandin's voice weaving through the voices of the others who were chanting around the monastery's main altar. Prayer flags strung along the roofline brushed against the monastery's dome, their ripple growing louder, and then softer, and then louder again.

The sounds were all so near, so flawless, so vibrant.

So alive.

Then suddenly, from the opposite direction, Ivar heard a rustling noise, faint at first but its pace quickening.

Ivar did not even try to open his eyes.

With the strength he had left, Ivar reached into the outer pocket of his sweatshirt and pulled out the letter he had been writing, holding it up in the direction of the approaching footsteps.

"You saved me the postage, *ngay drogmo.*"

CHAPTER 31

Andie took the letter, fell to the ground, and pressed her lips as hard as she could against Ivar's swollen face.

"It's good to see you too," Ivar said, letting his arm drape across Andie's shoulder.

Andie took off her jacket and used it as a cushion behind Ivar's head.

"Tell me you're not alone," Ivar said through a weak cough.

Andie smiled and shook her head.

Ivar forced one eye open, looking up the trail as Andie swept her palm across his forehead. He saw no one.

"It looks to me like those giant slalom legs haven't lost any of their spring," Ivar said as he struggled to sit up.

"Slow and easy, Professor," Andie said, wiping the icy sweat from Ivar's brow. "They'll be along soon enough."

Andie assisted Ivar as he took a couple of slow sips from her canteen.

"They?" Ivar asked, regaining some of his voice.

"Myles, to start with," Andie said.

"I didn't know he owned a passport," Ivar said after clearing his throat.

"It had a coat of dust on it, along with a bunch of empty pages between the covers," Andie said as she capped the water bottle. "But still valid, believe it or not. So we did manage to load Myles onto the plane."

"And the rest of 'we'?" Ivar asked.

"Dr. Morgan, along with your partner in all things avian," Andie said.

"I thought I spotted a cloud of Cuban smoke a while ago," Ivar said, struggling to draw in a breath. "And the four of you traveling all the way here . . . finding this place . . . being here now . . ." Ivar fell back and squeezed his eyes shut.

"Andie, I never wanted this," Ivar said faintly. "I cannot imagine what it took for you to get to Bhutan to find me. Andie, you need to know something. There are things I must tell you . . ." Ivar was trembling, his breaths becoming progressively more shallow.

"Slow and easy, Professor," Andie repeated as she again pulled Ivar close. "Slow and easy." After letting a long moment pass, she said, "Besides, your disappearing act wasn't all that good. After a round of breaking and entering, followed by computer hacking, bio waste sifting, nine thousand air miles, and an evening with a tribe of your friendly neighborhood yak herders, finding you was no problem at all."

"So if Joel is wandering around puffing dark fumes into the air, I suppose Martin is out there somewhere in search of the black-necked crane," Ivar said, looking up into the sky.

"The bird of which you speak is known as the *thrung thrung*," Karma said, having appeared out of nowhere. "The *thrung thrung* is seen only during the autumn months, along the high mountain valleys, farther to the east."

Andie sat up, reached out, and grasped Karma's hand.

"*Kuzuzangpo-la,*" Karma said as she offered Ivar a slight bow. "*Ngiming Karmaing.*"

"*Chhoe gadebe yoe?*" Ivar said in return.

"I am quite fine today, Dr. Ivar," Karma said as she sat down. "Thank you, I am quite fine indeed. And if I may."

Karma produced a thermos and three small bowls from a satchel that she had strapped around one shoulder. "Please, some butter tea," she said, a trail of steam rising from the bowls as she poured. "This shall ease our pace and awaken our thoughts. Butter tea stirs the heart and mind, yet serves to quell one's emotions," Karma said as she sipped from her bowl. "And today, we drink also to celebrate the meeting of new friends and the rejoining of old ones. The others are finding our windy paths a bit arduous, but please do not worry. They shall find their way, and soon we will all be gathered."

"The trail that leads to the monastery, Karma," Ivar said, again straining to speak. "Do you see anyone heading this way?"

Karma looked along the length of the trail that led to Taktsang, an early-afternoon fog shrouding some parts of path.

"I see no one, Dr. Ivar," Karma said.

"Tandin," Ivar said after drawing in another deep breath.

"Who?" Andie asked, not letting on that she knew who this man was.

"I have been staying in the home of a man by the name of Tandin Lehto," Ivar said through a spasm of cough. "Tandin and his wife, Dru . . . their house has been my home since I arrived in Bhutan a few weeks ago. Their home has also doubled as a medical clinic for years. These two, they are one remarkable couple. The problem is that right now Tandin . . . Tandin is still at Taktsang. I visited the monastery with him earlier today, and when I left just a while ago, he was meditating with the others in one of the temples. Tandin . . ."

"I believe I see the cause of your concern," Karma said, placing her hand on Ivar's shoulder. "Tandin's delay in returning will likely cause distress with his family, as doubtlessly people in need continue to arrive at their dwelling."

Ivar nodded, unable to speak.

"The solution here is quite simple," Karma said as she poured more butter tea. "I shall go and retrieve Tandin, and as the hour is late, I will remain at the monastery for the night. The walking trail that leads to and from Taktsang is treacherous after dark, but do not fret. I will bring Tandin back to his home at morning's first light."

"*Kadinchhey-la,* Karma," Ivar said.

"*Ta do-ran-sha,*" Karma said as she stood to leave. "As there is still adequate light, it is best I depart now. You mentioned, Dr. Ivar, that Tandin and Dru's dwelling is near. Hence, I am sure our two Sherpa guides can set up camp there. And should Dru need assistance this evening, no doubt Dr. Joel can lend aid."

"And, Karma," Ivar said, again clearing his throat, "if I could ask another favor. Earlier, when I hurried away to find Andie, I accidently left my belongings somewhere near the walkway that leads to the upper temples. It's a small gray knapsack, and I'm sure you'll find it there. There is not much in it . . . some papers, an extra shirt, a few medications, some herbs that Tandin gave me. If you could bring the knapsack back with you when you return with Tandin, I would be very grateful."

"Yes, yes, Karma, if you could bring back the rucksack," Andie said quickly, sounding somewhat alarmed. "Our friend at times loses track of his . . . medications."

"Of course," Karma said. "It would be my pleasure."

"Karma," Andie said as she refilled the third bowl with some fresh tea. "The butter tea awaits your return. And so do we."

Karma waved good-bye and disappeared into the low clouds that hung along the rim of the canyon.

As Andie looked back at Ivar, she noticed a large blotch of dark blood staining the base of a nearby tree.

"You sounded a little troubled," Ivar said, again prying open one eye.

Andie gave Ivar a blank stare.

"My medications," Ivar said. "The ones I left back at the monastery."

Andie remained expressionless.

"In my knapsack," Ivar said, holding Andie's gaze with his one open eye. "You seemed startled to learn that I carelessly misplaced my medications."

"You're bleeding," Andie said, her voice breaking slightly.

"And there isn't a medication in the world capable of fixing that."

"You're bleeding," Andie repeated, her jaw tight.

"So let's not concern ourselves over a couple of lost pills."

"Son of a bitch, Ivar, you're bleeding! You're bleeding out right in front of me. You need a doctor, Ivar. It's not too late. We can get you back to where you can be helped. We can."

"I saw your reaction when I mentioned what was in my knapsack, Andie. You practically jumped. I saw the look on your face, and I've only got half an eye to see with. Is that why you came here, because of what I'm carrying with me? Is that why you're here?"

"No!" Andie shouted. "Don't say that. Don't you ever say that!"

"What exactly do you think I was carrying that's so important?" Ivar asked, finding more strength in his voice. "Something I brought from home, or something I found here?"

Andie stood motionless, staring into the one eye that Ivar was struggling to keep open.

"Did we cross to the other side, Andie?" Ivar asked, his head starting to shake. "Is there something you came here to tell me, or is there something you came here to bring home with you?"

Andie held Ivar's gaze, not saying a word.

"Andie?"

"You," Andie said after a long pause, trying to keep a grip on her emotions.

"I can still see you, Andie, and I would like to know, did we make it to the other side?"

"I came here to bring you home," Andie said softly, looking up the trail for a quick moment. "We all came here to bring you . . ."

Andie heard a soft thud as Ivar let himself drop back into the tall grass. Andie fell on the ground next to Ivar and held him as tightly as she could.

Ivar pulled Andie in with both arms, pressing her toward him with whatever strength he had left.

When Andie took her bandana and cleared the drops of cold mist that had collected between them, Ivar beamed like a child as he silently mouthed the words: *"I love you, Andie Lynn."*

Through the fog that was closing in around them, Andie heard a voice—unmistakably Myles's voice—calling out Ivar's name.

Andie closed her eyes and cradled Ivar's head in her arms.

"'Weathered faces,'" she whispered.

"'Weathered faces . . .'"

"'Weathered faces lined in pain are soothed beneath the artist's loving hand.'"

CHAPTER 32

Against the dense moonlight that filtered through Taktsang, thin coils of smoke rose from the string of lighted butter lamps that lined the monastery's main altar.

Karma sat motionless, absent to everyone and everything around her.

"Meditation is cognition purified," a lama had instructed Karma some years earlier. *"As a skill, it must be refined, and as with the archer's aim, perfected by reiteration."*

With each passing hour, Karma's heart slowed. Her breathing became imperceptible.

"There is only here, there is only now." The master's wisdom was still vibrant in her mind.

"The past is an encumbrance—a collage of contorted memories."

As her senses became unaware, her consciousness became fully aware.

"One's future is the ultimate obscurity. When fully distilled, it is a hundred parts fear for every one part hope."

Within, all had slowed.

Within, all had eased.

"Discharge all conflict, expel all anguish."

Her energy was singular.

Her mind, robust.

"Dispel every negative thought. Subdue every emotional charge."

There is only here. There is only now.

"Isolate yourself from all sensation. Contemplate. Concentrate."

"Your mind is not your master. You alone are sovereign . . ."

The cymbals. Karma heard the cymbals.

She knew this sound, and she knew its origin.

The clash of the cymbals may have been low and faraway, but to Karma it had the boom of a carillon.

Karma did not have her lama master's mental fortitude.

She could not will away the sound she was hearing.

The chime in the distance was the first incantation of a *puja*—the yearlong ceremony that solemnizes the passage from life to death to life again.

Karma knew this music—its accent, its lament, its certainty.

She knew the first tones of a *puja,* and she knew its source.

And Karma now knew that Dr. Ivar Nielsen had left this world.

Chapter 33

"The incantation you heard last evening, you have no doubt as to its origin?" Tandin asked Karma, averting his gaze.

Making every attempt to conceal his emotions, Tandin hesitated for a minute or two before looking up again at Karma. Karma handed Tandin her scarf as she shook her head.

"During my childhood, I learned the art of lip reading," Tandin said, wiping his eyes. "Not by volition, mind you. Sometime prior to my ninth birthday, an affliction claimed some of my hearing, so I was left with little choice. When face-to-face, I can negotiate conversations quite well. But more distant sounds, such as music, are just that . . . distant.

"Last evening, after hours of meditation, I fell into a deep sleep on the floor of one of the upper temples," Tandin said, pointing to the adjoining walkway. "I heard not a single note— no cymbal, no drum, no melody of any sort. As with every night, last night was, for me, largely silent.

"Although Ivar and I met barely a month ago, it was as if we had known each other our entire lives," Tandin said as Karma led him back into Taktsang's main temple. "Ivar knew of our plight here, with so little to aid the sick and infirm. Dru and I, we did all we could, but for many ailments, our resources are limited. For many years, Dr. Ivar supplied us. And Ivar, his time here was so brief. With his heart and hands and intellect, Dr. Ivar adopted Bhutan, which to him was surely an alien land. And now that he is gone, who shall follow?

"This is why I journey to Taktsang," Tandin said, shaking his head. "Weakness. This is exactly what I said to Ivar, just yesterday, in this very place. My weakness of mind and feebleness of spirit are all pervasive, and in trying times such as these, they become yet more transparent. You listen now to the groans of a wallowing old man, as I stand here running over with self-pity and absorbed in my own sorrow. If ever there was a time to consider others . . ."

"Sir, if I am not mistaken, I believe this is yours," said the man who limped toward Tandin and Karma. "I was searching for the quietest of places, and in so doing I stumbled upon this as I descended the upper temple's stairway. If my recall is correct, I saw you carrying this around your shoulder last evening."

In the man's trembling hand was Ivar's tattered knapsack.

"Indeed, that is mine," Tandin said, throwing his arms into the air. *"Rog nang-wa tujay-chay* . . . my thanks for your assistance."

"Think nothing of it," said the man as he offered a slight bow.

"Please, allow me," Karma said to Tandin, taking the knapsack and securing it over her back. "You are loaded down with enough burden. Dru no doubt needs you now more than ever, with all that has transpired over these past hours. Please, go on without me. I will be along soon.

"Thank you again, sir, for your kindness," Karma said as she watched the elderly man shuffle down the hallway.

The man waved a hand without turning around.

"Did you see him?" Tandin asked Karma, looking in the direction of the stranger who had returned Ivar's property. "His features are grotesque, and as he waved back, you could see that he was missing several fingers. Such a crippled man, yet he considers his fellows before himself."

Chapter 34

"I heard someone call this place the Temple of Phorbu," Drapche said to Narayan as he surveyed the spare temple room. "And look what we have front and center, just like the travel agent told me."

Drapche approached the three-bladed dagger that was housed in the *chorten* that stood in the middle of one of Taktsang's temple rooms.

"The much-celebrated three-sided *phurba*," Drapche said, a glint in his eye as he stared at the weapon. "Legend tells that this was the instrument used to impale a whole cadre of local demons. Strange thing, though. I don't see a single speck of devil's blood on any of the three edges. Take a look with me here, partner. What do you see?"

Narayan stood as rigid as a statue, sweat pouring off his brow.

"I'll show you who ends up on the business end of the blade," Drapche said to himself, running the pad of his thumb along one edge of the dagger.

"You did real good," Drapche said, without looking up at Narayan. "You actually convinced all these wandering saints that I belong in here. Looks to me like they all bought into our sanctimonious little act, with you entering into a deep muse with the rest of the pilgrims."

From a small window on the opposite side of the room, Drapche spotted Karma walking along an adjoining passageway. Drapche stood on his toes and craned his neck, leering at Karma as she spoke in a soft voice to a small group of women who were standing nearby.

"Now there's a pilgrim I could get real cozy with," Drapche said, his eyes narrow. "Gotta admit, there's some seriously tight tush in this country. Kind of tragic, if you think about it—that little lass sending her grandpa on his way back home, and here she is, left behind with you and me and the rest of the saintly types. On the one hand, it's kind of a pity, erasing talent like that from the map. On the other hand, well, our devices are as painless as they are expeditious."

"Drapche, these . . . these people here in the monastery. Look at them," Narayan sputtered, speaking for the first time. "They bear the face of innocence. There are but a few souls here, so can we not clear the premises first and then proceed with your plan? What reason is there to—"

Before Narayan had completed the sentence, Drapche had moved to within inches of his face.

"There is no window-shopping here, chicken shit," Drapche spat, Narayan flinching as a waft of acrid air blew past him. "It's zero hour, and for anyone unfortunate enough to be stalking around in here, it's guilt by association, plain and simple. You think for a minute any of these imps ever bothered to meditate a little deeper after their king proscribed our entire bloodline to that rat infested pit? No Nepali with half a set of balls would feel an ounce of guilt for liquidating anyone within pissing distance of this place. *They're* the ones who should feel pangs of guilt. They assassinated our culture, stripping us of any last shred of dignity. They took our land, our lives, our fortune, our future."

Drapche glared at Narayan as he peeled the rucksack off his back. The package landed on the floor with a thud.

Narayan's blood jumped.

"Rest easy. It's all in the timing," Drapche said with unnerving calm. "Or should I say, it's all in the timer.

"Even the Chinese masters refer to this chemical combination as a 'volatile slurry,'" Drapche continued, looking down at the floor. "Personally, I prefer the term 'water gel.' That has a nice harmony to it, and it's rather innocuous sounding, don't you think? Just a blend of ammonium nitrate, a little borax, some guar gum, and a bit of fresh water from a nearby mountain stream. And oh yes, a generous dash of trinitrotoluene."

Drapche picked up the explosive and set it next to the three-sided dagger. "*They're* the barbarians, and *they're* expendable," he said, his eyes bearing down on Narayan. "Taktsang, this Tiger's Nest, a thousand years of myth and legend, vaporized in one breath. That's the price their sovereign pays. That's the price *they all* pay.

"Walk," Drapche said evenly. "Just like I told you while we were chatting over tea back there in Paro, you've got ten minutes. Ten. That's all the time in the world. So go back into the altar room, offer anyone who's in there your deepest respects, and then walk out that door. This is no time to attract any kind of attention to yourself, so don't scamper out of there like your ass is on fire. You'll get to see the main event; that much I can promise you. And if you have time on your way down the stairs, you can even practice looking real shocked about what you just witnessed. You know, rehearsing the moaning and grieving and all the carrying on that go along with such unforeseen catastrophes. And no need to fret about me. You and I, we'll meet up soon enough.

"One day soon, you'll be the stuff of legend," Drapche said as a sharp metallic click echoed across the room. "Did you hear something?" Drapche asked, cocking his head as he looked at Narayan.

Narayan lurched forward, his eyes darting toward the ceiling, and then toward the doorway, and then toward the window. And then Narayan saw Drapche's stubbled hand on top of the rucksack.

"Oh, did I say minutes?" Drapche said, a broad grin spreading slowly across his face.

Ten . . . nine . . . eight . . . seven . . .

"Apologies, Na-RAY-an." The arc across Drapche's forehead was now a blazing, fiery red sash. "I meant seconds."

Four . . . three . . . two . . .

"No, Drapche! No!" screamed Narayan as he ran toward the doorway. "No!"

Chapter 35

A massive fireball erupted from the center of Taktsang.

The monastery's central cupola flew into the air, cartwheeling up the black granite wall and disintegrating seconds later into shards of flaming debris. Taktsang's wooden façade sheared away from the foundation with a low, tearing sound, sending pieces of burning rubble tumbling into the Paro River below.

The deafening blast silenced the cries of anyone who screamed.

Several hundred meters away, Andie and Joel ran to the edge of the canyon. There they saw Tandin, and only Tandin, running along the final switchback.

"No. God, no," Andie said as the outer wall of the main temple tore free from its base, sending immense slabs of rock thundering toward the valley floor.

There were no distant voices or shrieks of pain or cries for help.

"My God, no, please . . . Karma," Joel said, watching billows of black smoke stream into the sky. Columns of dark ash began to rain down into the depths of Paro Valley.

"Karma!" Joel yelled, his shouts echoing through the canyon. "Karma! Karma! Karma!"

CHAPTER 36

Martin looked up into the sky, following the path of a second helicopter as it passed overhead and then landed in an open field just above Dru and Tandin's hut.

"That's either the military or the media," Martin said as Joel approached, "and if that's another army chopper, you won't have to wait more than five minutes before the press arrives. BBC, Reuters, CNN, they'll be tripping over each other trying to be the first to plaster this story onto their marquee."

"Do you see that procession across the way?" Joel asked, pointing to the line of police and army officers who were walking single file along the mountain path that led toward Taktsang. "I know they have to send in a search and rescue team, but the foundation of that building sits on a razor-thin ledge. In the next second, what's left of that monastery could slide off the cliff and into the river. Anyone setting foot in there is only going to compound this catastrophe."

Martin looked toward the gathering of uniformed officials who were huddled together in a nearby clearing. "You hear anything while you were up there?" he asked Joel. "All that brass milling around . . . they have any idea as to what just happened?"

"Not a clue, from what I take," Joel said. "Remember, not so long ago this was a closed country, so no military honcho is going to spill anything in the way of specifics to some Yankee stranger. Tandin told me that they were asking him all kinds of questions—had he seen anybody or anything unusual, did he hear any suspicious conversations, that sort of thing. Tandin, the poor man, he's shell-shocked. And the tall guy you see standing over there is from Bhutan's foreign ministry. He asked to see our passports and visas—very polite and professional, speaks perfect English. He did tell me that the royal family's personal envoy will do a flyover later today and report all he sees directly to the king. He also told me that the explosion was heard all the way back in Thimphu."

Joel and Martin heard a sharp ripping sound as a charred section of the monastery's roofline buckled inward. The upper eave of a turret, attached to the collapsing roof beam by what appeared to be no more than a thread, began to swing like a pendulum as it slammed against the cliff side.

"Any idea . . ." Martin said, pausing as he stared down into the canyon. "Do they have any idea as to how many were in the monastery?"

Joel pursed his lips and shook his head. "I put that same question to that official from the foreign ministry. He really doesn't know, Martin. He of course wanted to know if we had seen anything that might be helpful in their investigation, and I told him that all we heard was an ear-splitting boom, and all we saw was the monastery blown to bits. The man told me that he was briefed by the officers who interviewed anyone who left Taktsang earlier today, including Tandin. Tandin is certain that besides Karma and a couple other women, two men were left behind. One of the men was quite young, and the other middle-aged or older. There may have been others inside as well, but there's no way to know for sure."

"Is there any chance at all?" Martin asked without looking up at Joel. "I mean, how many disasters, natural or otherwise, have you seen in your career? You must know of rescue teams that found survivors after sifting through the rubble. I'm sure you've seen victims pulled from the wreckage before. Any chance . . ."

"Not after a blast like that," Joel said in a thin voice. "The force generated by a detonation of that magnitude, along the side of a mountain, that rescue team won't find so much as a molar up there. And let's face it, if you fall more than fifty feet, you might as well fall a mile. It was all over before you could blink, so I guess that's one bit of very cold comfort. I'm just praying that the search and rescue operation doesn't become part of the day's statistics."

A large wooden column, glowing red at one end and a mangle of smoldering char at the other, broke free from the base of Taktsang. The girder hurtled into the canyon as if it were a launched projectile, a stream of black smoke trailing off as it accelerated toward the valley floor.

"Land of the Peaceful Dragon," Joel said under his breath.

"Not this day."

"These are called *manidhars*," Andie said, walking past Joel and Martin with an armload of frayed sheets of thin yellow-and-red fabric. "Dru gave them to me. She says *manidhars* are the prayer flags flown to honor loved ones who have passed, and they're supposed to be paraded in batches of 108, something about invoking 'an immeasurable level of compassion to the deceased.' And check this out. The *manidhar* can only be flown on a precipice high above a river. So at least we've got one thing going for us.

"I haven't the first idea what this will accomplish," Andie said, her eyes welling as she began to string one of the flags onto the branch of a juniper tree. "But for me, it's either hang a stack of these beat-up old flags or go straight out of my . . ."

Andie gasped, gesturing for Joel and Martin to walk toward her.

Standing at the edge of the canyon, Andie, Joel, and Martin saw thousands of prayer flags hanging from the trees that lined both sides of the gorge.

"The prayers will waft with the wind." Andie recalled what Dru had just told her. *"And be carried by the perpetually flowing waters on their long and winding journey."*

"Here, let me help," Myles said, walking full stride past Andie and whipping one of the flags off Andie's shoulder. "Now, doesn't that make us all feel better," Myles said, his voice unsteady as he wrapped the prayer flag around the lower branch of an evergreen. "Only 107 more to go."

"Easy, Myles," Joel said, his tone heavy. "It's safe to say that it won't take anything more going wrong to make this one seriously piss-poor week, and you going daft on us isn't going to help anything or anybody. Like the rest of us, you need to rein it in and try to think as clearly as possible."

"Think?" Myles said, pulling another *manidhar* away from Andie. "Let me tell you what I *think*, Joel. Let me tell you *all* what I think. I think Ivar is dead. I think Karma is dead. I think other innocent people who we will never know are dead. I think a sacred shrine has been blown to smithereens. And I think a country that is supposedly the most tranquil place on the planet may well be under siege by homicidal zealots. And you know what else I think, Joel? You know what else I think? Nothing, that's what I think. I'm thinking about nothing because that's what I've got. *Nothing.* A lifetime of irreplaceable research just got incinerated, and as we stand here admiring the view, said research is on its was up into the clouds. Or maybe the better part of what was in Ivar's bird book latched onto some gravity and is now floating downstream. Hey, Geronimo!" Myles yelled into the canyon as loud as he could, "what you got down there?

"*That* is what I think. Now I don't know about any of you," Myles went on, pointing over his shoulder at the flaming debris that was draped across the base of the monastery, "but this blatant act of terrorism was plenty enough to fill my cataclysmic event quota for one lifetime."

"Stop," Andie said, yanking the *manidhar* back out of Myles's hand. "Stop it right now. You don't have the luxury of going bats on us, Myles. Imagine how Karma's family will feel when they get word about what just happened up here. The why of what happened here today . . . I'm the last person on earth to try and answer that question. And Ivar," Andie hesitated for a moment, swallowing hard, "we all knew that Ivar was one very sick man before we ever left Boston to come here. None of us expected Ivar to die right in front of us, but he did, and we all got to be with him when he passed. And he heard it from you, Myles: '*You did it, Professor. You did it.*'

"That was the last he heard. That was the last he knew," Andie went on, her voice tremulous. "We were with him, Myles. We were with him when he left, and for that, we are all blessed."

Myles took a step forward and looked along the length of Paro Gorge, its walls a sea of waving color. *Poppy jasper . . . its swirls of black reminiscent of tempest clouds.*

"Ivar's records mirror his research," Myles said eventually, having been lost in thought while staring down into the gorge. "They are peerless, impeccable. But those notes he carried with him all the time, they were his center. They were his orb. It was where he composed. It was where his craft came to life. And remember, all of us, meaning anyone and everyone involved in a given stage of research, are blinded. There is no way to pry the codes out of some computer chip. A backup? Sure, maybe, *somewhere.*

"Look, I know I'm not the first one in the door on a lot of things," Myles said, now pacing, "but I do get all this Bhutan business. Ivar's secret third-world life, in absentia for years, and then experiencing it all firsthand during his final days. With whatever time he had left, Ivar wanted to answer a life's calling in a land far from home. No doubt Ivar figured that one way or another, we would get all his personal effects, including his bird book and notes that contained all the trial codes. That way, we'd all be in the dark until the last possible moment. Everyone would remain blinded, and therefore every research phase would remain bias-free. And no one, at any point, would have access to the answer sheet.

"No access, all right," Myles continued as fragments of another wooden beam tumbled into the gorge and out of sight. "This mountaintop apocalypse never quite figured into Ivar's equation. Like the people we lost and the peace this country lost, those codes are gone for good."

"Maybe Tandin knows something that can help us," Andie said, looking at Myles and pausing before she spoke. "He's been working with Ivar day and night, and Ivar's been living under his roof for the past month. We all know the two of them were very close, Myles. And Tandin certainly knows more about Ivar's final weeks than anyone."

"Tandin?" Myles asked, shooting Andie a withered look. "What on earth do you expect Tandin to tell us? What good will it do talking to . . ." Myles edged closer to Andie, his face contorted. "Don't," Myles said, the muscles along one side of his face beginning to quiver. "Do *not* start in with your alternative theory about why Ivar came here, Andie. I don't want to hear it. There may be reasons we'll never understand . . . him choosing a place halfway around the world to donate his time. But don't try and tell me that Ivar came here in search of some fucking mountain weed, chasing around for a particular flower or stem that was going to supplant twenty years of peerless research. Tandin can't help us. I feel bad for Tandin, just like you do. But unless he can show me a long list of rock stars and Roman emperors, he can't help one damn bit."

Martin felt his limbs go numb. "What did you say?" he asked after a long pause, his voice barely audible as he looked over at Myles.

"I said Tandin can't help," Myles said, his tone caustic.

"No, not that," Martin said, his voice now trembling. "The Romans. What did you say about the Romans . . . the emperors?"

"I said . . . forget it," Myles answered. "Under the circumstances, it doesn't matter. Nothing really matters at this point."

As Myles pressed his eyes shut, he heard a dull thud at his feet. Myles opened his eyes and found Martin rummaging through the satchel that he had just dropped onto the ground.

"What are you doing?" Myles asked.

Myles then looked down at the copy of Ali's *Field Guide to the Birds of the Eastern Himalayas* that Martin was holding in his hand.

"I don't need your goddam bird book, Martin," Myles said.

"It's not my book," Martin said, his hands shaking as he began flipping through the pages of the guidebook.

"Then whose is it?" Myles asked.

"Ivar's," Martin said.

"Ivar's?"

"Yes, Ivar's."

"It's . . . how . . ." Myles said frantically, giving Martin a fierce look as he grabbed the book and began rifling through the pages.

"I thought . . . I . . . I . . . I thought it was Marty's homework," Martin said once Myles had pulled the genetic formula sheets out from between the pages of the birding book. "I was looking for a reference on one of the thrushes yesterday, and I saw those scraps of paper. I had no idea what they were. I figured my son Marty had put them in there by accident."

Joel, whose face was now white, looked back and forth repeatedly between Martin and Myles.

"That's Ivar's book?" Andie asked through the hand that was covering her mouth. "How did you get Ivar's book?"

"I have no idea," Martin said with both hands pressed on top of his head. "I have no . . ."

Martin stopped himself, looking straight up into the sky. "The power outage," he said, taking the field guide out of Myles's hand and opening the front cover. "I was at Ivar's lab that night early last month when the power went out. That's when he gave me a stack of birding books. They were all on top of his desk. I was fumbling around in the dark and dropped one of the books into Ivar's desk drawer, and I must have pulled out a different one by accident. Before we left that night, I remember Ivar looking into that drawer with a flashlight and then locking it. He would have never known that I had taken the wrong book by mistake."

Myles was ignoring the conversation going on around him, entranced by the sheets of paper he was holding in his hand.

"But Stacey turned Ivar's office upside down," Joel said, finding his voice after at least a full minute had passed. "When she searched through Ivar's desk, she would have found—"

"A book with my initials on it," Martin interrupted, showing Joel the initials IN written on the inside cover of the book he was holding. "When she unlocked Ivar's desk drawer, which I'm sure she did, Stacey would have found a birding guide with the initials

MNP on the inside cover. Ivar and I trade texts all the time, and a book with my initials on the cover would not ring any alarm bells. There are probably others in that drawer with my initials on them. I never in a million years would have thought that my book and Ivar's could have gotten switched around like that. And those notes . . . they looked like my kid's history lesson or something."

"History lesson?" Myles asked, clearly suspicious as he waved the sheets of paper in the air. "You thought this was a history lesson? Nothing else ever crossed your mind? And this 'switch' you mention . . . totally an accident?"

"No, nothing else crossed my mind," Martin said, giving Myles a stern look. "And given your present state of mind and what you've been through in the past few hours, Myles, I'll disregard that last inference. In case you didn't know it, I peddle toupees and fake tits for a living. How the hell was I supposed to know that Hadrian and Tiberius had anything to do with your research? 'Switch?' I'll chalk that up as your feeble attempt at humor."

Across the gorge, a member of the search and rescue team was rappelling onto the upper part of the temple complex from a cliff ledge about two hundred meters above Taktsang. Suspended from a belay rope, the officer was shouting down to the other rescuers who were approaching what was left of the lowermost section of the monastery. Belches of smoke were spewing out of every temple room.

"Look at those pages you're holding, Myles, and just be glad they're in your hand and not over there," Martin said, pointing over his shoulder, toward Taktsang.

"It looks like rock and roll is here to stay," Joel said, his eyes fixed on the person descending the mountain cliff.

"And so are the guys from Rome," Andie added, startled for a moment by the granite boulder that broke away from the foundation of the Tiger's Nest, the huge slab plummeting into the depth of Paro Gorge.

Andie closed her eyes, praying that she wouldn't hear any screams.

The air above Taktsang remained silent.

CHAPTER 37

"Sabbath!" Myles proclaimed, jubilant. "Andie, I knew this series of gene deletions and modifications was the Sabbath pattern. They *had* to be. Mind you, I had no advance knowledge of this, and don't think for a minute that I did. No peeking, nothing on the sly. But this had to be the Sabbath pattern. Pure deduction, Andie. A priori, and nothing else. So now I ask you, what other surface marker parent code would make more sense than this? Sabbath, Sabbath, Sabbath! Look for yourself."

With the formula codes in one hand and the satellite phone in the other, Myles had found a clearing along the edge of the gorge about a hundred meters away. Myles had every page of Ivar's notebook unfolded, using a collection of small rocks to weigh down each individual sheet along the trunk of a fallen tree. Andie had followed Myles over to the clearing, leaving Martin and Joel behind.

"But the Clash . . . the Clash . . . Clash 9 . . . Clash whatever . . . this arrangement right here." Myles's usually indistinct facial tic began to leak through as he lined up a row of Ivar's charts. "*This* sequence as the one promoting the Sabbath line? I would've been hired to sing cleanup at a German opera before I ever figured this one out. Never for a cold second did the genetic tweaks designated by the Clash ever cross my mind. But, Andie, who's that guy in our lab, the Bulgarian, his name is, you know . . . what's his name? The fella who always seems to sneak up on you when you least expect it. You know who I mean."

Andie nodded her head slightly.

"Ha! He knew it," Myles said. "The Clash. He knew it right from the start. It was written across his face like one of those medieval tattoos—you know, the ones with that tall, twisty gothic lettering. That Bulgarian, he's smart, man. Sharp. Always on top, that one. He's also a smoking devil. He'll end up blowing out a lung one of these days, I'm sure of it. Hate that. Tragic. He calls me something in Bulgarian every now and again. He says it means 'stallion.' I never bothered to look it up—probably means dork or prick-face or douche bag. Andie! Do you see what I'm seeing?"

Myles lifted up a stone and chased after one of the notebook pages as it started to blow away. "Gotcha, polecat," he said, wiping cakes of mud off the torn sheet of paper. "Chinatown. These modifications are the Chinatown pattern. What a dam buster! You can't believe it either, can you, Andie? You worked there, you saw all the pains, all the pieces, all the permutations. 'What sequence, my friends and colleagues, shall maximize viral replication within a given malignant cell?' Sound familiar? Heard the choir sing that refrain on Sunday mornings past?

"But even Ivar—even *Ivar*—even he wouldn't have seen the Chinatown succession as the transformation that allows the ideal titration of the replicating virus," Myles went on, crisscrossing down one of the marker charts with his index finger. "But there it is, Andie. Before you now, every last detail.

"How'd he ever do it?" Myles said, now looking at Andie, his face beginning to twitch uncontrollably. "How did he ever pull this off?"

"It was his life, Myles," Andie said, following Myles as he gathered up an assortment of notebook pages. "You know that better than anyone. It was Ivar's life."

"No, no, no, not Ivar," Myles said, cutting Andie off as he traced the intersecting lines drawn on another one of the graphs. "Martin. I meant Martin."

"Martin?"

"Yeah, Martin," Myles said. "How do you think Martin ever ended up with this?"

"With what?" Andie asked, catching a stray piece of note paper in midair.

"The code sequences. The keys. All of Ivar's notes." Myles held up two fistfuls of note pages. "All of this. The mother lode. The pages that hold the total sum labor of our collective lives. How in fuck's sake did Martin ever get it?"

"Myles, Myles," Andie implored, "it was an accident. You heard what Martin just told us. He hadn't switched the books or anything like that. It was complete happenstance. Now you walked over here to call Stacey, remember? Have you tried calling her? Have you tried to get through?"

"No signal here. Nothing. Zip," Myles said, slamming the phone against his thigh. "I recharged the battery last night, but without that signal from overhead, this bastard phone is deader than the pelts those yak herders were wearing. But if we wait another five minutes or so, that idiot tin-can satellite will pass overhead. Then I'll find her, all right. I'll track Stacey down. But back to Martin for a minute. Yeah I know, I know, he never meant to hide anything from us. At least he had the notes with him and eventually recognized what was jammed inside those bird book pages. He is clever, I always knew that. Very clever," Myles continued as he circled around the base of the fallen tree, fingered through another stack of notes. "He's a cagey one, that Martin."

"I'd say slithery is closer to the center," Andie said sharply. "Although he does appear to have his moments."

"Well, whatever," Myles said. "But for anyone to think that Ivar had somehow become derailed, that he came to Bhutan to wander around in the mountains in search of some magic herb that would save the day . . . Take no exception here, Andie, but that's heresy. Pure madness. Ivar took a few crude scraps from previous studies and created an entirely new science. It was his theory from the start. It was his research that was collated. It was his vision, his language. So to think that Ivar was hoisting the white flag . . . whatever possessed anyone, you or Joel or Martin or anyone we work with, to consider such a thing?"

Andie waited a couple of minutes before saying anything, watching Myles make circles and arrows along the margins of one of the code sheets.

"I do have one question," Andie said, trying to tread lightly, given Myles's frenzied state.

"This is it, Andie," Myles said, his eyes jumbling as he looked between Andie and the pile of data he was shuffling. "This is *it!*"

"Ivar didn't bring it with him," Andie said calmly. "His birding book, that is. He didn't bring it with him to Bhutan, Myles. You said that wherever Ivar traveled, he always brought a birding field guide with him, and inside he'd stash the notes that were 'his center, his orb.' You figured, as anyone who knew Ivar as well as you do would reasonably assume, that the genetic code sequences, along with the birding guide, were destroyed in the explosion. But Ivar didn't bring the book or the genetic sequence notes to Bhutan."

"Of course he didn't," Myles shot back without looking up at Andie. "How could he? Martin had the book."

"You're right, Martin did have the book," Andie said, slowly nodding her head. "But Martin thought the book he had with him was his, not Ivar's. He had no idea that the book he was carrying was Ivar's."

"That's irrelevant," Myles grumbled, his eyes darting between multiple sheets of paper. "All that matters is that we have the goods in hand."

It was then that Andie heard a trilling sound from across the gorge.

"Oh, no doubt," Andie said, now looking across the gorge. "The notes you've got lined up in front of you, Myles, they're what's critical here. But still, Ivar thought he had left all those notes, and the codes they contain, locked in his desk drawer at the lab. There is no way he could have ever known that the genetic codes on the pages you're looking at were *the* codes, the ultimate home run sequence. And Ivar certainly didn't know that Martin, unwittingly, had the code sequences with him. But still, why do you think Ivar intended on leaving all that back home instead of bringing the formulas here to study and tweak and modify?"

Myles was rearranging the notes that he had lined up along the fallen tree. He said nothing.

"I think Ivar wanted to leave it all locked up in his office because he had no use for the codes or formulas or anything else related to them," Andie said, watching the rescuer on the rappel rope lower himself to the level of the monastery's shredded roofline. "Ivar came here to find a triggering agent that could initiate the cancer treatment process that he and you and everyone else back home have dedicated their lives to. Native healers have for years known about certain substances, certain herbal remedies, that have a positive effect on reducing the size of cancerous growths. And they also know that these herbs can't really cure anything. But they don't have to cure anything, Myles. They just have to reduce the size of the tumor, even if for only a short time. *That* is what Ivar was looking for, a natural means of compressing the cancer load so as to allow virotherapy a chance to work. I wish I knew the exact name of this local medicine, but I don't. I can tell you that it was a big part of why Ivar came to Bhutan."

Myles had jolted to attention while Andie was speaking, and he was now giving her a hard, unblinking stare.

"You just can't let this one go, can you, Andie?" Myles asked. "You and Joel and Martin and God knows who else, all under this same spell, trying to sell me a bill of goods on how Ivar came here to . . ." Myles stopped, staring up into the sky as if he had heard something.

Andie neither heard nor saw anything unusual.

"And he is a curious sort, isn't he, that Martin?" Myles said, looking back at Andie. "Never figured it out, you know. It never made much sense to me, Ivar spending whatever painfully little free time he had with Mr. All-Profit. And since when did Martin ever give two shits about science and research?"

Myles was becoming unhinged, and Andie knew it. Any further consideration of Ivar and his reasons for coming to

Bhutan would likely send a tidal wave toward a level of balance that required no more than a ripple to disrupt. Andie wanted to show Myles the letter that Ivar had handed her, but under the present circumstances, she thought better of it. That would be for another day, as reading the letter now would be one torpedo too many for Myles, whose world of order, reason, and empirical study had already been shaken in every direction.

Andie again looked across the canyon, watching one member of the search and rescue team crouch down low and point at something.

"Ivar was Martin's friend, Myles," Andie said slowly, still looking across to the opposite cliffside. "I think Ivar was Martin's only friend. I think Ivar was the only person in Martin's world who didn't want something from him. Or want to kill him. Or both."

"I can see that. Can see it," Myles said as he again circled around the tree trunk. "What's he got, a couple hundred million? A billion? Maybe two? Maybe more? I'm sure everyone besides Ivar has their hand out at every turn. Everyone, every minute, every day. Kinda almost feel sorry . . . Andie! Valens, Licinius . . . they rule. They rule, they rule!

"The key is here. It's right here," Myles said, knocking his fist against the base of the fallen tree. "The genetic alterations that allow the virus to produce the most effective chemotherapeutic agents within the cancer cell, they're designated by Valens and Licinius. Or to be more precise, Valens four and Licinius five."

Andie watched the rescuer crouch lower, his chest now flat to the ground.

"Truth be known, Andie, there's a lot more swinging room when it comes to these cancer toxins. Mind you, I'm not minimizing this. The impact here, it's colossal. But the mechanics of the first two stages—getting our virus to clasp onto the cancer cell and then getting it to replicate—that's where the real plunder lies. Because once we're inside, Andie, it's a stadium. The Valens and Licinius transformations, they can then begin to lay waste . . .

"Oh shit . . . shit, man," Myles said, jumping as if an electric shock had shot up his spine. "That satellite. Stacey. I've got to call Stacey."

The rescuer began to crawl forward, toward the base of the monastery.

"And here I was, all this time, thinking Titus was our top liner, our megastar," Myles said, patrolling in all directions, searching for a satellite signal. "Titus, Titus . . . where are you, my Titus?"

Andie heard a voice from inside the monastery.

"Call her, Myles," Andie said, her eyes fixed on the man across the canyon. "Stacey. Call Stacey."

"Titus, Titus, is that you?" Myles sang, holding the phone at arm's length. "You are disappointing me here, Titus."

The voice from within Taktsang grew louder.

"Andie, there's a signal. I've got a signal."

"No telling how long that signal will last, Myles," Andie said as she watched the current of gray smoke that flowed out from under the monastery. "So just give Stacey the bottom line, the imperatives. That's what she's looking for."

"Andie, Andie, who do you think you're dealing with here? I practically have it all memorized."

The man who had been crawling toward the base of the monastery began to pull back.

"If it's all the same to you, Myles, it might be best if I spoke with Stacey first. For all we know, she may be watching this scene live on cable news."

"Of course. Yes, of course. As soon as I get through, you're on," Myles said, waving the satellite phone in the air. "She misses you so, Andie. Stacey misses you being there. We all do. And this, all this, today—"

Someone screamed.

"What the fuck was that?" Myles asked, dropping the phone.

"Call her, Myles," Andie said calmly, watching as someone tried desperately to crawl out of a window along the lower level of the monastery. "Pick up the phone and call her. Stacey needs to know that Ivar has died and that the rest of us are all okay. I'll speak with her first, and then you can decode everything. Then Stacey will have every particular, so it's all safe, secure, and in the right hands."

The man trying to escape from the burning monastery was an army officer who had entered Taktsang in search of survivors. Andie saw the man drop out of a smoke-filled window that was facing away from the cliffside along the base of the monastery. The man threw himself on the ground and rolled in the dirt until the flames that were covering the lower half of his uniform were extinguished.

"Stacey? Stacey?" Myles said, holding the phone with both hands.

Two other members of the search team raced to aid the injured officer. The man on the rappel line moved up the side of the cliff as quickly as he could, and the rescue team's leader, waving his arm in a wide arc, signaled everyone to evacuate the Tiger's Nest.

"I've got her!" Myles shouted. "It's Stacey. I've got her."

They would find no survivors.

"No, no, no . . . from my voice to your hand, Rads," Myles said, his face twisted in a dense spasm. "No texts, no graphics. Lord only knows who might intercept a written message. Anyone could be following us, tracing us, trying to steal it all from us. Anyone. But you have to speak with Andie first, Rads. Have to . . ."

All that remained were the ruins and the desolation and the fear.

"Andie . . . Andie . . ."

And somewhere, deep within Taktsang, is a light whose silent flame would never fade.

ChAPTER 38

Paro, Bhutan
Many years in the future

Although our world may have become smaller over the past hundred or so years, finding one's way to Bhutan's eastern border remains about as convenient as getting to the moon. Yet somehow, three months ago, I found my way to Sakteng, a town that is far to the east along Bhutan's border with India. And at long last, later today, my journey through this land will come to an end. I am now standing in the middle of Nyamai Zam, the covered wooden bridge that spans the width of the Paro River. On the riverbank to my right is Rinpung Dzong, the imposing white monolith that for centuries defended this country against Tibetan invasion. At the far end of the bridge, along the western bank of the river, I can see a foot trail that continues off into the who-on-earth-knows-what-lies-in-the-wilderness beyond here.

Below me, the Paro River is raging.

I have spent the last ninety days on foot, traversing the succession of mountain passes that weave through the eastern Himalayas. To the Bhutanese, the towering peaks I have wandered past are sacred; many are unnamed, and nearly all remain unexplored. These mountain slopes may be the last place on earth where the human imprint remains unknown.

About three weeks into our trek, I began to show early signs of altitude sickness. This was no surprise, as I had spent my entire life at sea level. Lhendrup, my guide and more than once my savior, brought me to a small outpost that even the most seasoned adventurer would typify as off the beaten track.

I thought Lhendrup had brought me there so I could get some rest. I did get *some* rest, about an hour's worth. That's when a local physician walked in, completed a cursory exam, and placed an intravenous line in my arm. And whatever that man ran into my system worked in a hurry, because within a couple of hours, I was vertical again. I thanked the doctor and left a donation on a tray next to the door, eyeing the faded *thangka* above the threshold as Lhendrup and I waved good-bye and headed out on our way.

Although that may have been the first mountain clinic we happened upon, it certainly was not the last. Nearly every village and town we passed through, no matter how isolated, had a medical volunteer somewhere to be found. The majority of the volunteers we encountered were not foreigners but native Bhutanese, each working in concert with any number of international aid organizations. And they treated everyone: every pregnant mother, every infant in need of immunization, every lethargic toddler, every injured farmer.

And every dehydrated mountaineer—be he accomplished, or otherwise.

North of Paro town, along the trail that leads to Mount Jomolhari, a simple white *chorten* stands as a memorial to four people who long ago peered into this remote world and saw more than just the timeless beauty that surrounded them.

Galen Vossner, Ivar Nielsen, Joel Morgan, and Andrea Lynn McKillnaugh all have their names forever etched into the north-facing wall of that small monument.

Dr. Joel Morgan, who never again traveled outside the United States, spent the rest of his life training medical specialists who went on to do volunteer work in Bhutan, Nepal, India, and at least a dozen other countries.

Dr. Andie McKillnaugh, who went on to complete her medical education and specialty training, returned to Bhutan and has in fact never left. Dr. McKillnaugh has helped train two generations of Bhutanese physicians, and to the best of anyone's knowledge, she still lives and works in the eastern districts of Mongar and Tashigang.

The inscription on the *chorten*'s dome, written in native Choekey, can be read as one circles the memorial in a clockwise direction:

> *A single lamp*
> *Upon an unlit room*
> *Vanquishes one thousand years*
> *Of darkness*

This was their vision, their passion, and their charge.
This was their life.

Although he never again returned to Bhutan, Myles Carnot did make at least one more transatlantic crossing during his many remaining years.

On a December evening that was far colder than any he had experienced in the Himalayas, Dr. Carnot, standing in the Main Hall of Stockholm's Konserthuest, reached for the extended hand of Sweden's King Carl XVI Gustaf. Next to Myles stood Stacey Ravelle, Neville John, and Luc dul Tran, the other three recipients of the Nobel Prize in Medicine.

During their acceptance speeches, the honorees dedicated their award to Dr. Ivar Nielsen, as the Nobel committee does not bestow their awards posthumously. To honor Ivar, the four recipients committed the proceeds of their Nobel Prize to the Nielsen Scholarship and Research Fund.

As was customary since the inception of the Nobel awards, each of the laureates delivered a lecture summarizing the evolution of their work. Years of trials, failure, and more trials were recounted, tracing tumor virotherapy from its infancy to its eventual use in the harnessing of a child's own immune system in the treatment of high-grade malignancy. They presented the regression of tumor load in the first twenty-two patients, each patient having highly resistant soft tissue cancer.

If those gathered were at all moved by the evening's presentation, their reaction paled against the sea of emotion that overwhelmed my family all those years ago.

The first patient ever treated was me.

"Mr. Duran?"

I turn around, a little startled and at least a little embarrassed. I saw two people standing at the near end of the bridge, but I didn't hear them approach. Either the torrent of water below me is louder than I thought, or my hearing, like the rest of me, is beginning to show signs of wear.

"I am Yoeden Penjor," says one of the women as she offers me her hand. "*Kuzuzangpo-la,* and welcome to Bhutan."

I corresponded with Yoeden via e-mail many months ago, but I must not have mentioned that I would be traveling far and wide prior to the day of our meeting. She clearly thinks I have just arrived.

"Jackson Duran," I say as I clumsily remove my hat. "It is truly a pleasure to meet you."

The gentle smile with which I am greeted seems almost inborn amongst the Bhutanese, and it never grows old. Although Yoeden is at least my age, she beams like a schoolgirl and seems genuinely happy to meet me. Her attire is classic: a deep maroon *kira* and a toga jacket that is as white as snow.

"Please, allow me to introduce Khandra Pelden, our curator," Yoeden says as the woman standing next to her takes a step forward.

"Greetings, Mr. Duran," Khandra says, placing her hands together and bowing slightly from the waist, a formal greeting that I promptly return. "It is an honor to meet you at last."

At last? This is a curious choice of words, and they linger for a moment, resonating in my mind like the words written in the letter I received last year. I again ask myself—how would the National Museum's curator, who I now know to be a woman named Khandra Pelden, know anything about Joel Morgan, Andie McKillnaugh, Myles Carnot, or Martin Phyte? In my reading and research prior to coming here, prior to my "Bhutan pilgrimage," as my family calls it, I was able to find plenty of information on all four of the American visitors—biographical publications, interviews, online references to their professional careers, and innumerable stories related to Myles receiving the Nobel Prize. And it is very possible that Khandra has read all of this same material. She is, after all, an authority on the nation's antiquities and a historian. Khandra is without doubt very well read. But her letter, or rather Yoeden's letter, speaks of Khandra's "intimate knowledge" of the American visitors. I cannot imagine how Khandra could have met Joel, Myles, Andie, and Martin all those years ago, as she appears, at first glance, far too young. This brings me back to what I have at times suspected ever since I first read Yoeden's letter: the connection between Khandra and the American visitors is Andie. Andie, I know with certainty, has spent nearly her entire adult life in Bhutan. And Khandra, somewhere in the years after the explosion at Taktsang, must have met Andie and formed a close bond with her.

Specifics about what happened in the days and weeks following the terrorist attack on Taktsang are very spare, with no published details concerning the remains of the victims who perished in the explosion. And whenever they were interviewed about the events of that day, none of the four Americans who were witness to the bombing ever mentioned Karma in the context of any personal relationship or affection. Joel, Myles, Andie, and Martin would all speak of how they were "traumatized by the savagery of the attack" and how "life was never the same afterward," and given the barbaric nature of the assault, I would have to believe that these testimonies were, if anything, understatements. But in reading and rereading their accounts of that day, it struck me as odd that none of them made any mention of Karma as a close companion. In one interview given by Joel several months after returning home from Bhutan, he spoke of "our guide, along with an untold number of other innocents, falling victim to this senseless and cowardly act." Maybe Joel was deliberately trying to distance himself from his own tortured memories of that day. Maybe they all were. But still, in any of the interviews given by Joel, Andie, Martin, or Myles, recollections about Karma sounded to me as having been rehearsed, with a detached and at times evasive undertone.

"Your shoes," Khandra says as she looks down at my feet, "they speak of many miles and surely many tales."

I am now aware of the thick layers of mud encasing both of my hiking boots. I look as if I've been running laps through wet concrete.

"Yes," I say as I begin kicking off some of the debris against the floorboards of the bridge. "Three months' worth, to be precise."

"Three months?" Yoeden says, visibly startled. "Mr. Duran, I had no idea that you arrived in Bhutan so long ago. So few visitors ever allow adequate time to travel about our kingdom. Your committing the many weeks needed to experience our land and our culture . . . this is quite remarkable."

As Yoeden is speaking, a sudden gust of wind sweeps aside the scarf that she's wearing around her neck. I can't help but notice that nearly all of her right ear is missing, with the surrounding skin having a dark and leathery appearance. Yoeden makes no attempt to hide what is likely scarring from an old injury, casually redraping her scarf as she adjusts her hair.

"After such a long and arduous journey, allow me to welcome you all the more to our centennial celebration," Yoeden says as she again offers me a broad smile. "As I mentioned in my original correspondence, our festival begins later this afternoon, and therefore you must forgive me for departing so hastily."

High on the hill above the Paro River is Ta Dzong, the ages-old circular watchtower that now houses Bhutan's National Museum. A parade of dancers is beginning to gather in front of the tower, their costumes so colorful that they can easily be spotted from this distance. Along the side of the dzong, an enormous *thangka*, known as a *thondrol*, is being unfurled. Yoeden goes on to tell me that this *thondrol* is a sacred relic, as it bears the likeness of Guru Rinpoche and his eight manifestations.

"I understand completely," I say. "You must have many details to oversee, and I do not mean to delay you any further. It has been a delight meeting you, Yoeden, and your inviting me here today was most thoughtful."

I hand Yoeden a pile of photographs, which are hard copies of many of the ones I previously sent her by e-mail. I included pictures of my wife, Kelly, seated next to our two daughters and five squirming grandchildren. Along with a few shots of the characters that make up Provincetown's inimitable street scene, I included several photos of the storm surges that continue to grind away at the not-so-endless dunes of outer Cape Cod.

Yoeden expresses her thanks, waving good-bye as she heads up the hill toward Ta Dzong.

"Traversing on foot from our eastern edge all the way to Paro town," Khandra says evenly. "Remarkable indeed."

Khandra is an elegant and strikingly tall woman—certainly tall by the standards of this part of the world, where the average height of an adult female is no more than five foot one or five foot two. To me, she seems poised and serene, with an ageless beauty about her. Her accent and manner of speech have a refined, almost formal quality to them.

"Getting to the eastern border may have been the toughest part of my entire trip," I say, still trying to knock some of the mud off my boots. "It took three days, six airports, a bus, and a pair of rickshaws to get from my home to the town of Sakteng. That's where I met Lhendrup, the man who guided me through every step of this trip. I've been huffing and puffing for the past three months while Lhendrup made the whole thing look like a stroll through his backyard. Of course, for him, I guess this is his backyard."

"Where is Lhendrup now?" Khandra asks.

"Heading to Thimphu," I say, doing my best to force a grin. "He's meeting up with a group of trekkers who are, no doubt, far more capable on their feet than the trekker he just suffered with these past many weeks."

"As your journey began in Sakteng, and concludes here in Paro, then surely you trekked through the Luana District," Khandra says, studying me for a moment. "The Luana District is the most northern reach of our land, and tracking through such terrain is challenging, formidable even for the most robust of travelers. This would therefore seem an awkward time, Mr. Duran, for you to display such unfounded modesty. You have accomplished a most noteworthy feat, trekking the entire distance of Bhutan."

"Please, Khandra," I say, shaking my head and holding up one hand. "First, it's Jackson. Please, call me Jackson. And second . . . well, second, I just took my time, walking very slowly. And I stand corrected. For me, getting from my home to Bhutan wasn't the hardest part. Saying good-bye to Lhendrup was. In all my days, that's one of the most difficult things I have ever had to do."

"Good-byes always bring us pain, but you and Lhendrup may one day meet again," Khandra says.

I notice the color of Khandra's eyes. Or more to the point, I now notice that Khandra's eyes actually *have* color. Instead of ebony black, they appear to have bright tinges of green or grayish green. There is something different about this woman that I just can't place.

Khandra walks to the edge of the footbridge and stares down into the river.

"The glaciers that blanket Jichu Drake are the source of these waters," she says. "Perhaps in recent days you saw this sacred peak, greeting the day's first light. Jichu Drake is best seen north of Paro, along the trail you took near the end of your journey. At dawn, the glaciers that cap this great peak are an unforgettable sight."

Khandra turns back toward me, her eyes searching.

"Did you go to Taktsang?" she asks.

The question startles me a bit, and no doubt she notices.

"No," I say quickly. "Over the past few days, Lhendrup and I trekked along an offshoot of the Druk footpath. We were east of . . . east of the monastery."

Khandra considers this, her expression unchanged.

"To be honest, the whole idea of going there . . . going to Taktsang," I say after an uncomfortable silence has passed, "I don't know, I can't quite explain it. Lhendrup brought the possibility up in conversation a couple of times, but I always found a way to change the subject. The thought of going there made me very uneasy."

"Why?" Khandra asks.

"I guess, like most human fears, it doesn't make a whole lot of sense," I say. "Fear is an irrational emotion, at least most of the time. And Lord knows I might never have another chance to experience such a historically significant site. That said, something about visiting Taktsang disturbed me."

I look away for a moment and draw in a deep breath.

"I have lived a separate life since coming to Bhutan, Khandra," I say. "The tranquility here is more than I ever could have imagined. But Taktsang . . . Taktsang has not been spared the hate and savagery that the rest of our world knows far too well."

"There is nothing at all to fear," Khandra says. "There is great evil in our world, and such evil has in the past descended upon Taktsang. Throughout its history, Taktsang has been razed many times, only to be rebuilt on a date deemed most fitting by the holy lama. The structure one sees, which to one's eye appears as a child born of the sky and mountains, it is but a shell. If a human hand strikes against us, we are only fortified. Adversity gives birth to all potential for doing good, both for oneself and for those around us. The Tiger's Nest is a casement for what lies within, and what lies within can never be extinguished by hate."

The sky above us is a flawless blue, the midmorning sun reflecting into the depths of the river below. The Paro River is a torrent, with spirals of water cascading over the boulders that line both its embankments.

"Perhaps then you could visit the Tiger's Nest before you depart," Khandra says. "Given the distance and terrain you have just traversed, such a walk would present little challenge."

"I just don't know, Khandra," I say. "After the festival today, I do have a few more days before I fly back to Kathmandu. Maybe I can . . . visit the monastery."

"Have no concern," Khandra says as she approaches me. "Taktsang shall endure, and you may yet have the chance to visit one day."

We are standing eye to eye, with less than two feet between us.

"After all you just told me, I have little doubt that Taktsang will endure," I say, trying my best to appear relaxed. "But I'm not so sure that I will."

Khandra reaches out and hands me a small envelope.

"Long ago, I believe, you proved otherwise," she says, her voice barely audible above the churning waters.

As Khandra looks away, I open the envelope. Inside is a single photograph, clearly quite old but nevertheless well preserved. In the picture, five people are standing in a row along the edge of Paro Canyon. On the far left stands a lumbering, bearded figure who seems to take up half the frame. Next to him is a balding and thoroughly uncomfortable-looking man whose image is slightly blurred. I can almost feel this man shivering. In the middle stands a rail-thin man with a shock of flame-red hair that is blowing in every direction. Standing to his left is a tall and stunning young lady with very long auburn hair. On the far right is an even younger girl, very petite, with a round, angelic facial contour.

In the distance is the Taktsang monastery, with a single faint light visible along its outer edge.

After taking a long, hard look at the photograph, I look up into the sky and shake my head.

"I guess you must know that I know who these people are," I say eventually. "Joel Morgan, Martin Phyte, Myles Carnot, and Andie McKillnaugh. You know, I have never seen another picture of Andie anywhere. What a gorgeous girl.

"And the girl on the far right," I add, a rush of emotion running through me as I pull the photo in closer, "that must be Karma."

Khandra remains silent.

"I never met any of these people, you know," I say. "Not once. I never met . . ."

I feel as if a meteor just knocked me down.

I walk to the edge of the bridge, looking up the hill toward Ta Dzong. I don't notice the dancers, or the musicians, or the giant *thondrol*, or the gathering crowd. All I see is the lone figure ascending the footpath that leads to Ta Dzong.

All I see is Yoeden Penjor.

"Khandra," I say, my hand trembling as I point to the last person in the photograph, "this has to be the young girl who served as a guide for the four Americans. Her name was Karma, and I'm sure that's her."

I lean over the rail of the bridge, blocking out the sun with one hand as I look up at Yoeden. Then I look back at the picture, trying to somehow make a whole out of a scattering of very improbable parts.

"At some point in her life, Yoeden sustained a serious injury," I say, staring at Khandra with what must be a desperate look on my face. "A very serious injury. I could not help but notice that she has deep scars across her face and along her scalp on one side."

Khandra remains still and silent.

"Khandra, I have read every account of that day," I say. "The explosion at Taktsang, all those years ago. No survivors found. No remains. The attack was thought to be the work of a suicide bomber, some Nepali fanatic with a serious grievance against your country and in particular against your king. The residue found along the mountain ledge gave evidence as to just how powerful that blast was. Eyewitnesses saw the roof of the monastery disappear into the sky."

I again lean over the railing and look up at Yoeden. My heart is racing.

"Khandra, I read all of it . . . every official report, every unofficial report, and every detail recalled by every witness," I say, staring at the figure in the photo, looking up again at Yoeden, and looking back at the photo. "There is no way . . . no one could have ever survived such devastation."

"You are quite correct," Khandra says with complete calm. "The day to which you refer was a horrific day in our history, and as you state, there were no survivors found. As a young girl, Yoeden was indeed severely injured, but she is not the girl you see in the photograph. The girl you see in the picture you are holding was never found."

"This picture, has anyone else ever seen it?" I ask, squinting in the bright light. "And who in the world ever took this? In an article Joel Morgan wrote, he said there were only five in their group, and all five are in this frame. Whether this was an auto-shoot or taken by one of the Sherpas, this shot is an image from one of five possible cameras. And if you don't mind me asking, where did you ever get . . ."

I hear two sharp clacking sounds against the wooden bridge planks.

When I look to my right, I see that the hem of Khandra's *kira* dress is now draped in a circular pile at her feet. Next to her are the two impossibly large elevator boots that she just removed.

Khandra unwinds her coiled hair, reducing her standing height by at least another inch and a half.

The world around me freezes.

"Karma," I say, staring wide-eyed at the person across from me. "*Karma.*"

Khandra-Karma tilts her head and slowly nods.

My mind, like the rest of me, goes numb.

"This just isn't possible," I say eventually, having mouthed the words a couple of times before actually uttering them. "I saw pictures of what was left of Taktsang after that blast. The rescue teams, one after the other, found no sign of life anywhere. No one could have survived a detonation of that magnitude. There is no way . . ."

I stop myself, running it all back through my mind.

"Up," I say, again looking into the sky. "The force from the detonation was transmitted upward. A black granite cliff . . . the path of least resistance."

Taktsang . . . a wooden frame.

A shell.

Only a shell.

"The cave," I say. "The Dubkhang. You were in the Dubkhang."

Karma again gives a slight nod.

I look up the hill once again, watching Yoeden as she begins to greet guests at the entrance to Ta Dzong.

"She was with you," I say, looking back at Karma. "Yoeden, she was with you, wasn't she? You hid Yoeden in the cave."

Karma remains still and silent.

"Were there others?" I ask, still in total disbelief. "Besides you and Yoeden, were others there with you?"

"Two others," Karma says. "We were four in all."

Karma replaces her boots, straightens her *kira*, and recoils her hair. She then takes several steps away from me, stopping at the entrance of the bridge.

"There was very little time," Karma says as she turns back toward me. "When I saw those two men speaking to each other in the monastery that morning, I knew something was terribly wrong. At that very moment, pure terror ran through me. The look in the one man's eyes was the most frightening sight I had ever seen. I signaled the others to follow me, and we crouched as low as we could in a recess adjacent to the Dubkhang. We could not evacuate in haste, as such a move would have attracted the attention of our enemies. Concealment, as I saw it, was our only course of action. After the explosive was activated, all of the wooden debris piled above us. The heat, no doubt, overwhelmed the rescue teams. It was days before the inferno abated, and as I told you, we were never found."

"Besides Yoeden, was anyone . . . anyone else injured?" I ask.

"Not as severely as Yoeden," Karma says. "For the first two days, Yoeden drifted in and out of consciousness, and more than once I was sure that we had lost her. The two others that were with us sustained only minor injuries. Myself, it was many months before I could again walk without pain, and I lost nearly all of the sight in my left eye. As unusual as this may sound, my visual loss has in fact afforded me an advantage, as the lenses I require bear shades of green. As one might imagine, such eye coloring is quite rare amongst our people."

"But changing your name, your identity, your appearance," I say, still struggling to pull all this in. "Why?"

"As one is never certain where one's friends lie, one is also uncertain as to the whereabouts of the friends of one's enemy," Karma says. "Those that struck upon us that day were not alone, and it was far better to deceive any fellow conspirators with a false sense of triumph than to taunt them with evidence of their failure. I feared most for my family, as reprisals against them may have ensued if it was known that I, along with the others, had survived. And apart from the lack of native casualties that day, the treasures of our great monastery, in particular the precious relics buried within, were largely preserved. The assailants failed in their attempt to diminish the vitality of our land, and such knowledge, if disseminated, would only serve to empower the radicals who plot against Bhutan. Even to this day, there are factions of Nepalis who wish to avenge what they see as a wrong against their people."

"Does anyone else know who you are?" I ask. "After all these years, who else knows?"

"Members of my family, of course," Karma says. "I have so feared for them that when we meet, we must do so in total secret. And besides Yoeden and the two others who survived the attack upon Taktsang, there have been a handful of foreigners who knew of my true identity. These foreigners are all, in fact, quite near to both of us right now."

After a moment or two of feeling even more befuddled, I realize that I am still holding the photograph that Karma gave me just a few minutes ago.

"Andie and Joel and Martin and Myles . . . they all knew that you survived?" I ask, unable to tone down the shrill in my voice. "I know that Martin and Joel passed away some years ago, and Myles . . . he died just last year. But Andie, you still see Andie?" I ask, looking at Andie and Karma standing side-by-side in the picture. "Is she still alive, still here in Bhutan?"

"Yes to all of your questions," Karma says, letting out a laugh. "Andie has dedicated her career to the people of Bhutan, and to me she is a friend unlike any other. As you may be aware, Andie has long credited the success of her work to a renowned philanthropist who is now deceased."

"Martin Phyte," I say without hesitation.

"Indeed," Karma says. "Mr. Phyte's benevolence has fostered charity programs in many countries, including my homeland. And for her part, Andie's perseverance and resolve have seemed nearly inexhaustible."

I again look up the hill toward Ta Dzong, where the musicians, all dressed in formal native costume, begin to play for the crowd that continues to assemble around the circular fortress. The *thondrol,* now fully unfurled, waves slowly in the breeze.

"How did you ever find me?" I ask, now looking at Karma. "I sent letters and e-mails to everyone and every place I could think of, looking for any information that would help me find . . . help me find *you* . . . or help me find out what really happened to you on the day Taktsang was destroyed. But you found me first, Karma. How did that ever happen?"

I look down and swallow hard.

"How did that ever happen?" I repeat.

"Your original inquiry to our Tourism Council, asking for any information concerning a group of American visitors," Karma begins, "this at first, I suspect, attracted very little attention. However, with your repeated inquiries, a member of the council sent around an e-mail that included copies of your letters, asking if any member of another government branch might be able to assist you. Tourism represents a large percentage of our economy, and the council encourages our assisting visitors, or potential visitors, in any way we can.

"Yoeden was astonished when she read your many letters of inquiry," Karma continues, "and when she showed me the letters, I was equally shocked, as you might imagine. In all these years, neither Yoeden nor I had read or heard of a single request for information concerning a girl named Karma whose remains were never found in the ruins of Taktsang. Given the unique nature of your interest in Bhutan's history, it seemed inviting you here today, to our festival, was most appropriate."

"And with some good fortune, afford us an opportunity to meet," I say. "To meet and to talk, with as little fanfare as possible."

"Indeed," Karma says, nodding. "And if I may ask, Jackson," she says, her eyes intent as she meets my gaze straight on. "You said that you were looking for information about me, or if my remains were ever discovered at the Tiger's Nest."

"That is correct," I say. "That is in fact the real reason I came to Bhutan, to find someone who could tell me more about you."

"Why?" Karma asks, a glimmer of light from the river's reflection shining in her eyes. "What is the source of this interest, prompting you to travel such a distance? You mentioned a moment ago that you studied all reports concerning the attack upon Taktsang, just as you have spent years reading about the lives of the four Americans who I guided during their first days in Bhutan. Did you not conclude, as did all the others who reviewed many of these same documents, that I perished when the monastery was destroyed?"

"I am here, I am alive, because of you, Karma," I say immediately, getting the words out before my emotions get the best of me. "I had a terrible disease when I was a child . . . a cancerous growth that was treated with an experimental method after every known form of conventional therapy had been exhausted. That experimental method was called virotherapy, which has been well established for many years now but at the time was novel and almost completely unknown in the medical world. And the man who originally introduced virotherapy, Ivar Nielsen, was the same man who came to Bhutan to find an herb that he believed could be used to induce the virotherapy pathway, making this form of treatment far more effective. That herbal remedy, *Lobelia nubigena*, was in the knapsack that you went to retrieve at Taktsang on the day of the attack. And no matter how many times I have stirred in the middle of the night wondering about the chain of events from that day, I always come up with the same three possibilities. The first and what would seem by far the most likely is that you died in the fire, and neither your remains, nor Ivar's knapsack, were ever found. But how could that be, if shortly thereafter the *Lobelia* herb found its way into wide use at major medical centers in the United States? The second is that you died but the knapsack was found, but that doesn't add up either. If that knapsack was somehow found beneath the rubble, it would have been of no value to anyone. It would have been inspected, catalogued, and tossed aside. That leaves us with the third possibility, which although objectively seems an impossibility, is in fact the only possibility: the *Lobelia* seed made it out of there because *you* made it out of there, Karma. If you had died in that explosion, the potential power and utility of the *Lobelia* herb would have never been considered. Through all these years, there has been a voice inside me that couldn't be kept quiet. Even though I could not envision any possible way you made it out of Taktsang alive, that voice just would not leave me alone. If anything, it grew louder and became more insistent. And it told me that you survived, Karma. You must have survived, because I survived. And because of you, so have a lot of other people."

After staring out toward the far riverbank for a long moment, Karma again considers me.

"The rescuers, as I told you, never found us," Karma says, "as we were buried very deep beneath the ruins of the monastery. The four of us, we eventually crawled our way out of the wreckage, and I did indeed have Dr. Ivar's small backpack with me. During my convalescence, I found the backpack in the corner of my hospital room. I knew of Dr. Ivar's passing the evening before the attack on Taktsang, and since he could never retrieve the backpack himself, I opened it as I thought it may contain something of importance. Although at first the contents appeared unremarkable, I noticed several small cloth containers that had seeds and fine granular material within them. There was also a series of notes, presumably written by Dr. Ivar, that referenced the seed pouch marked LO. I knew very little of our native herbs, and as you might imagine, I knew even less about Dr. Ivar's medical work. But in my one and only encounter with Dr. Ivar, it was evident to me that whatever was in the knapsack that he left at Taktsang was of significance.

"While I was recovering, I knew that I needed to locate Myles, as Myles was closest to Dr. Ivar's work," Karma continues. "But Myles, who by his nature seemed apprehensive and somewhat distrusting, might have considered any contact by someone claiming to be me as a hoax. I knew Martin was a man of considerable means, and hence I contacted Martin's business headquarters through e-mail, using the name Khandra and expressing interest in an import/export venture. Eventually, through a secure phone line, I was able to speak with Martin directly. I told Martin who I was and how I feared of retribution against my family, particularly if it was known that I survived the assault on Taktsang. And I told him the real reason for my contacting him, specifically, was the contents of Dr. Ivar's knapsack. A few days later, Martin visited me at the small hospital where I was being treated. He flew here himself to retrieve Dr. Ivar's belongings. I was overjoyed to see him, although his stay, by necessity, was brief. Asking my permission, Martin told Andie and Dr. Joel of our meeting, and of course he told Myles when he gave Myles the knapsack. Martin swore he would never tell anyone else of our meeting, and likewise all of the others kept this in the strictest confidence."

"But Myles," I mutter, trying to put together a coherent thought, "Myles had no interest whatsoever in traditional herbal medicines. He was militant against their use. So even if Martin gave him the backpack, which he clearly did, how was Myles ever convinced that *Lobelia* would be a critical part of the cancer treatment pathway? The only other person Myles knew of that had any knowledge of the *Lobelia* herb's use was Tandin, the Bhutanese doctor that Ivar worked with. But Tandin would have never been able to convince Myles to use *Lobelia* in the course of cancer treatment. Not in a million years. Tandin didn't even believe in it himself. From what I gathered, Tandin used the *Lobelia* herb to treat people who had tumors caused by use of the betel nut. He saw it as a temporizing agent, nothing more. Ivar, for whatever reason, was convinced that *Lobelia* would have some positive effect when it came to treating cancers in children. But at the time of Ivar's death, Myles didn't know any of this. Something must have persuaded him, even though he appeared to be beyond persuasion."

"You need look no further than Andie," Karma says with a shrewd look on her face. "The last thing Dr. Ivar ever wrote was a letter to Andie, which told of his belief in our traditional means of healing. Between the letter Dr. Ivar wrote to Andie, and the *Lobelia* seed salvaged from Taktsang, Myles, it would seem, was duly swayed."

"Ivar's letter to Andie!" I say, slapping the top of my head with my hand. "That's right. Even though he didn't mention *Lobelia* by name, Ivar spoke of all he had learned from Tandin, mentioning how Tandin had given him some of the traditional herbs while they were in Taktsang."

"And ultimately, I would imagine, there some level of faith," Karma adds, nodding slightly. "Faith that may have overshadowed any tangible evidence that Andie, or I, or anyone else, could have ever produced."

"If Myles had faith, it's because you handed him something to have faith in," I say, taking a step closer to Karma. "I can only imagine the thoughts that ran through Myles's head when Martin handed him Ivar's knapsack. At that moment, Myles knew you were alive, Karma. *Alive.* And you kept part of Ivar alive with you. And the part of Ivar you kept alive was, right then and there, staring Myles straight in the face."

Karma has a distant look in her eyes, gazing up briefly toward the musicians on the hill before again considering me.

"I believe you will find our celebration today a joyous occasion," Karma says as she puts her hands together and bows slightly from the waist. "And perhaps, Jackson, just perhaps, we shall one day meet yet again."

My head is whirling and my heart still pounding.

"I just cannot fathom any of this," I say as Karma begins to walk away. "That monastery was vaporized . . . vanished in the blink of an eye. No rational person would ever believe that there were survivors at Taktsang that day. No one. It just does not seem possible."

Karma turns back and gives me a long look, tilting her head slightly as she offers me one last smile.

"It is all possible," Karma says as she again bids me farewell.

I stand there, alone with all of this, watching as Karma walks up the hill toward Ta Dzong. Eventually I look over to the opposite side of the footbridge, again eyeing the meandering trail that fades off into the outland. Suddenly it seems as if I have just arrived, setting foot in Bhutan for the first time. And just as suddenly, the thought of leaving here seems unimaginable to me. All I can think of is wandering farther . . . farther and farther . . . if only for a bit longer.

Before tucking it away, I look at the photograph one more time. In it I see four people who fell into a world they never could have imagined, and next to them stands someone who would forever change the course of their lives.

And a distant glow. A distant light. A light burning somewhere in Taktsang.

Life restored to so many.

Life restored to me.

The song of a nearby prayer wheel dances in the morning breeze, its music drifting over the waters that surge forth from the sacred Himalayan peaks that gave birth to this land. A group of monks gathers along the outer wall of Rinpung Dzong, but to my surprise, they do not begin to sing. Nor do they begin to chant.

They listen. They only listen.

The chorus in our midst summons all to listen.

Acknowledgments

I would like to recognize, with my sincerest thanks, Kevin Grange, Balaram Chakravarti, Bill Frelick, Robert Worden, Ian Baker, Dr. ALK (personal communication), Bradley Mayhew et al., and Barry Clark. Their knowledge of Bhutan's history, religion, and culture, as evident in their writings, proved to be an invaluable resource in making this story come together.

In particular, I would like to express my gratitude to Katie Hickman, author of *Dreams of the Peaceful Dragon*. This beautiful journal of her time in Bhutan served as an inspiration to me from the very beginning. *Kadinchhey-la*, Ms. Hickman.

If I learned anything about the science of cancer virotherapy in writing this manuscript (and believe me, I did), I can thank the Department of Biochemistry and Microbiology at the Mayo Clinic, along with Drs. D. T. Curiel, Robert Martuza, Russell Kelly, and Mr. Sean McNaughton. I thank you all for introducing me to a world that I knew nothing about.

The editorial staff at iUniverse has seen me through every step of this project. I salute you for your professionalism, attention to detail, expertise, and above all, your patience.

I would have never experienced Bhutan's splendor without the many efforts of my lifelong friend and trusted colleague, Dr. Robert F. Ward. This toast is for you, Bob.

Although I never had the pleasure of meeting him, singer Don McLean performed many of his best known songs, including "Vincent," at a small café in the same town (in fact, on the same street) where I grew up in upstate New York. I am honored to include some of his lyrics in this story.

And above all, I would like to express my heartfelt appreciation to Kathy Gantz, Dr. Andrew Kurban, Mr. SL, Dr. Gary Ruggera, Drs. RD and TDG, Diane Bush, Carol Valdez, Dr. James Howell, Nicole Gakidis, James Davis, Janette Barber, Liz Desmarais, Suzette O'Farrell, Ann Howell, Lee Ann Sweet, and Roberta Anslow. Your encouragement, support, insight, comments, ideas, and suggestions, along with your *many* hours of assistance with copy and editing, mean more to me than you will ever know. Without all of you, this project would still be sitting on a shelf—or collecting dust somewhere inside my head. My hat is off to each and every one of you.

DS
8-17-13

About the Author

Dr. Dennis Snyder is an otolaryngologist and head and neck surgeon based in the greater Boston area. He is one of the founders of Medical Missions for Children, a volunteer organization that provides free surgical care to children with severe congenital deformities and burn injuries. One hundred percent of the royalties for *Taktsang* will be donated directly to Medical Missions for Children. Visit the organization online at www.mmfc.org.